IT STARTED
with a
COWBOY

JENNIE MARTS

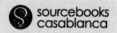

sourcebooks
casablanca

Published by Sourcebooks Casablanca, an imprint of Sourcebooks, Inc.
P.O. Box 4410, Naperville, Illinois 60567-4410
(630) 961-3900
sourcebooks.com

Printed and bound in the United States of America.
OPM 10 9 8 7 6 5 4 3 2 1

This book is dedicated to my sons:
Tyler & Nick
There aren't enough words to express
How much I love you both
—Never give up on your dreams—

Chapter 1

FLUFFY FLAKES OF SNOW SWIRLED AGAINST THE WINDOW as Chloe Bishop raced into the kitchen and grabbed the travel mug of coffee she'd set to autobrew at exactly 7:00 a.m. Several inches had already accumulated, but it was too late for the school district to call a snow day. A few of her students would most likely be absent or late today, but dealing with snow and cold was a normal part of life in the small mountain town of Creedence, Colorado.

"Fudge nuggets," she swore as a bit of coffee splashed over the edge of the mug and splattered across the counter. She didn't have time for this, but she grabbed a paper towel and quickly swabbed at the mess anyway. Nothing in her DNA would allow her to leave the house in disarray—even if she was running late.

Which she also did *not* do. Not usually. And this morning, she *should* have had plenty of time, had she not stepped out of bed and into a squishy pile of cat vomit. Hauling out the steam cleaner and dealing with the disaster had eaten away twenty minutes of valuable currency in the measured moments of her morning routine.

She tossed the soiled paper towel into the trash, then poured a perfectly measured scoop of kibble into a bowl for Agatha, the carpet-contaminating culprit. Stuffing her feet into her snow boots, Chloe caught a glimpse of red out the window.

Rubbing at the thin layer of frost, she peered through the pane and sighed, her heart breaking as she saw Madison Johnson, one of her third-grade students, standing ankle-deep in the snow and awkwardly brandishing a broom as she tried to clean the snow off her mother's car. Her scuffed sneakers had to be soaked through, and Chloe recognized the thin winter coat as the same one Maddie's brother had worn a few years before. Her blond hair was pulled up on either side of her head in uneven ponytails.

Chloe leaned out the front door, her cheeks tingling with the bracing cold as she called to the girl, "Just leave it, Maddie. I'll give you a ride to school."

"I got it, Teach," Tina Johnson, her neighbor and Maddie's mom, yelled, her voice carrying the slightest slur as she stumbled out onto her front porch.

That hint of a slur hit Chloe like a punch to the gut, taking her back in time to the sound of her father's voice. She gripped the doorjamb for support.

Stop it. Those days were over. She wasn't a child anymore. And her father was gone. He couldn't hurt her anymore.

She let out her breath, and it shimmered in the air as a shiver coursed down her back.

It was freezing out here, and Tina wasn't dressed much warmer than her daughter in a denim jean jacket over a pair of mismatched flannel pajamas. At least she had on a tattered pair of snow boots. And maybe it wasn't a slur. Maybe Tina had just woken up, and her tone was still tinged with sleepiness. Chloe hated to judge, but she wasn't taking a chance on Maddie getting in the car with her mom if she'd been drinking.

"It's okay, Tina," Chloe called back. "It's no bother for me to take her. I'm going to the school anyway."

The woman yawned and nodded. "Okay, if you're sure. If not, I can take her," she said, but she was already turning and heading back into the house.

"I'm sure," Chloe said to Tina's retreating back as she waved Madison up to her porch. "Come on in, honey. I just need to grab my bag, then we can go."

The girl dropped the broom and scrambled through the snow-covered front lawn, a smile spread across her rosy-cheeked face. "Thanks, Ms. Bishop," she said, stomping her feet on the mat before clambering inside.

"Where's your scarf?"

Maddie's smile fell as her shoulders shrank inward. "I think I left it at school," she mumbled as she bent down to pet Agatha, who had meandered out from under the sofa to grace them with her presence.

Chloe made it a point to knit each of her students a scarf every year, knowing that for some, it would be the only winter gear they would have. And there was a deep, inner part of her heart that knew the reason she took such good care of her students was because she worried she'd never have children of her own. She was missing the key ingredient, and going after that ingredient took guts and the kind of courage she didn't possess.

It was one thing to dream of getting married and creating a family; it was another thing entirely to step out of the safety of her comfort zone and go about making it a reality.

An image of the blond cowboy she'd met that summer filled her mind, but she shoved that thought away as she pushed the door closed against the cold. Colt James was so far out of her league, they weren't even in the same ballpark. Sure, he'd been nice to her the few times they'd met, but he was nice to everyone, even slightly overweight grade-school teachers with mousy-brown hair.

She let out a sigh. She didn't have time for maudlin daydreams about cute cowboys—not when she had actual kids to take care of and a class to teach. Grabbing her down parka from the hook on the wall, she quickly pulled it on, then drew her pink scarf from her pocket and wrapped it around the small girl's neck. "You can borrow mine for now." She tugged the matching hat and mittens onto the girl's head and hands. There was nothing Chloe could do about Maddie's feet for now. There was no way her boots would fit the girl, but she added "snow boots for Maddie" to her mental list of things to look for the next time she was in the local thrift store.

A quick glance at the wall clock told Chloe she didn't have time to rummage for a hat and gloves for herself, but she had an extra set at school. She'd make do until she got there. Her school bag sat prepared on the bench by the door, and she hoisted it and her purse onto her shoulder.

"Let's go," she said, pulling the door shut behind her and shepherding Maddie toward her car. The silver sedan had belonged to her dad. It and the house full of stuff were the only things of value she'd inherited when he'd passed away a few years back.

She helped Maddie climb into the back seat and buckle her seat belt. Chloe had taught second grade the year before but had been moved to third grade this year, so she had several students who had remained in her class, even though they were now a year older. Maddie was one of them, and she was thankful the girl had grown enough over the summer to not have to use a booster seat.

Grabbing the snow scraper from the back seat, she gave the car a quick brushing as she plodded back around to her side.

She dropped the scraper in the back as she got in and rubbed her hands together before starting the car. The radio blared out a heavy metal song, the thump of the bass rumbling through the car.

Maddie's eyes went wide and then she cracked up. "This song is in my brother's video game," she said, completely oblivious to the irony of her bashful teacher jamming out to metal as she lifted her hands and did a decent air-guitar impression.

Chloe laughed with her, doing her own head-banging impression as she switched on the wipers and defroster. The music might be out of character, and she didn't always listen to it, but something about the powerful, thunderous rhythm could give her a boost when she needed a shot of courage. She thought herself quite clever for using a little metal when she needed a little mettle.

Squinting through the frosty front window, she knew she should get out and completely clear the windshield of ice and snow, but the wipers had swished most of it off. She could see well enough, and besides, they were going to be even later.

With the radio blaring and the defroster whirring at full blast, she put the car into gear, looked over her shoulder as she pulled out into the road, and crashed right into the snowplow that had just turned onto the street behind her.

Colton James swore as the silver car pulled out in front of him. He hit the brake, but there was nothing he could do. The car crashed right into the thick snowplow blade affixed to the front of his truck with a sickening thud.

Well, shit. He wasn't even supposed to be on this street. He'd been called out early this morning to help plow the school parking lot. But spending time at the school had him thinking about a certain cute, curly-haired third-grade teacher, and he'd figured as long as he was out, he could swing by her street and make sure it was plowed as well. It seemed like the neighborly thing to do.

Not that they were neighbors. She lived in a house in town, and he lived in a cabin in the country on ranchland that his family owned. The Triple J Ranch had been in his family for years, and he, his mom, his brothers, and a slew of ranch hands ran it.

Speaking of his brothers, Rock and Mason were going to give him a ration of crap for this debacle. Even if it wasn't his fault. He'd been helping out the city by plowing roads for years now and hadn't ever had an accident.

But his mind hadn't usually been preoccupied with a woman. A woman who'd so far only offered him bashful smiles and a few kind words.

He swore again as he peered through the side window of the car that had hit him and saw that same woman behind the wheel. And from the frustrated look on her face, it didn't seem like she was saying any kind words now.

He cut the engine and grabbed his gloves as he climbed

from the truck. The frigid air stung his cheeks, and he pulled up the front of his scarf and dipped his cowboy hat to protect his face from the biting wind.

The edge of the plow was smashed into the driver's side door, so he scrambled to the other side and yanked open the passenger door. "You guys okay?"

A small girl blinked at him from the back seat. He recognized her as a girl in his nephew Max's class. "We're okay, but Ms. Bishop said a curse word."

"I most certainly did not," Chloe said, leaning her head on her hands, which still clutched the steering wheel.

"You said 'son of a beach chair.'"

"Which is not *technically* a swear word." Chloe's face was still buried against her fingers.

"Then can I say it?"

"No, you probably shouldn't." She pushed her bangs from her eyes as she leaned toward him. "I'm so sorry. I didn't even see you."

"It's okay. No harm done to me. But your car isn't going anywhere." He pulled the scarf down from his mouth. "But I'd be happy to give you all a ride to school."

Her eyes went wide as she looked up at him. "Oh, son of a nutcracker. It's you."

"You did it again," the girl helpfully pointed out.

He tried to keep the grin from cracking his face, somehow knowing that breaking into laughter would not help the current situation. "Let's get you out of there and into my truck. I've got the heat on, and it's colder than a witch's t—teeth out here."

Chloe arched an eyebrow. "Good save." She nodded to the girl. "This is Maddie. She lives next door and is in my class. I was giving her a ride to school."

"Nice to meet you, Maddie. I'm Colt. I'm a friend of your teacher." He looked down at her sneakered feet, then at the new accumulation of snow. "You're going to get your feet even more soaked trying to walk to my truck. Why don't you put your arms around my neck, and I'll carry you?"

The girl scrambled over the seat and into his arms, and Colt carried her to his truck. She weighed less than a bale of hay. "Stay right here, and don't touch anything," he instructed the girl. "I'll be right back with your teacher."

He trekked back through the snow to where Chloe was trying to climb over the center console and into the passenger seat.

"Son of a bacon bit. My foot is stuck," she gasped, her body spread halfway across the seat.

Colt leaned into the car, intent on helping, but was instead struck dizzy by the nearness of her and the honeysuckle scent of her hair. She had on black pants, which were tucked into her boots, and her coat and pink sweater had ridden up to her waist. He had the sudden urge to reach out and run his hand along the perfect curve of her butt.

Dang. What was wrong with him? Was he looking to get slapped? He shook his head and tried to focus. He could see the problem—the heel of her boot was wedged between the crumpled door and her seat. He reached his arm out, acutely aware of how close he was to her body, and tried to tug on the top of the boot.

"Ouch."

He snatched his hand back as if he'd touched a hot surface. *Double dang.* Now he was thinking about her body as a hot surface. "Sorry. You okay?"

"Yeah, I'm fine, I just can't twist my foot in the boot."

"No, I think your boot's good and stuck. Can you just pull your foot out?"

She yanked her leg up, then fell against him, her head knocking into his chin as her foot popped free of the trapped boot.

His arms automatically went around her, the slight bump to his chin ignored with the warm press of her body. "I got ya."

She held on to him for a second, then straightened up in the seat. "Oh my gosh, I'm so sorry. Did I hurt you?" Her cheeks went as pink as her sweater.

"No, darlin'. You did *not* hurt me," he said with a light chuckle. "I'm a lot tougher than that. But you look half froze." He guessed by the oversize accessories Maddie had on that Chloe had given the girl her scarf, hat, and mittens. His cowboy hat might not warm her head, but he could at least offer something to warm up her face and hands. He pulled his scarf free from under his coat and wrapped it around her neck. "There, that should help a little. Now you better put your arms around my neck like Maddie did so I can get you to school."

She sat frozen, blinking at him, her cheeks partially covered as the color drained from her face. "Oh, no. I couldn't."

"Sure you can. I won't drop you."

She shook her head, her eyes wide and round.

He arched an eyebrow. "Now, Chloe, we can sit here and debate this for another ten minutes, but you've met my mother, and you know Vivienne James would tan my hide if I let you walk through foot-deep snow in your stocking feet, or foot, or sock, or whatever." Now he felt his cheeks heating. His efforts at sounding cool and convincing were coming out as full-on dorkster. But he still wasn't about to let her walk through the snow without a boot. He needed to appeal to her more rational side. "Besides that, the longer we fret about it, the later you're going to be to school, so come on, woman, just let me carry you to the truck."

"Valid point." She sighed, then slid her arms around his neck and let him lift her from the car. "Sorry about all the potty-mouth talk before. I don't usually use such inappropriate language, and especially not around kids."

A grin tugged at the corner of his mouth. "It was pretty bad, but I can take it," he teased. And he was pretty sure that growing up with three older brothers, Maddie had heard much worse as well.

"I was just so frazzled. I never run late. But with the snow this morning and Agatha being sick and seeing poor Maddie out in the storm with no boots, then running into you—" She clasped a hand to her mouth. "Oh no. Should we be calling the police? Exchanging insurance information? Is this going to raise my rates? I've never been in an accident."

He could barely keep up with the way she jumped from subject to subject, but he liked to hear her talk. "Don't worry about it. We're on cold reporting this morning anyway, so the police only want you calling in if someone is hurt. And no one was hurt."

"Thank goodness." She shook her head, sending another wave of honeysuckle scent swirling through the air. "I wouldn't be able to live with myself if anything had happened to Maddie." She looked up at him from under dark snowflake-dotted lashes, her eyes round and sincere, as she whispered, "Or you."

A hard pull of protectiveness and need spun through his gut. This woman got to him. He wanted to pull her close, to hold her against him and protect her, while at the same time he wanted to capture her pretty, pink bow-shaped lips with his and kiss her proper—and thoroughly.

It had been a long time since a woman had gotten to him—a long time since he'd *let* a woman get to him. He'd learned years ago that it was easier not to take a chance at all than to risk taking a chance and having his hopes destroyed. He lived his life like that now—freewheeling through his days, taking life as it came, but never letting himself hope for something more. Until he'd met Chloe.

Something about Chloe Bishop was poking the edges of his heart, as if looking for a soft place to sneak in. And he could feel those rough edges giving in—not breaking, but bending a little each time she offered him a bashful smile.

He knew better than to hope though. The Colton Curse—the self-inflicted jinx that kept good things from happening to him—had hit too many times. Best to stick to the details, the everyday minutiae, and keep matters like feelings and possibilities at bay.

"Don't worry. No one got hurt. And the damage isn't that bad. You weren't even going fast enough for the air bag to deploy. We can worry about filing a report later." He had no intention of reporting the accident. He was sure it hadn't done any damage to his truck, and he didn't want her to incur any kind of loss with her insurance. "I've got a buddy who runs the auto body shop in town, and he owes me a favor." Justin really owed him about seventeen, but they'd quit counting a long time ago. "If you want to leave me your keys, I'll have him come over and take a look at your car. He can tow it in to his shop if he thinks it needs it."

"You don't have to do that."

"Would you quit arguing with me, woman, and just let me help you out? I'm trying to be the hero here, and you're seriously messing with my man card."

She grinned and pushed the keys into his hand. "Fine. I already crashed into the front of your truck. I don't want to be responsible for wrecking your man card too. But make sure your buddy sends me the bill."

"Will do." Not really. He doubted Justin would charge him for anything more than parts.

Colt shielded the side of the car from her view as he opened the truck door and got her settled in the cab. He knew the car was going to need some major repairs— the front of the heavy plow had hit it just right, and the driver's side door was completely crumpled in.

Chloe and Maddie were buckled in by the time he got back around to his side and climbed into the truck. He'd left the engine running, and the cab was plenty warm. Although he imagined he was feeling warm for another reason—a petite-curly-haired-brunette-crushed-against-his-chest reason.

He put the truck in reverse, and they all cringed at the screech of metal as the plow implement separated from the smashed-in side of the sedan.

"Son of a beach chair. That's loud," Maddie cried, pressing her hands to her ears, the too-big mittens flopping over the tops of her fingers.

Chloe looked down at her, a stern teacher expression on her face.

"Sorry." Maddie shrank back against the seat, the impish grin on her face implying that she wasn't really that sorry.

Colt pressed his lips together to keep from laughing as he pulled out and drove toward the school.

Chapter 2

THE FINAL BELL RANG AT THREE O'CLOCK, AND AFTER GIVING the children a last reminder to push in their chairs, Chloe dismissed them for the day.

Relief flowed through her that this school day was finally over. Not that she didn't like her job. She loved being a teacher, loved the kids, but this day had gone from bad to worse. She just wanted to go home, put her comfy sweats on, and curl up on the sofa with a warm cup of tea.

Not that she would. Between grading papers, making two dozen cupcakes for the bake sale the next day, and figuring out what the heck she was going to do about her car, she still had hours of work ahead of her. She wasn't ready to admit she also wanted to go home to where it was quiet so she could relive and analyze every moment of the time spent that morning with Colt. She still couldn't believe she'd crashed into him. Of all the people in Creedence, Colorado, she had to run into the guy she'd been crushing on for the past two months, but had been too timid to say more than a few words to.

Not that a guy like Colt James would ever take notice of her. She knew he was just being friendly and doing that gentlemanly thing that all the James brothers were known for, but she certainly took notice of him.

She let out a dreamy sigh and clutched her planning book to her chest as she remembered how it had felt to be cradled in his arms as he'd carried her to his truck. He'd picked her up like she weighed nothing, and she'd wanted to cuddle against him, wanted to bury her face in his neck and inhale the scent of his aftershave. Heck, she'd wanted to lick him and claim him as hers.

Stop it, she admonished herself, rolling her eyes at her own foolishness. Hadn't she just established that there was no way a guy like Colt would be interested in her licking anything of his?

Lord have mercy. Now all she could think about was licking him. Heat flared to her cheeks, and sweat gathered in the center of her back. She fanned herself with the planning book and let out another sigh as she looked around her classroom.

Her brain had been too fuzzy with thoughts of Colt and her damaged car, and she'd let the last half hour of arts and crafts go longer than usual. Trails of gooey glitter and scraps of construction paper littered the craft table, and piles of books lay scattered on the floor in the reading corner. Normally she wouldn't let the kids out until they'd cleaned all the stations and returned the room to its tidy state, but today she'd figured it would be easier to clean it herself than make the kids stay after the bell rang.

It took her only a few minutes to wipe the tables clean and return the books to their assigned shelves. She pushed the last book neatly into place, then ran her fingers over the straightened spines. Her chest eased as she scanned the neatly ordered book corner. An over-stuffed chair sat in one corner, and she'd arranged carpet squares in a perfect rectangle in front of the bookshelf.

Each section of her classroom was organized and

arranged so everything had a place and a purpose. She tried not to think too much about her need for tidiness, preferring to brush it off as a quirky part of her personality, but she knew the more she felt in control of her surroundings, the more she felt in control of her life. Her mom had left when she'd still been a kid, and the duties of cooking meals and keeping the house had fallen to Chloe. It didn't take her long to figure out that the best way to keep her dad happy—to control his moods, to keep him from going to the dark place—was to keep the house clean and the chores done. And even though her dad was gone now, it still settled her to straighten and tidy and keep her surroundings neat. It wasn't a full-blown obsession, but she couldn't quite bring herself to go to bed with dishes left in the sink or leave for the day with her classroom in disarray. Even if she did have a million things she still needed to do that afternoon.

A timid knock sounded at her door, and she looked up to see one of her former students standing just inside the room.

"Hi, David," she said, pushing to her feet.

"Hi, Miss Bishop." He stared at the floor as he shifted from one foot to the other. After a few seconds, he looked up and glanced around the room before nodding at the black-and-white guinea pig rustling in the cage sitting on the counter. "I was just wondering if I could come see Oreo."

"Yes, of course. Would you like to feed him a carrot?" She crossed to the mini-fridge behind her desk, pulled out a bag of baby carrots, and dumped several into a bowl.

The boy shrugged and crossed to the cage. "Sure, I

guess." His coat was threadbare and hung loosely on his small frame. His dark hair was in need of a cut, and he brushed his bangs from his eyes before taking the bowl of carrots.

"You know Oreo only likes to eat carrots if you eat one too," she reminded him, her heart breaking as she watched him gingerly push a carrot into the cage before stuffing one in his mouth.

David was in fourth grade now, but he had been one of her most challenging students a few years before. Not that he wasn't bright enough; he was smart as a whip, but his home life often prohibited him from turning in his homework or, at times, just staying awake in class. He'd made excuses for a long time, then finally admitted that his family didn't always have electricity and sometimes slept in a car or in the homeless shelter.

Poverty was an issue for several of Chloe's students, and she tried to bring in healthy treats once or twice a week. Plus she always kept extra snacks and protein bars in her classroom.

She opened the cupboard above her head and drew out a box of graham crackers. She tore open the top of a fresh pack and held it toward him. "I was just about to have a cracker. You want one?"

He shrugged again but took a cracker. She left the rest of the package on the counter and busied herself with straightening the art supplies next to the cage.

"So what's new? Anything exciting happening in fourth grade?" She kept her tone nonchalant, her focus on the tubes of glitter she was arranging by color.

"Nothing much." He kept his eyes trained on the guinea pig, pushing his finger through the bars of the cage to pet the end of the animal's nose. His voice was soft, and he seemed to be talking to the guinea pig instead of her. "I got an A on my math quiz last week."

"Wow. That's awesome. Good for you." She expected to see his shoulders pull back with pride, but they stayed slumped forward. There had to be something else going on. "How's your little sister doing?"

"Fine."

Hmm. That wasn't it. She tried a lighter approach, knowing he'd eventually get around to what was troubling him. "Read any good books lately?"

He shook his head, and his eyes cast to the floor. "Nah. Miss Ledbetter doesn't have as many books in her room as you do."

"Would you *like* to read a book?"

He shrugged again. "Kinda. I'm supposed to read one at home and do a book report on it."

Chloe patiently waited, holding her tongue in hopes his would loosen.

"But...ya see...we moved again, and it didn't work out to bring all our stuff...so I don't really have any books at my house right now." He scratched at a small scab on the back of his hand. "And I don't have my notebook anymore either."

Chloe pressed her lips together as a ball of anger burned in her chest. What was wrong with that Miss Ledbetter? How could she give out an assignment that some of the kids in class couldn't complete? Joyce Ledbetter was new this year and seemed more concerned with hanging out and gossiping in the teachers' lounge than taking her turn for recess duty. She'd tried to share some tidbit of a rumor with Chloe earlier in the year, but Chloe had shut her down and hadn't spoken to her much after that. But this was unacceptable. So she'd be speaking to her now.

Chloe tried to keep her own shoulders from slumping because she knew she wouldn't actually confront Joyce. No matter how outraged she was, she didn't have the guts it took to challenge another teacher. She avoided confrontation like the plague.

But she was fearless when it came to helping her kids. And she could help David. She nodded to the book-shelf in the reading corner. "I've got plenty of books. Probably too many. In fact, you'd be doing me a favor if you took one or two of them home with you. It would make more room on my shelf. And then you'd have one to do your report on."

The boy let out his breath, and the tightness in his shoulders eased. "Yeah, I guess I could do that. If it would help you out and all."

"It really would. And I think I've got an extra note-book around here that's cluttering up my cupboard." She opened another cabinet and peered inside. Every summer, she combed the back-to-school sales and stocked up on extra supplies. Grabbing an extra pencil and a blue notebook from the stack, she passed them to David, then nodded toward the bookshelf. "Why don't you go take a look and see if there are any books that interest you?"

He tucked the notebook under his arm and grabbed the remaining graham crackers before crossing to the reading corner and plopping down in front of the books.

Chloe busied herself with rinsing the carrot bowl as David pulled almost every book from the shelf and thumbed through them, scattering cracker crumbs across their pages as he tried to pick which two to take home.

She didn't care, didn't even cringe, didn't give a second thought to the mess she'd have to clean up or to the fact she'd be even later getting home. The smile on David's face and the soft chuckle of laughter he gave as he found a book he liked were worth everything.

"I found a couple," he told her, holding up two.

She peered at the books. "Great choices. But that one is the first in a series, so you should take the second one in the series too. In case it ends with a cliffhanger." She handed him an extra book. "Let me know what you think, okay?"

"Okay, I will." He stared down at the toe of his shoe, a pink flush coloring his cheeks. "Thanks, Miss Bishop. You're the best."

"You're the best, David. I know your book report is going to be great." She crossed to her desk and pulled out her drawer, then gave him the all-natural protein bar she'd been saving to eat after her classes ended for the day. "I always like to have one of these while I read. It helps me think clearly. You better take this one. Just in case."

He nodded. "Okay. Just in case."

She followed him out the door and watched him head down the hallway before turning and bumping directly into the hard-muscled chest of the object of her earlier licking fantasies.

He grunted as he grabbed her shoulders to steady her. "Woman, you are bound and determined to wreck into me today, aren't you?" he teased.

"Colt, what are you doing here?" Her skin flushed. Her cheeks burned warm enough to roast marshmallows over.

"I thought you might need a ride home." He held up her snow boot. "And, since it hasn't stopped snowing yet, I figured you'd be needing this."

Thankfully, she kept a pair of sneakers at school to wear when she had recess duty, so she hadn't had to go shoeless all day, but her day had been so crazy, she hadn't given much thought to what she was going to wear after school. Or to how she was going to get home.

She took the boot from him. "Thank you. That was really thoughtful."

He shrugged. "It was no big deal. I was out anyway."

Of course. He was just being nice. He would do the same for anyone, she was sure. That's just the kind of guy he was. Why would she think it had anything to do with her? She did nice things for people all the time. It didn't mean she was attracted to them.

"I just have a few things to finish up, then I'll be ready. If you don't mind waiting a few minutes."

"I don't mind." He sauntered into her classroom and gazed around at all the things she had on the walls. "Your class is nice. Everything is so neat."

She flushed again. Like he'd just told her she was pretty instead of complimenting her on her organizational skills. "Thanks. I like to keep things organized." She sidestepped around him as if trying to block the messy reading corner. "Usually, I mean."

He took a few steps closer and knelt down to gather a handful of books. His forearm brushed the side of her leg as he reached to put them back on the shelf. "I heard you with that kid before. You did a great job convincing him to take a few books *and* something to eat."

He was listening? Her cheeks burned hotter, and the

side of her leg where he'd touched her felt like it was on fire.

She should laugh off his compliment, dazzle him with her sparkling wit—do something, anything. But she couldn't. Besides the fact that she was woefully lacking in sparkling wit, even when she wasn't trying to talk to a devilishly handsome cowboy, her body felt so hot that if he said anything more, she was afraid she might spontaneously combust.

But she had to say something. She swallowed. *Focus on the student*. "Thanks. He's a good kid. He's just had a rough life."

He nodded, obviously understanding. Holding a book up by one edge, he shook cracker crumbs from its pages. "He got a few crumbs on some of these."

"It's fine," she said, trying not to cringe as he pushed the rest of the books back onto the shelf. It *was* fine. She could always go back and straighten them tomorrow.

He stood and turned to survey the rest of the room. "I like the bookworm." He pointed to the segmented creature that circled the top of the room, each part of its body listing a child's name and the book they'd finished reading.

She caught her breath as his arm skimmed her shoulder when he pointed. She stared at his chest, her mouth dry. His jacket was unzipped, and a stray thread had broken in the seam on his shirt. She wanted to reach up and pull it. Maybe his shirt would come apart and fall off. That could happen.

But she didn't reach up, didn't pull it. She kept her hands at her sides and tried to act natural. Like she had handsome men in her classroom every day. "Thanks.

It's a contest thing—anything to get the kids excited about reading." Her voice was too high. It sounded stiff.

He studied the bookworm. "It looks like my nephew makes up a significant portion of your worm."

She laughed and tried to relax her shoulders. This was more in her wheelhouse. She could talk about reading. "Yes. Max is definitely my best reader. I was glad to see him in my class again this year after they switched me from teaching second grade to third. His reading improved quite a bit over the summer. And he does a good job of getting the others excited about the books he's just finished. Do you like to read?"

"Not the way Max does, but yeah, I enjoy it."

"What are you reading now?"

He named a popular thriller that his mom had lent him. "How about you? What are you reading?"

Her cheeks warmed again as she thought about the western romance she'd been lost in the night before. For some reason, she'd been drawn to books lately about ordinary women and the swoony, hot cowboys who swept them off their feet.

Um, yeah. The reason is standing right in front of me—looking hot as heck in his snug Wranglers and cowboy boots.

She was saved from answering by the arrival of Maddie and two of her older brothers as they burst into the classroom.

"Can we get a ride home with you, Miss Bishop?" Maddie asked. "Jesse didn't show up to get us today."

The oldest Johnson boy, Jesse, was seventeen and wasn't always the most responsible, but it seemed to Chloe that he took on more than his share when it came to raising his younger siblings. He'd worked the whole summer before to buy an old beater Toyota that he usually drove the kids to and from school in.

"You don't have to," Charlie, the older of the two boys, said, staring down at his feet. His canvas sneakers were shabby and ragged, and the corner of his dingy white sock poked through a small hole in the end of one. "I told her we could walk. It's not that far."

The junior high school that Charlie and his brother, Jake, attended was across the street from the grade school, and although it started earlier, it let out at the same time.

"Where's Jesse?" she asked.

Jake shrugged. "Not here."

"Well, I would love to give you all a ride home, but unfortunately, I had a little accident in my car this morning, and I'm having to beg a ride home myself." She nodded toward the tall cowboy leaning nonchalantly against her desk. "And I don't think Colt...er, Mr. James's truck has enough room for all of us. Let me see if I can find another teacher."

"I can take them," Colt offered. "Didn't you say you had a few things to do anyway?"

"Yes, but—" But what? She couldn't very well say she'd rather have Colt give *her* a ride home than the three kids. And she wouldn't dream of ever letting that happen. No, it would be easier for her to find another ride or just walk to her house.

"It's no problem. I can run them home and come back to pick you up—take me twenty minutes tops. Will that give you enough time to finish up what you need to do?"

"Yes, but...you don't have to do that," she stammered.

"I don't want to put you out. I'm sure I can find a ride with someone else."

"Don't worry about it. You're not putting me out at all. I'm glad to do it." He winked at her, and her insides went a little gooey. "Hey, what are friends for?"

Her mushy insides turned into a solid mass that landed hard in her stomach like a punch that drove her securely back into the boundaries of the friend zone.

What had she been thinking anyway? That Colt had shown up here because he was romantically interested in her—a neurotic, chunky schoolteacher with unruly curly hair and poor driving skills? She smoothed the front of her sweater over her stomach. Okay, so she wasn't *so* chunky—not anymore. But she wasn't thin, and the label still haunted her after spending the majority of her growing-up years known as Candy Bar Chloe after her classmates had discovered a stash of chocolate bars in her desk.

"Yeah, of course," she stammered. "That sounds great. I'll just finish up here and wait for you to come back."

"Back in twenty," Colt called over his shoulder as he herded the kids out the door.

Chloe sagged into the reading chair, realizing she was still holding her snow boot in her hand. She dropped it to the floor and fought the urge to thump her head against the bookshelf.

What are friends for?

His words echoed in her ears as she rearranged the books, then finished cleaning up her desk and gathered her things together for the night. Being friends with Colt was better than nothing, she decided as she slipped her feet from her sneakers and pulled on her snow boots.

She'd just need to keep her emotions in check when she was around him.

Her classroom door opened, and she looked up expecting to see the handsome cowboy, a traitorous smile already crossing her face. So much for keeping her feelings in check.

But it wasn't Colt.

She tried to keep the smile in place. "Hi, Hugh."

Hugh Nordon bounded into her room. He was the PE teacher and did almost everything with an energetic zeal. Fit and toned, his upper body bulged with well-defined muscles, and he was always willing to share a new fitness or healthy-eating tip he'd just heard about or tried. His dark hair was thick and wavy, and a mustache covered his upper lip.

"Hey, Chloe, did you get your tickets yet?"

"Tickets to what?" Oh great. Had she missed a memo about a school event?

He pressed his fists together and flexed his muscled arms. "Tickets to the gun show."

She tried not to roll her eyes as she offered him the same kind of patient smile she'd give a second grader who'd told her a corny joke. "Good one, Hugh."

"Seriously, I can't even wear a jacket without a concealed weapons permit."

"And the jokes just keep coming…"

"No, for real now, I heard you wrecked your car this morning and figured I'd give you a ride home. My SUV does great in the snow," he said with his usual confidence in everything he chose to own, use, or wear.

"Thanks for thinking of me, but I've already got someone picking me up."

"It's not a problem for me," he said, oblivious to what she'd just said. "I could even come in when we get there, in case, you know, you have anything around the house that needs some *heavy lifting*." He smoothed the edges of his mustache and arched an eyebrow as if *heavy lifting* was code for something else.

She shook her head. "No, really, I'm good. I can't think of anything like that. And like I said, I've got someone picking me up."

"You sure? Because this is my 'arms' week for lifting, and I wouldn't mind a little extra workout. I've been working on bulking up my biceps." He took a step closer and grabbed her hand, then set it on his flexed bicep. "How do you think it's going?"

Before she could answer, a deep voice spoke from the doorway of her classroom. "Am I interrupting?"

Chloe snatched her hand away as Colt walked in. "No, of course not. We were just fooling around. I mean, we weren't *fooling around*. Hugh was just showing me his muscle." She clamped her mouth shut—she was only making it worse.

But Hugh wasn't fazed. He took a protective step in front of Chloe and lifted his chin. "Hugh Nordon. I teach physical education."

Colt held out his hand. "Colt James—friend of Chloe's. Nice to meet you, Huge."

"It's Hugh, actually," he said, firmly grasping Colt's hand.

The two men looked like they were sizing each other up as they crushed each other's hands in viselike grips.

Oh brother.

"Hugh, this is the friend I was telling you about, the

one who is giving me a ride home. Speaking of which, we'd better get going."

"Good to meet ya," Hugh said, extricating his hand from Colt's and casually dropping his arm around Chloe's shoulder. "I'm a friend of Chloe's too."

Oh, for heaven's sake. She could almost taste the testosterone flying around in the air. She ducked out from under Hugh's arm and grabbed her coat and Colt's scarf from the peg behind her desk. She stuffed her arms into her jacket, wrapped the scarf around her neck, and grabbed her bags from her desk. "You ready to go?"

"Yup."

"See you tomorrow, Hugh." She turned off the light, then stood by the door as she waited for Hugh to leave. Finally getting her not-so-subtle hint, he gave her a nod before heading out the door and down the hall.

"Yeah, see you later, Huge," Colt called, then looked down at her. "I like that guy. He seems nice."

"Yeah, sure." She playfully nudged him in the side with her elbow, shaking her head at his terrible efforts to conceal his grin.

She followed him outside, any more of their conversation cut off with the force of the blowing snow.

"My buddy towed your car in today," Colt told her once they were in the truck and headed toward her house. "He runs Bud's Auto Shop. He said most of the damage was to the door, and it wouldn't take too much to fix it. But he's going to have to keep the car for a few days at least."

"Oh no." That's what she'd been afraid of. "Now I'll have to file the accident with my insurance. Otherwise, I won't be able to get a rental car."

"You don't need a rental. I can give you a ride the next few days until you get your car back."

"Why would you do that?"

Please don't say that's what friends are for again.

"Because I feel partly responsible for the accident, and because I'd like to help you out."

Ugh. She didn't know which was worse—that he was doing it because he wanted to be her friend or because he felt responsible for her dumb driving mishap. "It's too much. You really don't have to."

"Do you have another car in the garage?" he asked, completely ignoring her protests.

"No. In fact, all I have in there are boxes of junk and stuff from my dad that need to go to Goodwill." She swallowed, the mention of the garage hitting her like a blow to the throat. For all her efforts at keeping her life tidy, the garage was the one place that she couldn't quite sort out. It was the one area of her home—of her soul—that she truly couldn't summon the courage to face.

It wasn't just her dad's old recliner and his collection of sports magazines. It was boxes of junk and layers of guilt packed in with a few remnants of shame and self-loathing. And every time she walked into the garage, she was reminded that it was the one area of her life that she still needed to "clean up," to deal with, to finally lay to rest.

She'd tried many times—had gathered trash bags and boxes and set her mind to dealing with her dad's stuff. Except it wasn't just his physical stuff. It was all the *stuff* that he'd damaged in her, that she didn't know how to fix or get rid of. No matter how much she prepared herself to stomp into the garage and hurl boxes into the trash or burn the magazines into charred ashes, she couldn't do it. Couldn't break the hold her dad and his "things" still had over her.

"Then it's settled. I'll pick you up tomorrow at seven." He grinned, oblivious to the inner war of regret coursing through her, then dipped his gaze to the scarf around her neck. "My scarf looks good on you, by the way. It matches your eyes."

"Th-thank you," she stammered, so flummoxed by the compliment that she forgot about the garage, forgot to keep arguing about him giving her a ride, forgot everything except the gloriously handsome man whose grin had just flipped her stomach inside out. She twisted the handles of her purse in her lap, trying to think of a more appropriate response than "I think you'd look good on me too." She hadn't said the words out loud, but just thinking them had heat darting up her spine.

"So, how was your day?" he asked, slowing for the one stoplight in Creedence.

"Crazy," she answered, thankful to change the subject. "As if it hadn't started out bad enough with the accident and running late, I also had to deal with three meltdowns, a glitter explosion, no recess because of the snow, two kids who called in sick, and one that should have, judging by the way he tossed his lunch all over his shoes." She glanced over at him. "Were you actually asking how my day went, or was that one of those rhetorical questions where I was supposed to say fine?"

He chuckled. "No, I was really asking. Hopefully, your night will get easier."

"Not hardly. I've got papers to grade, a load of laundry to do, and two dozen chocolate cupcakes to make for the bake sale tomorrow." She pressed her lips together again—*must stop blabbering on*. What was wrong with her? Standing next to him in her classroom, she could barely force out two words, and now she suddenly had diarrhea of the mouth. "How about you? How was your day?"

"About the same. Except that no one threw up on their shoes. I helped Mason with some downed fence line this morning, then did quite a bit of plow work this afternoon, trying to keep the streets and parking lots cleared for the downtown businesses."

She'd met Mason, Colt's older brother, earlier that summer and had spent a little time with the James family when she'd helped run the snack bar for the annual alumni hockey game. Creedence loved its hockey and its most famous hockey player, Rockford James, Colt's oldest brother, who played for the NHL. Rock had made headlines recently for his whirlwind wedding with his high-school sweetheart, Quinn Rivers. Now she saw Rock and Quinn frequently since it was Quinn's son, Max, who was in her class again this year.

"Do you work for the city?" she asked.

"No. I just fill in when they need an extra hand. It's one of about seven odd jobs that I fill in for."

"That's nice of you."

He shrugged. "I like to stay busy, and I like helping people. Plus the extra cash doesn't hurt."

Extra cash? She wasn't familiar with the term. Her teacher's salary barely covered her expenses plus the endless additional supplies she frequently purchased out of her own pocket for her classroom. Thank goodness her dad had left her the house, which was bought and paid for, or she didn't know what she'd do.

Chapter 3

COLT TRIED NOT TO LAUGH AS HE FOLLOWED CHLOE INTO her house. She was just so dang cute. He loved to watch her blush. Heck, he loved to watch her do just about anything.

He held the door for her as she fumbled with the lock. Were her hands shaking? Maybe he made her as nervous as she made him. He doubted it. Something about Chloe Bishop had him feeling like an adolescent teen with a crush on the prettiest girl in school. Whenever he was around her, his heart started racing and his palms began to sweat.

They stamped their feet on the rug, and she took their coats, hanging them both up neatly in the closet.

"Should I take my boots off?" he asked, glancing at the fresh vacuum tracks on the carpet of the living room.

She waved his concern away as she tugged her own boots off. "Oh, no. Don't worry about it. This carpet is so old, it's seen much worse than your boots." She gestured to the living room. "Have a seat. I need just a second to check on Agatha." She padded quickly down the hall in her stocking feet.

He wiped his boots one more time, then wandered around the immaculately kept living room. An over-stuffed blue sofa sat on one side of a heavy coffee table, and a large rocking recliner sat on the other. A purple tote bag brimming with multicolored skeins of yarn and knitting needles sat on the floor next to the recliner, and a paperback with a brooding cowboy on the cover perched on the corner of the end table.

A neat row of three pictures lined the oak mantel above a small fireplace, and Colt leaned in to study them. The first was a faded old photograph of a handsome, dark-haired man laughing as he held a chubby toddler high in his arms. The second was of Chloe in her college graduation cap and gown, smiling as she held her diploma, one arm wrapped around a tiny white-haired woman he assumed was her grandmother. And the third was a recent picture of Chloe sitting cross-legged on the floor of her classroom, laughing as she read a book to a group of students.

"Your nephew gave me that for Christmas last year," Chloe said as she stepped back into the living room. "I think it's the only picture I have of me teaching. I guess Quinn took it one day when she was volunteering in the classroom and had it framed for me."

He spotted Max in the circle of kids around her, his gaze rapt with attention at either the teacher or the story she was reading. Knowing Max, it could have been either, or both. "It's a great picture. You have a pretty smile."

She ducked her head, a pink blush rising to her cheeks. "It's one of my favorite gifts. But don't tell my other students."

He nodded toward the hallway. "Everything okay?"

"Yeah."

"So do you live here with your grandmother?"

"My grandmother?" She tilted her head. "I don't think so. Not unless she's a ghost. Then I guess, maybe."

"Oh, sorry. You said you were checking on Agatha, and I saw the…" He looked down to the bag of knitting supplies.

Chloe mimed a dagger to her chest. "Ouch. Agatha is my cat, named after my favorite author, Agatha Christie, and that mess of knitting and too much yarn is mine. And plenty of young—or youngish, in my case—women knit as a hobby." An embarrassed grin creased her face. "Although talking about my cat and my yarn obsession in the same sentence is not making me *feel* any younger at the present moment."

Oh shit. Good going, Colt. Open mouth, insert foot. "It's not making me feel so great either. If you'll excuse me while I try to unwedge the size thirteen boot I just stuck into my mouth. Sorry about that."

"It's okay. I'm just teasing you. And my grandmother is the one who taught me to knit when I was little. I probably haven't gotten much better since then, but I love the patterns, the colors, and the process of turning skeins of yarn into something beautiful. I guess I'm kind of old-fashioned."

Colt shrugged. "Me too. My grandfather taught me to play the harmonica and to whittle, both skills a bit on the antiquated side, but I still enjoy them. And I think knitting is cool. My great-aunt Sassy knits, and she's one of the coolest chicks I know."

"I've never actually met her, but I've seen your great-aunt at a couple of Max's school functions, and I would have to agree."

He held up the romance novel and offered her a teasing grin. "Good reading?"

She snatched the book from his hands and pushed

it between the cushions of the sofa. "I wouldn't know. That one belongs to the cat."

He cocked an eyebrow. "Does your cat have a thing for handsome cowboys?"

"We'll know in a minute. She just waltzed into the room." Chloe nodded to the black-and-gray tabby meandering its way toward him. The cat jumped to the corner of the sofa next to him and tilted her head up as if assessing him with her cool gaze.

He reached out his hand and let her sniff him before offering her a scratch under the chin. She purred loudly and rubbed her head against his palm.

Chloe shook her head. "Apparently she does."

"And apparently you just put me in the handsome cowboy category."

A grin tugged at the corner of her lips, and a surge of heat shot down his spine. Dang, but she had a cute grin.

"How about that warm drink? You want tea or coffee?"

"Tea sounds good. Got any Earl Grey?"

She narrowed her eyes. "I wouldn't have pegged you for an Earl Grey hot tea kind of guy."

"I'm quite the man of mystery, you know." He laughed at her eye roll, then followed her into the kitchen. "Before you start to think I'm too cultured, when I come in from the cold after doing chores, I'll drink about anything hot that someone hands me in a cup. Really, it's just my mom's favorite kind, so it's the only tea that I know the name of, and I was trying to impress you. But I'll take whatever you've got."

She grabbed a light-blue kettle from the stove and poured water into it as he studied the rest of the room.

The kitchen was big with a long center island. A white farm table with four chairs was tucked into a windowed breakfast nook. The cabinets gleamed a glossy white, and a row of robin's-egg blue canisters shaped like mason jars lined the soft-gray counters. A KitchenAid mixer in the same shade of blue sat in the corner next to the sink, a chocolate cake mix and tub of frosting next to it. Everything coordinated to the decor of white and the same light blue.

"Nice kitchen."

"Thanks." She ran a hand over the countertop. "I love it too. I like to cook, and it just makes me feel happy to be in here. Now."

"Now?"

"It didn't always. I lived here with my dad, and this kitchen didn't always hold the best memories. He died a few years ago and left me this house and a little money. I toyed with the idea of selling the house, but instead I used the money to do a couple of little remodeling projects, including the kitchen, and I'm slowly making it all mine. It's amazing how a little paint, a lot of Pine-Sol, and some sandpaper can change the look and feel of a place."

"You did all this yourself?"

"Most of it. I hired out some of the big stuff, but I refinished and painted the cabinets myself and put in the wood flooring. I'm pretty handy with a screw gun."

"I'm impressed."

"It's amazing what you can learn from the internet and watching do-it-yourself videos. And Pinterest."

It was amazing how much he was starting to really like her.

"I like all the blue stuff."

"It's aqua. And it's one of my favorite colors. I couldn't believe how much stuff they make in this color. I guess it's kind of the 'in' color right now. Not that I care about that stuff. I just love the shade. It's a happy color." She took a box of tea and two matching aqua mugs from the cupboard and set them on the counter.

The kettle whistled, and he watched her as she prepared the cups and poured hot water over the tea bags. He studied her, trying to figure out what was so special about this woman. Her movements were concise and controlled, and she kept things tidy as she worked.

She was average height and average weight, but somehow Colt felt there was really nothing average about Chloe Bishop.

"One Earl Grey for the cultured mysterious cowboy." She grinned as she handed him the cup, then gave a soft inhale of breath as his fingers brushed hers.

He noticed how close she was now standing. He could feel the heat of her, smell the scent coming off her skin. She smelled like vanilla and honeysuckle and something else flowery. His body leaned closer, almost as if they were connected by a fishing line and he was being reeled in toward her.

She pursed her lips to blow on the hot beverage, and he couldn't take his eyes off her mouth. She had great lips, kissable lips.

Dude. Step back. He did not need to get involved with this woman—with any woman. And there was no reason to think Chloe was even interested in him. She'd made a point of introducing him to her coworker as her friend, so maybe she was just interested in being friends.

He took a swallow of his drink and regarded her over the top of his cup. "So what's the deal with you and Huge?"

She choked on the sip of tea she'd just taken. "There's no deal at all. We just work together."

He raised an eyebrow.

"I guess he's asked me to go out with him a few times, but I always say no."

"How come?"

She shrugged. "He's not really my type."

"What is your type?" He leaned in, just the slightest, the fishing line drawing him closer.

She gazed up at him, her eyes wide. Her lips parted as she inhaled another soft breath, and he imagined how her mouth would taste, how her body would feel if he pulled her against him and crushed her lips with his.

His eyes were drawn to her slender neck as he watched her swallow.

Before she could answer, an urgent banging sounded at the back door, startling them both. A small face peered into the kitchen through the glass in the top half of the door.

Chloe pulled away, practically dropping her mug on the counter as she hurried to open the door. "Maddie, are you okay? Where's your coat?"

The girl barreled into the kitchen, her cheeks red and her eyes wide with fear. The bottom half of her pants and her sneakers were soaked from running through the snow. She grabbed Chloe's hand and pulled her toward the door. "Miss Bishop, come quick! Charlie started the house on fire!"

Chapter 4

A FIRE? CHLOE'S HEART JUMPED TO HER THROAT. "WHERE are the boys?"

Maddie tried to catch her breath. "In the kitchen," she gasped. "They were trying to make dinner, but the pan caught on fire."

"Is the whole kitchen on fire or just the pan?" Colt asked, his voice remarkably calm.

"I don't know. Just the pan, I think." Her lip trembled like she was trying not to cry. "I got scared and ran."

"You did the right thing." Chloe pointed to the pantry door next to Colt. "I've got a fire extinguisher in there."

"Got it," he said, opening the door and grabbing the red canister. "Let's go."

"Maddie, stay here. We'll be right back," she told the girl, then raced out the back door after Colt.

The back door opened at the side of the house in front of the garage, and they ran across the driveway and through the yard. Wet snow seeped through her socks, but Chloe ignored the cold as she raced up the porch steps and threw open the front door. "Charlie! Jake!" she called as she ran toward the orange glow in the kitchen.

The acrid smell of greasy smoke filled the air and burned her eyes as she entered the room. It was bad— but not as bad as she'd feared. A flaming frying pan had been pushed into the sink and one of the curtains around the window had caught fire.

The two boys were trying to swat the flames with towels, but they were only making the situation worse. The fire was starting to spread across the top of the window to the other curtain.

"Stand back," Colt shouted, already pulling the pin of the extinguisher as he entered the room. He pointed the nozzle at the sink and sprayed the thick foam across the curtains and the pan.

Chloe pulled the boys toward her, holding their backs against her chest as they watched Colt douse the flames.

It took less than a minute, but the foam from the extinguisher made a mess of white powder all over the sink and countertops.

"Everybody okay?" Colt asked, turning toward them, his face flushed with the heat of the blaze.

The boys huddled against Chloe, their eyes downcast and their shoulders slumped forward.

"I'm sorry," Charlie said, his hands gripping his elbows as he wrapped his arms around himself. "It's my fault. I was trying to fry some eggs for dinner. I put some bacon grease in the pan and turned it on to heat up, then I started watching this show with Jake, and I forgot about it."

"We smelled the grease burning and came in to get it, but it just caught fire," Jake explained, taking a protective step in front of his older brother. "It happened so fast. We tried to throw water on it, but it just got bigger."

"It usually does. But if anything like this happens again, you never want to put water on a grease fire," Colt explained. "You either try to smother it by covering it with the lid, if it isn't too big already, or you throw salt or baking soda on it. Waving a towel at it will just make it worse."

Charlie nodded. "I didn't know what else to do."

"I know. Fire is scary. I'm a volunteer firefighter so I've seen lots of fires, but they still scare the crap out of me. This one wasn't too bad. We got it out quickly, and the important thing is nobody got hurt." He narrowed his eyes. "Are you sure you're both okay? Did either of you get burned?"

Charlie held out his hand. "I think I burned the ends of my fingers a little when I pushed the pan into the sink. I tried to use the towel, but it burned through it."

Colt turned on the cold water in the sink. "Hold your hand under here, and let me take a look."

The boy obeyed, and Colt examined Charlie's fingers as he held them under the water. "No blisters," he told Chloe as she anxiously peered toward the sink. "Skin's just a little red. He'll be okay."

She let out her breath. This could have been so much worse. She didn't want to think about what could have happened if Maddie hadn't come to them for help. "Everything's okay now. Where's your mom?" she asked Jake.

"She's at work."

Tina tended bar at a dive out by the highway and often kept odd hours. But Charlie and Jake were in junior high, old enough to be left alone and in charge of their sister. Chloe had been babysitting other people's kids when she was younger than they were now. And Jesse was usually home with them at night.

"What about Jesse?"

"He's still not home."

Chloe looked around the sparse kitchen. There wasn't much on the counters, but other than the powdery foam from the fire extinguisher, they were clean. No dirty dishes in the sink or trash left out. The door to the pantry stood open, and the shelves held some paper plates and a few boxes of macaroni and cheese. Tina did try—she kept the house clean—but she didn't always remember to go to the grocery store.

"That's okay. I was thinking of asking you all over for dinner at my place anyway."

"What about all this?" Charlie asked, his chin tucked down to his chest, his shame-filled expression conveying his misery.

Colt clapped a hand on his shoulder. "When a man makes a mess, he cleans it up. This stuff is nasty, but I've got some gloves in my truck. I'll grab 'em if you can find the vacuum, and we can get this cleaned up pretty quickly."

Emotion welled in the back of Chloe's throat. She was sure the fire and the fear for the children's safety was contributing to it, but watching Colt as he treated the boys as young men and took care of this situation so simply squeezed at her heart.

Her own dad would have pitched a fit, yelling and screaming, then blistered her backside if she'd done anything like this, and she was sure the boys' dad would have acted the same way if he were still around.

But Colt wasn't mad at all. He was perfectly calm.

He winked at her and gave her a reassuring nod. "We've got this. Why don't you head back and get warmed up? Your feet have got to be freezing."

She'd forgotten all about her wet socks, but now a

shiver ran through her. "Good idea. I'll start dinner and check on Maddie. I'm sure she's got to be worried."

"No, I'm not," Maddie said from the doorway of the kitchen. "I'm right here."

Chloe brought her hand to her throat. "I thought I told you to stay at my house."

The small girl shrugged. "I needed to see if my brothers were okay." Her lip trembled, and she ran across the kitchen and flung herself into Charlie's arms.

"It's okay, Maddie," Charlie told her, hugging her against him. "That was smart to get Ms. Bishop. But it's okay now. We're just going to clean this up, and it'll all be fine."

Chloe's heart twisted with compassion for the girl. It was obvious these kids were used to taking care of each other.

Another feeling snuck in there—she couldn't quite place it. Not jealousy exactly, but maybe a little envy at the close relationship the kids had. She couldn't help but wonder what it would have been like if she'd had a sibling or two growing up. If she'd had someone to share the burden and the misery of being raised by Butch Bishop.

She shook off the memories. Butch was gone, and she was a grown woman. He couldn't hurt her now. She pasted a smile on her face. "Maddie, as long as you're here, why don't you quick go find some dry clothes and put on some shoes and fresh socks. I'm making dinner for everyone at my house."

"Yay," Madison cheered, obviously putting the trauma of the fire behind her in the anticipation of a hot meal.

"Don't get too excited," Chloe said, mentally running

through the items in her pantry. "We're just having grilled-cheese sandwiches and tomato soup."

Jake nodded at the foam-covered pan perched sideways in the sink. "Sounds a heck of a lot better than burnt eggs covered in fire-extinguisher spray."

He made a valid point.

Thirty minutes later, Chloe flipped the last crispy, browned sandwiches on the griddle as Colt and Charlie came through the back door, both of them stamping the snow from their feet.

"Sorry, that took a little longer than we'd planned because we stopped to shovel the driveways and the sidewalks in front of both houses," Colt said, clapping the boy on the shoulder. "Charlie here's pretty good with a snow shovel. He was keeping pace with me the whole time."

Chloe had looked out the window earlier and seen them shoveling, so she was over the initial shock of one more thoughtful thing Colt had done for her today, but she couldn't help noticing the way Charlie's shoulders pulled back and he stood a little taller next to the cowboy. "Wow. Great job, guys. I know I really appreciate it, and I'm sure your mom will too."

Charlie shrugged off the compliment, but a shy smile tugged at his lips. "It was no big deal."

"We got everything cleaned up in the kitchen as well," Colt said. "Except for the missing curtain, you'd never know anything happened."

"Our mom probably won't even notice," Jake said from his seat at the kitchen table.

"That's what I said." Charlie nodded his head in agreement. "One time this summer, I had a zit the size of a pizza right in the middle of my forehead. It was there for three days, and Mom never said a word. I don't think she even saw it."

"I'm sure she noticed. Maybe she was just trying not to hurt your feelings," Chloe said, making an effort to stick up for Tina.

"Yeah right," the boy mumbled. "I'm sure that's it. She's always worried about not hurting our feelings."

Chloe didn't know what to say, so she let the comment go as she glanced up at Colt. "You staying for supper? I made you a couple of sandwiches." She'd also brought in two extra folding chairs and had already set the table for five.

He grinned. "Well, grilled cheese just happens to be my favorite sandwich, and I don't think I've turned one down yet." He and Charlie washed their hands, and the boy took a seat at the table next to his brother. "Anything I can do to help?" Colt asked, drying his hands on an aqua-colored towel.

"I can't imagine what. You've already helped so much." Chloe studied him as she ladled soup into mugs. What was Colt still doing here? He did say he liked to help people, but come on. Everything he'd done today—from giving her a ride to arranging for her car to be taken in to putting out a fire in her neighbor's house—seemed like more than a regular guy would do.

Colt James was proving to be more than just a regular guy.

She handed him the platter of sandwiches as she picked up the mugs of soup and passed them to the kids.

She carried the last two over, then slid into the empty seat he'd left between him and Maddie.

Charlie reached for the platter of sandwiches as his sister bowed her head. He glanced sheepishly at Colt but followed suit when the man also bowed his head and clasped his hands together.

Maddie's small voice filled the kitchen. "Dear God, thank you for my family, even my brothers. Thank you for not letting our house burn down. Thank you for Miss Bishop and her friend Mr. Colt. And thank you for this good soup and these yummy sandwiches." She dropped her voice to a whisper. "And please help Momma to get better, and bring Jesse home safe. Amen."

"Amen," Colt repeated, then passed the platter to Charlie.

Chloe took a sip of water to quell the burn of emotion building in her throat. She took a napkin and focused on spreading it neatly across her lap, trying not to imagine this as her family, her kids and her husband. Trying not to think about how it would feel to sit down to dinner every night with them, to listen to them laugh and say their prayers, and to tuck them in at night, then crawl into her own warm bed next to Colt.

Oh geez. Criminently. What was wrong with her tonight? She wasn't usually this sappy. Okay, she was usually pretty sappy, but not over her own life. She got teary-eyed over sentimental commercials and could go through a whole box of tissues weeping over a great book or a heartbreaking movie, but she didn't usually let herself get mushy over her own circumstances.

Her life was what it was. She was happy. The kids in her class brought her joy, and she had Agatha to come home to every night. And the cat did occasionally seem glad to see her.

So what if she didn't have a man. Her dad had repeatedly reminded her she'd never be pretty enough or good enough or thin enough—or whatever "enough" he fancied at the moment—to catch a husband anyway. As if she were trying to lure one on the end of a fishing line with her wiggling around on the hook as bait.

"…and then the car exploded," Jake said loudly, spreading his arms and drawing Chloe's attention back to the group just as his hand hit his glass and sent it sailing across the table.

Maddie shrieked and grabbed her sandwich as water splashed onto her plate and dripped over the side of the table.

"Sorry," Jake said, trying to sop up the water with a handful of napkins.

"It's okay. It's just water." Chloe grabbed a towel. Maybe having kids and a family wasn't all sunshine and roses. Kids were messy. She didn't need that kind of chaos in her life.

Yeah, keep telling yourself that, sister.

The rest of the meal went off without a hitch, or a spill, or anything catching on fire. Chloe stood to clear the table. She couldn't believe it was already past seven. "I'd better get you guys home. Give you time to take showers and finish your homework before bed."

Colt rested a hand on her arm. "Why don't I do this while you take the kids back and get them settled in for the night?"

"You don't have to. You've already done so much."

He squeezed her arm reassuringly, and she felt the heat of his palm through her sweater. "I want to."

"Why? This has got to be a crazy night for you."

"Nah. I grew up with a single mom and two older brothers. A fire and something spilling or breaking was just a normal Tuesday night for us. This is nothing—just par for the course."

It made sense now how he was so unfazed. She didn't realize until much later that he hadn't answered the question of why.

It took Chloe longer than she'd planned to get the kids settled in for the night, and she fully expected to see Colt's truck gone by the time she slipped out of her neighbor's house and trekked across the driveway toward her own.

What she didn't expect was to open her kitchen door to the heavenly scent of chocolate in the air and the sight of a ridiculously hot cowboy standing next to the counter licking cake batter off the side of a beater.

He offered her a sheepish grin as he held the other beater out to her. "I saved this one for you."

She shrugged out of her coat but was so stunned she didn't even hang it up. Instead, she just tossed it on the chair and took the offered beater. "I don't get it."

Although the evidence of the warm stove, the smell of chocolate, and the mixing bowl soaking in the sink were all in front of her, she couldn't believe Colt had made the cupcakes.

"You did say you had to make two dozen cupcakes tonight for the bake sale tomorrow, right?"

"Yes, but I never dreamed you would make them for me."

He shrugged and licked another dollop of chocolate from the side of the beater. Watching his tongue dart out and lick up the batter was doing funny things to Chloe's insides, and she was getting tingly in spots she hadn't felt tingles in a long time. "It was no big deal. It's not like I made them from scratch. All the stuff was sitting on the counter, so I figured this was the one you wanted to make. And your kitchen is so well organized, it was pretty easy to find the rest of what I needed. I finished cleaning up and figured I'd get them in the oven for you. I hope that's okay."

She leaned back against the counter next to him, still holding the beater in her hand. "It's more than okay. I think it's the nicest thing anyone's ever done for me."

His eyes widened. "Lord, I hope not. All I did was toss a few eggs and some oil into a bowl and mix it up. If that's the nicest thing anyone's ever done for you, old Huge needs to step up his game."

She let out a bark of laughter, then clapped her free hand over her mouth.

He laughed too, and suddenly Chloe couldn't hold it back, the events of the day swirling in a crazy haze around her. She'd started her morning with cat yak between her toes, then wrecked her car into a cute cowboy who had put out a fire, washed her dishes, and just made a batch of cupcakes for her. It all seemed too ridiculous, and a gush of laughter bubbled out of her.

She held her stomach and bent forward as she tried to catch her breath. "This day has been something else," she wheezed as her laughter finally died down.

"Sometimes all you can do is laugh about it," Colt said. "And you have a great laugh."

She shook her head. "Stop it. My dad always told me that my laugh sounded like the bark of a seal."

His eyes widened. "That's crazy. And mean. And just plain wrong. You have an awesome laugh. It makes your whole face light up." His gaze dropped to her mouth.

She caught her breath, suddenly imagining how it would feel to have his lips pressed to hers. Would she be able to taste the chocolate of the cake batter on his tongue? Would his lips be as soft as they looked?

"So, are you ever gonna lick that?" he asked, his voice huskier than it had been before.

She blinked and swallowed, moistening her lips as her mouth went dry. "What?" she managed to croak.

"The beater. You know, the one you've been holding in your hands for the last five minutes. Aren't you going to lick it?"

Oh, for the love of cake. Every time he said the words *lick it*, flames of heat shot down her back. "Uh no," she said, passing him back the beater.

His forehead creased as he took it. "No? Why not?"

"I don't really eat many desserts. Too many calories."

"In a lick of cake batter?"

She shrugged. "It all adds up. And sometimes it's better not even to try it. Then you won't know what you're really missing out on. And you can just imagine it was awful and you didn't miss something great."

"What kind of crazy philosophy is that?"

One she'd lived for most of her life. And one she was trying to remind herself of now—and not just about the chocolate. "When you grow up as a chunky kid, you learn all sorts of crazy philosophies and tricks to keep you from eating."

His gaze traveled over her body, and she could almost feel the heat of his inspection. "You're not chunky now. You've got a great body." Pink flooded his cheeks. "I mean, you look great to me. Like, you know, just right. You're not chunk…er…heavy." He slapped his hand to his forehead. "Please save me from saying anything else."

She laughed, although she could feel the heat in her own cheeks at his compliments on her figure. Why had she just told him she used to be a chunky kid? He had to think she was a total dork. Although, maybe this was the kind of thing *friends* talked to each other about, so maybe he thought it was normal. So why was *he* blushing? And why did her skin feel like it had just been skimmed over with a light caress? "Okay, okay. I could easily argue, but I'm happy changing the subject too, so I'll just say thank you and let's go back to talking about the chocolate."

"Yes, chocolate." He grinned, then dragged his finger across the beater, scooping a dollop of batter onto the end, and held it out to her. "Come on. You've got to at least try it. Just one taste. Otherwise you really are missing out."

She peered down at his chocolate-smeared finger and swallowed again. There was no way in heck that she was licking that batter off the end of his finger. It was too intimate, too personal. Too freaking sexy. Just imagining it had warm currents of heat swirling between her legs.

This was not her. She did not lick things off men, especially gorgeous men like Colt James.

Why not? her inner vixen asked. *What would it hurt? He offered.* His hand was held midair, his finger extended, the smear of cake batter glistening on its tip. All she had to do was lean forward and lick.

Otherwise you really are missing out, he'd said.

How many times had she missed out, just because she was afraid to try, to put even a toe out of her comfort zone? Although it wasn't a toe. This was her tongue, and possibly her heart.

Shoving *that* thought aside—she certainly wasn't letting her heart get involved with Colt—she took a deep breath, gathered every ounce of courage she could muster, then leaned forward and wrapped her lips around the end of his finger and sucked the batter into her mouth.

Chapter 5

THE BURST OF FLAVOR HIT HER TONGUE, AND CHLOE moaned softly at the delicious chocolaty taste. She glanced up at Colt. This time, it was his turn to swallow as the teasing gleam in his eyes darkened to a flash of hunger—and not for chocolate. For her.

Oh boy.

"Good?" he asked, his voice low and deep.

Caught in his gaze, all she could do was nod, and that was only the barest movement of her head. "Yes," she whispered, and knew she was answering more than his query about the chocolate.

"You've got a little…" He reached up and ran his thumb along her bottom lip, presumably to catch an errant smudge of chocolate.

She couldn't breathe, couldn't move, as heat and want surged through her veins. It had been so long since a man had touched her lips, and the soft pressure of his thumb against her chin felt more delicious than a thousand tastes of chocolate.

He leaned forward, just the slightest bit, his gaze locked on her lips.

Her nerve endings stirred and tingled as a swarm of butterflies swooped and swirled in her stomach. Was he really going to kiss her? She could feel her lips trembling, even as they parted in anticipation.

Closer still—his breath warm on her cheek as he

tilted her chin up to meet his. He smelled like chocolate and soap and some kind of musky, manly aftershave that seemed to wrap itself around her like a warm cloak.

Another bit closer—she could almost feel the pressure of his lips against hers.

Her eyelids fluttered, ready to close for the kiss, then popped open wide when the loud beeping of the timer rang through the silent kitchen.

Colt pulled back, shaking his head as if to rouse himself from a daze, and turned to press the timer button on the stove. Chloe grabbed the edge of the counter to steady herself, her knees suddenly gone weak.

He opened the oven, and chocolate-scented heat poured into the room. "Do you..." His voice cracked a little, and he cleared his throat as he shoved his hand into an oven mitt and pulled the rack toward them. "Do you want to check these?"

"Yeah, sure," she answered, her voice a little unsteady as well. She pulled open a cupboard next to the stove, grabbed a toothpick from a box inside, and then leaned in next to him to poke a cupcake with the pick. The heat of Colt's hip as she brushed against it seemed as hot as the oven—or maybe that was just her body's reaction to anything of hers touching anything of his right now.

Pulling the toothpick free, she examined it for batter. "They're done." She reached around him, opening the cupboard next to the oven, and pulled out a couple of cooling racks and placed them on the counter.

He removed the two muffin tins and set them on the racks. "Now we just need to let them cool, then we can frost them."

Which would mean at least another hour of Colt

James being in her kitchen. The thought had Chloe's knees turning to jelly again. *Get ahold of yourself.* She was acting like a silly schoolgirl, not a full-grown woman who was, in fact, the person who taught those silly schoolgirls. And boys.

Which reminded her she still had papers to grade. Which would take at least a little bit of concentration. And all hers was currently being taken up by the cowboy in her kitchen.

"Colt," she started to say, then got caught on the sound of his name in her mouth. How could she be on intimate enough terms with him that she was saying his name with such familiarity? Like they were actually friends. How could this night even be real? "Really, you've done so much already. And I've still got papers to grade. You don't have to stay."

But please say you will. Please stay. Stay for an hour, stay for the night, stay for our whole lives.

She clamped her lips together to keep herself from saying the words.

"I want to, but I don't want to get in the way if you need to work." His voice rose a little at the end of the sentence, almost like he was asking her a question, or asking if she really wanted him to go.

She didn't want him to go. Ever. But she knew she was kidding herself. He'd said it himself—he liked helping people. All kinds of people. And she knew he was the go-to guy for a lot of people when they were in a bind. He'd spent the last month filling in at The Creed—the local pub and burger house—for the owner, whose wife had delivered their first child. And Chloe had seen him just last week shoveling the walk of his aunt's house when she'd driven down her street. Half the town owed him favors because he was always pitching in and helping friends out.

That's what friends are for. His words echoed in her ear, and she convinced herself that the moment before, the moment she'd thought he was going to kiss her, had just been in her imagination.

She glanced at the clock on the wall, surprised to see how late it was. "It's already past nine. I've kept you long enough. Even though I absolutely appreciate everything you've done, I think I should probably finish up on my own."

His shoulders slumped just the slightest, but he kept the smile on his face. "Oh yeah, sure, of course. I'll let you get to it then." He nodded to the overflowing trash bin next to the counter. "Least I can do is take this out before I leave. You keep your trash cans in the garage?"

"Yes, but you don't have to..." she stammered, her heart crashing against her chest at the mention of the garage.

"It's no big deal," he said, pulling the bag from the container and striding through the door connecting the house to the garage.

Chloe hurried after him, sweat erupting across her lower back as she waited for his reaction to the mess, waited to hear his judgment on the stack of boxes she should have thrown away a year ago.

"I can see why you can't park your car in here." He shimmied around the side of the boxes to get to the large trash receptacle. Lifting the lid, he dumped the bag in, then surveyed the stacks of stuff.

She twisted her hands together, holding them so they

didn't flutter to her face. "I know it's stupid. It's just a bunch of old junk. I've been meaning to get rid of it. None of it matters. I'm just busy and haven't had time to arrange to get it hauled away." She was rambling, the words tumbling out of her mouth faster than she'd meant them to. Trying to explain it—or in this case, avoid explaining it—to Colt made her chest tight and her palms itch.

Why couldn't she just let the stupid boxes go? The recliner was threadbare and probably had a family of mice taking up residence in its hollow center. She would never sit in it again. The boxes were filled with junk. Old clothes, worn-out shoes, stained and useless kitchenware, things she would never need or use. She hadn't opened any of the boxes in years.

All it took was making one phone call to Happy Hauling, and they'd pick everything up and take it away. But she'd made that call before. Several times. And always followed it with another call frantically trying to cancel the pickup.

"I get it. You're busy. I have tons of stuff I need to get done at my place and can't seem to find the time to get to." Colt circled around the stuff and started to lower himself into the recliner.

"Don't!" Chloe took a step forward, her hand outstretched, unable to bear the image of Colt, a good man, sitting in the chair of her father, who could be a good man but could also be a monster.

Colt jerked upright and backed away from the recliner. "Sorry."

She yanked her hands back, wrapping them securely around her body. "It's fine. *I'm* sorry." She let out her breath, trying to go for an easy laugh, but fearing she sounded on the brink of hysteria. "I didn't mean to yell. That chair is just filthy. And probably has spiders in it. I just didn't want you to get dirty."

He took another few steps away as he cringed at the chair. "I hate spiders." He turned to her and his face changed, his earlier flirty grin returning. "But I don't mind getting a little dirty."

Her eyes widened, and she let out a bubble of laughter. A real laugh. "You're terrible." She followed him inside, trying to calm the panic in her chest. He *was* terrible, in the sense that he was terribly good-looking, terribly charming, and could tear her heart into tiny terrible shreds.

But at least they were out of the garage.

She trailed after him to the front door, trying to control her breathing while struggling to think of something clever to say. "You've been amazing tonight." *You are amazing*. "I couldn't have done all this without you. Thank you so much." So, maybe not clever, but nice, at least. She could always do nice. Which was probably why he wanted to be her friend. Guys always liked to be friends with the "nice" girl.

But he just flirted with me. Didn't he?

Maybe that wasn't actual flirting. Maybe that was the way he acted around all women. She didn't have enough experience with men flirting with her to know. Except for Hugh. But he didn't really do subtle flirting. He wouldn't know subtle if it whacked him in the side of his huge, egotistical head.

"You don't need to thank me. It was nothing, really." Colt shrugged into his coat and pulled up the zipper.

Chloe headed toward the closet. "Let me get your scarf."

"Keep it," he said, flashing her a panty-melting grin. "At least until you get yours back. It looks good on you."

You'd look good on me. On me with my legs wrapped around your waist.

She swallowed and hoped another blush wasn't coloring her cheeks. Geez, her mind was in the gutter tonight. One minute she was sure he just wanted to be friends; the next she had him naked and thumping her headboard.

"I had a lot of fun tonight."

A chuckle escaped her. "I'll bet. I don't know if 'fun' would be the way I'd describe it. 'Chaotic' and 'crazy' come to mind. But we all appreciated everything you did." Why did she have to say *we*? *She* appreciated everything he'd done—more than she could say. But somehow telling him how much his gestures meant to her seemed too intimate, too much like she was suggesting he'd done something special just for her, instead of helping out some kids and their teacher.

Colt reached for the doorknob, then turned back and held out his hand. "I'll see you in the morning."

Chloe wasn't sure what to do. Was he offering to shake her hand?

He brought his other arm forward, and she realized he was going in for a hug just as she reached out with her hand to shake his. They meshed in a super-awkward one-armed hug with their hands smashed between them.

"Thanks again," she mumbled into his chest, ready now for him to just leave and for this humiliation to end.

"Yep. I'll pick you up at seven." Cold air whooshed in as he opened the door. Then he was gone.

She turned around and sagged against the door, wrapping her arms around her middle as she relived every embarrassing mishap she'd made over the last several hours.

Colt drove away from Chloe's house, shaking his head as he did the same thing. That last clumsy attempt at a hug goodbye had been the final act of humiliation for him. What had he been thinking? Thank goodness he hadn't tried to kiss her good night.

He hadn't known what to do when he saw her reaching out to shake his hand. It had been too late to switch it up at that point, so he'd just gone for the weird hug.

She had to think he was a total idiot. He *was* an idiot—an idiot for getting involved with this woman. Although spending one night with her and making her a batch of cupcakes hardly qualified as getting involved. Right?

So why couldn't he stop thinking about the honeysuckle scent of her hair or the way her lips had parted when he'd leaned in to her? And, Lord have mercy, when she'd sucked his finger into her mouth, he'd been afraid he was going to have a coronary. Her mouth was warm, yet her eyes held an innocent, almost astonished look, as if she couldn't believe she'd just done that.

Chloe's move had teased the hell out of him, but he somehow felt like she hadn't done that intentionally, and she'd been just as surprised by the reaction it created—in both of them.

He spent the rest of the drive home alternately reminding himself why he didn't need to start anything with Chloe Bishop and imagining what would have happened if he'd had the guts to actually lean down and kiss her.

Squinting through the light flurry of snow, he made the turn onto the dirt road that led to his cabin. His dad had built the cabin for him and his mom, Vivienne, when they'd bought the ranch. They'd been newlyweds and had dreams of eventually building a big house to raise their family in.

They'd finished the house and all moved in right after Colt was born, and the cabin had helped pay the new mortgage as a small rental usually occupied by one of the ranch hands.

The last renters had moved out several years ago and Colt had taken over the cabin, spending his free time remodeling the interior. It had needed a complete overhaul to update and modernize it. He'd hired a little help, but most of the stuff he could do himself, with the help of one or both of his brothers. He'd helped Mason remodel one of the bunkhouses on the main part of the ranch, and his brother had pitched in on several of the projects Cole had done in the cabin.

It had taken him over a year, but now the cabin was completely renovated and made a comfortable home for him. The main area was a combined living room and kitchen with a long butcher-block-topped island in the center. A stone fireplace rose up the side of the far wall, and the opposite wall held a row of tall windows surrounding French doors that opened onto a large deck. The view out the back was of the mountains and one of the small ponds on their property.

The layout was all on one level, and Cole had added a master suite and a huge bathroom onto the back of the cabin.

Everything was done in cedar or stone, and the furniture was big and overstuffed and comfortable enough for a guy over six feet tall. His mom had done a little of the decorating and kept everything within the log-cabin motif. He swore every time she saw something with a cabin theme, she bought it and found a place to put it up or stick it in the cabin. He didn't mind. She had great taste, and he sure as heck didn't have time to decorate, so he appreciated her efforts.

He liked having his own place, yet still being on the family property and only a few minutes from the main ranch. Over the years, they'd cut a dirt road through the fields, giving him an "as the crow flies" back way to the ranch. He could be there in three minutes in his pickup, seven on foot.

His golden retriever, Watson, met him at the door when he came in from the garage. The dog stretched his body, and Colt was pretty sure he'd been passed out on the sofa only moments before. He'd texted his brother earlier, and Mason had promised to stop in and toss some food in the dog's bowl.

Watson sniffed Colt's legs and jacket as he pulled off his boots. He rubbed the dog's head. "Hey, boy. You smell that cat on my boots? Her name was Agatha, and she thought I was handsome."

Watson was unimpressed.

The next morning, Colt pulled up in front of Chloe's house at five to seven. He didn't want her worrying that he would be late. She struck him as the punctual type.

He'd borrowed his mom's SUV, figuring the third

seat in the back might come in handy if he needed to haul the neighbor kids to school as well. Since he was coming into town, he'd offered to bring his nephew, and Max had regaled him with interesting dinosaur and insect facts during their drive.

"Stay in your seat, Max," Colt told his nephew. "I'm just going to get your teacher, and I'll be right back."

"Okay."

Colt hurried up the walk, not because he was worried about leaving Max in the car—he knew his nephew would stay there; he was a good kid, a rule follower—but because he was eager to see the cute schoolteacher.

Over the course of a long, mostly sleepless night, he'd convinced himself he was being stupid about this woman—that Chloe wasn't anything special, and he'd just gotten caught up in the high of helping someone out. He did like to help people, but not just for altruistic reasons. Somewhere, deep down—in that place where he knew things but didn't like to say them out loud—he knew he often agreed to help others in an attempt to break the curse. He wanted to do his penance for screwing up his life and finally break free of the belief that good things might come to those who wait, but they didn't come to Colt James. Well, they came; they just didn't last.

He'd had good things offered to him, but they'd all been taken away just as he reached to grab them. He could look, but he couldn't touch. He could dream, but he couldn't take hold of the reality.

Geez, why was he getting all maudlin? He needed a good night's rest and to put this silly notion that Chloe Bishop was anything special out of his head.

He'd barely rung the bell when the door swung open, and the object of his late-night musings stood there, already wearing her jacket and his blue scarf around her neck. "Hey, Colt. Thanks for picking me up this morning."

She offered him a warm smile, and his stomach did a hard flip. He swallowed, his mouth suddenly dry, then his lips curved into an answering grin. He couldn't have stopped them if he tried. He had been completely wrong about this girl.

Chloe *was* something special. All she'd done was smile, and it felt like the sun had just come out after several cloudy days.

"And thanks for being on time. You could probably guess from my crazy behavior yesterday that I hate to be late. And by crazy, I mean that thing where I ran my car into you. And now I'm rambling. Shutting up now." She pressed her lips together, then grabbed her purse, a bulging tote bag, and a clear cupcake carrier, and pulled the door shut behind her. "You ready?"

"Uh…yeah, sure." Colt realized he'd been standing there like a dope, not saying anything, just staring at her as if he couldn't decipher whether she were real or not. He reached for the bag and the cupcakes. "Let me carry those for you."

She hesitated, probably battling her sense of independence and the need to not put anyone out that he'd discovered the day before, then handed him the cupcakes and the bag. He grunted at the heavy weight of it.

"Geez, what have you got in this thing? Rocks?"

"Books. And homework papers. And something for you." She ducked her head and offered him a shy grin.

"For me? What do you have for me?"

Before she could answer, the screen door on the neighboring house slammed open, and the three younger Johnson kids came clamoring out and ran toward them.

"Can we get a ride to school with you?" Maddie asked, her breath coming in hard gasps from sprinting across the lawn.

"Yeah, sure," Colt answered, opening the front door for Chloe and the back door for the kids. "That's why I brought the SUV. Climb in."

They all climbed in, saying hello to Max as they buckled their seat belts and got settled.

"Nice car," Chloe told Colt, running her hand along the leather seat.

He squashed the mental image of her hand making the same motion as she ran her fingers along his bare chest. "Uh, thanks. It's not mine. It's my mom's. Rock bought it for her a couple years ago. I figured I'd bring it in case the other kids needed a ride today too."

"That was really nice of you to think of the kids as well, and to bring all of us to school," Chloe said.

He wished she would stop saying how *nice* he was. If she only knew the wicked and downright sinful thoughts he was having as he imagined what would have happened if she would have answered the door wearing his blue scarf…and nothing else. She wouldn't think he was so *nice* then.

"No problem. I was bringing Max in anyway." He pulled away from the curb and headed toward the school.

"Colt's my uncle now, aren't you, Colt?" Max said.

"Yep, I sure am, buddy."

"And he's teaching me to skate, and we're starting a hockey team."

"Is that right?" Chloe asked. "Just the two of you?"

"No." Max giggled. "A whole bunch of kids. Our first practice is tomorrow after school."

"I want to play," Maddie piped up from beside him in the seat. She was squished in between Max and Charlie, while Jake sat in the third row.

"You can't," Max told her. "Girls can't play hockey."

"Of course they can," Chloe said. "They have entire women's hockey leagues. In fact, the U.S. women's team took gold in the last Olympics."

Max eyed her skeptically. "Is that true, Colt?"

"Yep."

"But girls can't play on *our* team."

"Why not?" Maddie asked, her small brow creased.

Chloe crossed her arms over her chest. "Yeah, Colt. Why not?"

"Hey now, how did I get in trouble? I didn't say it. He did." Colt jerked a thumb at his nephew. "Thanks a lot, kid."

"So girls *can* play on the team?" Chloe pressed.

"Honestly, I have no idea. I haven't had any girls want to be on the team, so it hasn't even come up. But I'm totally good with it. The more the merrier."

"Yay," Maddie cheered and held up her hand to Max for a high five. "I'm going to be on your hockey team."

He looked at her hand and tilted his chin as if he were thinking it over, then shrugged and smiled as he smacked her hand. "I guess I'm totally good with it too."

"Before everyone gets too excited, you better let me check with the league to make sure they don't have any special rules about coed teams. I'll call them later this morning and let you know what I find out when I pick you up after school." Colt turned into the school driveway and parked by the sidewalk.

"Thanks for the ride, Colt," Charlie said as he opened the car door. The other kids piled out with more murmured thanks and headed toward the school.

Chloe turned in her seat. "Really, thanks so much for giving us all a ride."

"I was happy to do it."

"Before I forget…" She reached into her tote bag and pulled out a small plastic container. "I told you I had something for you."

"I remember. It's all I've thought about the whole way here." He grinned. "Well, that and how I'm going to add Maddie to our hockey roster."

Chloe smiled and held the container out to him. "It's nothing, really. I just wanted to give you a couple of the cupcakes. You left last night before they were frosted."

An impish grin covered his face as he opened the container. The scent of chocolate filled the interior of the car. "I know. And that's the best part. We could have had fun with that frosting."

Her cheeks went pink, and her face paled.

Idiot. Why did he say that? "I just meant because doing the frosting is the fun part." He cleared his throat, searching for something else to say, something that didn't come out sounding flirty and dirty like that stupid frosting comment. "Are you sure you have enough to give away? I thought these were for a bake sale."

She swallowed and pushed her shoulders back, as if the change in topic helped her regain some of her composure. "They were. But I'll donate a dollar for the two I took. They're worth the buck." Grabbing her bags and the cupcake carrier, she slid out of the car.

"You want me to help you carry that in?"

"No, I've got it." She leaned her head in and offered him a shy smile. "And just for the record, I thought the cake batter was the best part." She slammed the car door, turned on her heel, and headed toward the school before he had a chance to respond.

He picked up a cupcake and watched her walk away, the curvy sway of her hips making him hunger for more than chocolate frosting.

The frosting comment stuck in Chloe's head all day. Had he really been flirting with her, or was the comment an innocent misinterpretation? Just the thought of what she could do with Colt's muscular body and a tub of chocolate frosting had her flustered and making silly mistakes throughout the day.

Which seemed about par for the course, since she hadn't been able to get him out of her head the night before either. She'd been so distracted with thoughts of him and the cake-batter moment that she'd absently squeezed toothpaste onto her finger and rubbed it onto her cheeks instead of her normal night moisturizing cream.

And today she'd been so busy daydreaming, she'd almost walked into the men's bathroom, and she'd left her room keys in the teachers' lounge after lunch. She needed to get it together, needed to put Colt James out of her mind.

Yeah right. That was like telling someone who'd just started a diet not to think about food.

Chloe somehow made it through the day and had convinced herself the cowboy wasn't all that cute as she, Madison, and Max stood on the sidewalk in front of the school waiting for Colt to pick them up. Charlie and Jake were having a snowball fight on the lawn behind them but stopped as the SUV turned into the lot.

"How was your day?" Colt asked, flashing her a panty-melting smile as she opened the car door and slid into the leather seat next to him.

"Great," she answered, her palms already sweating as she clutched her tote bag in her lap. What had she been thinking? Not that cute? Holy hot buckets of gorgeous. His jacket pulled across the defined muscle of his bicep as he leaned over the seat to make sure all the kids got buckled in, and she wanted to run her hand along the side of his arm.

He pulled back so his face was even with hers and offered her a grin. "Thanks for the cupcakes. We do good work. They were amazing."

He was amazing. The scent of cinnamon gum mixed with his aftershave, and she wanted to close her eyes and bask in the pure masculine scent of him as she melted into her seat. But that would be weird, right? *Yes, definitely weird.*

"You're welcome," she finally managed to say.

"I've got good news." With everyone buckled in, he put the car in gear and pulled out of the parking lot. "I called the league, and they said we can absolutely have girls on the team. In fact, they encourage it. But there has to be a female coach on the roster and at the games and practices."

A cheer went up from the back seat.

"That's great," Chloe said. "But why do you need a female coach? Don't you treat all the kids the same when you teach them to play?"

"Yeah, of course. It's not that. It's just because the kids will be in different locker rooms. So Maddie will need someone to be in the girl's locker room with her and to take her to the bathroom if she needs help, and whatever other dark, mysterious things women do."

"I can go to the bathroom by myself," Madison stated. "I'm not a baby."

"I know, honey. I think Mr. Colt just meant like if you were sick or something," Chloe said, smoothing over his statement. "So who are you going to find to help you coach at such late notice?"

He pulled up to the stoplight, then turned toward her and raised one eyebrow.

She held up her hands. "Oh, no. Not me. You've got to be kidding. I don't know the first thing about hockey. The only game I've ever seen was the charity alumni game that you played with your brothers last summer."

"Well then, you do know something about hockey. You've at least seen a game."

"But I don't know anything about the rules or how to play. I don't even know how to score."

A playful grin covered his face. "I can teach you how to score."

Oh, for fritter's sake. Had she really said that? Heat flamed in her cheeks, and she peered out the front windshield. "The light's green."

She didn't look at him, but she heard him chuckle as he turned his head back to the road and drove through the intersection.

"If you were on our hockey team, then you'd get to be our coach *and* our teacher," Max pointed out. He had a gift for stating the obvious.

"Oh please, Miss Bishop," Maddie pleaded. "I really want to play hockey with Max's team. It would be so fun. And you don't have anything else to do."

Chloe turned in her seat, thankful to no longer be talking about her lack of scoring knowledge. "How do you know?"

The girl rolled her eyes and let out a sigh that gave Chloe an early indication of how she was going to act as a teenager. "Because I live next door to you. And I know you're *always* home. Plus, you have time to knit scarves for every kid in our class."

Point taken. She glanced over at Colt. "Why not one of the moms whose kid is on the team? Or how about Quinn? She knows everything about hockey, and she's good at this kind of stuff."

"She already said no."

Chloe's shoulders fell as she slumped back in her seat. "Oh great. A second ago, I didn't even want to do it, but now I'm somehow miffed about being your second choice."

"You're *my* first choice," Maddie said.

"Mine too," Max agreed.

They pulled up in front of her house, and Colt put the SUV in park. He turned to her and grinned. "Mine too."

Dang. Why did his grin turn her insides to mush? Still, she wasn't letting him off the hook that easily. She gave him her best teacher stare.

"Just because Quinn said she wouldn't do it doesn't mean she was my first choice. She was just there at my mom's when I was on the phone with the league at lunch. And she told me to count her out as soon as I hung up. She didn't give me a chance to tell her I already had someone else in mind."

"Good save. Although if you had asked her, she might have changed her mind and decided to do it. Women are funny like that."

Colt smiled but wisely chose not to comment.

"Please say you'll do it," Maddie begged. "It'll be fun."

Chloe held her hands up in surrender. "Okay, fine. I'll do it." Her stomach did another flip as Colt's face broke into a smile. "Except I have one slight problem."

"What's that?" Colt asked.

"I don't know how to skate."

"Oh, that's no problem," Maddie said matter-of-factly. "Neither do I."

Chapter 6

LATER THAT NIGHT, CHLOE FOUND HERSELF STANDING outside the ice arena while she waited for Colt to unlock the door. Her breath froze in the air as she blew on her hands and stamped her feet.

What had she gotten herself into this time? It was past nine, and she was out with a man she barely knew. And it was a *school night*.

She should be home in bed, her cat curled up on her shoulder, her newest paperback propped on her chest. Except now, instead of reading about a heroine having an adventure with an oh-so-hot cowboy, she was actually having the adventure herself.

It didn't feel real. Yet every moment she'd accidentally brushed against him or he'd touched her back to help her into his truck seemed to hang in the air, suspended in a flash of time she wanted to grab on to and stick into her pocket to keep and bring out later to examine and touch and relive.

He hadn't come in when he'd dropped her home after school, but he'd said he would pick her up that night for her first skating lesson. She had done all her work and graded her papers early, then sat down for a light dinner—or what should have been dinner but had instead been twenty minutes of pushing her food around on the plate because she was too nervous to eat. She hoped her stomach didn't growl during the lessons. It already felt like it had a horde of grasshoppers hopping and flipping around inside it.

Why had she agreed to this dumb idea? She'd googled the rules of hockey that afternoon, but no amount of internet searching could teach her how to skate. Which was exactly what she'd told Colt that night when he'd come to pick her up. He'd said it didn't matter. He would teach her. He'd assured her he could teach *anyone* to skate.

Well, he hadn't seen her skate. She had made one hideously embarrassing attempt back in high school and hadn't tried again since. She was fairly certain he was overestimating his skating-lesson expertise since he hadn't had her as a student.

She'd also tried to tell him she didn't have any skates, but he'd said they could borrow a pair at the rink. He'd easily knocked down that argument, just as he had every other argument she'd tried to come up with as to why this was a really bad plan. It seemed the guy wouldn't take no for an answer.

Colt unlocked the door and held it open for her. The arena was dark inside, so he flipped on the light switch next to the door.

"Where is everybody?" Chloe whispered, which was dumb because her question had just established that no one else was around. So why was she whispering?

"The rink closes at nine. But I've got a buddy who works here, and I offered to run the Zamboni and clean the ice tonight if he let me have the rink for a private lesson."

She gulped. Why did *private lesson* sound so dirty and delicious when Colt said it? The guy was seriously so good-looking. And with that deep voice and the flirty spin he put on his words, everything that came out of his mouth sounded sexy. He could ask her to pass the salt, and she swore she would swoon.

Which was one more reason why this whole idea of Colt being interested in her was so ridiculous. Sure, he oozed charm, and it sometimes felt like he was flirting with her, but the more time she spent around him, the more she realized he was simply a charming guy who acted that way with everyone. He'd tipped his hat and grinned at the mom who had crossing guard duty that afternoon when he'd picked them up from school, and the woman had almost tripped off the curb.

He was just that kind of guy—attractive, polite, and nice to everyone. Heck, he probably flirted with the grocery store clerk and the waitress at the diner, but she didn't see them going off all half-cocked imagining they had a chance at a relationship with him.

Oh, for heaven's sake. Who said anything about a relationship? She was standing in an ice arena. She needed to chill out. What did it matter what his intentions were, or if he was just being nice or wanting to be her friend? Why not just enjoy the attention of a hot cowboy and quit overanalyzing every moment they spent together?

She stuffed her hands in the pockets of her coat. "What's a Zamboni? And how do you clean the ice? Like with Windex?"

He broke into laughter. "I do like you, Chloe Bishop. You make me laugh."

Heat flamed in her cheeks and up her spine. *Stop it.* He said he liked her because she made him laugh, which was exactly the thing to say to a *friend*. He didn't say he liked her because she made his heart race or his lips tingle because he wanted to kiss her so bad.

Oh geez. He didn't say that, because nobody says that. *Lips tingle?* For crying out loud. Did that even happen? Maybe she *had* read too many romance novels.

Walking through the lobby of the arena, Chloe marveled at the display cases filled with trophies and at how many times she saw Rock's name. "Your brother has really done a lot for this arena."

"Yeah, it was pretty run-down when we skated here as kids. He said if he ever made it big, he was going to renovate the place and put in a nice sheet of ice."

"So, he did all this?" She noted the new carpet, the shiny aluminum bleachers, and the glossy wood countertops of the skate-rental window.

"Nah. He's not that generous. But he donated a huge sum, and the town put up quite a bit for it too. Our family and several others really wanted the hockey and figure-skating programs for the kids to continue and flourish, so we did a ton of fund-raising to help make it happen."

Chloe had only been back in town the past three years, and the skating rink had already been finished by then.

Colt carried a duffel bag containing his skates and dropped it on the floor next to the skate-rental booth. "The Zamboni is down here," he said, opening a door next to the booth that led down a hallway and into a large room. The floors were concrete, and rows of workbenches and pegboards neatly hung with tools covered the back wall. The cavernous space was a cross between a workshop and a garage and probably ten degrees cooler than the ice arena had been.

She shivered as Colt walked toward a machine that looked like a giant rectangular box with wheels. On the back end, it had one seat in front of a steering wheel and another smaller backward-facing seat next to it.

He patted the side of the machine. "This is our Zamboni. We call her Bertha. She's the one who does the heavy lifting when it comes to actually cleaning the ice. In layman's terms, she sprays water on the ice, then shaves off the top layer and collects the shavings and debris like blood and broken teeth, then sprays another layer of water on top, which freezes into a perfectly smooth 'clean' sheet of ice."

Chloe wrinkled her nose. "Blood and broken teeth?"

He grinned. "Hockey humor." He opened the big doors in front of the machine. "They had practice in here tonight so I thought we'd clean the ice before your lesson. That way, you'll have smooth ice to learn on and not have to worry about chips or dents that could trip you up."

"I appreciate that. But did you say 'we' would clean the ice?"

"Yep. I'll drive, but you can ride next to me."

"I'm not getting on that thing."

"Oh come on. We've actually made good money auctioning off chances to ride on the Zamboni between periods. It's perfectly safe. The thing tops out at twelve miles an hour, but I'll keep it down to an even five."

Chloe eyed the small cushioned seat on the back.

He reached into the front of his jacket and pulled a small silver thermos from the inside pocket. "I figured you might be nervous about tonight, so I brought you a little liquid courage."

Oh dear. She'd been hoping for hot chocolate when she saw the thermos, but now worried it contained something more ominous. "What does that mean?"

Colt chuckled. "Nothing crazy. Don't worry. It's just some of my mom's homemade strawberry wine. I mixed it with a little lemonade, so it's not real potent, but it may be able take the edge off your nerves."

"I'm not much of a drinker." Although strawberry wine mixed with lemonade hardly had an ominous ring to it.

"Neither am I." He opened the lid and the scent of strawberries, with a hint of lemon, filled the air. "I promise, it's not that strong. It's probably on par with a wine cooler."

She'd tried a wine cooler at a barbecue that summer just to see what it was like. Her face had flushed and she'd gotten a little giggly, so she'd stopped after two. It's not that she never drank; she'd only done so sparingly and with abysmal results. Like the time she'd had a couple of glasses of wine at a teacher function and had ended up with a terrible headache the next day. No time that she'd tried drinking had ever seemed like it had been worth it.

Her philosophy of controlling her surroundings included her body, and she knew the effects of alcohol when it came to losing control.

Chloe peered into the cup as he poured the pink liquid. She wasn't so sure about this. Then again, she wasn't sure about the whole idea of learning how to ice skate so she could help coach a sport she knew virtually nothing about. When she looked at it that way, what could one little cup of strawberry-flavored courage hurt?

"You said your mom made this?"

He handed her the cup. "Yeah, but it's my aunt Sassy's recipe. She and my mom make up a batch every summer."

She swirled the liquid around and took a small sniff. "So it's like moonshine?" She conjured up an image of Vivienne James and Colt's aunt Sassy running an illegal still in the mountains behind the ranch. In her mind, they both had on overalls and floppy felt hillbilly hats, and Sassy was smoking a corncob pipe as Vivi filled a crockery jug with homemade liquor.

"I'd say it's more like sunshine."

She took a deep breath. She wouldn't know if she didn't try it. And what if all this time, her stupid life motto of playing it safe was just that…stupid? What if her motto was really just an excuse to not have to try anything new?

Oh, to heck with playing it safe. What was an adventure anyway, without a bit of risk? She offered Colt a brave smile. "Bottoms up, or down, or whatever that saying is." She took a tentative sip, then tossed back the drink.

It was surprisingly good. The sweet flavor of strawberry mingled with the tart taste of lemon. It didn't really taste like alcohol—except for the slight prickle in her throat and the warm feeling in her chest.

"It tastes like Kool-Aid. With a kick." She held out the cup, hoping he didn't notice the slight tremble in her hand. If she was going for brave, she might as well go all in. "I'll have another, please."

He arched an eyebrow. "You sure?"

She nodded. "I'm sure I'm very nervous, so yes. Just one more."

"Okay." He refilled the small cup, and she drank this one a little slower. But it was so delicious, it didn't take her long to finish. She handed him the cup and patted the side of the Zamboni. "Okay. I think I'm ready to conquer Big Bertha now." She studied the back of the machine. "How do I get up there?"

Colt laughed as he helped her climb up into the seat, then settled into the driver's seat next to her.

Her face was flushed, but she thought it had more to do with the feel of his hands on her waist as he helped her up than the effects of the strawberry wine. Or maybe it was a little bit of both. "Where are the seat belts on this thing?"

She might be giving in to a little alcohol, but she hadn't completely lost her senses. Although they were becoming quite disoriented by the scent of Colt's aftershave as he leaned over to snap the seat belt across her hip.

"There you go. You're buckled in, but if you get nervous, you can hold on to me." He winked at her as he started the engine.

They pulled out onto the ice, and she grabbed his arm as they slid around the first corner. The Zamboni really didn't go that fast, but she kept her fingers gripped around his bicep as they took the first lap. By the second circle, she had relaxed a little and was starting to enjoy the ride. It was fun to see the shiny, smooth layer of ice appear beneath her feet.

Colt finished the ice and pulled back into the garage and cut the engine. He turned to face her. "Well, what did you think?"

"I liked it." She bounced a bit in her chair. "And this seat is great. I could feel the engine under it, and the rumbling gave me tingles in my cupcake."

His eyes widened, and a grin spread across his face. "Your cupcake?"

Chloe clapped her hands over her mouth. "Did I say that out loud?"

"Oh, yeah you did."

"Son of a birthday."

He laughed and helped her down from the Zamboni. "Let's go get you some skates."

She followed him back to the skate-rental booth.

"What size shoe do you wear?"

She told him, and he handed her a pair of white figure skates. "You usually go one size smaller than your shoe size. You can try these tonight and hockey skates next time to see which work better for you, then we can get you a pair of your own."

He grabbed his duffel bag and led her over to the row of carpeted benches. She sat down and pulled off her boots.

Kneeling in front of her, he held up one skate. "With your skates, you want to get a good, tight fit. Start by loosening the laces all the way to the toe. Your heel should fit snugly, and your toes should barely touch the end of the skate." He took hold of her ankle and guided her foot into the skate.

Chloe's mouth had gone dry when he'd said, "You want a good, tight fit," and she tried to breathe and focus on the fit of the skate instead of the feel of his big hand around her shin.

"Start tightening the laces from the end by your toes." He methodically moved up the skate, tightening the laces with each step. "You want your laces to be super tight around your ankles. That's what gives you the most support and keeps your ankles from rocking in. So, when you think your laces are tight enough, tighten them again." He repeated the same steps with her other skate. "You're going to want to help Maddie with this. I'll get you a lace puller to help you tighten her laces. It's a little metal tool that helps you pull on the laces."

Colt took her hands and helped her stand. "When you stand up and bend your knees, your toes shouldn't touch the end, and your skates should be snug but not painful. How do they feel?"

She bent her knees and wiggled her toes. "Good. I think."

"Okay, now before we go on the ice, I want you to walk around a little on the carpet. You can practice while I get my skates on. Just walk up and down here. Get a feel for the skates. Make sure you feel comfortable and balanced."

"I feel comfortable out here," she said, which wasn't entirely true. She felt mostly like a dork who had forgotten how her feet were supposed to work. "But the carpeted floor isn't a slick sheet of ice."

He stood and took her hand as he steered her to the door of the ice rink. "You ready?"

"No. I think I need another dose of that liquid courage."

He shook his head. "I don't think so. After that tingly cupcake comment, I'd say you seem courageous enough." He winked and stepped out on the ice in front of her. "Besides, you're going to want some coordination and balance."

"Well, that's just craptastic. I don't have coordination and balance even when I haven't been drinking."

Colt chuckled. "Take it easy. Step out onto the ice— hold my hand and use the boards to hold on to. When you take your first step, always make it a small one, not like you're walking. Otherwise, your foot will slip out from under you. Hold on to the boards, but don't lean too far into them, or your feet will slide out from under you on the other side."

"Got it." Her knuckles turned white as she gripped the barrier wall around the ice. "Small steps. Hold on to the boards, but not too tight, and don't lean into them. How about if I just stay here all night. Can't I coach from here?"

"'Fraid not."

She peered out over the glistening sheet of ice. "Why don't you take a practice lap around? Show me how it's done."

"You didn't come here to watch me skate." Her legs were shaking, but he was totally at ease as he circled around so he was facing her.

"But I want to. Come on. One quick lap." Or twelve slow ones. Anything to delay her having to get out there with him. "Show me how fast you can go."

Colt narrowed his eyes as he glided a few feet away, but a grin tugged at the corners of his lips. "I'm pretty fast."

Her heartbeat quickened at the idea that he might want to show off for her. "Prove it."

He laughed, a hearty laugh that rang out in the empty arena. "You're on." He kept his eyes locked on hers as he drifted backward. The sharp scrape of his blades on the ice sounded as he turned and took off. His body doubled over, and his feet seemed to be running over the ice as his arms swung from side to side, pumping the air as he picked up speed. He rounded the corner, sprays of ice spitting up from his blades as he crossed one foot over the other to make the turn, then he was sprinting again down the long side of the rink.

His movements were fluid as he glided across the ice like a speeding train. Chloe lifted one hand from the boards to press it to her chest. Her heart hammered against her hand, the sight of Colt flying across the ice both terrifying and exhilarating.

He let out a whoop as he rounded the far corners, his feet crossing over each other again and again as he sped around the turns. Then he was barreling toward her, a joy-filled smile creasing his face. Just before he reached her, he suddenly turned his body, bringing his feet together and shooting them out to the side, spraying a plume of ice crystals in the air as he came to a stop.

Tiny bits of ice sparkled in the air around her like it was snowing, and she clapped her hands together and blinked back tears. She'd always been sentimental, and watching him skate—like he was one with the ice, so comfortable, as if he were born to do it—pulled at something in her heart.

"That was amazing," she said, letting out her breath. She felt like she'd been skating with him, even though she hadn't taken a single step.

He offered her a humble shrug, but pride sparkled in his eyes. "Now it's your turn."

Chloe let out a laugh. "My turn to fall on my face."

"I've got you." He took her hands and glided around so he was facing her. He skated backward as he pulled her slowly forward on the ice. "When you're on your own, stick your arms out. It'll help with your balance. For now, hold on to me, bend your knees, and move your feet like you're marching."

Clutching his hands, Chloe took a couple of tentative march steps.

"Good job. Now once you're feeling comfortable and balanced, turn your toes out a little and start taking baby steps forward. Make sure your feet are underneath you and your shoulders are straight. Don't let your knees knock together. Keep your legs apart and your knees straight over your feet."

Her knees were already knocking together, but it didn't have anything to do with the skating. It had to do with the cute cowboy whose hands held hers as he said things like "Keep your legs apart."

"You're doing great. Now gently push one foot forward while you push off with the other so you glide along the ice. Keep your weight on your back foot when you push off, then transfer your weight to your front foot when you glide. Always push your weight onto the foot you're pushing forward. Then bring your feet back together and switch. Push off with your other foot, and glide forward. And just keep going. Push and glide, push and glide. As you get comfortable, you push a little bit harder, and glide a little bit longer."

"This sounds complicated."

"It's not as difficult as it sounds. You'll get the hang of it, and I won't let you go until you're comfortable."

She swallowed, knowing what he meant but still wishing he was talking about something else when he promised not to let her go. She followed his instructions, focusing on her feet and where she was putting her weight and trying to freaking glide. She blew her bangs off her forehead. "You make this look so easy."

"It is easy for me. But I've been on skates since I was

four years old, and I started playing hockey with my brothers when I was younger than Max."

"Do you miss it? Playing hockey?"

His gaze flicked to the scoreboard above the ice. "Yeah, some days."

"I once heard Rock say that you were better than him when you were in high school—that you had a chance to go pro."

Colt shrugged. "I don't know. I guess I was pretty good. I had scouts coming to my games and offers to play for a couple of colleges."

"That sounds like you were better than just good. What happened?"

"The Colton Curse," he muttered.

"The what?"

He shook his head. "Nothing. I got in a car accident. It was my own stupid fault. Dumb kid, too full of himself, driving way too fast, didn't make the turn and skidded off the side of the road. Rolled my car four times, and when it finally stopped, my leg was shattered and pinned under the dash."

"Oh no. How awful."

"Thank God I didn't hurt anyone else." He looked away, into the bleachers, but she had a feeling he was gazing into the past. "I don't remember a lot of it. I woke up in the hospital, and my whole life had changed. In that one stupid moment, in an accident that happened in less than thirty seconds, I lost everything. Up until then, I thought I had it all—colleges throwing money at me, the perfect girlfriend, a chance at a career in professional hockey. After the accident, it all disappeared—hockey, the girl, the scholarships." He let go of her hand and tapped the side of his leg. "But I did get a super-sexy scar and this nifty titanium rod in my leg that still aches when it rains, so that's something."

Chloe didn't know what to say. There was nothing she *could* say—nothing that could change the outcome or make any of it better. "I'm sorry."

He shrugged. "It was a long time ago. And nothing is going to change it." He narrowed his eyes. "Are you trying to distract me so I won't notice you haven't tried to skate yet?"

"Is it working?"

"No." He pulled her to the center of the ice and walked her through the steps again. He was a patient teacher and encouraged her as she cautiously practiced the moves. Push and glide. Push and glide.

She kept her gaze on her feet. "How do I stop?"

"Just push your knees apart while kind of pushing your toes together. Try to scrape the top layer of the ice with your skate as you slide one foot out diagonally, kind of like a snowplow, until you come to a stop."

"Shall I remind you that I don't have a lot of luck when it comes to snowplows? I tend to crash into them."

Colt chuckled. "You won't crash with this one."

She took a few glides forward, then turned the front of her skates in toward each other and shuddered to a clumsy stop.

"You did it."

"That's not how it looks when you stop."

He shrugged. "Yeah, well, we can work on the hockey stop later when I'm teaching the kids. Tonight, let's stick with the basics and just get you comfortable on the ice."

She gripped his hands, afraid to let him go as she glanced up at him. His body was relaxed, completely comfortable on the ice. He'd taken off his jacket and rolled up the sleeves of his flannel shirt to reveal muscled forearms. The blue stripes in the fabric brought out the bright-blue color of his eyes, and looking into them made it hard for her to breathe. "What if I fall?" she whispered.

"It's okay to fall." He gazed down at her, his expression sincere, and it felt like he was talking about something else, something deeper. "If you think you're going to fall, just go with it. Relax your body, and take the fall." He pulled her along the ice, keeping his gaze fixed on hers. "Besides, falling isn't so bad."

"Falling is how you get hurt."

He gave her a slow wink followed by one of his charm-filled grins. "Don't worry. I've got you. I won't let you fall."

Too late.

Chloe swallowed, her heart racing as her stomach swirled with nerves and the thrill of being alone in the ice arena holding Colt's hands. Time to pull it together and figure out this skating thing so she could spend more time hanging out with him as his assistant coach.

Dropping her gaze to her feet, she focused on pushing and gliding, shifting her weight, and trying to relax into the movements.

After another twenty minutes of practicing, she was easily gliding across the ice and actually skating without Colt's help. She hated to let go of his hands, but she liked the freedom of being able to skate on her own. He stayed in front of her, skating backward as he encouraged her to keep going.

"You got it," he said. "Now, try going a little faster, smooth it out." He skated further away until he reached the end of the rink and backed up against the boards.

"I'm doing it. I'm really doing it." Her feet picked up speed as she skated toward him. Right toward him. Faster than she'd skated before. "I forgot how to stop," she cried, pinwheeling her arms out at her sides.

"Go into the snowplow," Colt instructed, laughing as he held his arms out toward her. "I've got you."

She tried to turn her toes inward and slowed a bit before she crashed full-on into him. His strong arms wrapped around her, pulling her against him as she planted her palms on his chest and gripped the front of his shirt.

He gazed down at her, the laughter still curving his lips into a smile. "See, I told you I wouldn't let you fall."

She couldn't take her eyes off his mouth. Tearing her gaze away, she sucked her bottom lip under her teeth as she looked up into his eyes.

He glanced at her lips, and the laughter in his eyes changed to something darker—intense with desire.

Or at least in her strawberry wine-induced mind, she thought it was desire. That would be the only rationalization she could offer later for why she decided to let down her perfectly constructed defenses and stretch up to press a kiss against his beautiful mouth.

Chapter 7

CHLOE DIDN'T JUST PRESS HER LIPS TO HIS. SHE WRAPPED her arms around his neck and pressed her whole self against his muscled chest.

The ice rink was cold, but his lips were warm and soft, and he tasted like spearmint gum. She tangled her fingers into the hair at the nape of his neck and melted into him. Her body came alive at the touch of his lips, her breasts tightening. If she'd thought the engine of the Zamboni had given her cupcake a tingle, it was now a full-on cake explosion of heat and desire. Every cell, every nerve bursting with want and need and desire.

In the stacks of romance novels she frequently devoured, the first kiss was always her favorite part to read. She loved the last kiss as well, the one where they overcame all the conflict and knew their love was worth it. But there was something special about that *first* kiss, that very first moment when the hero and heroine connected. Not with their eyes or their personalities or their sparkling wit—but with their lips, their bodies.

The first kiss held a certain kind of magic. Chloe hadn't had a lot of first kisses, only four to be exact. And the first one didn't really count because she'd been a kid on the playground, and it had been a dare.

Kiss number two had been in high school, and she was fairly certain it had been a dare as well. She'd been visiting her cousin in Nebraska, who had given her a makeover, then dragged her to one of those parties out in a field where everyone was drinking and pretending to have the time of their lives around a keg and a tiny firepit. Even though she didn't understand the depths of his disease, Chloe had known her father was an alcoholic, and she didn't often drink. But that night she'd had two beers and had let some friend of her cousin kiss her and clumsily feel her up. She didn't remember his name, never saw him again after that night, and the things she remembered the most about the kiss were the hoppy flavor of beer and the faint coppery taste of blood where his braces had cut her lip.

Kisses three and four had been in college, one from an awkward and horrible first date and the other from a boy she'd actually ended up dating for several months, but in the end, it hadn't worked out. So far, none of her first kisses had held up to the hype and fantasy of the ones she'd read about.

Until now—this moment—with this man. And this holy-buckets-of-hotness kiss.

It was glorious. For about ten seconds.

In those ten seconds, his arms wrapped around her waist, and he pulled her tightly to him and kissed her back. With tongue even.

Which was what made the whole thing ten times more embarrassing when he suddenly pulled back and dropped his hands from around her as if her skin burned his.

She saw his Adam's apple bob in his throat as he swallowed before she turned away, unable to look at him as heat flared in her cheeks. What the heck had she been thinking? Throwing herself at him like that?

"I'm sorry. I shouldn't have done that." She pushed

herself away and haltingly skated toward the door of the arena. Forget the smooth push and glide. She just wanted off this ice and out of these skates so she could go home to pull the covers over her head.

She marched across the carpet, dropped onto the bench, and yanked at the laces. Why had Colt tied them so dang tight? Oh yeah, to protect her ankles. Right about now, she couldn't give a fig about her ankles. It was her pride that was wounded, damaged, hauled out, and tromped on. She tore at the laces as if the skates were burning her feet and she couldn't get them off fast enough.

Colt had followed her, stopping to close and secure the door to the ice. "Chloe…" He said her name, but that was as far as he got.

She kept her head down but held up her hand, stopping him from saying anything else, from saying some stupid, pitying words that would make a worse fool of her. "I think I'd like to go home now."

"Yeah, sure," he muttered, sinking onto the carpeted bench next to her. Not close enough to touch her, but she was acutely aware of him anyway.

Her feet were finally free of the skates, and she tugged on her boots. She stood up—apparently way too fast for a woman unaccustomed to strawberry wine, and her knees threatened to give way. That and the unfamiliar feel of regular shoes instead of thin blades of metal had her swaying to the side.

Colt was up in a second, and he reached for her arm to steady her. She pulled it away, punching herself in the other shoulder as she did. It didn't matter. The ache in her shoulder was nothing compared to the pain in her heart and the sting of humiliation.

"I'm fine." Had she slurred a little? Maybe she should have slurred more, just to make sure he knew she was inebriated and the wine was to blame for the kiss, not her.

She reached for her skates, but he grabbed them first. "I'll take care of these. Then I'll take you home."

"I'll wait by the door." She walked away, trying to hold her head up, but feeling the weight of shame and embarrassment digging into her shoulders. She had to fight to keep them from slumping in defeat.

In the truck, on the way to her house, he tried again. "Look, Chloe…"

She shook her head. "Please don't. You don't have to say anything. I shouldn't have done that. I got caught up in the moment. I'm sorry. It was a mistake."

"I know," he said not quite under his breath.

But she'd heard it, felt it, like a stab to the heart. He'd known it was a mistake as well and was just too nice to say anything more. He was probably just as embarrassed. How humiliating it must have been to have her throw herself at him!

But she'd really thought he liked her, thought he was flirting with her.

Thought he was different.

He had seemed special—not just because he was crazy cute and the little dimple in the side of his cheek made her want to swoon, but because he was also sweet and kind and helped others, and because when he looked at her, she could forget for a moment that chunky girl nobody wanted. She could almost imagine all he saw was her. The Chloe she was now, who could almost pass for attractive.

But that's all it was, all this whole thing between them

was—in her imagination. Colt didn't desire her, didn't dream of kissing her. Sure, he'd kissed her back for a few seconds, but that was probably just a reflex. Or maybe he didn't want her to feel *too* embarrassed. Too late. If a giant hole appeared in the floor of this truck, she'd happily sink right through it.

They pulled up in front of her house, and she opened the door and slipped out as soon as he'd put the truck in park. "Thanks for the skating lessons. Bye, Colt." She slammed the door and hurried up the sidewalk and into her house before he had a chance to say anything more.

Thanks for the skating lessons? Really? She might have fled his truck in mortification, but she was still going to be polite as she left.

She let herself into the house and kicked off her boots before padding into her living room. Agatha slept curled on the recliner but opened one eye, then stretched out a paw to acknowledge her.

Chloe swallowed against the burn in her throat. She flung herself onto the sofa and pressed her face into the cushion as she let out a frustrated scream.

The next morning, she took extra care with her hair and makeup. She dabbed concealer on the dark circles under her eyes, telltale signs of the sleepless night she'd had. Colton James didn't need to know she'd lost an ounce of shut-eye due to him.

She glanced at the clock as the hands inched closer to seven. She had no idea if he'd even pick her up this morning, but if he did, her plan was to act like the night before had never happened. She would be cordial and polite. Maybe she could thank him for teaching her how to skate again. *Head slap*. But she in no way, shape, or form would let on that the previous night's kiss had affected her or their "friendship."

Status quo. That's what she was going for. She might be riddled with embarrassment, but she didn't want to never see the guy again. Friendship was enough for her. If he still wanted to be her friend.

She could do this. The sound of an engine pulling up in front of her house had her hands clenching into fists, her fingernails digging into the skin of her palms.

She was wrong. She changed her mind. She couldn't do this.

Stop it. It wasn't that bad. It was just a kiss. It wasn't like she'd stripped naked and done a *Blades of Glory*–style ice-skating striptease. Now *that* would have been embarrassing.

She took a deep breath, unclenched her fists, and pasted on a smile before opening the door to face him.

Except that it wasn't him sitting in the cab of the SUV. It was Quinn.

The day had started off so beautiful, the bright sun glinting off what was left of the snow, but Chloe felt like a cloud had just passed over the sun, her insides going as dark and gloomy as a thunderstorm. She'd been nervous about seeing Colt and how she was going to act, but she hadn't expected this. Hadn't expected him not to show up at all.

He was still Colt, after all—the guy everyone could count on to come through for them, everyone's friend. Except now apparently not hers. She'd had her doubts, but in her heart, she'd been sure he'd show up, which was probably why she hadn't arranged another ride home for herself. But maybe this was his way of saying he didn't really want to be her friend.

She gulped and tried to keep her smile in place as she gathered her things and walked to the curb. Max waved happily to her from the back seat.

Quinn's window slid down, and she stuck her head through. "Colt had an issue at the farm, and he asked me to pick you up this morning. Hope that's okay."

"It's great. I really appreciate it." She needed to get her own car back. And soon. She'd make some calls on her break today to price how much a rental would be. Even if insurance wasn't covering it, having her own transportation would be worth it. It had been different when Colt was giving her a ride, and it felt like he was doing it because he wanted to see her. But now accepting a ride just felt like an imposition.

Quinn looked gorgeous, as usual. Even with her long, blond hair pulled up in a messy bun and wearing an oversize, faded brown Carhartt jacket that probably belonged to Rock, she still looked like a model. She lowered her aviator sunglasses and darted a glance at the house next door. "Any more passengers for the Quinn-Tank Taxi?"

As if on cue, the front door of the Johnson house opened, and Maddie, Jake, and Charlie tumbled out, a mass of coats and backpacks as they raced toward the car. "Can we get a ride?" Maddie asked breathlessly, her hand already reaching for the back door.

Her brothers waited for Quinn to nod before they piled in the back after their sister.

"Still no Jesse?" Chloe asked the boys as she slipped into the passenger seat and closed the door.

Charlie shook his head. "He started hanging out with this new kid, and he's been staying over at his house. Mom isn't happy about it, but at least he's texting her and telling her where he is now. Which is better than him not showing up and her not knowing where he is at all."

"True."

"It's okay with me," Jake said. "Last time he came home, he stunk up the whole room. He smelled like a skunk with BO."

Max made a disgusted face, but worry snaked through Chloe. She didn't like the sound of this new kid. Or the fact that Jesse apparently wasn't showering and was smoking pot. She might be naive about taking drugs herself, but she lived in Colorado and knew that the scent surrounding someone who had recently smoked marijuana often smelled similar to the spray of a skunk. Jesse had always been a good kid. He might have complained about the extra responsibilities of his siblings, but he'd always put their well-being first and hadn't ever shirked on making sure they were taken care of. She might need to chat with Tina this weekend.

"Sorry, I know I'm not the James you were expecting," Quinn said, leaning toward her.

"You're fine. I'm glad to see you." The other woman might not be Colt, but Chloe truly was glad to see her. She really liked Quinn. They'd made some tentative attempts at friendship, and she could use a female friend.

"I'm still not quite used to calling myself a James." Quinn smiled and lowered her voice as she put the car in gear. "Even though I am technically a James now, I know I'm no substitute for a six-foot-four cute cowboy named Colt."

Heat flared in Chloe's cheeks at just hearing his name. "Really. It's fine. He's not my personal taxi." She tried to keep the emotion out of her voice, but her words cracked the slightest, and Quinn gave her a concerned look.

"Everything okay? Did something happen between you two?"

"No. Of course not," she stammered. "Did *he* say something happened?"

Quinn arched an eyebrow. "No. He just asked me to give you and the kids a ride to school. Was there something for him to say?"

"No. I'm sorry." Chloe waved her hand at the other woman. "I'm just tired. It's been a long week, and I'm ready for my Friday to be over and the weekend to be here. Don't worry about me."

"I'm actually glad I'm getting a chance to see you. I desperately need a girls' night out, and I was wondering if you'd like to join me and Tessa for a drink. You remember Tess from the hockey game? Mason's girlfriend?"

"Sure." She'd met Tess when she'd helped the James family run the snack bar at the alumni hockey game earlier that summer. The other woman had just started dating Colt's brother Mason, but Chloe had seen her around town several times since then. They'd chatted amicably every time they'd run into each other and always left with a promise to get together for lunch or dinner sometime soon.

"It wouldn't be anything fancy. Just a chance to get a little dressed up and go out for some Mexican food. And by Mexican food, I mean street tacos and frozen margaritas. You look a little like you could use a marg and some girl time."

Chloe wouldn't know. She'd never had a *marg* and some girl time before. But she was up for it. In fact, it sounded like a great way to get her mind off a certain cowboy. "It sounds great. Count me in."

"Good. Rock's got a meeting in Denver this week, and The Creed has a Taco Tuesday night, so I thought we'd shoot for going then."

"Sounds good."

"It'll be fun. Just a group of cool twentysomethings going out on the town."

Chloe's shoulders fell. "Are you sure you want to invite me? I hate to break it to you, but I am neither cool nor a twentysomething. Not after my birthday last year."

"Really? I thought you were younger than me." Quinn waved her hand through the air. "But it doesn't matter. I was just teasing about that. And I'm right behind you anyway. Plus, I'm the mother of a third-grade boy, so my 'cool' status is highly questionable as well."

Not hardly. Quinn might be a year younger, but she had a family and had just taken one of Denver's most sought-after bad-boy bachelors off the market. Her life seemed pretty perfect to Chloe. It was different for her. She had all the makings of a cliché spinster—unmarried schoolteacher with an obsessive knitting habit *and* a cat.

Ugh. She looked down at her khaki pants and the comfortable but far from fashionable boots she wore. No wonder Colt had pulled away when she'd thrown herself at him the night before.

What a fool she'd been to imagine a guy like him would be interested in a frizzy-haired, former fat-club frump like her.

Quinn pulled the car up to the curb. "I'm not sure who will come in this afternoon to pick up Max, but one of us will be able to give you all a ride home."

"We don't need one," Charlie told them as he climbed out of the car. "Our mom said she's picking us up after school. She gets paid today, and we're going out for hamburgers, then coming to watch Maddie's first hockey practice."

Chloe held in a groan. What was she supposed to do about hockey practice? Would Colt still want her there? Did it matter? She couldn't very well back out now. Maddie needed her to be there, and she couldn't let the little girl down. She applauded her bravery and gumption for wanting to play hockey, and she certainly didn't want to stand in the way of that or mess up Maddie's chances of being able to play. Maybe she could go tonight and try to find a mom who might be willing to help.

She waved to Quinn. "You don't have to worry about me either. It's nice today, and I have a few errands in town, so I'll just walk home." In her unfashionable but sturdy boots.

"Are you sure?" Quinn peered at Chloe over the top of her sunglasses.

"Positive."

"Okay. I'll text you about Tuesday, and I'll probably see you at Max's practice. Colt told me you were helping him coach. I think that's awesome. My brother, Logan, is helping with the team too. You all are going to have a lot of fun." Her impish grin gave away how much *fun* she thought coaching a bunch of little kids would be. She waved and pushed her sunglasses back up her nose. "See you tonight."

Chloe focused all her energy on forming her lips into a bright smile. "Yep. Can't wait. See you tonight."

The scent of Vivi's famous fried chicken filled the air as Colt dropped into a chair in his mom's kitchen for lunch that day. His mouth watered as she set a steaming bowl of creamy mashed potatoes on the table next to the platter of chicken.

Meals tended to be larger and more substantial on the ranch. Vivi knew she had several hungry men who had already put in numerous hours of physical labor, and she did an amazing job of providing a great spread for their crew. It was hard to know who would come in for the noonday meal, but Vivi always had plenty to share.

Today's attendance was fairly light, with only his mom, his brothers, one ranch hand, and Quinn. Which was fine by Colt since that meant more chicken for him. And the anticipation of fried chicken and mashed potatoes covered in his mom's country gravy had been the highlight of his day so far.

The heavy snowfall earlier in the week had caused a few problems on the ranch, and Mason had dropped by the cabin that morning to say he really needed Colt's help. A huge section of fence line had been downed by broken and fallen tree limbs and the chicken coop's roof had sprung a leak.

There was always something to do around the ranch, always something to fix or change or check on or feed. And the weather or the health of an animal or herd could ruin any number of well-laid plans. Like the ones he'd made for how he was going to talk to Chloe when he picked her up that morning.

He couldn't get the kiss out of his head. His sheets had been a tangled mess this morning because he'd tossed and turned the night before, unable to sleep for thinking about her warm lips and her soft body pressed against his. Even though kissing and touching her had been all he could think about during the entire skating lesson, she'd still taken him by surprise when she'd planted one on him.

It hadn't seemed real. But her lips against his had been real, and she'd felt amazing. He'd wrapped her in his arms and pulled her close, the needs and wants of his body overriding any rational thoughts his mind might have tried to interject. Everything else fell away, and all he could focus on was Chloe and the way she'd fit perfectly against him like she were the other piece of his puzzle.

Her mouth was soft and yielding, and she'd kissed him with a hunger and desire that he hadn't felt in a long time. But it was the enormity of his feelings for her, the need to touch and taste and the crazy impulse to strip off her jeans and take her against the boards that had him pulling back to regroup and catch his breath.

Colt couldn't remember the last time he'd wanted anything so much or felt the tight grip he usually kept on his feelings loosening. It had scared the daylights out of him. He hadn't wanted to stop. He'd just needed to catch his breath, to take it down a notch before he did something he regretted, like getting naked on a sheet of ice wearing hockey skates.

But he knew the second he pulled away, knew the

instant he saw the shift in her expression go from sex kitten to deer in the headlights that he'd made a terrible mistake.

Because that subtle shift in expression told him all he needed to know—that he wasn't the only one who'd made a mistake, and Chloe had just realized hers. Hell, she even admitted it. First words out of her mouth before she ran—or stumble-skated off—were "Sorry" and "This was a mistake."

He'd tried to talk to her, but he didn't know what to say, and she'd made it quite clear she didn't want to talk. She'd seemed embarrassed, and who could blame her? She was whip smart, college-educated, and so pretty. Why would she be interested in a guy like him? She probably thought he was an idiot, hanging out at her house the whole night before, and making those cupcakes... What a dope.

He never should have brought that wine. It was obvious she was an inexperienced drinker. She'd even admitted the wine had made her do it.

Up until that moment, he'd thought things were going so well. She had to know he was flirting with her. And the way she would blush, then playfully tease him back made him think she was really interested too.

But the words *This was a mistake* kept ringing in his ears, and he knew the curse was alive. Things had been going too well. He was really starting to like this woman. They had fun together, and she made him laugh. Already, in the few short weeks he'd known her and especially in the last few days, she'd awoken something in him, some part of him that had been shut up tight and sealed off, a dream he didn't think could ever be his—a dream of having a real relationship, of a woman to love.

He figured he'd give her a night to think about it and to recover from the strawberry wine. When he picked her up this morning, he'd planned to charm her into smiling and talking to him again. But nothing about his day had gone as planned.

He bowed his head as Rock said grace, then filled his plate as the food was passed around. Trying to sound casual, like it didn't matter to him one way or the other, he tipped his chin to Quinn. "Thanks for picking Chloe and the kids up today. I appreciate it."

"It was no problem. I was glad to get to see her. I've been wanting to touch base with her about getting together for a girls' night out anyway, and this gave us a chance to plan something."

"Oh, yeah. Good. That sounds fun. So…did she seem okay?"

"I'm not sure what you mean by 'okay.' I think she was a little flustered that I showed up instead of you. I don't think I'm a great substitute for a tall, hunky cowboy."

Colt glanced down at his plate, suddenly intent on getting the perfect ratio of gravy to his bite of mashed potatoes. "It's not like that," he muttered.

"Oh?" she asked faux-innocently as she leaned her chin into her hands. "What *is* it like?"

"Yes, Brother," Rock chimed in, a teasing grin on his face as he pointed a chicken leg at Colt. "What is it like?"

Chapter 8

COLT TOSSED A CHUNK OF BISCUIT AT ROCK. "SOMETIMES I can see the appeal of being an only child."

"Uh-oh," Mason said, never one to miss a chance to rib his little brother. "He's evading the question *and* getting defensive. He must really like this girl."

"Shut up. I never said I liked her."

"You never said you didn't."

"She's a friend. And I feel obligated because I told her I would give her, and the neighbor kids, a ride to and from school. I was hoping we could finish by two today so I'd have time to get cleaned up before I picked her up."

"You don't have to," Quinn said.

"What do you mean? Why not?"

"She said she didn't need a ride today. Said she had some errands to run in town and was going to walk home."

Was that true? Or was that just an excuse to get out of having to see him?

Mason was watching him. "That's a pretty unhappy expression for someone who claims to not like this girl."

"I didn't say I didn't *like* her, I just didn't say that I like-*like* her." This was getting ridiculous.

"Well, I like her. I think she seems cool. She's smart, and funny, and pretty"—Mason paused, obviously for dramatic effect—"which is why I don't understand why she would be interested in a chump like you."

"Hilarious. You should really rethink that career as

a comedian, Mace. Except that one was a little weak. Good delivery, but you could do better."

"Quit giving your brother a hard time," Vivi scolded. "Plenty of smart, funny, pretty girls have been interested in him." She reached across the table and squeezed Colt's chin. "Just look at him. He's cute and charming. Any girl would be lucky to have him."

"I think you just found the new line for your dating profile, Bro," Rock chimed in. Which wasn't surprising. When the three brothers were together, it was always two against one. Rock made air quotes with his hands and fluttered his eyelashes. "Hi, I'm Colt. I'm cute and charming, and any girl would be lucky to have me. Just ask my mom."

"Hey, it worked for you," Colt shot back. "Didn't it, Quinn?"

"Leave me out of this," she said, shaking her head. "I think you're all dorks. And besides, I think Max is already planning to marry her, so she's off the market for the next decade at least."

"Speaking of Max," Colt said, thankful for any excuse to change the subject, "don't forget, tonight is our first practice for hockey."

Quinn rolled her eyes. "Oh, I couldn't forget if I tried. It's all Max has been talking about this week."

"I'm glad he's excited."

"He's beyond excited," Rock said. "And so am I. I can't wait to watch him play. I'll try to come out and help with some of the practices if I'm around."

"That would be cool. I'm sure the kids would love it. Logan offered to help too. He said he'd be there tonight."

"Seriously, Brother. Thanks for taking on this coaching thing. I really appreciate it. And I'm glad Logan is helping. Max will get to hang out with two of his uncles."

"So, if Logan is helping you coach, do you really need me to be there tonight?" Quinn asked Colt.

"No. I guess not."

Rock wrinkled his brow. "Why can't you go? Do we have other plans that I forgot about?"

"I don't know what your plans are, but I could use a date with a bubble bath and a good book."

Rock's mouth curved into an impish grin. "I can change my plans. I've been thinking I should do more reading."

She arched an eyebrow in his direction, then turned back to Colt. "I feel guilty because I told Chloe I would be there."

"Chloe? Funny how this woman's name just keeps popping up." Mason chuckled. "But why would she be at hockey practice? Does she have a kid too? A secret love child we've never heard about?"

"No kid. And no secret love child. At least that I know of. She's going to be there because she's helping me coach."

"Huh? I thought you just said Logan was helping you coach."

"He is. But so is Chloe."

"Why do you need three coaches? And does she know much about hockey?"

"Nope, and apparently she barely knows how to skate. But she *has* been to a game."

"*A* game? As in one?" Mason let out a low whistle. "Wow. Well then, that should qualify her to teach the nephew how to play."

"Logan and I will be teaching the nephew how to play. But we've got a girl on the team, so the league told me I need a female coach. And Chloe offered to help." *Sort of. Offered* might be a bit of an overstatement.

"Nice." Mason tapped the side of his head. "Very ingenious to get a girl player so you could coax Chloe into coaching and hanging out with you. You're smarter than you look, Brother. So, who'd you talk into joining the team?"

"I didn't talk anyone into it. In fact, she talked me into it. She's a girl in Max's class. Her name is Maddie."

"She's one of the Johnson kids," Quinn said. "They live next door to Chloe."

"Speaking of the Johnsons, I heard Rank Johnson is out of jail and back in town," Vivi said. She had a way of hearing about everything that happened in Creedence. "I hope he doesn't try to show up at any of Maddie's practices."

A sliver of worry jabbed into Colt's gut. The last thing he needed was a dirtball like Rank Johnson showing up at the ice arena. Or hanging around Chloe's house.

"He'd better not," Quinn said. "Last I heard, Tina had a restraining order put against him after she filed for divorce. He can't come anywhere near her or the kids."

That hadn't stopped him before.

It was close to three that afternoon when Chloe finished her lesson plans and finally left the school. She'd been stopped in the hall by Huge…er, Hugh—geez, now Colt had her doing it too—and he'd offered to give her a ride home. She had told him no, claiming she wanted the exercise, and as the gym teacher, he could hardly argue with her reason.

She breathed in the clean, brisk mountain air as she walked toward the main area of town. Rivulets of water trickled across the sidewalks and along the gutters as the bright sun melted the remaining snow. It was commonly said in Colorado that if someone didn't like the weather, they could just wait an hour, and it would change. Coloradans had been known to have rain, snow, and sunshine all in the same day, and she loved that about her state. A big dump of snow could hit one day, and the sun would melt it away the next. Colorado residents liked to boast that the state had three hundred days of sunshine a year, and she thought that was pretty close to the truth.

Normally, all that sunlight would put her in good spirits, but Chloe was having trouble coming out of the gloomy mood she'd been in most of the day. She'd told Quinn she had errands to run, but that was just an excuse so the other woman wouldn't have to schlep her home.

Walking past the storefronts, Chloe tried to think if there was anything she did need. She passed Claudia's Clothing Boutique but wasn't in the mood to shop for clothes. The Book Nook was normally a place she couldn't pass without popping in, but the last thing she wanted to do today was browse the romance section. Looking at all those happy couples on the covers would only make her heart hurt more.

A list of groceries she needed ran through her head, but it could all wait until her normal Sunday shopping trip. Although it wouldn't hurt to pick up a half gallon of milk, and she could probably use more eggs. And she could carry those home.

She wandered past Carley's Cut and Curl and caught a glimpse of herself in the reflection of the window. A crazy mess of curls hung past her shoulders, and she reached up to finger a mousy-brown tendril as she perused the trendy photos circling the window. The hairstyles looked so glamorous. Especially compared to her usual style of letting her hair air-dry and wearing it down until about the middle of the day when it started to drive her crazy, and then she pulled it into a ponytail or twisted it into a bun and jabbed a pencil through the twist to hold it in place.

Carley Chapman, the owner of the shop, popped her head out the door. "Hey there, Miss Bishop."

"Hi, Carley. You can call me Chloe now. I haven't had one of your kids in my class for two years."

"Sorry, Miss… I mean, Chloe." Carley grinned, then tilted her head toward the pictures in the window. "You thinking about getting a haircut? I just had a cancellation and could fit you in now if you want. I've got time to do a cut, and we could give you a little color too. I find a few highlights tend to chase away the winter blues."

How did Carley know she had the blues? Was it written all over her face? Or was that just the standard line hairstylists used to lure unsuspecting bystanders into their chairs?

Could a simple haircut and a few highlights really help her mood? Chloe looked back at her reflection. Maybe a new look was just what she needed. She'd had the same hairstyle since she'd left for college. And she'd never used color in her hair. Her dad had forbidden it. But her dad wasn't in charge of her anymore. She was in control of her own life. And her own hair.

Normally, she liked things to stay the same. She knew what to expect when she kept her life in consistent order. But maybe it was time for a change. Time to shake a few things up. Heck, just in the last few days, she'd tried strawberry wine, ridden on the back of a Zamboni, and licked cake batter off a hot cowboy's finger. A new hairstyle might be exactly what she needed to give her the confidence to face Colt James again after she'd thrown herself at him the night before.

She took a deep breath and lifted her chin. "Yes. Actually, I would like a haircut. And I think a few of those blues-chasing highlights sound good too."

Carley grinned. "Come on in then."

Chloe stepped into the salon. It smelled like shampoo and permanent solution, but it was clean and cheery. The decor was fashioned after the old fifties-style beauty shops with cotton-candy-pink-and-white-striped wallpaper and hot-pink leather chairs. The floor was tiled in black and white squares, and a large framed print of Audrey Hepburn wearing pearls and a diamond clip in her hair adorned the wall over the small row of hair dryers.

She settled into a chair, and Carley draped a pink-and-white-striped cape around her neck. "What do you think?" Chloe asked. "Is there any hope for my drab hair?"

"There is always hope when you've got a good stylist. And I am a very good stylist." She lifted Chloe's limp locks and ran her fingers through the curls. "You've got great hair. It's healthy and thick, and these curls are to die for. You just need a better style and a little direction on how to use a roller brush, and your hair could be utterly gorgeous. If you're up for a change, I could take a few inches off, layer the back, put in a few blond highlights, and give you some wispier bangs, and you'd feel like a totally new woman."

Was she really up for a change? She'd had the same hair, the same routines for so long that Chloe wasn't sure she was capable of change. But suddenly the thought of keeping things the same felt more like being in a rut than being in a routine. And the only way to make a change was to take a leap. She could do this. It was only hair.

But she knew it was more than just hair—it was a step. And not just a small step, but a giant leap toward breaking the chains her dad and her history held over her. She squeezed her eyes shut and summoned her courage, not from a strawberry-flavored liquor, but from somewhere inside her. *I can do this. All I have to do is say yes.*

She took another deep breath, then opened her eyes and smiled at Carley. "Yes. Let's do all those things." With those words, she could feel the resolution, the glimmer of bravery, flowing through her like water soaking into a sponge. She was doing something. Taking a chance. And it felt good.

But as good as it felt, she tried not to hope for too much. She couldn't imagine how a new haircut could do all that, but she wanted to feel like a new woman, to *be* a new woman. She was tired of the old one.

Chloe winced. She wasn't *old*. She was just *older* than a certain someone she knew.

Quit thinking about him. Yeah right. Like that was going to happen. But maybe she could put him out of her mind for a little bit. Just long enough to enjoy the experience of letting someone else pamper her for a while.

"I could do your nails too, if you want," Carley said.

"It wouldn't take but a minute to paint them while we wait for the color to take."

Hair and nails in the same appointment? Why not? In for a penny, in for a pound, as her grandma used to say. "A manicure sounds wonderful."

Two hours later, Chloe walked out of the salon, her steps—and her wallet—as light as her bouncy new hair. Apparently getting a new cut and color *was* a mood lifter. She caught her reflection in the glass of the Creedence Country Store and marveled at the change of her new look. Wispy bangs brushed her forehead, and the sun gleamed off the light strands of blond.

The new do was trendier and did make her look younger, more in style. She felt younger too. Fresher. And the hot-pink nail polish added a bit of sass. Carley had spent extra time with her, teaching her how to use a round brush and a hair dryer to create the soft waves. Armed with those instructions and the bag of expensive hair products she'd purchased, Chloe even felt fairly confident she'd be able to create the look again.

As she ran her fingers through her frizzless tresses, she noticed the sign for Bud's Auto Body reflected in the glass. That's where Colt's friend had taken her car. Might as well check on it while she was in town. Maybe it would be finished, and she could drive it home today.

She crossed the street and poked her head into the open garage bay. The sound of a pneumatic drill came from underneath the engine of a blue Chevy pickup, but she didn't see anyone else around. The air smelled of car grease and motor oil.

She spotted her car in the third bay of the shop. It didn't look bad, other than the front driver's side door being missing. Which dramatically lessoned the likelihood of her driving it home today. She was pretty sure that was a moving violation of some kind.

An oily puddle of melted snow had formed on the concrete floor, and she gingerly stepped around it.

"Hello," she called, the word echoing in the cavernous room.

"Be with you in a sec," a man's voice answered from beneath the pickup.

Chloe rounded the back of the truck and spied a pair of coverall-clad legs sticking out from beneath it. He gave one last burst of the drill, then slid out and stood up. "Sorry about that. What can I do ya for?"

He had dark hair and an easy, friendly smile. His coveralls were smudged with dirt, but the collar of a bright-white undershirt shone above the buttoned front. He looked to be around Colt's age, so younger than her. *Stop it.*

"Are you Bud?"

"Nope. Bud's my dad. I'm Justin. My dad retired a few years ago, so the shop is mine, but you know small towns. Everyone gets used to a name, and nobody wants to change." He held up his grease-stained palms. "I'd shake your hand, but…"

"It's fine. I'm Chloe Bishop. Nice to meet you." She pointed to the doorless vehicle. "That's my car."

He looked her up and down, and a knowing grin spread across his face. "Ahhh, so you're the one."

"What one?"

"The one who got Colton James to finally take me up on my offer to let me do a favor for him."

"Well, I can tell you I really appreciate your help, but I'm planning to cover the damages myself." She had no idea how much it would cost to repair a door, but she knew she wasn't going to let Colt pick up the tab, no matter how big or small the amount was.

Justin waved a hand in her direction. "Your money's no good here, Chloe."

She tried to keep her mouth from dropping open. "You can't mean that."

He narrowed his eyes at her. "I can assure you I do. I've known Colt a long time, and I'd do anything for that guy. He did something for me that I can't ever repay. I owe him big time, but he's never asked for anything in return. Until now. Until he needed a car towed and fixed... for a woman. For you. You must mean a lot to him."

Not hardly.

"Well, I wouldn't know anything about that, but I do know that I can't let you fix my car for free. You've got to let me pay you something. I know with parts and labor, car repairs can get expensive. And I can't imagine what kind of favor Colt could have done that would make you want to give away your services."

Before Justin could answer, the door between the garage and the office opened, and a gorgeous copper-colored golden retriever padded into the garage and sniffed her hand.

"Hello, puppy." She scratched its ear. "Who's this guy?" she asked Justin.

The dog turned at the whirr of a motor and raced back to the door as a child maneuvered an electric wheelchair through it. The boy looked to be about Max's age and had curly blond hair. He pushed his round glasses up his nose and offered her a sweet grin. He looked like a cherub, an adorable angel with no wings.

Justin smiled at the boy. "This is my son, Spencer. And you already met his dog, Milo."

She waved at the boy. "Hi, Spencer. I'm Chloe. I'm a teacher at the grade school. I know a lot of kids your age, but I don't think I've met you."

The boy rolled his eyes. "That's because my parents are ridiculously overprotective, and my mom insists on homeschooling me."

Chloe chuckled. "From the sounds of your vocabulary, I'd say your mom is a pretty good teacher."

He shrugged. "I guess. But I'm still trying to talk her into letting me switch to the grade school. Especially now that I have Milo."

Chloe peered down at the dog, who was sitting obediently next to the boy's chair. "He's a beautiful dog."

"He's the best." Spencer rubbed the dog's head as he looked toward his dad. "Mom wanted me to tell you dinner's going to be on the table in thirty minutes."

"Okay, thanks, buddy. Tell her I'll wash up and be there in a few."

"Nice to meet you," the boy said as he turned the wheelchair around and eased back through the door.

"You too, Spencer," she called, then turned back to Justin. "He seems like a great kid. And smart. Your wife is doing a great job with him. If she ever needs any support or teaching materials, she can call me. I'd be happy to help."

"That's kind of you. I can see why Colt likes you."

Heat flared to her cheeks. What the heck had he told this guy about her? She wished she could ask. For now, it was easier to change the subject. "I love golden retrievers. Milo seems to do really well with Spencer. Is he a service dog?"

Justin nodded. "He's the best. That dog has changed our lives. Besides being the first friend my kid's ever had, he's allowed Spence to be more independent and given him a purpose. He's a different kid now that he has Milo. It used to be there were days when he didn't want to leave his room, and we could forget getting him out of the house. Now he jumps out of bed to feed Milo, and he begs us to take the two of them to the park."

"That's wonderful."

Justin narrowed his eyes and tilted his head as if he were taking her measure. She must have passed his squinty-eyed test, because he nodded his head slightly before he spoke. "Milo was sired by Colt's golden, Watson. Colt sponsored the pup and spent six months training him to be a service dog. Then he spent another six months working with Spence and Milo together, teaching them how to work as a team and training the dog to do tasks specific to our son's needs."

Oh.

He glanced toward the doorless car then back at her. "Do you understand now?"

She nodded, unable to speak around the emotion clogging her throat. Yes, she understood now.

"I had to order a couple of parts for the door, but they'll be here Monday, and I should have the car back to you, good as new, by the middle of the week."

"Thank you." There was nothing else for her to say. No other choice. How could she take this away—this chance he had to finally do something for the man who had given him an immeasurable gift? "And thank you for telling me. It was really nice to meet you. And Spencer and Milo. I'll let you get back to work."

He smiled. "It was really nice to meet you too, Miss Bishop."

"You'll tell your wife? To call me at the school? Or just drop by. I meant what I said. I'm happy to help."

"I'll tell her."

———

Later that night, Chloe paced her living room, glancing at the clock for the fifteenth time. The minute hand crept closer to seven, and she resisted the temptation to nibble her freshly painted hot-pink nails.

By this time on any other Friday night, she'd already be in her comfy flannel pajamas curled up on the sofa with a frozen pizza and bowl of popcorn big enough to make it through several hours of binge-watching some series on Netflix.

But tonight, she was dressed in jeans and an over-size sweatshirt and had finished eating dinner twenty minutes ago. She'd also spent the last thirty minutes studying the rules of the game of hockey. Which might be all for nothing. Who knew if Colt still wanted her to help coach?

She caught her breath as she heard an engine pull up out front. *Crud. What now?* Should she act like she wasn't expecting him or like she was? She rushed over to the sofa and plopped down, crossed her legs, and nonchalantly threw her hand over the back of the cushions. No—too prim. She uncrossed her legs, slouched against the pillows, reached for her knitting.

Oh, for the love of bean dip. This was ridiculous. It didn't matter how she was sitting. If he came to the door, she'd have to get up to answer anyway. It's not like he was going to waltz through her front door and find her casually sprawled on the sofa working a purl stitch.

A soft knock sounded at the door. She caught her breath and cocked her head, trying to interpret the intensity of the noise. Was it a hesitant knock like "I hope she doesn't hear me. Then I can leave and say I tried"? Was it a questioning knock like "I have no idea if she still wants to do this or if she's going to be glad, or mad, to see me"? Or was it a confident knock like "Last night didn't matter, and we're going to pretend it didn't happen anyway"?

Another more insistent knock sounded, and she jumped. "Chloe?" Colt's deep voice came through the door.

Get up and answer the door before he leaves.

She pushed off from the sofa and rushed to the door, her knitting project still clutched in her hand and oblivious to the ball of yarn that fell off the sofa and trailed behind her, unraveling as it rolled. "Be right there," she called.

She sucked in her breath and pulled open the door.

Chapter 9

CHLOE'S BREATH CAUGHT AS SHE TOOK IN THE TALL COW-boy standing in the pool of light on her porch. He wore jeans and boots and a brown felt cowboy hat pushed low over his forehead. His tan Carhartt coat was unzipped and open, and he wore a faded denim shirt over an ivory thermal Henley. He looked good enough to eat.

He offered her a shy grin, almost as if he didn't know what to expect from her either. It was a small smile, no teeth, just the slimmest curve of his lips coupled with a slight inquisitive tilt of his head, but it was enough to twist her stomach in a nervous knot and have her mouth going dry.

Quit looking at his lips and say hello.

"Uh, hi. Colt," she stammered, then took a step back. "Come on in."

She must have been shadowed by the light behind her, because when he stepped into the house, his mouth dropped open.

"Wow, look at your hair," he said, his eyes going wide.

Her free hand fluttered to the side of her head, the knot in her stomach rolling over. With her other hand, she clasped her knitting to her chest, as if the stitched yarn could somehow muffle the sound of her heart pounding against her chest.

What had she done? Had changing her hair been a dumb decision? Did it make it seem like she was trying too hard? She cursed Carley and her mood-lightening highlights. "I had it cut this afternoon."

"It looks amazing," he said, then held up his hands. "I mean, it looked good before, I liked it the way it was, but it looks really great now." He stopped, took a breath, and let it out. "I don't know why my mouth is not connecting to my brain tonight. Your hair looks nice, Chloe. You look real pretty."

She bit her lip to keep the beaming smile from completely taking over her face. "Thank you." They stared at each other, both smiling, but neither offering anything more to say.

"Meow." Thankfully, the cat saved them as she strolled into the room and rubbed herself against Colt's legs.

Lucky cat.

He bent down and stroked Agatha's back, then straightened and nodded his head toward the door. "We should probably get going. You ready?"

"Uh, yeah. The hockey thing. Sure." She twisted the knitted yarn in her hands. "I didn't know... I wasn't sure if you still wanted me."

"Of course I want you. I mean...of course I want you to help me coach the team," he stammered. "Why wouldn't I?"

She stared down at her hands. "Because of last night."

"You mean because you can't skate that well?"

Yeah, Colt. That's what I mean. I was worried about last night because of my skating abilities. Nothing at all to do with the lip-locking kiss I awkwardly forced on you while we were on the ice.

But, if that's how he wanted to play it, she'd go

along with the "ignore it and maybe it will go away" option.

"Don't worry about it," he said. "Half the kids on the team can barely skate. You'll learn with them. You just need more practice."

He could say that again. She needed more practice with a lot of things. Like how to deal with handsome men who made her palms sweat and her chest tight.

His brows knit together. "Do you still *want* to help with the team?"

"Yes. I do. Maddie really wants to play, and I want her to have that chance. I don't want to let her down." She held up the scrunched wad of yarn in her hands. "I wasn't sure if you were going to pick me up, or if I was still coaching, so I was just doing a little knitting." Yes, of course, if she couldn't *look* nonchalant, she should clumsily try to *explain* how relaxed and unconcerned she was about whether he was going to show up or not.

"It looks like Agatha is helping you." He gestured behind her, and she turned to see the cat batting and chasing the ball of yarn that had trailed behind her. A long line of purple yarn was now wrapped around one leg of the coffee table and had unrolled willy-nilly across the room as the cat pursued it like a hunter stalking its prey.

"Oh Mylanta," Chloe cried, shooing the cat away and trying to gather the yarn as Colt chuckled behind her. Tossing the whole wad on the sofa, she turned back to him. "I'll deal with this later. Let's go." She grabbed her coat off the hook by the door and shoved her arms into the sleeves.

He peered into the tote bag sitting on the bench by the

door, then offered her a teasing grin. "For not knowing if I was coming to get you or not, it's a good thing you were ready."

She gave a noncommittal shrug, trying to ignore the surges of heat his grin sent racing down her spine. "I like to be prepared."

"I can tell. It looks like you conveniently prepared a notebook, a clipboard, a *Hockey for Dummies* handbook, *and* a first aid kit, and had them ready by the door."

She playfully glared at him, then grabbed the bag and nudged him on the shoulder as she walked out the door. "Oh, hush up." At least he was grinning and teasing her again. She'd take that over awkward and embarrassed any day.

As she walked to the truck, Chloe let out a small sigh of relief that they didn't have to talk about the kiss or what had happened the night before. She was good with pretending it didn't happen and going back to being friends. She knew how to pretend. She'd spent a lifetime pretending everything was okay. And she could do the same with Colt. Even if hanging around him had her body heating up like a solar panel on a sunny day, she'd take the burn if it meant being with him, hearing him laugh, and having him occasionally touch her back or brush against her hip.

If being Colt's friend was all she was going to get, then she'd take it.

Fifteen minutes later, Colt held the door open for Chloe as they walked into the ice arena. The smell of her hair had him wanting to drag her back to the pickup and have his way with her, but that wasn't going to happen. Not just because they had a dozen kids and their parents waiting for them, but because Chloe had made it clear the night before that she wasn't interested in their relationship going in that direction.

She'd still seemed nervous when he picked her up, but that was most likely due to the awkwardness of the botched kiss. He'd done his best to tease her out of it, and he felt like they were okay again. Even if she didn't want to steam up the windows of his truck with him, he was happy just being around her. She had this thing about her—he couldn't describe it—it was kind of like the way sunshine felt warm against his skin.

Geez, man. Get a grip on yourself. Since when did he think about women as sunshine and rainbows? Chloe was a nice person, and he felt good when he was around her. He also felt like he had a swarm of angry hornets buzzing in his gut when she smiled at him, but he'd think about that later.

Right now, he had a bunch of kids to get laced into skates and a practice to run. He led Chloe toward the skate-rental booth where he'd left her skates the night before. Logan and Max were standing in front of the booth.

Colt introduced Chloe to his neighbor. "Have you met Logan Rivers? He's Quinn's brother, our neighbor, and next to my brothers, probably my best friend."

She nodded. "We've met at some of Max's school functions and when we all went out after the alumni game this summer. Hi, Logan."

He tipped his head and smiled warmly. "Hey, Chloe. Thanks for helping out. It's great that we'll have a girl on the team. I wish Quinn could have played as a girl.

She used to mess around on the pond with us when we were kids, and she could stickhandle better than me."

"My dog can stickhandle better than you," Colt ribbed him.

"Hi, Miss Bishop." Max shouldered his way in front of his uncle and held up a gleaming red-and-black hockey stick. "Isn't this cool? Rock gave me this new stick, just tonight. I'm gonna score a goal with this one. I just know it."

"I'll bet you do," Chloe agreed.

Colt liked the way she encouraged everyone. "First we've got to get the team together, buddy. Can you help me round everyone up?"

Five minutes later, Colt stood in front of the bleachers where Chloe, Logan, a handful of parents, and twelve excited and nervous kids sat.

He introduced himself, Chloe, and Logan, and had the kids say their names and what position they'd like to play. He caught most of the names, trying to memorize them as the kids said either their desired position or mumbled a version of "I don't know." He knew Max and Maddie, so he was good with two. He noticed Chloe was furiously scribbling notes on her clipboard as he mentally ran through the other kids' names—Brock, Dillon, Ryan, Brady, Keith, Floyd, kid with the taped glasses, red-haired set of twins, and a taller heavy-set kid named Gordy, who thankfully said he wanted to play goalie.

As far as Colt was concerned, the kid could have the position. It was much harder to assign the role, so he was thrilled at least one kid had stepped up.

Maddie had claimed she wanted to be the quarterback, and he was fairly certain he'd seen Chloe jot that down. "You don't have to write that one," he told her. "We don't have a quarterback in hockey."

"I know." She nodded wisely, then casually erased a line on her page.

"This is a twelve-week season," Colt explained to everyone. "We'll practice once a week on Mondays and an occasional Saturday if I can get the ice time, and we'll have games every Wednesday. I know this is Friday, but tonight is kind of a special deal since we're doing this meeting and passing out equipment and making sure everyone's skates fit. I got us an extra hour of ice time because I wanted to give us enough time to skate and go through a couple of basic drills and see where everyone's skating abilities are." He raised his gaze to the parents. "We'll email you with the final schedules, so make sure we have your correct email address and a good phone number to reach you." This was also how he was planning to get Chloe's number without having to come out and ask her for it.

"As you know, our sponsor, Rock James, is donating pads and equipment to everyone on the team. We took the measurements and sizes you turned in when you registered, and we have a bag for each of you that contains your skates, helmet, and all your pads." He patted the line of a dozen roller bags that he and Logan had brought in earlier. "We're not using sticks tonight, but you all have a certificate to use at the Skate Shop next door to get one free stick of your choice. Otis runs the shop, and he'll cut your stick to the right height and show you how to tape it up.

"Once you know everything fits and is going to work for you, I want you to have it all labeled with your name before you come to practice on Monday night. Before I pass out the bags, I'm going to go through the uniform and show you how to put everything on." He held up each piece, starting with the breezers, then moving through the pads, socks, and gloves. Some of the items were self-explanatory, but Colt didn't want any of the kids to feel dumb for not knowing how something worked or how to put it on. "Gordy will have a few extra pieces, like a blocker and a catcher, and he'll have extra leg pads since he's the goalie."

Gordy grinned, and his shoulders pulled back as the other kids looked at him with envy.

"Everybody wears a helmet and a mouth guard, no exceptions." He held up a piece of white plastic. "Also, everybody gets one of these. This is an athletic cup, and it protects your family jewels. Trust me on this one. You do not want to forget to put this on. And everyone *has* to wear one." He glanced at Madison who was listening intently. "Well, almost everyone. You don't have to worry about this piece of equipment, Maddie."

The girl pulled her head back. "Why not? Why don't I get to wear one too? I'm athletic, and I like to protect my family's jewels. My mom might not have a lot of diamonds, but she still has some pretty jewelry."

The boys around her smirked and tittered, some of them knowing what a cup was for and others just knowing what their family jewels were.

"It's not those kind of jewels, honey," Chloe told her. She leaned closer and must have whispered the true purpose of the cup into the girl's ear.

Maddie wrinkled her nose and gave Colt a scathing

look. "No thank you. I've decided to pass on wearing a cup to practice. Or anywhere."

"Good choice." He offered a grateful smile to Chloe, who was holding her clipboard in front of her mouth and trying not to laugh. "Everybody gets a bag, a helmet, and skates tonight. We'll pass out the bags, and we want you to spread out and get dressed and get your skates on. We'll come around to help adjust your helmets and answer questions and make sure everything fits."

He motioned to the older man sitting in the bleachers above them. "This is Otis. He was kind enough to be here tonight to help as well." Although the giant profit his store made on the sale of all the equipment probably carried a little swaying influence. Colt pointed to a couple of the dads he knew from the alumni team. "And Brock and Dillon's dads also played hockey so they can help too. If that's cool with you guys?" Both dads nodded, and the kids clamored off the bleachers in search of their labeled bags.

It took close to an hour, but all the kids finally had their equipment on and made it onto the ice. Colt and Logan led the kids around the rink a couple of times to assess their skating abilities, then broke them into two groups. The more experienced skaters followed Logan to work on drills on one side of the ice, while Colt worked with the less experienced skaters, and Chloe, on the other side. After half an hour of skating, he brought the team back together, and after getting twelve high fives, he sent them off for the night.

He'd had fun. The kids cracked him up, and he enjoyed being out on the ice and talking about the game. Granted, it was only one practice and it didn't take a lot to impress eight-year-olds, but their first practice had gone well. Everyone had seemed to have a good time. He'd been especially impressed with Maddie, who had attacked skating with the enthusiasm of a shark swimming after its prey. Maybe it was because she was used to hanging out with three brothers, but she fit right in with the other kids, and none of the boys seemed to treat her any differently or think anything odd about having a girl on the team.

"What did you think of your first hockey practice?" he asked Chloe as he collapsed onto the bench next to her. She'd already taken her skates off and changed into her boots while he finished up with the parents.

"It was fun," she said, straightening the pages of notes on her clipboard. "I learned a lot. And all the parents verified their phone numbers and email addresses with me before they left."

"Awesome. That reminds me..." He casually pulled his phone from his pocket. "We should probably exchange numbers too. Just in case we need to talk. About the team, or practice, or something." *Real smooth, dude. Real smooth.*

"Sure." She recited her number as she pulled out her phone.

He punched it in, then sent her a text. This is Colt. Hi. *Wow.* He was on fire tonight with his lady-killing moves.

She tapped at her phone, and then his buzzed in his hand. He read her return message. Hi. This is Chloe. Thanks for asking me to coach. You did great with the kids. ☺

He typed a message back. Thanks. So did you. He

held his finger over the emojis, hesitant to add one to his message. He never knew which one to use. The smiley face? The thumbs-up? Both seemed too generic. The heart was too forward, and there was no way he was using the kissing lips, even though he half wanted to. Where was the emoji for "I'm interested in you but am too big of a dork to know how to tell you"?

How could he face down twelve hyper eight-year-olds and inform them they all needed to wear a cup, but get nervous sending a single text message to a woman?

Oh, forget it. This was stupid anyway. She was sitting right next to him. He pushed Send.

"Hey, you ready to go?" Logan ambled over as the last of the kids were leaving.

Quinn and Rock had shown up halfway through practice—Colt had known they wouldn't be able to stay away from the first practice—and had taken Max home with them.

He stuffed his phone into his pocket. "Just finishing up."

"We're heading over to The Creed to get a celebratory first-practice beer," Logan told Chloe. "You wanna come with us?"

"Oh, gosh, no." She shook her head. "I don't want to intrude." Her gaze traveled around the ice arena. "I can grab a ride home with one of the other parents. Maddie's mom might still be here."

Colt narrowed his eyes at Logan. *Idiot*. He'd wanted to be the one to ask her—to ease her into the idea. "I'm still planning to take you home," he said, leaning forward to unlace his skates. "I'll meet up with Logan after I drop you off." Unless he could still convince her to

come with them. He'd give it another try when they
were in the truck.

— ∿∿ —

Chloe walked between the two men, their hockey bags
slung over their shoulders as she, Colt, and Logan left
the ice arena.

She studied them as they talked strategy for the next
practice and who they thought should play what position. Quinn's brother was almost as tall as Colt and had
the same lean, muscular body. He wore cowboy boots
and jeans like Colt, but instead of a cowboy hat, he had
on a blue baseball cap advertising a local feed store. His
hair was darker than Colt's, more of a chestnut brown,
but she remembered this summer it had been a bit
blonder, probably from the sun and spending so much
time outside.

The two old friends talked and joked easily with each
other, and she smiled up at them as her stomach swirled
and spun. How had this become her life? Logan and
Colt were both ruggedly handsome, and here she was,
a petite, quiet schoolteacher hanging out with them as
if she were in on their jokes. And if that weren't crazy
enough, her world had somehow tilted on its axis so she
was going to partner with these two ridiculously hot
guys to coach a bleeping hockey team.

"You sure we can't convince you to come have a beer
with us?" Logan asked, holding the door for her.

She knew he was just being nice. Why would they
want to have a beer with her? Surely, having a third-
grade schoolteacher hanging out with them would cramp
the style of two single guys at a bar on a Friday night.

Besides the fact she didn't even like beer, she'd already made the humiliating mistake of drinking around Colt the night before. She wasn't going to make that mistake twice. "I'm good. You two go on and have a good time."

Logan shrugged. "Maybe next time." He nodded at Colt, who was tossing his skate bag into the back of his pickup. "See you in fifteen."

The ride home went quickly as they talked about the kids and how the practice had gone. "I was proud of Maddie," Colt told her as they pulled up in front of Chloe's house. "She really held her own tonight. I thought the fact that she had no idea how to skate would hinder her, but it didn't seem to bother her at all. From what I saw tonight, she'll be skating better than some of the boys soon." He grinned at her. "She's gonna make a great quarterback."

Chloe laughed and playfully shoved his arm. "I knew that quarterback thing was wrong. I was just nervous, and I was trying to write down all the kids' names and preferences. I knew it was wrong as soon as I wrote it." But she would be studying the rules and positions more this weekend so she didn't make a rookie mistake like that one again.

"Oh yeah, I'm sure you did."

Another car came flying down the street and screeched to a halt in front of her neighbor's house. The back door opened, and a teenage boy fell or was shoved out. Then the car took off, its tires squealing on the street.

"That's Jesse," Chloe said, her heart pounding as she scrambled from the truck. She heard the other truck door slam but was already hurrying toward the teenager.

Jesse stumbled across his front lawn and fell onto the

grass. She heard him groan, but couldn't tell if he was drunk or if he'd been beaten up. He curled into a fetal position and wrapped his arms around his stomach.

"You okay, son?" Colt's legs were longer than hers, and it had taken fewer strides for him to reach the boy and kneel down next to him. He put a hand on Jesse's shoulder, but the teenager jerked back.

"Who are you? Get away from me." His words were slurred, and his eyes widened as he scrambled back.

"Jesse, it's me. Chloe. Miss Bishop. From next door. This is my friend Colt. We're trying to help." She kept her voice low, her tone soothing. "Are you okay? Are you hurt?"

"I'm fine," he slurred, rolling over and crawling toward his porch steps.

"Let us help you inside, at least." She reached under one of his arms and Colt reached under the other, and they hauled the teen to his feet and helped him up the steps. He smelled like stale beer and weed, and his hair stunk like smoke. "Hello, Tina," Chloe called as they pushed through the front door.

"Miss Bishop," Maddie said, running from the kitchen. "What are you doing here…" Her joyful smile fell, and she turned back when she saw her brother. "Mama, you better come in here. They've got Jesse."

"Jesse?" Tina came through the door, drying her hands on a dish towel. She hurried forward and threw her arms around the boy's neck. "Where have you been? Are you hurt? Oh dang—you smell like a brewery. Are you drunk?"

He pulled free of Chloe and Colt and shrugged off his mom's arms. "Just leave me alone." He staggered to the sofa and fell into it, his face planted into the cushion and his arm hanging limp off the side.

Tina rolled her eyes. "I will *not* leave you alone. I'm your mother. It's kind of in my job description to take care of you."

"Can I do anything to help?" Colt asked Tina. "Want me to take him to his room?"

She shook her head. "No. He'll be fine. I'm just glad he's home. Thanks though. And thanks for everything you're doing with Maddie on the hockey team."

"No problem." He looked at Chloe, then leaned his head toward the door. "I'm just gonna go."

She nodded absently, her concentration focused on Tina as she rested a hand on the other woman's arm. "I'm going to stay here for a bit and try to help Tina. I'll talk to you later."

"Oh. Yeah. Okay. I'll see ya later then." He turned and slipped out the door, pulling it closed behind him.

"How about if I help get the other kids to bed while you talk to Jesse?"

Tina's shoulders slumped, and it seemed as if her whole body shrank into itself. She let out a heavy sigh and scrubbed a hand across her forehead. "That would be great. Thank you."

Chloe walked toward the kitchen and realized she'd left her bag in Colt's truck just as she heard him pull away from the curb. Oh well, she'd get it at the next practice. She'd checked the *Hockey for Dummies* book out from the school library and had been looking forward to studying it, but she was sure she could find plenty of hockey information on the internet until she got the book back.

Jake and Madison were standing inside the kitchen door, but Charlie was elbows deep in a sink full of soapy water. He turned as she came in. "Mom let us have ice cream after Maddie's practice. I was just cleaning up the mess so she wouldn't have to worry about it. Sounds like she's got enough on her plate dealing with Jess."

"That was thoughtful of you," Chloe told him, wondering if he usually did the task or if Colt's influence had rubbed off on him a little. "I was going to read a book to Maddie, if you and Jake want to come in when you're done."

Charlie shrugged and pulled the plug from the sink. The water made a gurgling sound as it drained. "Maybe." He turned toward the window as another car roared up in front of the house.

Chloe could see the shape of the car around Charlie's head. It was a late-model muscle car with a spoiler and obviously no muffler. The passenger door opened, and a man got out and stood at the curb studying the house. The car drove off with a squeal of tires.

Geez. What is it tonight with people being dropped unceremoniously at the curb of this house? Before she had a chance to ask, Charlie turned back to her, his knuckles white as he gripped the kitchen counter, his face pale as the color drained from it. "It's my dad," he whispered.

Maddie let out a whimper and clung to Chloe's leg as Jake raced past her into the living room.

"Mom," he cried, his voice filled with terror. "It's Dad! Dad's here!"

Chloe picked up Madison and followed Jake. Tina's

eyes were wide as her head whipped toward her. "Get the kids out of here." She shook Jesse's shoulder so hard, he almost fell off the sofa. "Jesse, get up. Your dad's here. You've got to run."

Chapter 10

SWEAT BROKE OUT ACROSS CHLOE'S BACK, AND THE HAIR lifted on her arms as she jumped back in time twenty years to her own kitchen, her back to a corner, her arms wrapped tightly around her stomach, trying to make herself as small as possible as she waited for her father to walk in the door after a night out with his pals.

But she'd been alone, no nice neighbor lady, no mother to protect her. Her mother was already gone. Which was one of the items on the list of things her father blamed and punished her for.

She sucked in a shuddering breath. *Stop it*. This wasn't *her* father standing on the curb. Her father was gone. And she was a grown woman and had a chance to do something, to help these kids, even though no one had ever helped her.

Jesse pushed himself up from the sofa, weaving as he tried to stand. "No way. I'm not leaving you here with him."

"I'll be fine. But you've got to go." Tina pulled him tightly against her in a quick hug, then pushed him away, her voice trembling as she ordered him to go. "Run, Jesse. I mean it. If he finds you here, he'll kill you."

Even in his alcohol-induced state, the teenager knew fear. He stared into his mom's eyes, then stumbled forward and sprinted for the back door.

"Call me later, and I'll pick you up," she called as the back door slammed.

Maddie's head was buried in Chloe's shoulder, the little girl's body trembling as Chloe raced back into the kitchen where Charlie still stood frozen at the sink. "Come on, Charlie. We've got to go." Her hand was shaking as she reached for the boy. "I need you to help me with your brother."

The mention of his siblings must have broken his stupor because Charlie nodded and hurried into the living room. "Come on, Mom. We've gotta get out of here."

Jake was stuck to his mother's side, his eyes round and blinking like a trapped animal. Tina wrenched his arms away and pushed him toward Charlie. "Go with your brother, honey."

Jake clung to her hands, his voice shaking as he begged. "Come with us. Please, Mom."

A fist hammered at the front door, and Maddie whimpered again, pulling her hands free to press them tightly against her ears.

Tina pushed Jake toward Chloe. "Go!" she hissed. "Get them out of here. I'll be fine. I can handle him."

"Come on, Teeny. Open the door. I know you're in there. I just want to talk to you. I heard Jesse's been looking for me."

Tina's hands shook as she waved them toward the back door. Chloe grabbed Jake's hand and ran through the house and out the back.

She heard Tina yelling as Charlie quietly eased the door shut behind them. "Go away, Rank! Or I'm calling the police. I mean it. Go home!"

"This is my home!" he roared back, his voice booming

through the dark as Chloe and the kids snuck across the yards.

Thankfully, Chloe hadn't taken a purse tonight and had shoved her wallet, phone, and house keys into her jacket pocket instead. Closing her fist around the keys, she tried to pull them from her pocket without letting them jingle as she motioned for Charlie to carefully open her side door.

She knew the feel of her house key and shifted Maddie on her hip so she could slide the key into the lock and gently push the door open. The boys slipped through the door in front of her, and once they were all inside, she pushed it shut and turned the dead bolt.

Leaving the lights off, they crept toward the living room. She tried to set Maddie on the floor, but the little girl wouldn't let go of her neck. The boys instinctively stayed low and huddled on the floor behind her recliner. She crouched next to them, then pulled her phone from her pocket and tapped 911.

Jake put his hand on her phone. "Don't call the police. That'll just make it worse."

She glanced up at Charlie, not sure why she was looking for direction from a thirteen-year-old-kid. He nodded, his eyes wide with fear, but certain. She hit Send.

"Nine-one-one operator. What is your emergency?"

She quickly explained the situation and was told the police were on their way.

"Does the assailant have any weapons?" the operator asked.

Chloe glanced at Charlie. She kept her voice low, barely above a whisper. "Do you think your dad has a weapon?"

"He doesn't need one," he said, then raised his fisted hands in front of his chest in a mock fighter's stance.

Bile rose in Chloe's throat, and she swallowed it back. This wasn't her dad, wasn't her life. "We don't know for sure, but he has been known to be abusive to his wife." She gazed at the circle of kids around her, their eyes all wide and frightened. Tina's words came back to her, telling Jesse to run or Rank would kill him. "And his kids."

Charlie lowered his eyes, shame surrounding him like a dark aura. She wanted to pull him close and take away his pain. Take away all their pain. "This isn't your fault," she told them. "No matter what he says. This has never been any of your faults. He's the one to blame. Dads aren't supposed to hurt their kids."

She prayed her words sank in. Would it have made a difference if someone had said them to her? Or would the constant barrage of blame her father drilled into her have overridden any words of comfort from someone who wasn't there? Who didn't know the truth—that her mom had left because she didn't want to be a mom anymore.

As an adult, and after years of therapy, Chloe could see now she wasn't to blame. Her mom had made the choice to leave, whatever her reasons were. But as a frightened child, Chloe hadn't seen it that way. And neither had her dad.

The operator asked her to stay on the line, but she declined and hung up. She'd rather support the kids than wait on the phone. "The police are coming. It's going to be okay."

"Will they take my daddy away again?" Madison asked in a tiny voice.

"Probably."

"He's not supposed to come to the house or near my mom or us kids," Charlie explained. "So, if he's here, he's probably drunk."

Chloe could imagine that Rank Johnson was a mean drunk. She'd never met him. He'd already been gone when Tina and the kids had rented the house next door. But even in the shadows of the front yard, she could tell he was a big guy, and the anger in his voice when he'd pounded on the door struck terror in her bones.

Her back ached from carrying Maddie, so Chloe sat on the floor and shifted the girl into her lap. She hadn't seemed that heavy when Chloe's adrenaline had spiked and she'd lifted her onto her hip, but now she could feel the strain on her muscles. Maddie laid her head on Chloe's chest, and her thumb had snuck into her mouth. That had to be some kind of trauma trigger, because she'd never seen the girl suck her thumb before.

Relaxing her shoulders, Chloe tried to calm her breathing while she prayed for Tina and for the police to get here quickly.

She let out a shriek as a fist hammered her door, and Rank's voice came through the wood. "Open up. I know you've got my kids in there. Open the door, lady, or I'll break it down."

A tremor ran through Chloe's whole body, and every one of her muscles tensed as panic flooded through her. The kids huddled closer to her, and Maddie squeezed her neck so tightly that she could barely breathe.

Not that she could breathe that well anyway. Her chest was so tight that each shuddering breath she tried to pull in felt like she was trying to suck air through one of the thick wool scarves she knitted.

"Open this damn door!" Rank roared again. "Don't say I didn't warn you."

Maddie screamed as a hard slam rammed into the door. A loud crack sounded as the wooden frame split around the dead bolt.

Chloe's gaze frantically searched the room for a weapon—anything she could use to protect the kids. She wasn't a child anymore. This wasn't her dad. She didn't have to take this abuse. She could fight. She could stand up for herself and for these kids.

Another loud crack as he slammed into the door. But the frame held. For now.

Chloe's knitting project lay wadded up on the sofa where she'd tossed it earlier, and she leaned forward and grabbed one of the knitting needles. She buried her mouth in Maddie's hair and whispered in her ear, "Go to your brother. I won't let your father hurt you."

The little girl shook her head and pressed her face harder into Chloe's neck.

Chloe pushed to her feet and pointed to the hallway. "Go hide. Get under the bed or hide in the closet. The police are coming."

Charlie nodded, but before the kids could move, another blow hit the door, and the frame cracked and gave way as the door crashed open. It hit the wall with such force that a framed picture of a pansy fell from the wall, the glass shattering and spilling out onto the floor.

Chloe pushed the boys behind her, holding the knitting needle out in front of her as if it were a sword instead of a thin, pointy stick. She might not be brave when it came to herself, but she could be when it came to these kids. She could stand up for them. "Stay away," she shouted.

Rank filled the doorway. He had long, dark hair that stuck out around his head, making him look like an eighties rocker who'd had a hard night. A heavy beard and mustache covered the lower part of his face, and a scar slashed through the edge of his right eye, causing it to droop just the slightest, as if his eyelid was in a permanent squint. He wore jeans, heavy black motorcycle boots, and a thick leather jacket adorned with patches. Tall and broad shouldered, he seemed as big and as mean as an angry grizzly bear.

"Who the hell do you think you're talking to?" he demanded. "Who is this chick anyway?" he asked Tina, who tried to push past him to get inside.

Her right eye was swollen and red. She kept her tone even, but Chloe heard the slight quiver in her voice. "She's nobody, Rank. She's just the neighbor. I told the kids to come over here."

He held out his arms. "Hey, kids. Daddy's home. Why don't you come over here and give me a hug?"

Madison's whole body trembled against Chloe's chest. One of the boys had the back of her jacket clenched in his fist. None of them moved.

Rank's eyes narrowed as he searched the room. "Where's Jesse?" He shouted toward the hallway. "Jesse! Get out here, boy! You've got some explainin' to do."

"He's not here," Chloe said, trying to keep the tremor out of her voice. "And I already called the police. They're on their way."

"You what?" Rank's head jerked from side to side,

as if he were looking for the police inside her house. "Why'd you do that? You don't even know me." He took several menacing steps toward her, and Tina slipped inside behind him.

Chloe tried to push her shoulders back, but her every instinct was to curl up and hide. "I know men like you," she stammered, taking a step back.

"You've never met anyone like me," he sneered, his lips pulling back from his teeth in a snarl. He looked down at the knitting needle brandished in her hand and scoffed. "What are you planning to do with that? Knit me a scarf?" He reached out, his movement quick as a snake, and snatched the needle from her hand. He threw it across the room, and it bounced across the carpet.

He grabbed her arm, his fingers digging into her bicep as he dragged her against him. Spittle flew from his lips as he shouted into her face. "These are *my* kids. *My* family. And they are none of your damn business. You hear me, lady?"

She wanted to fight, to pull her arm away, to do anything. But she couldn't. She couldn't move. She was frozen with terror—her blood like ice in her veins—frozen with the memories of her father grabbing her the same way.

Rank's eyes were cold and full of rage as he stared down at her. She couldn't look away. Tears burned her eyes, but she refused to cry, to give him the satisfaction. They hadn't turned on the lights, and her knees went weak as his features blurred and transformed in the dimness of the room. Instead of Rank's snarled scowl and beady eyes, she saw the face of her father.

The slightest whimper escaped her lips, and she

shrank back, her brave stance shriveling into the weak posture of a frightened child.

As she blinked her eyes, Rank's face reversed back to his own, but something changed in his glare, the slightest movement, but enough to show that he knew he had her, that she was terrified and would submit to his demands.

He let go of her arm and snaked his hand around Madison's stomach, yanking the girl toward him. "Come on, Maddie. Come to Daddy."

Maddie hugged Chloe's neck, the skin of her arm rubbing against Chloe's throat as Rank pulled her away. The little girl teetered between them like a human tug-of-war battle, except that Chloe was no match for his strength.

Tina reached up, trying to get her arms around her daughter, and Madison let go of Chloe and grabbed for her mom.

The scream of a siren filled the air, and Rank lifted his head like a dog sniffing the air. He let go of Maddie, and Tina stumbled back against the sofa, her daughter clinging to her chest.

The scent of stale tobacco filled Chloe's nostrils as Rank leaned toward her, his face an inch from hers, his eyes narrowed and mean. "Don't go causing trouble for me, lady, or I'll be back. And you'll never see me coming." He planted his thick palm on her chest and shoved her toward the floor. Chloe went down—hard—her teeth clacking against each other as her body hit the floor. She scuttled backward, away from him.

He turned to Tina. "I'll be back. And tell Jesse I'm looking for him. He's got some shit to answer for." As the sound of the siren drew nearer, Rank took off, running out the door and across the yard, away from the approaching police car.

Jake and Charlie scrambled to their feet and threw themselves against their mother. She wrapped her arms around them, pulling them to her in a tight hug. Maddie cried softly against Tina's neck.

Red and blue flashing lights reflected off the walls as the police car pulled up in front of the house next door. They heard two car doors slam as the officers exited their car.

Tina held the kids to her for another second, then pushed up from the sofa. "Come on, we need to tell the police we're here." She glanced down at Chloe. "Thank you for calling them. Are you okay?"

Chloe nodded but kept her arms wrapped around herself, afraid she might break apart if she let go. She tried to arrange her features into what she hoped was a brave face and forced her lips into a tight smile. "I'm fine. You go. They'll be looking for you."

The boys circled their mother, both of them touching either her arm or her hip, while Maddie still clung to her neck. Envy rose in her throat as Chloe wondered what it would have been like for her if she'd only had one other person to cling to, to hold their hand, to ride through the trauma with. Splintered fragments of the doorframe were scattered across the floor, and the Johnsons tried to pull what was left of the door closed behind them as they left.

Chloe drew her knees up and pressed herself against the wall, not realizing she was crying until the tears dripped off her chin.

She let out a terrified whimper and buried her head

in her knees as the door burst open again and a tall man filled the frame. All pretense of putting up a brave front vanished, replaced by the terror of the past and present colliding and flooding her body with the anticipation of pain.

Chapter 11

CHLOE HUGGED HERSELF TIGHTER, TRYING TO DISAPPEAR into the wall.

The man yelled her name into the house, pieces of the doorframe cracking under his boots. "Chloe!"

She raised her head, unable to believe he was here. "Colt," she croaked, her throat raw, her mouth dry as cotton.

His head whipped left and right, and then he saw her. Relief filled his voice as he repeated her name, softer this time. "Chloe." His long legs carried him quickly across the room, and he knelt beside her and reached to pull her to him.

Instinct had her shrinking back, flinching away from his outstretched hands.

He stilled and turned his palms over as if beckoning a skittish animal. "It's okay, darlin'," he whispered gently. "I've got you."

She let out a shuddering breath, forcing her fear behind her as she leaned toward him. Willing her clenched fists to open, she wrenched her arms from around her middle and threw herself into his arms, a sob escaping her throat.

He lowered himself to the floor and pulled her into his lap, rocking her gently as he smoothed her hair and cooed into her ear. "It's okay now. I'm here. Nobody's gonna hurt you."

She melted into him, shaking as she let the tears out and sobs racked her body. He held her close, and she buried her face in his neck, clutching his jacket as she cried herself out. Taking another shaky breath, she drew strength from his solid chest and his strong arms wrapped around her. "I tried to protect them, but he was so strong. He broke down the door."

He pulled back the slightest, tenderly touching her cheek as he studied her face. "Are you all right? Did he hurt you?"

"I don't know. I was trying to shield the kids and keep them behind me. He grabbed my arm. But he didn't hit me. I'll be okay." Her body still felt numb. She'd probably have a bruise or two, but dealing with a few bruises was getting off easy. "Tina's eye was swollen, so he must have hit her."

"Bastard," Colt hissed between gritted teeth. His fists clenched against Chloe's back. "I should go next door and let him know how it feels to get hit in the face with a fist."

"He's not over there. He ran off before the police got here."

"Damn. They never should have let him out."

Chloe laid her head on his shoulder. How could he be here, holding her in his lap? "I can't believe you're here. How did you know?" How did he know how much she needed him?

"Logan and I were sitting at the bar at The Creed waiting for our drinks, and a cop was sitting next to us having a burger. We heard the call on his radio, and I recognized the address."

"And you came to check on me?" she asked, her voice holding a measure of awe.

"Of course. I didn't even hesitate. Neither of us did. Logan and I jumped in our trucks and raced over here so fast, I thought we might beat the police car."

She glanced around the room. "Logan is here?"

"Not here. When we pulled up, I yelled I was coming to find you, and he went to check on Tina and the kids."

"That's good. The kids were really scared."

"I'm sure they were. Rank Johnson is a mean son of a bitch. When we heard his name, we figured he'd be coming after Tina. My mom told us he just got out of prison, but we'd hoped he'd steer clear of her for a while."

"I think he came looking for Jesse."

Colt's brow knit together. "That makes sense. I heard he blames Jesse for ratting him out and getting him sent to jail."

"Did he? Rat him out?"

"No. But if he had, it would've served the guy right, and whoever did probably saved Tina's life. I think Rank has been serving time for dealing drugs and assault, so him getting sent to jail was the best thing to happen to that family."

Chloe let out a breath, her heartbeat finally slowing to a normal rate. Colt's arms felt so good around her that she wanted to stay wrapped in them forever, but she couldn't. "I should probably go talk to the police. I need to give them my statement."

Instead of loosening, Colt's arms tightened around her, drawing her closer to his chest. "They can wait a few more minutes. I'm not ready to let you go yet."

Oh.

He bent his head forward, resting his chin on top of her head. "My chest feels like I just ran a marathon.

When I heard your address on the radio, I thought my heart was gonna stop. It was pounding so hard on the way here, I'm not sure it's slowed down yet. I couldn't stand the thought of something happening to you."

She didn't know what to say, so she held on tighter, burying her face in his neck, inhaling the scent of him. His words worked like a salve to her heart, soothing the pain caused by something deeper than just Rank's wrenching grip on her arm.

A knock sounded on her damaged front door. "Hello, Miss Bishop?" a male voice asked. "I'm Officer Russo. I'd like to ask you some questions, if that's okay." He nodded at Colt, but didn't seem that surprised to see him. "Hey, Colt. Saw your rig outside, and Logan told me you were over here." He stood back and took a couple of photos of the door.

He was of average height but broad-shouldered, and his thick forearms indicated a regular weight-lifting routine. His dark hair was cut close to his head, and the crisply ironed fabric of his uniform showed he took his position seriously.

"Hey, Mike," Colt said, then looked down at Chloe. "I've known Mike a long time. He's a good guy. You ready to talk to him?"

She nodded and let Colt go. He helped her stand but kept his arm wrapped around her waist as he guided her to the sofa. She waved the officer in as she sank onto the couch. "Are Tina and the kids okay?"

"Yeah, they're packing up some stuff to go stay at a friend's house tonight. An EMT is checking Tina out now, then Logan's going to take her and the kids over there."

"He's a good guy too." It seemed she was surrounded by good guys right now. So why did she still feel terrified from her encounter with one bad one? She knew why, but was stuffing that down inside herself to deal with later.

Mike entered the room and tried to push the door closed as best he could. Cold air seeped through, and Chloe pulled the edges of her coat tighter around her. Mike sat on the chair across from her and pulled a notepad from his pocket. "Can you tell me what happened?"

She told him everything she could remember, starting from the time Rank first pounded on Tina's door. Colt's grip tightened on her waist as she relayed how Rank had kicked in her door. And he sucked a breath in through his teeth when she got to the part about Rank grabbing and threatening her before he tried to wrestle Maddie from her arms.

"Sounds like you did the best you could, and frankly, things could have gotten much worse. I've dealt with Rank before, and he can get pretty violent." Mike glanced at the door as he closed his notebook. "We'll have a squad car do a couple of drive-bys of the neighborhood tonight, just in case he comes back."

Chloe's breath caught in her throat, and she shrank against Colt's shoulder. She hadn't thought about the fact that Rank could return.

"Do you have someplace safe you can stay tonight?" Mike asked. "Maybe with a relative or a friend?"

"She's staying with me," Colt said before she had a chance to answer. "And I'll take care of the door before we leave."

Mike nodded and passed her his card. "Feel free to call me if you think of anything else or if you hear from Rank. We're going to run by a couple of his usual haunts, see if we can pick him up tonight."

Colt stood. "Thanks, Mike. Let me know if you find him, would you? Just for the peace of mind."

"Sure thing. You take care, Chloe. Nice to meet you."

Colt studied the doorframe, then turned back to her. "I've got some tools in my truck. Why don't you get some things together, and I'll patch this up until I can come back and put in a new door and frame."

She mechanically did as he said, moving through the motions of grabbing a bag and tossing in a change of clothes and her sneakers. She didn't travel much, but she had a small case she kept stocked with a few basic toiletries, and she threw that in the bag along with her cellphone charger. The plastic sack of new hair products still sat on the bathroom counter, and she stuffed it in as well. Hefting the bag over her shoulder, she jumped at the sound of hammering coming from the living room.

Colt had brought in some tools and was nailing a board across the doorframe. "I had some old lumber in the back of my pickup. It isn't pretty, but nobody is getting through this door tonight." He glanced at her bag. "You ready?"

"I think so."

"What about Agatha?"

"She's got food and water. She'll be fine overnight."

His brows furrowed. "I'd feel better if we brought her with us. Do you have a little carrier we can bring her in?"

Chloe swallowed at his thoughtfulness for her cat. Most of the men she even considered dating shied away from any talk of the cat, preferring to act like she didn't have a pet rather than seeing her as a thirty-year-old single cat-owner, as if the furry beast was equivalent to a spinster's loom.

Not that she was considering dating Colt. *Ha*. She'd done more than *consider* dating him. She'd full-on fantasized about marrying him and having his babies. And most of those fantasies included numerous variations on the act of making those babies.

Chloe sighed, then set her bag on the edge of the sofa and went back to pack up the cat. Agatha wasn't any more excited about this impromptu field trip than she was. The idea of going to Colt's house and spending the night there had Chloe's already frayed nerves unraveling at a rapid pace. Crawling under the covers of her bed and curling into a ball sounded like a much better idea.

"Let me get that for you," Colt said, reaching for the cat carrier as she stepped back into the living room. He hoisted her duffel on his shoulder. "You need anything else?"

She gave the room a cursory glance. Colt had swept up the fragments of wood from the splintered doorframe, and the broken door was secured back in place. Other than the two boards nailed across it like a caution symbol over an abandoned mine shaft, it looked back to normal. She hadn't ever taken her jacket off, so she checked the pockets for her cell phone, wallet, and keys. She hesitated at the kitchen door, worried that Rank would be waiting outside, hidden in the darkness, watching for his chance to attack her. If only she had a way to pack an ounce of courage or a measure of bravery in her bags! She took a deep breath. "I'm ready."

Colt had to have been thinking along the same lines

because he narrowed his eyes as he stepped outside and surveyed the driveway and neighboring yards. Nothing must have seemed amiss because he held the door open and led her toward his truck.

The drive to the ranch was quiet, with only the *whoosh* of the heater and the occasional unhappy yowl from Agatha to fill the void. But it was a comfortable silence, and Chloe leaned against the back of the seat, her body suddenly heavy with exhaustion. Her eyelids fluttered and closed as she gave in to sleep.

"We're here," Colt said, gently shaking her arm.

She struggled to sit up, the weight of sleep still pressing her down. "Sorry. I must have dozed off." Wiping her chin with the back of her hand, she prayed she hadn't drooled.

"It's okay. You've had a pretty rough night." He slid out of the truck and hurried around to open her door and lift the cat carrier from the floor in front of her feet. He took her hand to help her out, and she wanted to hold on to it and not let go.

It had begun to snow while she'd slept. She climbed from the truck and gazed in awe at the cabin set against the side of the mountain as light snowflakes floated down around her. Towering pine trees framed the cabin, and their evergreen scent filled the air. A long front porch ran the length of the cabin, complete with a porch swing and two rockers framing a large bay window. A light dusting of snow was already settling on the railings leading up the porch steps, and two neat stacks of firewood sat next to the front door.

Even in the dark, Chloe could feel the magic surrounding the place. If she believed in that sort of thing.

Which she did not. She'd given up on believing a long time ago, after wishing as hard as she could and having no fairy godmother—or any mother at all—appear.

It was so quiet. The only sound was the soft *whoosh* of the wind in the trees. No traffic noises, no hum of streetlights—not that Creedence had a lot of traffic to begin with, but out here in the country, the absence of sound only intensified the feeling of isolation. Which was usually a good thing, unless someone was concerned that a huge, pissed-off biker was on the hunt for them.

A shiver ran through Chloe as she looked back toward the cabin. A movement, something subtle, had caught her eye.

The curtains in the front window of the cabin swayed, and she grabbed Colt's arm, the hair on her neck standing on end. "Someone's in there."

Chapter 12

CHLOE SUCKED IN A BREATH AS EVERY NERVE IN HER BODY told her to run. But run where? Into the pasture? Into the trees? Up the side of the mountain?

Colt didn't seem the least bit alarmed. He tucked her hand into the crook of his arm and led her up the steps. "It's okay. It's just Watson."

She pulled back, his calm demeanor settling her nerves. "You have a studious sidekick living here who helps you solve crimes?"

"I wish." Colt chuckled and pushed open the front door to let the golden retriever run excited circles around Chloe's legs. She could tell the dog was barely controlling his yearning to jump as he sat in front of Colt and nudged his free hand. His whole doggy body seemed to radiate excitement, his bottom wiggling and his tail thumping happily against the wooden porch floor while Colt scratched his neck. "You're a good boy," he told the dog, then glanced back at her. "I guess he is a devoted sidekick, but I don't solve many crimes, other than figuring out how a skunk got into Mom's chicken coop last week. But I like the idea of you imagining me as a crime-fighting superhero."

Oh, she was imagining it all right. He was totally a hero in her eyes—smart, muscular, compassionate, and someone who swooped in when she needed him. He was her Captain Cowboy.

He pushed past the dog and into the cabin. "Welcome to the bat cave. Although as a super-cool hero lair, it may leave a little to be desired."

Chloe's mouth dropped open as she stepped into the cabin and gazed around the room. It was all so gorgeous—from the cedar accents to the stone fireplace surrounded by river rock, to the French doors framing a scene out of a magazine as the moonlight and snow-flakes glittered off a small pond. "I can't think of a single thing left to be desired," she breathed, caught up in the stunning home.

A proud grin snuck across Colt's face, making the dimple in his chin pop, and she swallowed as she real-ized the single biggest desire of her heart was standing right in front of her. She shook her head, bringing her focus back to the house. "It's wonderful, Colt. Did you do all this yourself?"

He shrugged. "A lot of it. Mason helped, and I hired out some of the really big stuff. But I did most of it, I guess."

"I'm impressed."

"Thanks." He dropped her bag in the chair and set the cat carrier on the floor. A loud yowl of protest sounded from inside. "I think Agatha would like out."

"Will Watson do okay with her?"

The golden was sniffing the metal bars of the carrier as he inspected its slightly miffed occupant.

"Oh sure. We have a ton of barn cats on the ranch. He's around them all the time." He patted the dog's head. "He's a pretty mellow dog. I don't expect any trouble."

"'Mellow' is not how I would describe Agatha." She opened the carrier door, but the cat stayed inside.

"Why don't we give her a little time to get used to the place?" Colt said, gingerly lifting the carrier. "I thought we could set up her stuff in the mudroom." He led Chloe to a small room that held a washing machine and dryer. The walls were lined with pegs for coats and cubbies for boots and shoes. Several cowboy hats rested on the shelf above the coats. A utility sink sat behind the door, and the floor was tiled with sturdy linoleum.

The cat carrier had come with a travel litter box, and Chloe got it discreetly set up while Colt filled Agatha's food and water dishes. She placed the dishes on top of the dryer to keep them out of the dog's reach. Nothing like fixing up a place for your cat to poop to set a romantic tone.

Stop it. It didn't matter if she was setting up a litter box or a jukebox. She wasn't here for a romantic tryst. She was here because she'd been attacked and threatened by her neighbor's crazy husband, and Colt was a good man who was giving her a safe place to stay for the night. He was acting like a friend, which was all he'd indicated he wanted to be.

They washed their hands, then left the cat and went back to the living room. "Can I get you something to drink?" Colt asked, detouring to the kitchen. "I've got soda, beer, coffee, or I could make you some hot tea. I've got Earl Grey." He grinned, and a flutter crossed her stomach at the thought that they had an inside joke. It seemed like something a couple…er…a couple of friends would have.

"Hot tea sounds great. Can I help?"

He shook his head. "You could help by taking off your jacket and acting like you're going to stay instead of looking like a scared rabbit that might dart out of here any second. You're safe here. You can relax."

Yeah right. Being able to relax around him had nothing to do with how safe she felt. It had more to do with how warm she felt observing the way his muscles flexed as he filled a mug with water and stuck it in the microwave. Maybe she would take her jacket off. Then find something to fan herself with.

The microwave dinged as Chloe took off her coat and hung it over Colt's on a peg by the front door. Maybe the scent of his aftershave would seep into the fabric of her jacket. And maybe she would wear that jacket as pajamas so she could lie in bed at night and drift off to sleep pretending his arms were wrapped around her. Or maybe she should just quit having fantasies about sleeping with him.

She wandered into the living room and sank into the corner of the couch. He dropped a tea bag and a spoon into the mug and carried it in to her. She stirred the tea bag, letting it steep, then took a small sip as she watched him build a fire. He really was like a superhero in motion, the way his muscles flexed and the denim of his jeans tightened over his toned legs as he loaded the fireplace with stacks of wood.

What was wrong with her? She'd had a traumatic event happen to her earlier that night. She should be feeling more traumatized instead of lusting after the nice guy who'd just made her a cup of tea. This must be the way her body was processing the stress—by pretending it hadn't happened.

Colt's phone buzzed, and he took it from his pocket as he stood. The fire blazed behind him, and Chloe could already feel the warmth. Or maybe that was the heat in her cheeks as she imagined that Cole was getting a text from another woman.

He tapped the screen and sent a return text before dropping onto the sofa next to her. "That was Logan. He said he got Tina and the kids settled at her friend's house, and he was headed home."

Chloe had to stop her eyes from rolling at the pettiness of her suspicions. "That was really nice of him to take the time to do that."

He shrugged. "That's one of the best parts of living in a small town. We're a community first, and we take care of each other."

Was that what he was doing with her? Just offering her a friendly hand because she was part of his community? Because that's what folks in small towns did for each other?

"I can't begin to tell you the outpouring of support I got when I had my accident in high school. It was like the whole town came together to help me and my family." He stared into the fire as if remembering that time in his life. "It especially helped my mom. I was in the hospital for weeks and physical therapy for months. My entire life changed in the span of four seconds. I lost my chance at a career in hockey, I lost the girl I thought I'd marry, and any plans for college scholarships went up in smoke. I was so angry and bitter about it that I was pretty much a jerk to everybody. But it didn't matter. They all still helped."

She suspected there was more to the story. Her ears had perked right up when he'd mentioned something about a girl he'd thought he'd marry. But a few things were starting to make more sense. "Is that why you're always going out of your way to do nice things for people? To pay them back for helping you and your family?"

He lifted one shoulder. "I don't know. Maybe. Although there aren't enough favors for me to do that could ever truly pay them back." His eyes cut to the fire again as he muttered, "Or to break the Colton Curse."

"The Colton Curse? What does that mean?" He didn't strike her as a guy who believed in the nonsense of some kind of curse.

"Nothing," he said, shaking his head. "Forget I said anything. It's stupid."

"No, I want to know." She started to reach out her hand, to rest it on his shoulder, but couldn't bring herself to do it. The gesture was too intimate, too comfortable, and she was neither of those things with him. "It obviously isn't stupid to you."

"Look, some guys just aren't meant to get it all. That's just the way it is."

"Do you think you're one of those guys?"

"I know I am. I've been so close so many times, then just when I start to believe that things are all going to work out, they always end up slipping through my fingers." He slapped his hands against his knees and cleared his throat. "Geez. This is depressing. Why are we talking about me anyway? You're the one who went through some crazy stuff tonight. How are you doing?"

Sucking her bottom lip under her teeth, Chloe was tempted to press the issue, to get to the bottom of Colt's idea of being cursed and try to convince him it wasn't true. But what right did she have to try to convince him of anything? She was no one to him beyond a new friend. And they hadn't been friends long enough for her to start digging too far into his psyche. She'd done that before with women friends and had it backfire in her face. No, better to steer clear for now. If he wanted to change the subject, it was okay. Starting an argument with him over his odd conviction wasn't worth the risk of losing his friendship.

Even though the last thing she wanted to talk about was how she'd failed the Johnson kids tonight because of her own weaknesses. "I'm fine, really," she told him.

He rested a hand lightly on her knee, and she swore she felt the heat of his skin through the fabric of her jeans. "I still can't believe how brave you were tonight. Standing up against Rank Johnson... That took guts."

She shook her head, the shame heating her skin as the memories of the night filled her mind. "Don't say that. I wasn't brave. I was a coward. I didn't do anything. I tried to stand up to him, but I failed. When he grabbed my arm, I froze. I looked up at him and saw my father's face, and I was like an injured animal caught in a trap. I couldn't do anything. I got snarled in this ambush of the past and the present blending together, and I was useless." She realized too late she'd let the mention of her dad slip out, and the shame burned hotter in her cheeks.

"Don't worry," Colt said, almost as if he could read her mind. "I figured it out when you cringed away from me like a caged rabbit. I wasn't sure who'd hurt you, but I figured it was a parent from the way you were trying to protect those kids." He squeezed her leg, his big hand practically covering her thigh. "You don't have to be embarrassed in front of me. It's not your fault. Men who hurt their wives and kids are cowards in my book. The blame rests solely on them."

"I know. I understand that. My therapist has said the same thing. But it's different when it's your dad." She swallowed back the emotion building in her throat. "If a stranger on the street backhanded you for spilling a glass of milk, you could fight back or feel hatred toward them. It's different when it's your dad, the guy you love, and in my case, the only parent I had left. You can call my dad a coward, and maybe he was, but he was also a good dad at times, when he wasn't drinking. He had a great laugh and a zest for life. He made everything fun, and all I wanted to do was please him, to be a good girl who didn't cause trouble, to keep my room clean and the house tidy, not to do anything that would make him angry.

"I think that's what people don't understand. When it was bad, it was very bad, but when it was good, it was wonderful. It made all the bad fade away, made a few bruises seem like a small price to pay. He'd go through periods where he'd attend AA meetings and pour all the liquor in our house down the drain. He'd hug me and swear he wasn't going to drink anymore. But alcohol is like a cruel and heartless mistress. And my dad couldn't stay away."

For her father, the booze had been a seductress, and one who didn't let her captives go easily. She'd show up in the worst of times and promise that she'd make everything better. Promise she'd make him forget.

Chloe offered Colt a thin smile. "No number of clean rooms or tidy kitchens could compete with something like that."

Colt hadn't said anything, just let her talk, and she

wasn't sure if he felt pity or compassion or horror at the thought that someone could say a man who abused them was also wonderful. She couldn't look at him, afraid of the tears that were threatening would spill over if she saw the true emotion in his eyes.

As she was talking, Watson had come to sit next to her, and he rested his head on her knee. She rubbed her hand over his furry head and took comfort in his soulful brown eyes. Funny how she could so easily accept compassion from a dog, but was hesitant to receive it from a man.

"I don't know why I just told you all that. I don't ever talk about it. And the only times I have has been with my therapist and my cousin, Leann, who is like my best friend and was there when my dad had one of his episodes."

Weird how they'd called it an "episode." She wasn't sure if she'd started that, or if it was her cousin. It was a terrible comparison. An episode made her think of a sitcom on TV, where a family might have trouble, but they solved it in thirty minutes with hugs and laughter and a few well-placed life lessons or jokes. That was nothing like what happened with her dad. There was no laughter, no jokes, no heartfelt hugs, not when her dad was snared deep in the arms of his mistress, when the dark clouds of depression and drink shrouded his mind. Then there was only fear, and yelling, and blame, and pain.

"Thank you for trusting me enough to tell me," Colt said, his voice low and deep, and the timbre of it settled something inside her.

She let out a trembling breath. She did trust him. "I guess I wanted you to understand why I feel like I failed with those kids tonight. I'm an adult now, and I finally had a chance to stand up to my dad... Well, their dad, but you know what I mean."

He nodded. "I get it. You wanted to protect them like you couldn't protect yourself before. Or like you wished someone would have done for you."

He did get it. She put her hand on top of his, gripping his fingers in hers, as she stared into his eyes, trying to make him understand. "Yes. Exactly. But I didn't do that. I failed them—failed myself. I tried, I swear I did, tried to stand up to him, then he grabbed my arm, and I was a little girl again, terrified and frozen, and couldn't do anything. How will those kids forgive me? How can I forgive myself?" She looked away, the humiliation tearing at her chest like a rat gnawing through her skin.

"Hey now, come on." Colt scooted closer and tipped her chin up to look at him again. His brow creased as he held her gaze. "You're being way too hard on yourself, darlin'. There is nothing to forgive. Those kids don't see someone who failed them. They see someone who put herself in harm's way to protect them. You took the focus of their father's rage and put it on yourself instead of them. You took the pain so they didn't have to. That isn't being a failure, or someone who is weak. Those are the actions of someone brave and strong who puts the safety of others above her own. That's what they see. That's what I see."

His words soothed her battered heart, touching a part of her that she normally kept locked away. She wanted to believe him, to see herself through his eyes, but it was hard to shake the years of being told she was worthless.

"Thank you," she whispered, not even realizing she

was leaning toward him until he pulled her into his arms. She rested her head on his broad chest and inhaled the clean scent of laundry detergent on his shirt.

He rubbed his hand over her back. "I hate the idea that someone put their hands on you and that you were scared. I know a few self-defense techniques I could show you, and maybe you'd feel stronger if you ever run up against him or someone like him again."

"I'd like that. But why did *you* need to learn self-defense techniques? In case you were attacked by a cow?"

He chuckled. "No. If I get attacked by a cow, I use the 'run like hell' technique. But I've done some training with the sheriff's department so I can help out as a volunteer deputy when we have big events or at the county fair."

She pulled back and looked up at him. "You are a volunteer fireman, a volunteer deputy, and you run a snowplow for the city. Is there anything you don't do?"

He lifted one shoulder. "I don't know. I told you I like to help, and I like to be proficient in a lot of different skills."

Oh boy. She couldn't let that one just sit out there without making some kind of comment. Her talent for flirting left a lot to be desired, but he'd plunked that one right out in the middle of the lake, and she couldn't resist at least reaching for the bait.

She lowered her voice and might have batted her eyelashes a couple of times. "So *are* you proficient in a lot of different skills?" Her voice was huskier than she'd planned, the desire and nervousness mixing together to tighten in her chest.

He raised an eyebrow as a slow, roguish grin pulled

at the corners of his mouth. "I like to think so, but it never hurts to brush up on my technique. They say practice makes perfect."

Rev. Rev. Her lady-part engines had just turned over, and fuel burned like fire through her veins. She wanted to say something back, some cute, teasing remark, but her mouth had gone dry and her brain refused to feed her any words as Colt's gaze cut to her lips.

What the hello am I doing? She'd tried to act like she was experienced at this—throwing down the flirting gauntlet like she was some kind of siren. And he'd picked it up and taken her dare. She licked her lips and swallowed back a nervous giggle.

The setting couldn't be more perfect—the fireplace sending a warm glow into the dim room, the snow falling outside the window, Colt's arm already around her waist. All she had to do was lean in...but she'd done that before. She'd practically thrown herself at him at the ice rink, and he'd pulled away.

What if she was misinterpreting this whole thing... again? She needed to let him take the lead, make the first move. She couldn't breathe, like there was literally no air coming into her lungs.

He leaned closer, his grip tightened on her waist. Her heart threatened to pound through the wall of her heaving chest. This was it. This had to be it. He was going to kiss her. *Please, please, for the love of gobstoppers, let him kiss me.*

Desire swirled and tumbled in her stomach, and she prayed she didn't throw up. She parted her lips in anticipation...and yawned.

Chapter 13

HOLY MARY, MOTHER OF PEARL. SHE DID NOT JUST YAWN.

Except she did. She totally did. At the very moment he was leaning in, at the pinnacle of the perfect kiss, a freaking yawn stretched Chloe's mouth into a gaping black hole. And now all she could do was hope another black hole showed up and sucked her into it.

Colt's eyes widened as he pulled back and blinked. "Geez. Sorry. You must be exhausted." He gave a nervous chuckle. "I should let you get to bed."

She shook her head. "I'm not tired. Really. That was a reflex. I just wasn't breathing deeply enough because…" What could she say? *I wasn't breathing because I was longing so hard for you to kiss me?* Yeah, that wouldn't make her sound desperate at all.

He stood, and the moment was lost. She collapsed back into the couch cushions, giving herself a mental head slap. Agatha chose that moment to slink through the room, giving her a cool stare as if to say, "Yeah, you blew it again, sis. You're trying too hard. You need to channel your inner cat and make him beg for your attention." Or at least that's what it seemed like the cat was saying. Her look probably meant something more like, "I'm not pleased to be here, and I just threw up in the middle of that guy's bed to prove it."

"You can take my room, and I'll crash out here on the sofa," Colt told her as he set their mugs in the sink.

"Oh no, I couldn't. You've done enough for me. I can't take your bed too. I'll be fine on the sofa."

He leveled a cool stare at her. "I'm nothing if not a gentleman, and there is no way I'm letting you take the sofa. Period. Besides, I'll probably have to get up early and take care of a few chores, and I wouldn't want to wake you."

She could see there was no use arguing with him. "Fine. And thank you."

"Don't mention it." He picked up the bag they'd left by the front door and led her to the bedroom. Setting her things on the bed, he gestured around the room. "Master bath is through there. Clean towels are in the cabinet next to the shower. If you need something, feel free to rummage through the drawers to find it. Extra blankets are in the chest at the end of the bed if you get cold."

"I'm sure I'll be fine." The bed was king-size and covered in a thick navy-blue down comforter. The cabin decor flowed into this room, and the headboard and dressers were made from heavy oak. A lamp sat on one bedside table, its base shaped like a pine cone, and a chunky ivory candle surrounded by sprigs of evergreen sat on the other. A paperback spy novel sat haphazardly on the edge of the nightstand, and she cringed at the dog-eared page.

He snagged one of the pillows from the side of the bed. "I'll probably be up reading for a little bit, so just holler if you need me."

I need you, she mentally hollered. *Don't go. Stay with me.* But all she managed to say was "Thanks."

Her shoulders slumped as Agatha jumped on the bed

and sniffed Chloe's bag. She knew she'd be up for a while too. There was no way she'd be able to fall asleep with Captain Cowboy in the next room, but she might as well go through the motions of putting on her pajamas and brushing her teeth. She unzipped the bag and peered inside. *Oh no.* She dug through the sparse collection of things she'd thrown in the bag, tossing out a fresh pair of socks and undies and her toiletry kit, but didn't find what she was searching for.

Well, Fraggle Rock. She'd remembered her toothbrush and her cell phone charger, but she'd forgotten to throw in some pajamas. That was great. She'd have to sleep in her clothes. Or…maybe she should sleep in the nude. Just the thought of it sent a thrill up her spine. Her normal sleeping attire consisted of a certain favorite jersey or a T-shirt, flannel pants, and occasionally a pair of fuzzy socks. She didn't think she'd ever slept in the nude. But there was a first time for everything, and slipping naked into the sheets of Colt's bed seemed like the perfect inauguration into birthday-suit snoozing.

And maybe she'd have a bad dream and cry out in her sleep, and Colt would come racing in to rescue her, only to discover she was naked, and he would be overcome with passion and not able to bear another moment without her, and he'd strip off his clothes and…

"You okay?" Colt asked, startling her as he leaned in the doorway.

"Wha… Yeah, yes, fine." A little warm, and her hoohaw was humming like a harmonica at the Grand Ole Opry, but other than that, she was totally fine.

"I forgot my book." He grabbed the paperback off the bedside table, then nodded to her bag. "There must be something pretty amazing in the bottom of that thing. You've been staring into it for the last few minutes."

She shook her head, heat flaming her cheeks, and her chest, and her... Well, never mind. "Nope, nothing amazing. Just got lost in thought." *Thoughts of you stripping off your jeans and climbing into bed with me.* "I was looking for my pajamas, but I must have forgot to throw some in." Why did she tell him that? So he'd imagine her sleeping in the nude?

He crossed the room and opened the top drawer of his dresser. "Here. You can borrow one of my shirts." He dug through the stack, pulled free a blue T-shirt, and held it out to her. "This is one of my favorites."

She took the shirt, a thrill already coursing through her at the thought of the soft cotton fabric of *his* shirt against her skin. Geez-o-pete, she was acting like a teenager, fawning over the cute boy who'd just given her his letter jacket. But she felt like a teenager, a lovesick adolescent with a crush on a boy who was totally out of her league.

That thought sobered her up, and she suddenly felt shy and awkward, like a stupid girl who'd been caught fantasizing about Prince Charming. And that's all it was, a fantasy. Hadn't she chastised herself earlier for this very thing? Her life wasn't a fairy tale, and she was certainly no princess.

"Well, I'll let you get to it," Colt said, after she'd spent the last several seconds silent as a mime. "Good night."

"Good night," she said to his retreating back, then buried her face in his shirt. She was such a dorkahontas.

It didn't take her long to brush her teeth and wash her face. She debated closing the bedroom door, but decided to leave it open, figuring if there was any hope of her fantasy coming true, she might as well give it a fighting chance.

She quickly took her sweater and shirt off and pulled Colt's T-shirt over her head. It fell almost to her knees. She shimmied out of her jeans but left her socks on, then neatly folded her clothes and laid them in a pile on the chest at the end of the bed. Now what? Bra on or off?

Leaning back on her heels, Chloe risked a quick peek into the living room. The lights were off, but the fire still burned, and in the glow, she could see the top of Colt's head as he reclined on the sofa.

The soft cotton of his shirt caressed her skin. She chewed her lip. No bra.

Reaching under the back of her shirt, she released the clasp and drew the strap out one sleeve, then tugged the whole thing out the other sleeve and dropped it on top of the pile. It was only a stupid shirt, but it belonged to him, and the light touch of the soft fabric against her breasts had her nipples tightening into pebbled nubs. Pulling back the covers, she slid between the sheets and laid her head on the same pillow where Colt laid his every night.

She tried to close her eyes, but every creak and groan of the cabin had her popping them open and straining her ears to hear if Colt's footsteps were headed for the bedroom.

There's no way I'll be able to fall asleep. I haven't even checked the locks, were her last thoughts before the exhaustion of the day finally caught up to her, and she drifted off.

The comforter fell off the sofa as Colt tossed and turned to his other side. Again. He'd taken plenty of naps and slept easily on this couch many nights before, but tonight he couldn't seem to find a comfortable spot. It wasn't the sofa's fault. He couldn't get his brain to turn off either. His brain and a few other parts of his body as well.

Not with having the woman who'd been haunting his dreams in the next room sleeping in his bed. Without him.

Something about this picture didn't seem right. Not right at all.

Forget it. He pushed off the sofa and padded barefoot into the kitchen. Staring out the window, he watched the snow fall on the lake as he leaned against the sink and drank a glass of water. The swirling flakes had a hypnotic effect, and he headed back to the sofa to try again. Except instead of his feet taking him toward the living room, they carried him toward his bedroom.

He didn't go in. Just stood in the doorway and watched her sleep, listened to the rise and fall of her steady breathing. It was the third time that night he'd checked on her, the third time he'd stood in this same spot and listened to her breathe.

He knew he shouldn't be standing there. It was probably some rule in the pervs' handbook about stalking women, but he couldn't help it. She looked so pretty while she slept—curled on her side, her hand tucked under her chin, wavy curls of hair spread out on the pillow. If he leaned down and pressed a kiss to her lips, would she be his forever?

Or would she slap him upside the head for even considering such dopey fairy tales? He knew that's what his brothers would do. Hell, he should slap himself silly for pondering the idea that he could be a prince to any woman. He knew better. And he knew that nowhere in his life did he get to have that elusive happily-ever-after.

He might get to see it, to picture it, even dare to reach for it, but experience and hard lessons had taught him that it didn't matter how much he dreamed of it, how hard he wanted it, or how close he got to it. That old brass ring was always snatched away before he could grab it.

Quit feeling sorry for yourself. Shut up and appreciate the beautiful woman sleeping like Goldilocks in your just-right bed.

No wonder she was sleeping so peacefully. She was surrounded by the coziness of both her animal *and* his as the cat lay curled on one side of her and Watson snoozed on the other.

A smile tugged at his lips at his dumb dog, all spread out in the middle of the bed and snugly cozied up to Chloe's back. *Traitor*. Watson was supposed to be his loyal companion, but one scent of a damsel in distress, and the dog deserted him faster than a bucking bronc. Although he had often wondered about the intuitiveness and compassion that his dog displayed. Some dogs acted aloof, some skittish, some only loyal to their alpha. Not Watson. For a scratch, or even the slightest hint that he might possibly get a scratch, he'd offer to be just about anyone's friend. And that dog was a great friend to have.

Watson had taken to Chloe from the moment she entered the house, as if he could recognize her kind heart and knew she needed him. That was okay. She could have the dog for the night. Colt wasn't concerned about the loyalty of his faithful companion—that dog had more than enough love to give—he was just jealous that Watson got to curl his body around Chloe to sleep.

Colt glanced around the room, not ready to go back to the sofa just yet. The pile of neatly folded clothes on the chest at the end of the bed made him smile. The black lacy bra draped over the pile did other things to him than just draw a smile. Somehow, he'd pictured her as more of a white-cotton-bra-and-undies kind of woman. This woman continually surprised him—and he liked it, liked the idea of exploring her depths to discover her secrets and the mysteries she hid. The idea of exploring her body encased in that black lace sent his thoughts to a darker place, and heat swept up his spine. Now he'd never be able to fall asleep.

Turning away from the door, he headed back to the couch. The embers had all but died in the fireplace, and his chest felt as ashen as the burnt logs. He could dream of Chloe all he wanted, but she deserved someone better than a guy like him, a guy with no future who screwed up every real chance he'd ever been given at securing any kind of success for himself.

The curse was real, but it was a curse of his own doing. He knew the accident was his own damn fault. He'd been driving too fast, too cocky and full of himself, so sure of his own destiny, as if fame and fortune were already his. Losing Ashley had been his fault too. He'd turned into an asshole of the highest order, treating her like crap and pushing her away instead of appreciating all she'd tried to do for him. No wonder she'd left him.

It was always the same. He'd come to accept it and just appreciate the good things in life he did have—friends, the ranch, a great family, and a good dog. He let out a sigh and punched his pillow into a different balled-up shape. It had been a long time since he'd let himself imagine something more in his life. Some*one* more.

Colt woke before the sun, his eyes scratchy with too little sleep and his back aching from a fitful night spent on the sofa. Not that he'd complain. He'd take itchy eyes and aching muscles any night if it meant knowing Chloe was safe and under his roof.

He'd considered skipping his morning chores and having Mason cover for him, but his brother had already texted he needed an extra hand that morning getting one of the stables patched up and the cattle fed in the south pasture. Colt had learned long ago a rancher had a duty to his land and livestock first. They were his livelihood, his responsibility. If he took care of them, they would eventually return the favor, one way or the other, through a plentiful crop or providing food for the table or money in the bank.

Thankfully, he had fresh clothes sitting in a basket in the laundry room, and he took a quick shower in the guest bathroom so as not to wake Chloe. He made coffee and filled a travel thermos for himself and left the rest of the pot for her. His mom had given him a plate of blueberry muffins the day before, and he left them in the center of the counter with a note telling Chloe to make herself at home, and he'd be back as soon as he finished his morning chores.

He considered whistling for the dog, but decided to leave Watson with Chloe. He might lick the freckles off the face of a friend, but he recognized danger and would do his best to warn and protect Chloe. Not that Colt thought Rank would have any clue she was out here, or dare to step foot on his land, but having the dog in the house would hopefully offer her some peace of mind.

So he added a bit to his note asking her to drop a scoop of dog food into Watson's bowl when she got up, then slipped quietly out the front door.

Chloe pulled the covers tighter under her chin and snuggled into the pillow. She'd been having the most delicious dream that Colt had brought her to his cabin and she'd fallen asleep in his bed. A warm breath of air caressed her cheek, and she opened one eye, wishing to see Colt's handsome face on the pillow across from her.

But instead of Colt's sandy-blond hair, she saw the copper-colored hair of his golden retriever as he lay with his head on the edge of her pillow. She cringed and reared her head back as a giant pink tongue tried to lap up her cheek. Not quite the kind of kiss she'd been dreaming of waking up to.

"Colt?" she called out as the dog stretched and groaned beside her. Her voice was scratchy and raw, and she tried again, a little louder this time. No answer.

The dog jumped off the bed and headed out of the room, and she padded after him, the scent of coffee leading her toward the kitchen. She read Colt's note, then dumped a scoop of food into the dog's bowl and filled his water dish. The muffins looked delicious, and she took a bite of one as she filled a mug with coffee. The taste of blueberries mixed with vanilla-flavored bread and just a hint of lemon had her groaning in pleasure as she stuffed another bite in her mouth. She hadn't realized how hungry she was. Although this muffin was so good, she probably still would have eaten two even if she'd already finished a four-course meal.

She found some sugar in the cupboard and creamer in the refrigerator, but couldn't find a measuring spoon, so had to make do with using a regular spoon to prepare her coffee, then wandered around the living room looking at framed photos and the bric-a-brac that made up Colt's life. A picture of him and his brothers when they were teenagers, all smiles and laughter with their arms wrapped around each other's shoulders. A sweet picture of Colt as a little boy with his mom in the kitchen next to a mixer, him standing on a chair holding a beater laden with cookie dough as he flashed a grin. One of his front teeth was missing, but the dimple in his chin was there.

Another picture of him and his brothers with a man she assumed was his father; he looked like an older version of Mason. They were standing in a row in front of a lake, all three boys proudly holding up a fish they must have caught. Colt's fish was the biggest, and his back buckled as he held the monster aloft. Rock was the tallest of the boys, but he held the smallest fish, a sheepish grin creasing his face. They seemed like a good family, like they were close and truly loved each other and got along. Chloe bit back the tiny pang of jealousy that liked to rear its ugly head whenever she saw or heard about a family who cared for each other and got along so well.

The dog whined at the back door, and she opened it and stood in the doorway as Watson ran out into the yard. *Yard* was putting it mildly. Colt's backyard was a field of snow with a lake covered in shimmering ice. She leaned against the doorjamb, cradling her warm coffee mug in her hands as she watched the snow fall. Another few inches had accumulated overnight, and the scene before her was like a winter wonderland. Everything was blanketed in snow, giving magical shapes to what might have been a farm implement lying in the grass, but was now a polar bear curled in slumber. White caps of snow on the tops of fence posts looked like frosting on cupcakes, and the branches of the trees were laden with glittering white icing.

The air was hushed, the only sound the far-off mournful bawl of a cow, and Chloe shivered as a gust of wind blew across her bare legs. Watson ran back into the house, and she followed, shutting the door behind him. Spying one of Colt's sweatshirts hanging by the door, she wrapped it around her shoulders, imagining it were his arms instead of his jacket.

Her imagination was really running wild this morning. Seeing cupcakes and polar bears in the snow, pretending she was being hugged by Colt instead of only wearing his clothes. That cow she heard was more likely bawling for food than because of any kind of mournful state. What would a cow have to be sad about anyway? She thought of the hamburger she'd had for lunch earlier that week. Okay, maybe there was something to be upset about, but the cow didn't know that.

Chloe wandered back into Colt's bedroom, resisting the urge to snoop through his drawers. The bathroom of the master suite was huge with double sinks, a separate shower, and a giant corner bathtub. Catching sight of herself in the mirror, she gasped. Thank goodness Colt hadn't been in the kitchen when she'd wandered out to find coffee. Her smudged mascara-rimmed eyes, combined with a curly mess of crazy bedhead, would have sent the guy running for the hills, or into convulsive laughter. She wasn't sure which was worse.

The shower, with its multiple jets, was tempting, but her body was sore and stiff from her run-in with Rank, and a hot soak in the tub seemed just the thing to remedy her aching muscles. She started the hot water, and even though she hated to take them off, pulled Colt's clothes from her body. Holding up her arm, she winced at the purple bruises in the shape of Rank's hand. She tilted her head to the side and checked her neck. The slight abrasion from Maddie was almost gone.

She ran a hairbrush through her hair, then pulled it up into a messy bun on top of her head. Rummaging through her bag, she found her earbuds and tucked them into her ears. She scrolled to the most relaxing playlist on her phone, and the sultry strains of a Norah Jones song filled her ears as she stowed her phone on a towel and stepped gingerly into the tub.

A bottle of shower gel sat on the edge of the tub, and she squirted some into the water rushing from the faucet. The scent of something woodsy and masculine filled the steamy air as she settled into the bubbly water.

It took Colt longer than he'd planned to help Mason repair the stable, and he still needed to run a couple bales of hay out to the cattle in the south pasture, but he'd been worried about Chloe and thought he'd stop at the cabin to see if she was okay and if she wanted to ride along with him.

Watson met him at the door, but there was no sign of Chloe in the living room. Two of the muffins were missing, but the counter didn't hold even one stray crumb. "Hello," he called. "Chloe?"

He walked down the hall and could see the empty bed through the doorway. No sounds of running water, so she couldn't be in the shower. His heart pounded against his chest as he imagined scenarios where Rank had shown up and taken her, or worse. "Chloe?" he called again, now rushing down the hall, poking his head into the door of his office, into the mudroom, then into the bedroom. He'd made it a few steps into the bedroom, just to where the double doors opened into the master bath, when he saw her—soaking in the tub.

Not kidnapped, not attacked, no run-in with a crazy dude, just her, neck-deep in a bathtub full of bubbles. Completely naked. *Yeah, dude. That's how most people bathe.*

Her head was resting on the edge of the tub, her eyes closed, her hair a sexy, curly mop on her head. An earbud cord snaked from her ears. No wonder she couldn't hear him calling for her.

Colt swallowed as he drank in the sight of her: her bare shoulders, her slender neck, the glistening length of legs that rose from the water as she rested her feet on the other end of the tub. Glittery pink polish flashed on her toes as she tapped them in time to whatever music played in her ears. A band of bubbles hugged the creamy skin of the tops of her breasts, but the suds had thinned in other places, just enough to give him glimpses of bare skin. What he couldn't see, he knew was there, and his imagination filled in the rest.

As much as he wanted to stand there—hell, he wanted to climb into the tub with her—he knew he should leave. He took a step back, slowly so he didn't disturb her. She never even had to know he'd been here. His foot landed on the dog's paw, and Watson let out a yelp.

Chloe's eyes popped open and grew wide as she saw him. She rose up in alarm, the earbuds popping out of her ears, then ducked back into the water, sending a spray of soapy water over the edge of the tub. The water hit the floor with a splash, but Colt didn't even notice.

He was too busy looking at her, dazed by the sight of her bare breasts as she'd risen out of the water. It was just for a moment, but the image of the soapy bubbles clinging to her skin and sliding down to rest on the pink nub of her nipple had his jeans tightening and heat shooting up his spine.

He gulped, trying to swallow, his mouth suddenly as dry as cotton. "Sorry," he croaked. "I got scared when I couldn't find you. I didn't mean to…"

"No, I'm sorry. You weren't here, and a hot bath sounded so good." She sank lower under the water, trying to cover herself with her hands.

"It's totally fine. I'm glad you did…are…using the tub."

"Do you think you could hand me that towel?" She raised just her finger out of the water and pointed to the towel.

"Yeah, sure." *Geez, dude, get a grip*. It's not like she was the first naked woman he'd ever seen. Although she was the first naked woman to be in his bathtub—and the woman he'd been fantasizing about seeing naked for the last few weeks. And now here she was, in all her glory, and he couldn't do a damn thing about it except hand her a towel.

He passed her the towel, then turned his back. He should leave, he knew he should, but he couldn't get his feet to move.

He heard the splash of water as she stood and stepped out of the tub. His eyes cut to the big mirror on the wall just in time to catch a quick glimpse of her wet, glistening body before she wrapped the towel around herself.

"You can turn around now," she said, her voice timid and soft.

He slowly pivoted until he faced her again. It felt like something was happening here, and he didn't want to ruin this chance. He opened his mouth to say something, anything. *I like you. You're beautiful. You have a great smile. I think you're funny.* Maybe best not to mention her sense of humor while she was standing practically naked in front of him.

Before Colt could think of the best thing to say to dazzle her with his wit and charm, his eyes fell on the top half of her arm and the row of purple bruises there. "Holy shit." He crossed the bathroom and gingerly lifted her arm to examine the marks. Flares of rage sparked through him, and he wanted to kill Rank Johnson. "I will never let that bastard put his hands on you again," he said through gritted teeth.

"I'm okay. They don't hurt that bad. And it could have been worse. Much worse."

She was right. Rank was as mean as they came, and

she was lucky he hadn't done worse to her or the kids. "He shouldn't have touched you at all."

"I know," she whispered.

The scent of her skin surrounded him, and he was caught between wanting to wrap her in a blanket to protect her and wanting to pick her up and carry her to his bed. At this point, either option would work for him.

He lifted his hand, raising it to cup the side of her face. Tendrils of her hair tickled the back of his hand. "I'm so sorry this happened to you."

She shook her head, just the slightest movement. Then she placed her hand on top of his and leaned her cheek into his palm. "I'm not. If it hadn't happened, I wouldn't be here with you now."

This woman was going to flat-out kill him. He ached for her clear to the marrow of his bones. He leaned in, fully intent on capturing that pretty little mouth in a kiss, but he couldn't bring himself to do it. He pulled back, shaking his head. "I like you, Chloe, but…"

Her face fell. Colt saw it and knew instantly that he'd blown it. Her shoulders shrank in, and she wrapped her arms around herself as if trying to cover the towel. "But not like that," she finished for him. "I know. I get it."

He shook his head. "No, I don't think you do. I *do* like you, *exactly* like that. You're all I've thought about for the past several months. And now you're finally here, standing right in front of me, and I can't do a damn thing."

Her eyes widened, and she looked like she didn't know if she should stay still or run—like a dang deer caught in the headlights. A beautiful deer. He knew he was screwing this up. Of all the ways he'd imagined this moment would go, this hadn't been one of them. He had to do something to save himself. As his dad used to say, it was time to fish or cut bait.

"Chloe, just listen. It's not that I don't want to…that I don't want *you*. I do. And it's killing me to say this, because I want you so bad, it freaking hurts. I want to kiss you and touch you. I want to take you to my bed and spend the whole day exploring every inch of your gorgeous body." He let out a breath, his brows drawn together as if saying the words actually pained him. "But you've just been through this whole traumatic ordeal, and I want to give you time to heal. Someone hurt you, and I don't want to be a jerk by not giving you the space you need. The last thing I want to do is make you feel uncomfortable. And I don't want to take advantage of you."

Chloe stood perfectly still, as if her feet were glued to the tile floor. A cool drop of water dripped from a tendril of her hair and trickled down the front of her neck and into the terry cloth of the towel. Her skin was so hot that she wouldn't have been surprised if the drop had evaporated into steam.

She tried to take in everything Colt had just said. She wasn't sure she'd heard it all over the rushing in her ears that sounded after he'd said he liked her *exactly* like that and had been thinking about her for months. Then why had he pulled away when she'd kissed him at the rink? Why hadn't he kissed her back?

Oh, for flint's sake, what the French toast was she doing wasting time analyzing what happened a few days ago? It didn't matter now. What mattered were the crystal-blue intensity of Colt's eyes and the passion behind his words. He'd said he wanted her, said he liked her.

His words touched her, and she could appreciate the sentiment, and the chivalry, behind them. But she wasn't a victim. She wasn't a poor, helpless woman who needed space. A flaming-hot cowboy had just told her that he wanted to take her to his bed and explore her body. *That* was what she needed. Not space, not coddling. Despite the chill of the wet towel, her body was on fire and she wanted him, needed him.

Something inside her snapped, the deep part of her that had been fantasizing about this moment. The part that had been dreaming this could come true. And she knew in her heart this was the moment she'd been waiting for—her chance to risk something, to be daring and fearless. She'd never wanted anything as much as she wanted Colt James, and this was her chance to grab him. No guts, no glory.

I can do this. I just need to pretend to be someone else. Someone who is brave and daring.

Her eye caught the swish of Agatha's tail from where she lay next to the vanity, and Chloe knew that was the answer. She needed to think like a cat. Cats were bold and didn't care what other people thought. They took what they wanted; they were adventurous and playful. She wrenched up her inner feline, brought her to life, and steeled herself to play.

I am woman, hear me roar. Or at least meow very courageously.

She reached for the knot securing the towel around her chest as she raised her chin and offered him her most seductive stare. "I like you too. And I love that you don't want to push me, that you want to give me space, but I don't *need* space. I need you. And I *want* you to take advantage of me. Right now." She inhaled a breath as she took a step back and released the towel, letting it drop to the floor.

Chapter 14

HOLY FLAMING-HOT CHEETOS. WHAT DID SHE JUST DO?

Chloe had never done anything so bold in all her life. What if he rejected her now? The light in here was too bright—every imperfection was on display. What if he took one look at her body and sneered in disgust?

And he *was* looking. His gaze traveled over every inch of bared skin. But he wasn't sneering. The look that glazed Colt's eyes was more like admiration and pure hunger. She pushed her shoulders back, standing just the slightest bit taller.

Her nipples tightened and sent a zing of pleasure to the spot between her legs. She was standing utterly naked in front of him, baring both her body and her soul, and he wasn't running or turning away. He took a step toward her. Anticipation, hot like the feel of the warm summer sun on her skin, coursed through her as her body yearned for his touch.

He raised his hands and circled her throat, driving his fingers into her damp hair as he drew her head toward him and captured her mouth in a ravenous kiss, drinking her in as if she were cool water and he'd been dying of thirst.

His lips were smooth and slick and faintly minty like he'd just applied lip balm. She wrapped her arms around his neck, his skin still cool from being outside. The whiskers on his chin scraped her as he tilted his head, but in a good way, such a good way. His tongue slipped between her lips, and he tasted like spearmint gum.

Bending his knees, he swept his arm down her back, over her hips, and picked her up, cradling her against his chest as he carried her to his bed. She couldn't believe this was happening. Things like this did not happen to her.

She clutched his neck, holding on and waiting for him to whack her head into a doorframe or stagger beneath her weight, but he did neither of those, and it was the most romantic thing that had ever happened to her. This whole sequence of events was so unlike anything in her scope of imagination. He was carrying her to bed, and she was completely *naked*. Just the idea of it made her head spin. Which was quite a feat since her stomach was tumbling and completing a spin cycle of its own.

Colt pulled back the comforter and laid her down. The sheets were cool against her heated skin, and she wanted to shiver, to curl up and pull the blankets over herself, but she didn't. She couldn't. She was caught in his gaze as he stared down at her, raking his eyes over every curve.

He was still fully dressed in jeans and a flannel work shirt with a white tee underneath. He still had his boots on, for goodness' sake. But he looked as sexy as any romance novel hero Chloe could ever have imagined. In fact, he *was* every romance novel cowboy, all rolled into one.

She thought he would undress, was dying for him to undress, to reveal the perfect muscled chest she knew had to be under his shirt, but instead he reached out and took her hand, lifted it to his mouth, and laid a tender kiss in her palm.

Trailing his lips along her wrist, her arm, stopping to kiss the sensitive skin inside her elbow, he slowly, methodically worked his way up her forearm, along her shoulder, and buried his face in her neck, inhaling her scent.

His hands splayed on either side of her body, not touching her, just holding himself up as he continued his exploration with his mouth. He lingered around her neck, his breath warm as he kissed the soft spot just below her ear.

She dropped her head back as his whiskers scraped along her collarbone and the top of her chest. His hair tickled the edges of her breast, as light and soft as the brush of a feather, as he moved his head.

Slowly, so achingly slowly, his lips skimmed around the tightened nub of her nipple. Her breasts ached with need—she'd never experienced such a sharp twist of pain and pleasure. She arched up, offering more of herself to him, dying to feel his lips on her, shaking with the craving.

Her body tensed as his tongue circled the edge of her nipple, not quite touching it, but so close she could feel his breath, hot and teasing. His teeth grazed the hardened tip, and she had to bite back a cry. Her arm splayed out to the side. Her fingers gripped a handful of the sheets, mangling them in her fist.

His tongue circled and teased, then finally, *ahhh* finally, sucked the tightened nub between his lips. A moan of pleasure escaped her, and a bullet of heat shot from her chest straight through to the ache between her legs.

She stole a glance at him and caught the slightest curve of his lips. He was enjoying himself as he tortured her. But it was the most delicious torture. Taking his time, he lavished her, licking and sucking, kissing and teasing. A hum of heat skimmed her breast as he let out a low growl, and it was the sexiest sound she'd ever heard.

Her head dropped back as she succumbed to the feeling of purest pleasure. Tingles and shimmers of heat flooded her body, rippling against her skin, and she thought she might die from the feeling. But he was only getting started.

He moved lower, trailing his tongue down the length of her stomach, stopping to press a kiss to her navel, then another and another as he moved lower. She parted her legs, a silent signal of consent, and sucked in a breath as his beard scraped the delicate skin of her inner thigh.

His breath tickled and teased. She was coming apart at the seams, and he hadn't even touched her yet.

He kissed her thigh before he stood, and she wanted to weep with missing the feel of him.

Balancing on one leg, then the other, he pulled off his boots, never taking his eyes from her. The soft whisper of his zipper sent a thrill through her belly as he unzipped his jeans and thrust them down his legs. Legs that still seemed tan, even partway into winter. A long, gnarled scar wound its way down one leg, a constant reminder of the accident that had changed his life.

Sucking her bottom lip under her teeth, dying to see more of him, she watched as he freed each button of his shirt and shrugged out of it. Grabbing the back collar of his T-shirt, he pulled it over his head, finally giving her the view of his muscled chest and ripped abs.

His body defied description. His legs were strong and toned, his stomach flat, his waist lean, and he had those funny vee things on either side of his navel that made a woman want to go exploring to see where they led.

He stood before her, wearing only a pair of black boxer briefs, and she could see the outline of his hard excitement through the thin fabric. And what an outline. Her inner core pulsed with want.

His eyes cut to the space next to her, and she wiggled over to make room for him on the bed. They hadn't said a word to each other since she'd dropped the towel, but they seemed to be communicating just fine. He lay down next to her and skimmed the backs of his fingers along her neck, down her chest, across her stomach, then flattened his palm over the curve of her waist.

"You are so beautiful," he whispered, his gaze traveling up her body before landing on her face. She'd never seen such naked desire in someone's eyes. Maybe in the movies, but never, ever for her.

She touched his cheek, ran her fingers along his chiseled whiskered chin, finally getting to touch him. She drew her hand down his neck and over the hard muscles of his chest, circling his nipple with her fingertips and drawing a hiss of breath from him.

He reached up and pulled the ponytail holder from her hair, letting the curls fall, and her hair tickled her bare shoulders. He slid his finger inside one curl and rubbed it with his thumb. "Your hair is so soft. I like the new cut."

"I was so tired of the old me." Her voice dropped to a whisper as she lowered her eyes. "I needed to be someone different." She swallowed and boldly raised her gaze to look into his eyes. "Someone brave enough to drop her towel in front of a hot cowboy."

A smile pulled at his lips. "Now I like it even better."
He brushed her bangs from her forehead and looked
deep into her eyes. "I meant it when I said I didn't want
to rush you. Are you sure you're good with this?"

She nodded. "So, so good with this." His hard body
radiated heat just inches from her own, and she draped
her shin over his, tangling their legs together and pulling
closer to him. Her breasts pressed to his chest, sending
ripples of desire through her. "And this," she whispered.

He scraped his lips along her jaw, then closed his
mouth over hers, kissing her so long and so deeply she
wasn't sure if she was breathing her own air or sharing
the breath from his lungs.

His hands roamed her body, skimming over her
curves, exploring, touching, caressing. His mouth was
on her lips, her neck, his fingers tangled in her hair. His
voice was husky as he growled into her ear. "More?"

She arched into him. "Yes. More," she whispered. So
much more.

He reached for the drawer of his bedside table and
fumbled for the box inside. He pulled free a plastic strip
of condoms. "I think we'll need these."

She swallowed, the vixen who'd awoken inside her
cheering for joy. "All of them?" she croaked.

A sly grin curved his lips. "Darlin', you might be
overestimating my abilities."

She grinned back, feeling flirty and reckless as she
lay naked in his bed, knowing her body was flushed with
heat and her hair was in a sexy, tangled mess around her
head. "You might be *under*estimating mine."

He chuckled, a low sound in the back of his throat.
"I hope not." He tore open a packet and tossed the rest

to the floor, then tugged off his briefs and covered himself.

She parted her legs and let out a shuddering sigh as he settled between her thighs. His arm muscles rippled as he braced his hands on either side of her head. He dropped his mouth to hers for another deep kiss.

She dug her hands into his thick hair, her breasts throbbing with need as she wrapped her legs around his waist. He moved with her, slowly at first, then increasing in tempo. She took what he gave and demanded more. It was as if someone else had taken over her body, someone brave and wanton who knew what she wanted and how to get it.

He let out a moan as his restraint slipped, and he gripped her waist, his fingers digging into her sides. She loved it. Loved that she could cause such a reaction in him. She matched his rhythm, taking everything, then giving it back.

Her body was all nerve endings, all sensation. She clutched his back, holding on, savoring the sweet torment as he drove her closer and closer. Throwing her head back, she clung to him, crying out and giving herself to the exquisite sensations as the waves of pleasure erupted through her.

His grip on her tightened, pulling her closer, his teeth grazing her shoulder as he tensed and shuddered. Letting out a shaky breath, he collapsed next to her and dragged her to him. She burrowed into his chest, loving the feel of her skin pressed against his.

Nothing had ever felt so good. So right. Ever. She felt sensual, awakened.

And ready for more.

―ᴧᴧᴧ―

They spent another hour in bed, exploring each other and making their way through the plastic strip Colt had retrieved from the floor.

"I hate to do it, but I've got a load of hay in the back of my truck that I need to get out to the pasture," he said, dragging a hand through his messy hair. "You want to ride along or stay here?"

"I'll ride along." She would go anywhere with him.

Half an hour later, Chloe was in Colt's truck, bouncing along the snow-covered lane, happily smooshed between him and Watson. They'd dropped off the hay and were headed back to the cabin. Colt had his arm around her shoulders, and Watson had his head on her lap. Country music played on the radio, and Colt sang along to an old Johnny Cash song. She couldn't be happier.

Colt pressed a kiss to the side of her forehead. "I was thinking about something, and I have a question for you."

"What's that?"

"You remember the other day when we were at the ice rink, and I took you for a ride on the Zamboni?"

"Yeah." Although she'd rather forget the rest of that humiliating night.

"I was just wondering how I compared this morning."

"Compared? What do you mean?"

He grinned. "You know, in the cupcake-tingling department."

She swatted him playfully. "I'd say you compared favorably, but I might need another demonstration to know for sure."

"That seems reasonable."

They parked in front of the cabin, and Colt helped her out of the truck. Light snow flurried through the air, and she stuck out her tongue to catch a few flakes. It was so beautiful. Watson jumped from the truck behind her and raced through the white powder in the yard. She laughed as he rolled on his back, making a smudgy snow-dog angel.

"Silly mutt," Colt said, shaking his head as he headed toward the porch.

Chloe watched him walk away, admiring the view. The man did look fine in a pair of jeans. A giggle bubbled up in her, and she felt deliriously happy. So much so that she grabbed a handful of snow, formed it into a ball, and tossed it at his back. It hit him square in the left butt cheek.

He stopped and slowly turned his head, a mischievous grin on his face. "Oh, so you want to play, do you?" He scooped up some snow and molded it into a ball.

She shrieked and ran for cover behind a tree as he let the snowball fly. It missed her head and splatted against the tree, sending a shower of snow down on her back. Before she could launch her own attack, another snowball was lobbed toward her. This one hit her leg, and she laughed as she bent down, scooping snow into her hands and trying to hastily make a ball as Colt inched closer.

Her hurried throw fell short of its target. Watson barked and jumped in the air, trying to catch the next snowball Colt tossed. Chloe threw another one while he was distracted with the dog, this one landing against his neck, and he hollered as snow fell into his shirt.

"You're gonna pay for that one, Miss Bishop," he teased, charging toward her.

She let loose another shriek and tried to run toward the cabin, but the snow in the yard was too deep. Colt easily caught her, grabbing her around the middle, and they fell into the soft powder. He grabbed a handful of snow and held it over her chest. "Do you dare me to dump this down your shirt?"

She laughed. "No, of course not. Why would I dare you to do that? You are obviously used to brothers." His face was flushed, and he'd lost his hat in the chase. A lock of blond hair fell across his forehead. He was so dang cute, it almost hurt her chest to look at him. "But I'll dare you to kiss me."

"My brothers never say that." He dipped his head and kissed her on the mouth. Light snowflakes fell around them, landing on her cheeks, but she didn't care. They only made this moment more magical.

Colt pulled back, his lips curved in a teasing grin. "I've suddenly got an awful craving for a cupcake."

She laughed and let him haul her to her feet.

Him having a cupcake sounded like a great idea to her.

They spent the rest of the afternoon in his bed, then in the bathtub and then back in his bed. Hunger finally drove them into the kitchen. Colt made ham and cheese omelets while Chloe perched on the barstool at the counter wearing only a pair of panties and one of his flannel shirts.

He grabbed the plates and nodded to the living room. "I'll make a fire, and we can eat in front of it." He followed her perfectly rounded butt into the living room. She might have seen herself as an ugly duckling when she'd been a kid, but those days were long gone. He thought she was perfect.

She carried in glasses of ice water and set them on the coffee table, and he put the plates down next to them. Grabbing the pillows from the sofa, she piled them on the floor and settled against them as he set to building a fire.

The fire crackled and popped, and she handed him his plate as he sank down beside her.

"I changed my diet when I left home and don't think I've had eggs cooked in bacon grease since I was a kid."

Oh crap. He hadn't thought of that. He should have offered her a healthier alternative. He leaned forward. "Sorry. I can make you another one."

She laughed and pushed him back. "No. I didn't mean that. This smells amazing. I was just making conversation." She hesitantly took a bite of the omelet, then shut her eyes and groaned in appreciation. The sight of her with her eyes closed and making that soft sound had Colt wanting to forget the food and carry her back to bed.

"I'm impressed with your cooking skills," she said, then took another bite.

"Don't be. I have about four or five things in my kitchen repertoire, and then I'm tapped out. I am fairly good with the grill though, so I pretty much survive on sandwiches, potatoes, and whatever hunk of meat I can find to toss on the grill. I stick with the basics. My mom spent a lot of time trying to teach us to cook and bake, hence my cupcake-baking skills. Now Mason wouldn't admit it, but he's a genius in the kitchen. He goes all out with the chopping of the vegetables and adding the spices. He makes these steak fajitas that'll knock your boots off. Wait 'til you try them."

"I'd like that." A grin tugged at the corner of her lip, and Colt realized he'd just inferred she would be around long enough to sample his brother's cooking. He paused, trying to decide how he felt about that. His chest was easy. The idea of her sitting at the table at a barbecue with his family was surprisingly simple for him to imagine and accept.

He wasn't sure how she'd feel about it. Getting the whole James crew at once could be a little overwhelming, especially for someone who already seemed a little timid. Although she'd sure lost some of that shyness during the last few hours they'd spent in the bedroom. Now she seemed more at ease, more comfortable with him.

And she was a teacher, so she was used to dealing with loud and immature people who could sometimes be assholes. So maybe she could handle the chaos of his brothers just fine.

She took her last bite, then set her empty plate on the coffee table. "I really admire your mom raising three boys on her own. And you were so lucky to have had siblings growing up."

"I can't imagine being an only child. Your house must have been so quiet."

Chloe cut her eyes to the floor, a veil of pain crossing them for just the briefest moment before it disappeared. "It was sometimes. When my dad wasn't angry or in one of his moods."

A hard knot of anger curled in Colt's gut at the man who had hurt his child. "I'm sorry that happened to you."

She shrugged. "It is what it is. I can't change it. It's just part of me now."

"I think the stuff that happens to us can affect and

maybe shape who we become, but I also think we can choose to either let that stuff destroy us or use it to make us stronger."

"Is that what you did with the death of your dad and the accident that ended your hockey career?"

He reared back. "Geez, you don't pull any punches, do you?" She really was getting more comfortable with him. He rubbed his stomach. "I thought we were talking about you. But that one hit me right in the gut."

"Sorry. I shouldn't have said that," she muttered, her eyes downcast as she twisted her hands in her lap.

Cole set his plate on top of hers, then reached for one of her hands and laced her fingers through his. "It's okay. You can talk to me about whatever you want. And yeah, those things did shape who I was, but if I'm being honest, I don't think I used either one of them to make me stronger. In hindsight, I probably used them as excuses to act like an asswad and push away the people who meant the most to me. Losing my dad happened *to* me, but the accident and everything that happened afterward were essentially my own fault. My actions and reactions to that accident and my injuries affected the trajectory of my life."

And still affected it. He was still letting the accident and his subsequent behaviors dictate the way he lived his life. All the favors, all the volunteer work, everything he did played a role in making up for that time and what a jerk he'd been. But was he really using those events to make himself stronger?

Colt swallowed, pushing down the answers that were forcing themselves up his throat. He didn't want to cough up all that garbage, all that history, didn't want to spew the filth of his bad decisions onto the new, clean landscape of their budding relationship. No, they could work on that stuff later. Or never. Yeah, never would work great for him.

Best to turn the focus to something else. "I'll admit having my dad die when I was a kid absolutely changed me. No kid should ever have to lose their parent."

Chloe huffed out a breath. "I wouldn't know about that. I didn't *lose* mine. She ran away, then chose not to be found."

His heart hurt for her. "Which is a real sucky thing to do to a kid. But that wasn't your fault."

She stared at him. "According to my dad it was."

"Speaking of asswads," Colt muttered not quite under his breath. He held up his hands. "Sorry. I shouldn't have said that."

"It's okay. He could be a…buttwad." She paused before saying the offensive name, then covered her mouth with her hand and tried not to laugh.

"Speaking of buttwads, I want to talk about Rank Johnson."

Her smile fell. "Ugh. Why? I'd be happy never to talk about that man again."

Colt let go of her hand and pushed back the coffee table. "We have to talk about him because we need a plan of attack for when he comes back. And like a bad penny, men like Rank always come back."

Chapter 15

A SHIVER RAN THROUGH CHLOE AT THE THOUGHT OF RANK coming back, of him entering her house or putting his filthy hands on her again.

"I saw that shiver," Colt said. "And I want you to hold on to that. Use all the rage and anger and disgust you have toward him to fuel your own attack."

"My own attack? I don't plan on attacking him." For the moment, she just wanted Rank to go away so she could pretend none of the scene in her house had happened. But she couldn't do that. Not to herself. Or to the kids who she had failed to protect. She took a deep breath. No, she couldn't let that happen again.

"I know you don't. And I hope the cops catch him before he gets a chance to come at you again. But in the meantime, I want you to be prepared just in case you have to face him."

"Okay."

He stood and looked down at her. "Have you ever taken a self-defense class before?"

She shook her head, silently admonishing herself for such a stupid mistake. She should have taken classes, should have done something, *anything* to learn how to defend herself. Instead of being the weak little timid mouse she was.

Colt narrowed his eyes and reached out a hand to pull her to her feet. "There's no blame or shame in that question. There are plenty of things we think we should have done or have never got around to doing. Hindsight is a mother. But we're going to do something about it now."

"Now?" She looked down at her bare legs and feet. "Shouldn't I put on some shoes or at least some pants or something?"

He grinned. "No." Then he waved his hand in front of her. "Sorry. Forget that suggestive grin. My mind wandered for a minute. I'm focused now—all business."

"Got it. All business." She nodded and pressed her lips together to keep from smiling. He was cute when he was serious.

"You never know when an attack could happen. You could be outside going for a walk, or at home in your pajamas. I want you to be prepared for whatever circumstance you might find yourself in."

Chloe swallowed, terrified at the thought of an assailant breaking into her home and catching her unprepared and in her pajamas.

Colt ran his hand up the side of her arm and gave her an encouraging squeeze. "That's why we're doing this. So you don't have to be scared."

Why did it feel like he always knew what she was thinking? "Okay, I'm ready. Where do we start?"

"With you. No disrespect intended, but most men are going to be bigger and stronger than you."

"Agreed."

"But that doesn't mean you can't be smarter and tougher than they are."

"I'll give you the smarter part, but I'm not sure about the tougher. I have a hard time killing a spider."

He shrugged. "That's because spiders are tiny, predatory,

eight-eyed assholes that can make even the most badass man scream like a girl and throw his boot across the room to kill one. Present company excluded."

She kept her expression deadpan. "Of course."

He cleared his throat. "Let's get back to talking about you." He motioned for her to stand next to him. "Your arms and legs are your best weapons. And sometimes your only defense. You don't have to be able to throw a punch or do some kind of karate kick, but a well-placed knee or elbow jab can sometimes startle or disable your assailant for a few seconds, and a few seconds may be all you need to get away."

"Am I launching an attack or just trying to get away?"

"That depends on where you are and how quickly you can get to somewhere safe. If help is in sight or you can run, then I think your focus should always be on getting away. But if you have no other way out, then you have to be ready to take him out. If it's him or you, you want to be the last one standing. Right?"

She nodded.

"One of the things that freaks out a lot of people is worrying they will freeze up in the moment because they don't know what to do or are worried they'll be too afraid to fight."

She cut her eyes to the floor, shame filling her like rain in an empty bucket. "That's exactly what I did. I froze and couldn't do anything."

His expression softened. "There was a whole lot of other stuff that played into that encounter. I don't want you to beat yourself up. I want to teach you some moves that will boost your confidence and have you trusting yourself and believing you can fight back. That's one of the most important things you can do in an attack situation—believe you have the power to do something, to fight back. I know you have a lot of anger wrapped up in the way your dad and Rank treated you, so use that anger to your advantage. Channel it into aggression against your attacker."

"I hear what you're saying, but anger isn't going to help me get away."

"Not by itself. But it will fuel your hits. When you're in a confrontation, you only have a few seconds, so you want to aim for the most effective body parts to hit, the ones where you can do the most damage the easiest. The eyes, nose, ears, neck, groin, knee, and legs. How close you are to your attacker determines which zone to strike first. If you're striking the upper part of the body, you want to use your hands and go for the eyes, nose, ear, and throat. Gouge, poke, scratch at their eyes." He picked up her hand and turned it over. "You might not be real tall, but your arm gives you another couple feet of height, and you can use your momentum to drive your palm up and under your assailant's nose. Throw your whole body weight into this move, and it will force him to loosen his grip on you."

He demonstrated the move and let her practice a couple of times. "Your elbows, knees, and head are also effective weapons, and those are among the most sensitive spots when hit. So whacking your assailant in their elbows, knees, or head is the best way to inflict damage. Jam your elbow into their gut, stomp on their feet, or kick the front of their kneecap as hard as you can. A knee to the groin is still a good move, but it's one assailants prepare for and try to block." He showed her a few more moves and walked her through various strike positions.

She listened intently, cataloging all the moves in her head and going through the steps he showed her multiple times. Some of the ideas seemed so simple, like the kick to the kneecap or jab to the nose, but when she thought about how much it hurt to get hit in the nose or the knee, she realized how effective those hits could be and how much damage she could do.

Every run-through of the actions made her feel more empowered, like she could actually do some of these things. Even in just a shirt and her undies, she felt like she could put up a fight.

"What if I don't have time to prepare? What if he surprises me and grabs me from behind?"

"Good question. And something that could actually happen, so I'm glad you asked." Colt stepped behind her and wrapped her in a bear hug. "This is a common hold an assailant will use. It's also something my brothers used to do to me, and still try, so I'm fairly proficient at this one. Granted, I'm not trying to hurt them...well, not much." He chuckled, then tightened his grip on her. "Mason and I taught Quinn and Max this move too, since they have to endure Rock now and his love of wrestling."

"Smart. And if Max can do this, so can I." Chloe lifted her chin and pushed her shoulders back to stand taller.

"That's right. You *can* do this. And it's not that hard. The first thing you want to do is bend your knees like you're going into a squat. Let the full weight of your body drag you down and out of his grip. Leveraging your weight is one of your best tools both to escape and for inflicting the most damage."

She dropped her weight like he'd said, but his arms were still gripped tightly around her chest.

"Now wiggle."

"Wiggle?"

"Yeah, wiggle yourself free."

She moved her shoulders, but his grip didn't budge.

"Come on, you're not even trying," he said. "You ever try to give your cat a bath?"

"Yes, I guess. But I fail to see what Agatha's hygiene has to do with me getting away from a bad guy."

"It has everything to do with it. Imagine how Agatha would respond if you were holding her over a tub of water. You want to act like that—squirm, wiggle, bite, kick, jab—make yourself as difficult as possible to control. And if you can get lower, you have more places you can strike."

She blew her bangs out of her eyes. *You got this*. She dropped her weight and wiggled. And squirmed and jabbed him in the side. And he let go with an *oomph* of air.

But he let go.

"I did it." She jumped up and down, causing Watson, who had been observing their odd behavior from his spot on the couch, to raise his head and let out a bark.

"It's okay, boy. We're just playing," Colt assured the dog as he ruffled his ears.

Adrenaline surged through her. She could do this. She could get away. Could fight if she had to. She wasn't a victim, wasn't weak.

But all these moves were designed for an attack. What if Rank really tried to kill her? Could she still defend herself? Could she really get away? The thought sobered her, and she flashed to the night before when he'd broken down her door and stormed into her house. She put her hand on Colt's arm. "What if he's really trying to kill me? What do I do if he gets his hands around my throat?"

His eyes narrowed to steely slits. "If he gets you around the throat, I'll kill the man myself." He shook his head. "Sorry, that image got me for a second, but this is about you protecting yourself, not me coming in to save you." He picked up her hand. "I'm teaching you these moves, and I want you to feel confident that you can use them if you have to. But I still want you to know I will do everything in my power to make sure you don't find yourself in a position to have to use this stuff."

"Thank you," she whispered. Tears burned her eyes, and she turned away so he wouldn't see how much his words meant to her.

"Despite my male pride getting in the way, you're right to ask. And I want you to be prepared for every instance, especially because this is a common tactic." He stepped behind her and wrapped his arm around her throat.

Even though she knew he was only acting the part, the feel of his forearm cutting across her windpipe and the strength of his biceps reminded her of how vulnerable she truly was. Rank was a big man, built of solid muscle, so a few jabs of her elbows weren't going to inflict much damage.

"If you are in a full choke hold, time is of the essence," Colt told her. "You don't want to mess around. Turn your chin into the arm that's choking you, and raise your shoulders while you dig your chin into his arm. If you can, use your teeth. Bite his arm, and try to stomp on his instep, anything to get him to loosen his grip and give you the chance to twist out of his hold."

She nodded, then pressed her chin into his arm while turning her body toward him.

"Ouch." He pulled back his arm, rubbing his bicep. "Dang woman, you have one strong chin."

It worked. She'd done it. She raised her shoulder and flashed him a teasing grin. "And I didn't even have to bite you. Not yet anyway."

He wrapped his arm around her waist, pulling her to him and nuzzling her neck. "You are stronger than you can imagine and tougher than you think. You can do anything you set your mind to. You just have to believe you can do it."

His words touched something inside her—some secret place that had been waiting to hear those declarations. She melted against him, finding his lips and kissing him with everything she had, telling him through her actions, her passion, how much his belief in her and her abilities meant.

She *was* stronger than she'd thought, and she *could* do anything she set her mind too. And right now, her mind was set on one thing—having him. Here. Now.

Once again, he knew exactly what she was thinking, and his hands scrabbled with the buttons of her shirt, unfastening each one, then opening the lapels and slipping his hands inside. His palms skimmed over her skin, caressing her stomach, her waist, her hips.

The fire crackled and popped, lighting the room with an amber glow as her shirt dropped to the floor and they sank onto the pillows. They kissed and touched and made out with the fervor of a couple of teenagers until they couldn't take it any longer, and he carried her to his bed.

Later, much later, they lay curled together, her back against his chest, his arm wrapped possessively around her rib cage, his palm cupping her breast as if he needed to hold on to it to make sure it didn't escape while he slept.

Her body felt sated, achy but good. She dipped her chin and pressed a kiss to the corded muscle of his forearm. "Good night, Colt," she whispered.

His voice was sleepy, but she could still hear the mischief in it as his breath tickled her ear. "Good night, cupcake."

––––

The snow had stopped by the next morning. Chloe stood in the kitchen, sipping coffee from a red mug with a picture of a cow on the side that read "Sorry for what I said when we were working cattle" as she stared out the big picture window. The sun danced and sparkled over the frozen lake, and the idyllic scene looked like something from a postcard.

Colt had made her breakfast, and they'd washed the dishes and cleaned the kitchen together. It had been a perfect morning, a perfect couple of days, and she wished they could stay here forever, just the two of them. And the dog and the cat, of course.

But that wasn't going to happen. Like every good fantasy, this one was about to come to a screaming end. She turned to Colt, who casually leaned against the kitchen counter and had just invited her to go to Sunday dinner at his mom's house.

"It's kind of her thing," he said. "Everyone's expected to show up on the first Sunday of the month. Logan and the Rivers' crew are invited as well. We have dinner together most every Sunday, but Communion Sunday is sacred. Unless you're bleeding or in the hospital, your butt had better be in a chair. Rock was the only one of us who ever got a pass. With him being famous and all, she figured his coach overruled her as long as he was paying Rock's check."

"I'd love to go." Love to like she'd love to get a root canal or a colonoscopy. Something told her that when they stepped through those doors, when they went back to the real world with other people, with his *family*, everything would change. "But I don't have anything to wear. Maybe I should just go back to town and let you go by yourself."

He shook his head. "Don't be silly. It's not fancy. It's just family. And you can borrow something of mine, if you want."

Yeah, she was sure that would go over really well. The first meal with his family, and she shows up in his clothes. They'd never guess she and Colt had been together or what they'd been doing. Heat rose to her cheeks. "I'll figure something out."

"I thought with all the snow, it would be fun to ride the ATV over, so jeans will be good."

The clothes she'd thrown into her bag on Friday night were still clean, since she'd spent most of the day before either naked or in one of Colt's shirts. She took a quick shower and realized her hands were shaking as she tried to apply a layer of mascara.

Why was she so nervous? These were perfectly nice

people, and this wasn't the first time she'd be meeting them. Because she'd been Max's teacher last year as well, she'd spent plenty of time with Quinn and Ham, her dad. And she'd worked with Vivi in the snack bar at the alumni hockey game earlier that summer. But that was as Chloe, the schoolteacher, not as Chloe, the vixen sleeping with her son.

The sun glimmered on the fresh layer of snow, which crunched under their feet as they walked out of the house and through the yard. The air still had a bit of a bite, so Chloe zipped up the front of her coat as she followed Colt to the garage where he kept the ATV.

It was a newer model, yellow and black with silver chrome trim and sleek in design. He patted the seat. "I call him Bumblebee."

She grinned. "Nice. Does he turn into a butt-kicking alien robot?"

He huffed and gave her a derisive look. "Not around civilians."

He held up a black helmet. "I usually wear this when I'm going on a longer ride, but not if I'm just going across a couple of fields to Mom's. The path is pretty easy, and I don't go very fast since Watson likes to run along beside the quad. But you're welcome to wear one, if you want."

She touched the side of her hair—she'd done pretty well duplicating the look Carley had created, and she wasn't thrilled about messing it up. But she did value safety first. Vanity won—she passed on the helmet. But there was still the matter of her fairly large purse. "What should I do with my bag? Stuff it inside my coat?"

"We can put it in the dry box with the other stuff I have to bring." He opened the heavy plastic box affixed to the back of the ATV, and she put her purse inside. He added his items, then buckled the box shut and climbed onto the four-wheeler.

She still had his scarf, and she looped it around her neck and pulled it up over her cheeks as she straddled the seat behind him. She wrapped her arms around his middle and held on as he revved the engine and pulled out of the garage, clicking the automatic door closed behind them.

The snow crunched under the wheels, and Watson ran alongside the ATV, appearing to revel in the race and the occasional spray of snow in his furry face.

They cruised over the fields, occasionally pausing for Colt to point out a favorite horse or something he had done on the ranch. The land owned by the Triple J Ranch was far-reaching, starting with fields and pastures and moving up the side of the mountain behind it.

As they drew near the house, Colt pointed to a road leading up the mountain behind the ranch house. "That's the road leading to Rock and Quinn's new house. It's on the other side of that ridge." He'd told her Quinn wanted to stay near family, so Rock had a house built for them that summer. They'd only recently moved in, and they split their time between the house up here and his house in Denver when he was in the middle of the season. Colt gestured across the fields to the neighboring ranch. "That's Rivers Gulch, where Logan and Ham live. It was fun growing up so close to other kids. Although our parents didn't always get along."

Quinn had told her that Rock had caught Vivi and

Ham seeing each other on the sly, so it would seem they got along just fine now.

They bounced over a small dip in the trail, and Chloe held on, pressing her head against Colt's back as he let out a whoop. She was tempted to give a whoop herself. She'd been apprehensive about going to Vivi's, but Colt didn't seem worried at all. He made everything seem fun, and his outlook was contagious. Letting go of her anxieties, she surrendered to the moment and let herself simply enjoy it. She felt alive and adventurous—totally different than the normal Sunday afternoons she spent curled on the couch with her cat, a knitting project, and a series binge on Netflix.

Cruising past a corral filled with cows, they pulled up in front of the house and climbed off the ATV. *Holy Cheez Doodles*. Her heart pounded in her chest. So much for letting go of her anxieties. Her feelings of freedom floated off in the winter breeze, replaced with feeling as though she'd just shown up to church in her undies.

She retrieved her purse and twisted the straps in her hands as she followed Colt up the porch steps. This was it. *Showtime*.

"Hey, Mom," Colt hollered as they walked into the house. He hung his hat and coat on the rack inside the door, and helped Chloe with her jacket before crossing to the kitchen. The inside of the old farmhouse had obviously been renovated, with new carpet and tiles and gorgeous new cabinets and appliances. The room appeared to have been opened up to make the kitchen and living room one, and a giant island sat in the center.

Colt set the plastic bag he'd been carrying on the

counter next to a cookie jar shaped like a smiling, chubby pink pig. "I brought some of that venison jerky you asked for."

Vivi had been at the sink, and she dried her hands on a towel as she came around the center island. "Thanks, honey. I'm glad you're here." She gave her youngest son a big hug.

Hadn't she just seen him a few days ago? Chloe's dad had only doled out one or two hugs a year, usually around Christmas and her birthday.

"Welcome, Chloe," Vivi said, her arms outstretched as she enfolded Chloe in a hug as well. "I'm glad you're here too." Colt's mom held on an extra moment, and Chloe was struck with a sudden longing for her own mother. Or for the woman she imagined her mother could have been. If she hadn't left.

"Thank you," she choked out, surprised by the emotion clogging her throat.

Vivi pulled back but didn't let go of Chloe's arms as she studied her face. "I was so sorry to hear about the incident with Rank. Are you okay, hon?"

Chloe nodded, not sure she could trust her voice. What was up with her? Why was she getting emotional over every comment out of this woman's mouth? She'd spent time with the James family before. But that had been at a rowdy hockey game, not a family dinner after she'd spent the last day and a half playing hide the salami with the youngest son.

She was saved from having to say anything by the arrival of Ham and Logan. They brought in a gust of cold air as they stomped their boots and took off their jackets. Ham headed for the kitchen to drop off a nine-by-thirteen pan, but Logan headed toward her and drew her into a hug.

Geez-o-pete. What was with these people and all the hugging? Not that she was complaining. It felt kind of nice.

"You okay, Chloe? I've been worried about you after the other night," he said.

"I'm fine. How is Tina? And the kids?"

"They're doing okay. She hasn't heard from Rank. And neither have the police, I guess. They think he's lying low, but I'm hoping he left town. They're all anxious to get back home. I think they're going back tonight so the kids can go to school in the morning."

Chloe nodded, knowing she'd be going home tonight as well, her weekend of playing house with Colt almost through.

"That was really sweet of you to help them."

Logan shrugged. "It's the least I can do. We've known Tina a long time. Right, Colt?" He nudged Colt's arm and gave him a teasing grin that implied a secret joke they shared.

What was that about? "Oh," Chloe said, going for casual nonchalance. "How did you know her? Were you *involved*?" Gah, what a stupid question. She tried to play the question off like a joke, but she was sure it fell flat. She was terrible at jokes. It was none of her business anyway.

"Uh, no. Not hardly," Colt said with a chuckle as he swung a punch toward Logan's arm.

"But you wanted to be." Logan ducked the punch, then waggled his eyebrows at Chloe. "She used to baby-sit us when we were kids. Our Colt had quite the crush on her." He turned back to Colt and jabbed him a couple

of times in the ribs. "And now she's just your type—
wounded sparrow in need of saving. Perfect pickings for
a do-gooder like you."

"Yeah right. I was a little kid," Colt told Chloe, then
turned back to cuff Logan on the shoulder. "That was
a long time ago. And the last thing I need right now is
another person to save."

Chapter 16

COLT AND LOGAN'S WORDS HIT HER LIKE A PUNCH TO THE stomach, and Chloe reached out to grip the chair in front of her. *Wounded sparrow in need of saving. Perfect pickings for a do-gooder like you. Another person to save.* Was that what Colt had been doing with her all weekend? Did he see her as a poor damsel who needed saving? Was she just one more of his projects—another way to do penance for his stupid notion of a curse?

All the pieces of the last few days came rushing back to her. She'd kissed him and he'd backed off. She'd been in the tub and he'd backed away. He'd almost kissed her, then pulled back. They didn't actually go to bed together until she straight up offered him her naked body. Maybe he was just too polite, and too much of a man, to decline the offer of a naked woman in his bed.

No, he'd said he liked her, said he wanted her. But liking and wanting someone didn't mean the same thing as a relationship—didn't mean anything more than a roll in the hay.

She thought back to everything she'd told him about herself, how she'd been chubby as a kid, how her dad had treated her. Colt was a great guy, always doing things for other people. Maybe this weekend, maybe *she* was just another one of those things, and he was having sex with her because he felt sorry for her and wanted to do her a favor.

Bile rose in her throat at the thought. She glanced at the door, thinking she should just leave before she embarrassed herself, or Colt, anymore. But she couldn't leave. Number one, because she had no vehicle, and she didn't think stealing the quad and hightailing it back to her house was a very sound plan, notwithstanding the fact that she had no idea how to start the thing. And number two, the door was currently occupied as Rock, Quinn, and Max came through it in a gust of wind and laughter.

A huge, brown furry dog tramped in after them and raced around the room, greeting everyone with sloppy kisses, including her. She knelt on the floor, hoping the act of stroking the dog's back would quiet the tremble in her hand.

Get ahold of yourself. Colt wasn't like that.

How do you know? her spineless inner conscience asked. *You barely know him.*

But she did know him. At least she felt like she did. And he wouldn't have spent the whole day in bed with her just to be nice. He wouldn't have done that thing in the shower, and he certainly wouldn't have done that thing with his tongue out of kindness or sympathy.

"Miss Bishop," Max cried, running toward her and practically falling on top of the dog as he threw his arms around it. "This is Truman. He's my dog. He's all mine. Aren't you, buddy?" He ruffled the dog's neck. "Isn't he so cool? We're not sure what kind he is. Rock calls him a Heinz 57 'cause he's a mix-up of different breeds, but some people say mixed breeds are healthier. And this guy sure seems healthy. You should see him eat."

Chloe's cheeks flamed as she pushed away the thoughts of Colt *and* the thing he'd done with his tongue.

She buried her face in the dog's furry neck, then turned her focus to the boy. She loved Max—loved to hear him talk in that too-old-for-his-age way of his, and she got a kick out of the random trivial facts he often dropped into a conversation. "I like him. He's very friendly," she said, cringing at the wet tongue Truman had just licked up her cheek.

Max lowered his voice. "He's kind of in trouble because he ate a pair of mom's underpants this morning." He screwed his mouth into a disgusted grimace. "I love him, but he's kind of a goofball."

Wasn't that true of all of them? She looked past the dog to where Rock and Colt were immersed in some kind of wrestling match. Rock had his younger brother's head clamped under his arm in a headlock.

"Wow. Chloe, I love your hair," Quinn said, crossing the room to give her a hug, then leaned back to admire her new style. "It looks great. So cute." She cut her eyes slyly toward the wrestling brothers. "What did Colt say? I'll bet he liked it. It's so trendy and stylish. And fresher and hipper than your last style."

Chloe shrugged, trying to keep her smile in place as her withered ego took another hit. How untrendy and out of style had she looked before?

"What? Did he say something?" Quinn asked, too intuitive for her own good. She leaned in, lowering her voice as Max and Truman tumbled off to join the wrestling fun. "Did he hurt your feelings? Are you two having trouble getting along? Do you want me to talk to him? Want me to slug him?"

Chloe chuckled, not used to having a woman friend who was so ready to go into battle for her. "No, he said he liked it. Everything is fine. You don't need to slug him. We're getting along great." Or they had been until a few minutes ago, when doubt and insecurity reared their ugly heads.

Quinn narrowed her eyes, studying Chloe's face, then an impish grin curled her lips and she waggled her eyebrows. "Ohhh, I see."

Heat flushed Chloe's cheeks, and her own lips tugged up at the corners. "It's not like that."

Quinn chuckled. "Oh yes, it is. It's *exactly* like that. I can tell. Colt doesn't date a lot of women, and he doesn't do casual, so I know you're special. And I can see by the blush on your cheeks that you took the Colt out of the stables and went for a ride. How was it? Was it like a quick jaunt around the corral, or was it like a long ride through the mountains with a stop at a lake?"

"Shhh," Chloe hushed the other woman, a giggle rising in her throat. Quinn had just said Colt doesn't do casual—so he wouldn't just be throwing her a bone— *ahem*—so to speak. She *had* to mean something to him. Whether or not they were true, she grabbed Quinn's words and held on to them like a lifeline.

"Oh, come on. One detail. You gotta give me something."

Chloe pressed her lips together, then finally gave in and whispered, "Okay. It was more like a 'hold-on-for-dear-life bucking bronco' kind of ride."

Quinn covered her mouth, holding back her laughter. "Attaboy, Colt."

Mason and Tess arrived then, ushering in an elderly woman wearing a bright-purple coat and hot-pink snow boots.

Quinn wrapped her arm around Chloe's waist and leaned in as they walked toward the door. "I'll expect more details after we get a couple of margaritas in you Tuesday night."

"Who's this?" the older woman said, eyeing Chloe. Mason had taken her coat, and she fluffed up the soft cloud of silvery-blue curls circling her head. "I don't think we've met, but you must be *somebody* if you've made it to Sunday dinner."

Colt had extricated himself from Rock's armpit and crossed to give the woman a hug. "Hey, Aunt Sassy." He pressed a kiss to her wrinkled cheek.

"Hello, darling." She fondly smoothed his mussed hair from his brother's headlock, then gave him a keen side-eye. "Are you the one who brought a lady friend to dinner?"

He chuckled. "Guilty." He took a step toward Chloe, a proud grin on his face as if he were showing off his prize pig at the county fair. "Aunt Sassy, this is my friend, Chloe Bishop. She's Max's teacher, and she's also helping me coach the kids' hockey team this season."

The pride with which he introduced her gave Chloe a warm feeling in her chest and helped ease her earlier insecurities. Not that being likened to a prize pig seemed like a good thing, but he appeared genuinely pleased to present her to the grand matriarch. Having been in Max's life the year before, she'd heard stories about Sassy and seen her at some of Max's events, but hadn't ever had the occasion to meet her. She seemed both warm and intimidating.

Chloe held out her hand. "Nice to meet you."

Colt's aunt kept a straight face as she held on to

Chloe's hand, her eyes narrowing in a shrewd study. "Have you ever coached hockey before, Chloe?"

"No, never." What an odd first question to ask her.

"Are you a big fan of the game?"

"I'm becoming one."

"What's your favorite subject to teach?"

"Reading."

"What's your favorite book?"

"*Harry Potter*."

"Which one?"

"All of them."

"Are you a morning person or night owl?"

"Morning."

"Favorite color?"

"Pink."

"Coke or Pepsi?"

"Diet Coke. Hands down."

"Favorite season?"

"Spring."

"If your house caught on fire, what's the one thing you'd save?"

"My cat," Chloe answered, without hesitation. Sassy's rapid-fire questions hadn't fazed her a bit. She was used to school-age children asking *why* seven thousand times a day. One little old lady with a few easy lobs didn't even compare.

A grin curved across Sassy's lips, and she patted Chloe's hand, then finally released it. She gave Colt a wink. "She'll do."

He chuckled and leaned down to speak into Chloe's hair. "She does that to everyone. You were awesome." His breath tickled her ear, and she wanted to lean into him, to wrap herself around him and go back to that warm feeling of being next to him.

Instead, she felt awkward and unsure of herself, afraid to touch him or give away the closeness they'd shared. Although she did feel pleased with herself about the Sassy introduction, like she'd somehow passed an important family test.

Despite Quinn's words, that pleasant feeling warred with the insecurity of how many other girls before her had run the auntie gauntlet and of Colt introducing her as his "friend." *But I am his friend.* And really—what else was he going to say? *This is Chloe—she's my latest lover, my weekend flame, my new mattress-mambo mate.* Was she expecting him to say: *She's my sweetheart*, or *She's my soul mate*, or how about *She's my bae*?

Okay, Chloe wasn't sure she knew exactly what that last one meant, but she'd heard the high-school kids say it. One of the girls had told her it meant "before anyone else," which sounded sweet, but the girl could have been making that up and it actually meant something more lurid. Either way, Chloe couldn't really imagine Colt using the term. But what term had she expected him to use? They'd only been together a day and a half. It's not like she was his *girlfriend* already. And *soul mate* felt a little daunting, even to her. Maybe *friend* was the best choice, and it wasn't a *bad* term. It was sweet. And they *were* friends. They'd just transitioned to *friends with benefits*.

Cheese and rice. Not everything Colt said had to have a double meaning or carry a negative connotation. Maybe he hadn't meant his earlier comment the way she'd heard it. She needed to quit overanalyzing every word out of the man's mouth and just enjoy spending time with him and his perfectly lovely family.

And she *was* going home with him, so they could talk it through later and she could simply ask him what he meant. *Yeah right*. A confrontation was just what she wanted when they left here. And she was so awesome at fearlessly broaching uncomfortable subjects.

But the only way she would find out was to ask him. She had to. But for now, they had to eat.

The group moved toward the table, which had already been set for the meal. Colt pulled out a chair for her, then dropped into the seat next to it. Warmth bloomed in her chest as he picked up her hand, until Quinn picked up her other hand, and she realized they were just preparing to say the blessing.

Ham bent his head, and his deep voice flowed across the table. "Father, thank you for this day. Thank you for the moisture, for these good folks around the table, and for the blessings we are about to receive. Amen." He was a man of few words, but he got the job done.

Chloe looked up in time to catch the quick wink and extra squeeze he gave Vivi's hand before he let go and reached for the platter of roast beef. Swallowing hard, she had to look away, feeling like she'd intruded on a private moment and fighting a twinge of jealousy.

Colt's thumb rubbed the back of her hand before the table erupted into the act of passing the food and filling plates. He let go as his brother passed him a bowl of mashed potatoes.

"So, how's the new team look?" Rock asked. "I'm going to try to come watch their practice tomorrow night."

"Good," Colt answered. "We've got a fun group of

kids, and a couple of them are pretty good. Don't you think, Chloe?"

"Uh, yeah. They all seem excited to play."

"That's half the battle," Rock said.

"The other half of the battle is finding a kid willing to play goalie, and we've got one of those. The Henderson twins are on the team, and they're both beefy kids *and* they can skate so I think I'm going to make them our defensive line. I can't remember their names, but they have red hair so I keep calling them Fred and George."

Chloe grinned at the reference to her favorite books. Okay, maybe Colt *was* her soul mate. Or getting closer to it anyway.

"I'm going to play forward because I like to score," Max announced.

"So does Rock," Quinn muttered under her breath, nudging Chloe with her elbow.

She almost choked on her sip of iced tea.

Rock must have heard it too. He grinned and waggled his eyebrows at his new wife as he proclaimed, "And I'm very skilled at scoring. I strive to get a hat trick in every game."

The table erupted in chuckles as Vivi swatted at her eldest son. "Stop it."

"What's a hat trick?" Max asked, wanting to be in on the joke.

"It just means you score three times in one night... er...game," Rock said, still grinning impishly at Quinn.

"Oh. I'm going to do that then."

Ham patted his grandson on the shoulder. "Sometimes it's easier said than done, son. Just go out there and do your best. It still counts if you give it your all."

"Absolutely," Vivi agreed, avoiding looking any of her children in the eye.

Chloe bit her bottom lip to keep from laughing. She liked this family. "Speaking of giving it your all, our lone girl on the team, Maddie, is doing great as well," she said, earning a thankful smile from Vivi. "She's really picking up the skills, and she skates better than some of the boys after only one night of practice. She has this confidence that she can do anything and throws herself into learning it all." She wished she could bottle up some of the girl's enthusiasm and courage and throw back a shot of it every morning.

The conversation moved from the kids' team to Rock's team, then on to the happenings of the ranch and how the recent snow was much-needed moisture. Even though she had a little trouble keeping up with all the conversations, Chloe enjoyed listening to the family's easy rapport. She liked the way they teased and joked with each other, yet the admiration and respect for each other, especially for Vivi and Hamm, was always present.

Between the time spent at the table, cleaning up, and having dessert, the afternoon flew by in a mix of laughter, teasing, and loud chaotic bedlam. Between the dogs—and the brothers—wrestling with each other and Max, and the constant clatter of dishes being served and cleaned up, Chloe's head was swimming. She tried to pitch in and help where she could, drying dishes, wiping down counters, and carrying things to and from the kitchen, but it seemed like as soon as they got one thing cleaned up, they messed up another.

Vivi and Quinn must have been used to the pandemonium because they didn't seemed fazed at all. They were perfectly relaxed and often jumped in with sarcastic remarks or a well-timed clever line, but Chloe's nerves were frayed and the introvert in her needed a little peace and quiet.

It wasn't as if she was unused to some chaos—she did teach grade-school kids. But that was controlled chaos, and at school, she was in charge, she made the rules. Here, she had no influence, no say in when or how things would go. Her classroom was the one place she did feel confident. She knew she was good with kids. If they were under four feet tall, she could handle them.

It was the over-six-foot hot-as-heck cowboy and his rowdy family that she wasn't too sure about. The disorder and commotion she had no control over coupled with the doubts about Colt's earlier conversation had her confidence fleeing to hide in the bathroom with the door locked and the lights off.

Colt hadn't been overly affectionate, but several times he'd brushed his fingers over her hand, and the side of his hip had always pressed close against hers when they were standing together or sitting on the sofa next to each other.

There were a few secret moments they'd shared, a smile or a wink meant just for her, and a dart of heat had spun down her spine when he'd made the offhand comment during dessert about how he'd been craving cupcakes lately.

Finally, ready to head back, she thanked Vivi for the meal. She and Colt went through another round of hugs before they made it to the door. Quinn promised to text her the next day to confirm their plans for Taco Tuesday girls' night out.

Colt was helping her with her coat when Aunt Sassy reached for her arm. "Hold on, honey. I've been thinking about you and this Rank fella, and I want to give you something." She gestured for her nephew to pass her the purple purse hanging from the rack.

Shame and regret washed through Chloe. She dropped her gaze to the floor, wishing she could just forget the whole ordeal. They certainly didn't need to talk about it anymore. And if Colt's aunt passed her a well-meaning crisis-hotline brochure, she would die. But surely the likelihood she'd be carrying one of those in her purse had to be fairly slim. Although, the woman's purse was about the size of the Front Range mountains, so who knew what she could have in there.

"Here we go," Aunt Sassy proclaimed in victory, handing the bag back to Colt and pressing a small canister covered in pink sparkly gems into Chloe's hand. "You take this, honey. It's pepper spray, and all you need to do is twist the lid to open it, then point and shoot. This baby has a sixteen-foot range."

"Oh, I couldn't."

"Sure, you can. Having this on your key chain helps gives you a sense of security. And I want you to feel more confident and have a way to defend yourself if that jackwad shows up again."

Chloe stared down at the small, sparkly canister, wishing it really did hold the power to give her confidence. "But what about you?"

"Oh, don't worry about me, hon. I've got another one just like this at home. I get these as two-for-one specials from Amazon. I think I have one rolling around in every drawer in my house."

Colt nudged his aunt's arm. "She likes to be prepared. Even though I can't imagine who would mess with a tough old bird like her."

Aunt Sassy raised an eyebrow at her nephew. "This tough old bird is going to give you a sock in the mouth if you dare to compare me to an overcooked chicken again."

He held up his hands in surrender as he chuckled. "Sorry, Aunt Sassy. What I meant to say was I can't imagine wanting to harm someone as sweet and kind as you."

"Damn skippy." She nodded and winked at Chloe. "Now you take that and hook it to your keys or the side of your bag, somewhere you can easily get to it if you need it."

Chloe closed her hand around the canister. "Thank you. It's very thoughtful." She unzipped her bag and strung it on her keyring, then dropped them back into the outer pocket and zipped it closed. Sassy was right. Having the canister in her bag did give her a tiny boost of confidence.

"As long as we're giving you things to take home, why don't you take this as well," Vivi chimed in as she headed across the room. She lifted a silver antique revolver from the mantel of the fireplace. "I got some new candles and a floral arrangement that I want to put up here, and this throws off the look of my decor." She hefted the gun into her hand and brought it over to give to Colt.

He grinned. "You know that's my favorite gun."

"I know. That's why I'm giving it to you. You can put it on display on your fireplace."

He aimed the gun out the front window toward the barn. "This thing has come in handy. I had to use it in a gunfight against a couple of low-life mobsters this summer," he told Chloe as he spun the barrel around his index finger.

"You were in a fight with some low-life mobsters this summer?"

"Not an actual fight, more like a showdown at high noon, where we fended them off gunslinger style." He grinned at his brothers and spun the gun again, landing the butt of it in his palm and handed it to her. "Here, you want to put this in your bag too? Just until we get back to the house. Then I'll tell you the whole story."

Chloe hesitated, staring down at the weapon, uncertain even how to hold it. Guns scared her.

"Don't worry, it's not loaded," he said with a chuckle.

She wasn't sure what was so funny about that, but everyone else seemed to be in on the joke, so she took the gun and set it gingerly inside her open purse, then zipped it back up.

———

Bundled back in their scarves and gloves, they headed out, Colt whistling for the dog as they walked down the front porch steps toward the four-wheeler. He brushed the seat off, and Chloe climbed on behind him, wrapping her arms around his middle. The afternoon had been full of crazy thoughts and confusing concerns about what was happening with them, and she struggled to make sense of it all as they rode back to the cabin. She had no idea what would happen when they made it back, so she savored the feeling of pressing her body to his and laying her head against his muscled back. The air smelled like pine and the distant earthy scent of the horse stable.

He took it a little slow, she assumed for Watson since he'd been playing with the other dogs all afternoon and should be worn out. But the golden raced along the trail next to them with as much enthusiasm as he had on the way there.

The sun was setting, and like the impending night, a darkness settled in her as she replayed the afternoon in her mind. It should have been great. They'd had such a wonderful weekend together, but her insecurities and doubts kept messing with her head. She analyzed every look and touch of the afternoon.

He hadn't come right out and told his family they were involved. But why would he? Maybe he assumed they would figure it out. Or maybe he simply wasn't big on public displays of affection. Or did he play down their involvement because he was ashamed of her?

Back up there, sister.

No one said the two of them were dating. In fact, neither of them had said anything about what was going to happen when they left the cabin and went back to their real lives.

They pulled up in front of the house, and she tried to shake off the darkness and not let her feelings show. But apparently she was even worse at disguising her feelings than she was at learning to ice skate.

"You all right there, darlin'?" Colt asked her as they walked into the cabin and hung up their coats. "You seemed awful quiet this afternoon."

"I'm fine," she said. *Tell him.* The easiest way to answer all her questions and doubts was to simply ask him what he was thinking—to tell him what was bothering her and clear the air. Just ask him what that crack about saving another person had meant, what this whole weekend had meant. She opened her mouth to speak, the questions on her tongue, but she couldn't do it. The anxiety of him confirming her fears outweighed the desire for the truth about his feelings. If she didn't ask him, he wouldn't be forced to tell her the truth, and she could go on pretending this was all real and that he really did care about her. "I've just got a little headache, that's all."

His brow furrowed. "Ah, hell, why didn't you say something? I could have found you some aspirin or ibuprofen."

This was the kind of thing that fed right into her insecurities. Why did he act so attentive, like he really cared? Because he really did care *about her*, or because he acted that way with everyone, because he was genuinely a nice guy?

"It's all right. But I think I should probably head home. I didn't bring any clothes for work, and I've got to be to the school early in the morning for a faculty meeting. It'll probably be easier for me to get there on time if I'm in town."

"Yeah, sure, that makes sense."

Wow. Her stomach turned at the ease with which he gave in. He didn't even *try* to convince her to stay. She tried to read his expression, but he'd already turned away. Her shoulders sagged as she made her way down the hall toward his bedroom. "I'll just get my things together."

"Okay. I'll pack up the cat's stuff."

"You don't have to. I can do it," she said from the bedroom.

As if she knew he was talking about her, Agatha crept

out of Colt's closet and sauntered toward her. Chloe was so frustrated by his silence, and maybe a little disappointed that he hadn't fought harder for her to stay, that a horrible part of her secretly hoped the cat had yakked in one of his shoes.

What is wrong with me? She didn't usually wish cat yak on anyone. Everything about her was out of sorts—like her whole rhythm was off-kilter. She knew what was wrong—her heart was breaking. And she felt like an idiot. Spending the day with his family, with this group of people who were so self-assured, so easy in their own skin, and so loving and supportive of each other only reminded her of how alone and screwed up she was. She didn't know how to handle, how to be around all of them. And she didn't know how to manage the wild extreme of feelings that had been rocketing through her the last week.

She didn't do impulsive, didn't throw things in a bag to spend a weekend with a hot guy. For that matter, she didn't spend weekends with hot guys at all. But the last few days, she'd thrown caution to the wind, let the chips fall, and every other cliché that basically equaled the fact that she'd done her best to act brave and let her defenses down, and this is what she got.

Leaving now was the best thing, before she sank any deeper into the idea that a future existed for her with a guy like Colton James. She needed to get home and get back into her routines. That's what made her feel strong, where she drew her confidence, in her schedules and making sure all the pieces in her life went exactly so. She understood order and routine. When she could control those, she felt more in control of everything.

The cat weaved back and forth between her legs and let out a soft mewl of affection. The show of unconditional love almost did her in, and she sank onto the bed as tears burned the back of her eyes. She pressed her palm against her mouth to keep Colt from hearing her cry.

They hadn't made the bed that morning; she'd tried, but Colt had made her leave it. The rumpled sheets only served to remind her of the amazing weekend they'd shared and what a fool she'd been to believe it was anything more than purely physical. She ran her hand across the soft cotton, whispers of their lovemaking sighing up from the fabric.

You've always known you weren't good enough, her dad's voice whispered bitterly into her ear. Her fingers closed, her nails digging into her palm as she twisted a handful of the sheets tightly between them.

Enough. Stop bawling and go home.

Chloe swiped the stray tears from her cheeks with the back of her hand, then pushed up from the bed and collected her things. At the last second, she dropped her bag and quickly made the bed. She couldn't help herself.

She'd thought the smoothed comforter and perfectly plumped pillows would help her to breathe a little easier. Instead, they shot a tortured ache through her heart, as if her time there with Colt had now been erased, as if Colt's room had been set back to normal and any traces of her and their weekend together had been dispelled.

Chapter 17

COLT WAS IN THE KITCHEN WASHING THE CAT'S FOOD AND water bowls as she came out of the bedroom. She set her bag on the sofa next to her purse. "I'll finish this," she told him.

It only took a few minutes to finish cleaning up and crating the cat. Agatha yowled her protest, telling her in cat terms that Chloe wasn't the only one who was unhappy about leaving the cozy cabin. Despite her cool attitude, the cat had seemed at home at Colt's, stretching out on the warm stones of the fireplace and lounging in the patches of sunlight that came through the big windows in the living room.

Colt was coming in from outside, his cowboy hat pushed low on his forehead, when Chloe carried the cat crate out of the mudroom. He was so handsome, it hurt her stomach, and she had to look away. Her knuckles turned white as she clutched the handle on the top of the crate.

He didn't seem to notice as he reached for the crate. "I took your stuff out and got the truck all warmed up for you."

Wow, that was fast. He must really want her out of there.

The wind had picked up and was as cold as the tendrils of anguish snaking around her heart. Colt whistled for the dog, and Watson jumped into the truck and settled on the seat between them. Neither moved to shoo him out of the way, and he laid his head on Chloe's leg.

The ride back to town was quiet, except for the soft rumble of Colt's deep voice humming along to the radio and an occasional disgruntled squall from the cat. Chloe looked out the window, dread settling in her stomach as they got closer to the house. What would happen then? Would he drop her at the curb and drive away?

She doubted it. No, he would be a gentleman and carry her things in. Then what? Offer her a chaste, "friendly" kiss on the cheek? How humiliating.

Should she thank him for the weekend? He had let her stay with him. *Hey, Colt, thanks for the warm bed and for all the hanky-panky that happened in it.* Yeah that sounded really clever. Maybe she could just tell him thanks for the ride and *the ride*.

She mentally groaned. Maybe she should try to laugh it all off—act like she knew it was all physical the whole time, and she was totally cool with it. *Hey, thanks for the two hots and a cot and that thing you did with your tongue. It was amazing.*

Yeah, that sounded like her. And she could follow it up with casual chuckle. *Ha ha. Don't worry, I do this all the time. I'm a totally cool and carefree chick.* Ugh. She couldn't even make herself buy that one.

Colt pulled up in front of the house and hopped out of the truck, saving her from having to imagine any more mortifying pseudo-conversations with him. As predicted, he grabbed her bags and the cat crate, and she and Watson followed him around to the side kitchen door, reminding her of the fact her front door was nailed shut.

A shudder ran through her, and she glanced nervously

around the yard. Rank was still out there. He could be watching them now.

Colt's eyes narrowed as he scanned the yard, apparently thinking along the same lines. "I don't see anything strange. And he knows the cops are looking for him now, so he's most likely to be lying low."

He was probably right. It still didn't keep the fingers of dread from tickling her skin. She passed Colt her keys, the sparkly pepper spray hanging from the ring, and tried to imagine being brave enough actually to squirt someone in the eye with it.

She let out a relieved breath as they stepped into the kitchen, and she saw everything neatly in its place. The countertops gleamed in the faint moonlight coming through the window, and the canisters were still perfectly lined up in a row against the backsplash.

Colt entered the house in front of her, turning on lights and checking the rooms and peeking into all the closets. "Everything looks okay. And there's no sign that he came back this weekend."

Bile rose in her throat at the thought of Rank being in her tidy home, touching her things with his nicotine-stained fingers.

"You all right?" Colt asked, reaching out a hand to steady her. "I swear the color just drained clean out of your face." He pulled out one of the kitchen chairs. "You want to sit?"

She shook her head. "No, I'm *not* all right. I'm creeping around my yard hoping my neighbor's ex doesn't attack me, my front door is nailed shut, and I'm afraid to walk into my own house. I just want my life to go back to normal."

A week ago, the most exciting thing that had happened to her was unexpectedly finding a ten-dollar bill in the pocket of a pair of jeans she hadn't worn in a while. This week, she was flinging her naked self at a sumptuous cowboy, coaching a kid's hockey team, filing police reports, and having the kind of sex she'd only read about in books.

Being home in her well-ordered environment brought everything to a head, and she wanted to crawl into bed, under the covers that she'd washed with exactly one level scoop of her favorite detergent.

"I'm sorry." She scrubbed her fingers across her forehead. "I don't mean to take it out on you."

"It's okay. It's been a rough couple of days. I'll get out of here and let you get some rest." He leaned toward her as if to pull her into his embrace, and she suddenly felt awkward and shy and wasn't sure even how to touch him.

She wanted to hug him, to melt into his arms and have him carry her off to bed. She wanted to put all this doubt aside and go back to the fun, easy way they'd been the past two days, but now something felt off, like they didn't quite know how to act around each other. She wasn't sure if it was her fault or his, or a combination of both, but she knew something felt different. Some slight thing had changed.

Watson nuzzled her hand and wiggled his furry behind against her, drawing a smile from her and a chuckle from Colt. But it was enough to break through at least the top layer of the awkward ice.

Colt leaned forward, gave her a quick hug, and pressed a light kiss to her forehead. "Get some sleep, and you'll feel better. I'll see you in the morning."

Locking the door behind him, Chloe watched him walk down the driveway. He did have some great swagger in those boots. Watson stayed next to him, and Colt must have been talking to him, because the dog's head tipped up as if he were listening intently, his attention solely on the tall man next to him. She knew the feeling.

I'll see you in the morning. The last thing he'd said before disappearing into the night. So, apparently he still planned to pick her up for school in the morning. That was something. Wasn't it? Or was it just another gesture of kindness?

All this second-guessing was making her head pound. She needed to turn her brain off, to go to bed and sleep. Flipping off the kitchen lights, she headed toward her room and spent the next twenty minutes going through the steps of her nightly routine, every practiced movement working to loosen the tightness in her chest. She washed her face, smoothed moisturizer onto her cheeks, and brushed her teeth for a full two-and-a-half minutes.

Quinn had given her a hockey jersey earlier that summer when she'd helped out in the snack bar at the alumni game. They'd all worn matching red and blue jerseys with the word "JAMES" lettered across the shoulders, and she'd been wearing hers as a nightshirt all fall. Stripping down to her panties, she slipped the jersey over her head, then stuffed her feet into a pair of fleece-lined slippers.

Tension stiffened her shoulders as she walked through the house checking all the windows and doors. Colt had already checked them once, but she needed to do it again, to pull on the knob, to verify the latch was secured.

Pulling back the curtain in the living room, she spied

Colt's truck still sitting at the curb. What the french fry? Why was his truck still here? Had he stopped in at Tina's? Had his battery gone dead?

The hair on her neck lifted as she feared that Rank had caught him on the way out of her house. Heedless of the threat of Rank waiting outside, she raced through the kitchen, ran out the side door, and down the driveway. "Colt!" she yelled into the chilly air.

A sharp bark answered her, and she jerked her head toward Colt's truck. Watson's head appeared in the back window, and she ran to the side of the truck, cold wet snow seeping through the thin soles of her slippers. Peering through the window, she saw Colt bolt up from the seat, the sleeping bag he'd been under falling to the floor of the pickup.

He pushed open the door, alarm registering on his face as he panned the yard behind her. "What's wrong? Did Rank show up?"

"No. I mean, not that I know of." She shook her head, as if to clear her thoughts. "What are you still doing out here? And why do you have a sleeping bag?"

"Get in," he told her, his gaze dropping to her bare legs.

A shiver ran through her, either from Colt's cool gaze or the cold night air whistling under the hem of the hockey jersey. She climbed into the truck, and he reached an arm around her to pull the door shut, then drew her close to him, unzipping his coat and enfolding her inside it and against his warm chest. Watson jumped to the floor of the cab, whining as he tried to find a place to lick her.

Colt rubbed his hands over her arms. "What are you doing out here? You've got to be freezing."

Her inner temperature had just spiked about ten

degrees as he pulled her bare legs up and under the sleeping bag and wrapped himself around her. "What are *you* doing out here? I saw your truck and thought something had happened to you."

A grin tugged at the corner of his lips. "So you thought you'd run out here in your slippers and night-shirt to save me?"

Okay, so it didn't sound like the smartest plan the way he'd said it, but it had made sense to her at the time. "I wasn't thinking. I was just reacting. I thought you were in trouble."

"I appreciate the effort, but you just put yourself at more risk by leaving the safety of the house."

"Forget about me and my safety for a minute. I'm fine. Except for being totally confused by what's happening here." She lifted the corner of the sleeping bag. "Are you sleeping out here?"

"Not yet. Especially not with Watson barking his fool head off. But I was planning to eventually get some shut-eye."

"In your truck?"

"Darlin', I've slept in a lot worse places." He patted the seat next to him. "This bench seat is downright comfy compared to sleeping on the ground with a rock or two digging into your back."

"But why? Why would you sleep out here?"

He raised an eyebrow. "Really? Have you forgotten about the newly released convict you recently pissed off who threatened to come back for you?"

"No, of course not."

"Neither have I. And I'm not about to leave you alone here without someone to watch your back."

Tears pricked the backs of her eyes, and she could hear the blood rushing in her ears. He was sleeping in his truck, in the cold, for her? Her skin tingled and she wanted to touch him, but she didn't know how, so she kept her hands clasped tightly in her lap. "Were you planning to sleep out here all night?"

He shrugged again. "Not all night. I figured I'd get out and walk around the house a couple of times, just to keep an eye on things."

That hadn't been what she'd meant. "Thank you," she whispered. "You didn't have to do this." She tipped her head up, realizing suddenly how close her face was to his. Even in the semidarkness, she could see the dirty-blond scruff of whiskers covering his cheeks, and her chest burned with the memory of those whiskers abrading her tender skin. His hat was wedged between the windshield and the dash, and his hair was tousled as if he'd just run his hand through it. She itched to run *her* hand through it, to feel the soft strands between her fingers.

"I wanted to," he whispered back, his voice huskier than before. "I told you I won't let anything happen to you."

She didn't know what to say. Couldn't speak if she tried. Her gaze was captivated by his as he looked down at her, his expression both hard and somehow soft at the same time. She swallowed and licked her lips. His glance dipped to watch the movement, and heat coiled in her stomach.

His hand rested on her leg under the sleeping bag, and he made the slightest movement with his thumb, raking the side of it against her skin. Her breath caught at his touch. He spread out the fingers of his hand, sliding them across her upper thigh. His pinkie brushed the hem of the hockey jersey, which had already ridden up her leg when she'd climbed into the truck.

"Chloe," he said, one word, one soft whisper. But she could see his breath in the air, and it was as if the crystalized mist cast a spell on her, drawing her closer, making her forget every other thing except this man and his palm pressed against her thigh.

She leaned in, powerless against his pull, her bare nipples tightening against the rough fabric of the jersey. Her lips parted, as if inviting him to kiss them.

His fingers tightened on her thigh, sliding up under the jersey to grip the curve of her hip as he dipped his head and captured her mouth with his. He didn't offer her a sweet peck or a gentle brush. He kissed her with the hunger of a man who hadn't eaten in weeks. His tongue pushed between her lips, delving, tasting, taking.

She forgot about her worries, her self-doubt, and responded with the same primal need, as her arms circled his neck and she pressed her breasts to his chest.

Sliding his hand under her butt, he pulled her onto his lap. She straddled him, her knees pressing to either side of his thighs as his hand slid up under her jersey and found her full aching breast. Cupping it in his palm, he squeezed and caressed, rolling the hardened nub of her nipple between his thumb and index finger.

A soft moan escaped against his lips, as she moved her hips, rubbing against the rough denim of his fly, the thin fabric of her panties the only thing between them. The friction and movement had heat and need building between her legs.

Both of his hands were under her jersey now, skimming over her skin, caressing, squeezing, touching her everywhere. She couldn't get enough of his hands on her, and she arched into him as he filled his palms with her breasts.

The windows fogged as their breath came in ragged gasps, and the cab of the truck warmed with the heat of their bodies. Either that, or she just didn't notice the cold. She couldn't seem to focus or care about anything more than getting closer to him. And he seemed to feel the same way as he lifted the front of her shirt, baring her breasts and slanting his head to savor them. His mouth burned a hot trail along her skin as he moved from one to the other, licking, kissing, then sucking each tender tip between his warm lips. She arched into him, planting her palm on the back windshield for support and smearing the condensation.

Watson let out a sharp bark, and she squinted at the flash of the high beams of a car driving down the street. *Holy fork*. She froze—like a half-naked deer caught making out in the headlights.

Then she did what any other sensible schoolteacher who had been spotted bare-breasted and straddling a hot cowboy in a pickup outside her house would do— she ducked.

Diving for cover seemed like a good idea, except the hem of her jersey was pushed up and twisted around her neck, and as she moved to the side, she got caught on his hand, which was trapped under the back of her shirt, so as the lights of the car flashed across the back window, she flashed them back with headlights of her own.

Colt's body shook under her as he tried to both pull his trapped hand free and lift the sleeping bag to cover her. She whipped her head back. "Are you laughing?"

He pressed his gorgeous lips together and shook his head, but his eyes crinkled at the sides as he tried to hold back his laughter.

"This isn't funny. I'm a teacher, for fox sakes. I'm supposed to set an example, and I just motherforking flashed my liberty bells at an innocent member of our community." She tugged the jersey down to her hips.

"Liberty bells, huh? Well, catching a glimpse of your bells probably just made their night. I know they just made mine."

She glared at him.

He tried to keep a straight face, but couldn't quite manage it. "Well, they did. They're pretty spectacular bells. I might even go so far as to call 'em real traffic stoppers." A laugh finally busted out of him.

A giggle bubbled up in her chest, and as hard as she tried, she couldn't hold it in. She buried her head in his chest as she laughed out loud. Watson jumped up, planting his feet in her lap as he tried to lick her laughing face. It felt good to laugh. Almost as good as it felt to be wrapped in Colt's arms, feeling the rumble in his chest and hearing the deep tone of his laughter.

"Maybe you should go back inside before somebody calls out the Neighborhood Watch. I don't want to be the one responsible for giving you a bad reputation."

If only. Whoa. Where did that come from? She'd never wished for a bad reputation in her entire life. In fact, she'd spent a considerable amount of her time doing just the opposite—trying to be a good girl, an obedient daughter, an excellent student. But something about the way this handsome cowboy made her feel inside had her throwing "good sense" and caution to the wind, as evidenced by the fact she'd been less than a minute away from getting naked and down and dirty in a pickup truck in her front yard.

"I think that's a wise idea," she told him, then laid a hand on his muscled chest. "Do you want to come in with me?"

"Try and stop me."

An impish grin pulled at the corners of her lips as she pushed open the door of the truck and slid out. A shiver ran through her, but she had a feeling it was more from Colt's promise than the winter night air. Tilting her head, she offered him a challenge. "Try and catch me."

A low growl sounded in his throat, and she let out a tiny shriek of laughter as she took off across the yard. Watson raced ahead of her, getting in on the game, and her heart leapt as she heard the truck door slam and Colt scrambling across the grass behind her.

He caught her right outside the kitchen door and swooped her up into his arms. She wrapped her arms around his neck and pressed a hard kiss to his lips. He responded with something hard of his own. "You better take me inside before I take you against the side of this house, and we really get in trouble with your neighbors."

Another giggle bubbled out of her as he set her down. *Holy hot Cheetos.* She didn't think she'd giggled as many times in a whole year as she had in the last twenty minutes with this man. But he had this way of making her feel giddy and light and like she was sexy and desirable. She'd never felt like that before, and the giggles were probably a cross between nerves and happiness, but as silly as it sounded, she didn't want them to stop. She was having fun, real honest fun, and she loved it.

Fumbling for the door handle, she pushed it open, letting the dog in ahead of them, then pulling Colt in behind her. She kicked off her slippers as he bent forward and pulled off his boots.

He pulled her to him, nuzzling his lips against her neck. His voice hummed along her skin as he whispered in her ear. "I'm suddenly feeling very patriotic."

She chuckled, then her laughter died, and she shivered as he ran his tongue along the rim of her ear. His words were meant to be funny, but the low, slow way he'd said them was pulse-pounding sexy. "'Give me liberty, or give me death.'"

He took a step back and tugged at the hem of her shirt. "As much as I love seeing you wearing my jersey, cupcake, I'd much rather see you *not* wearing it."

She swallowed, suddenly shy again as she clutched the hem of the shirt, holding it down over *her* cupcake. "Right here?" It had been one thing to have him pull it up in the heat of the moment; it was another thing entirely to whip it off in the middle of her kitchen.

His eyes went dark with hunger as his voice went deeper, a cross between a request and a command. "Yes. Right here. Right now."

This wasn't like her. None of this was like any semblance of her normal self. But who was her normal self? A shy schoolteacher who spent most nights hanging out with her cat, either knitting or reading romance novels and imagining what it would be like to have the kind of crazy-hot sex scenes that filled the pages of her books?

Well, sister, a six-foot, four-inch package of hot sex was standing right in front of her and telling her to take her clothes off. She had a chance to fulfill one of those scenes right now, if only she were brave enough to bare herself to him, quite literally.

She licked her lips and swallowed again as she clutched the edge of her shirt in her hands. Her knees threatened to buckle under her, and flames of fear mixed with desire swirled through her veins. Why was this such a big deal? It's not like he hadn't already seen her naked.

But this was different. This wasn't lying in bed or in the throes of passion. This was sensual and intimate and about something more. This was about trust.

He hadn't moved, hadn't taken his eyes from her. He stood still, his only movement the fall and rise of his chest.

A naughty grin pulled at her lips as she tightened her fists around the hem, then pulled the jersey over her head. She held it out in one hand before letting it drop to the floor. "Let freedom ring."

Colt threw back his head and laughed. Not *at* her, but *with* her, and the sound of it rippled over her bare skin like cool water on a hot summer day.

Shrugging out of his jacket, he let it fall onto the kitchen floor as he unbuttoned the first few buttons of his flannel shirt and pulled it over his head, not bothering with the last remaining ones. His hair was mussed, and his grin was devilish. She expected him to pull her to him or grab her and kiss her, but instead, he gestured toward the hallway leading to her bedroom. "After you." He might be a rake, but he was a gentlemanly one.

She took a deep breath, then pushed back her shoulders and walked through the living room. He followed and must have been stripping as he walked. His white T-shirt flew through the air beside her and landed halfway across the back of her sofa. His pants must have fallen off next because she heard them hit the carpet in the hallway.

By the time they made it to her bedroom, all he still had on was a pair of black boxer briefs. She had no idea what had happened to his socks. And she didn't even care.

Bending forward to pull the throw pillows from the bed, she felt the heat of Colt's hand as he placed it in the center of her back. He stepped closer, trailing the back of his fingers up her spine. He drew her hair to the side, exposing her neck. She tipped her head and sighed as his lips settled on the spot just below her hairline. His open hands glided around her waist, pulling her back against him as his palms cupped and teased her breasts.

Forget the throw pillows. Forget the bed. He could take her right here on the floor.

He bent his knees, trailing his lips in a line of hot kisses that led across the back of her neck and down her spine. His thumbs slid inside the elastic band of her panties, and he slid them down, the cotton gliding over her hips, her thighs, her knees, then drifting to the floor.

He lifted her and set her tenderly on the bed. She lay back against the jumbled pillows, the comforter askew beneath her, and watched as he dipped his head to her breast.

She let go of everything that had happened earlier in the day and just let herself savor the time with him. She was putty in his hands, and all she wanted was to have him touch her. She craved the feel of his hands, his lips, his tongue, as he explored and discovered what she liked and how she wanted to be touched, to be caressed, to be stroked. She came alive under his touch—arching and sighing, telling him what to do.

She'd never been so brazen, so bold, never experienced such raw sensual need.

This isn't me, she kept telling herself. But maybe it was. Maybe this was the woman she was always supposed to be. Maybe it was okay to be wanton and sexy and to stop overthinking this whole thing and just let herself feel it, experience it. Who cared if her perfectly made bed was messed up? Who cared if her lover—gah—her lover's clothes were strewn across her house? Seriously, what had happened to his socks?

This could be her. The new her. The new Chloe who had hot, crazy sex with a handsome cowboy, and coached a hockey team, and who stayed up way past her bedtime. Even on a school night.

Chapter 18

CHLOE OPENED HER EYES THE NEXT MORNING AND FOUND herself staring at Colt's muscular back. She sucked in her breath as she studied the definition of his broad shoulders, the dip and curve of his shoulder blades. The sun was barely up, and a soft glow of predawn light filled the room, giving it an almost ethereal feel, like the room itself was being held in a delicate balance and once she moved, her reality would tip and falter, and she'd be back to being the same frumpy schoolteacher she'd been the week before.

Except she wasn't the same. Nothing was the same. For one thing, there was a man sleeping in her bed, and by the warm pressure against her legs, she was pretty sure a dog was sleeping there too. She had no idea where her cat was—but Agatha could take care of herself.

She'd had an odd night, alternating between feeling wide awake and drifting into deep sleep. She'd only left the bed once, waking with a jolt as she remembered Colt's revolver was still in her purse. She'd slipped out of bed and hurried into the kitchen, taking the gun from her purse and setting it on the counter where she knew she'd see it and remember to give it to him in the morning.

Just having it in the house both made her nervous and imparted an odd sense of security. But the sight of the steel weapon on her white counter gave her the chills, so she'd wrapped it in a towel and stashed it in a drawer next to the workbench in the garage.

As she closed the drawer, she'd caught a movement out of the corner of her eye and almost screamed. Then laughed at herself as she realized it was only Watson. The dog must have followed her out to the garage to check on her.

Agatha couldn't care less about her nightly rovings, so it was nice to have the dog accompany her on her rounds as she checked the windows and locks. With a sigh, he'd settled on the floor by the bed as she'd slipped under the sheets, cuddled against Colt, and fallen back to sleep.

Now with the pale shimmers of light falling on Colt's body, Chloe held perfectly still, not wanting to wake him, not wanting to break the illusion. She only wanted to look at him, to study him, to memorize every feature, every hard plane of his body, so she could play it back in her head once he was gone.

A thin, white line of scar tissue marred the perfect skin of his shoulder. He'd told her about a time Mason had caught his shoulder with a fishhook when their dad was first teaching them to fish. It had happened the same day the picture on his mantel had been taken, and Colt had pointed out the scar with pride.

She reached up, wanting to run her finger along the edge of the scar. But she didn't. Didn't touch him at all.

Memories of the night before swirled in her mind, and now, in the light of a new day, as she needed to get up and return to her life as a schoolteacher, she felt confused and conflicted, embarrassed that she'd been so open and willing with this man. She didn't really even know him. Yet she'd let him... Well, it didn't matter now what she'd let him do. It was done, and all that was left were the soreness of her muscles and the tender ache between her legs.

She needed a hot shower, a cup of coffee, and a shot of perspective. Feeling out of sorts, she needed her routines, something to plan and organize, something she could control, or that would give her at least a measure of feeling she had a grip on something in her life.

Dropping her hand, she lifted the comforter and slipped naked from the bed.

Colt blinked against the sliver of sunlight shining on his face, disoriented for a minute by the unfamiliar feel of the sheets. Then he remembered, and a slow smile crept across his face. He felt a warm body against his back and turned over to greet her. "Good morning, beautiful."

He was met with a sloppy lick to his cheek from Watson, who'd made himself comfortable stretched out in Chloe's spot. Rubbing the dog's neck, Colt pushed him off the bed, somehow guessing Chloe wouldn't be thrilled to find the dog's head lying on her pillow.

The clock on the nightstand read half past six, and he yawned and stretched his arms over his head. His muscles were sore, and he was tired from staying up late, but it was a good tired and he welcomed the ache, because he knew what had caused it. And it had been worth it.

He couldn't seem to stop the smile from spreading across his face as he slid out of bed and pulled on his briefs. He listened for sounds of Chloe, but the house seemed quiet. Padding barefoot down the hall, he expected to see the trail of his discarded clothes, but instead saw them placed in a neat pile on the side of the sofa.

The scent of coffee led him toward the kitchen, where he finally spotted Chloe, sitting at the table, papers, books, and a giant white poster board spread out in front of her. Fanned out across the table were books with titles such as *Creating a Winning Culture*, *Hockey Skills & Drills*, and *How to Be a Great Coach in Seven Easy Steps*. Charts and diagrams filled the pages, and she'd made similar color-coded plans across the poster board. He recognized the names of the kids on the hockey team on the board and realized she was working out schedules and drills.

Her head was bent over the poster board as she used a colored pencil to shade in a section of a pie diagram. He leaned against the doorway, watching her. Her attention was focused on the papers in front of her. Her lips were set in a tight line as she concentrated on the diagram. A lock of hair fell across her forehead, and she reached to push a loose strand behind her ear.

She was so damn beautiful. She didn't know it, didn't see herself the way he and other people did, and that was part of her beauty. She had about the biggest heart of anyone he knew, and in the short time he had known her, he'd seen numerous occasions that she'd put others before herself.

Something twisted in his chest as she chewed on her bottom lip, pulling it under her top teeth as she worked to neatly fill in the space on the diagram with color. He liked this woman way too much. He knew it, but he couldn't help it.

He only wished he could tell her—tell her how beautiful he thought she was, how kind and thoughtful he found her, how much he loved kissing her and holding her and…well, doing lots of other things to her as well. Last night had blown his mind. Every time they were together, she grew more comfortable with him, more comfortable with herself. It was like watching a flower bloom in his hand. A wildflower.

And like a wildflower, she'd planted something in him. And it was growing stronger every day he spent with her. But he hadn't told her.

He wanted to—wanted to take her face in his hands and tell her all the crazy emotions he was feeling. But he couldn't. Not because he didn't know—he knew what he was feeling—knew how hard he was falling for her. Falling like a paratrooper with no parachute. But he couldn't tell her. Couldn't say the words. Because as soon as he said it out loud, it became real, and that's when it could be taken away. When it would all start to go wrong.

No. Best to keep his feelings to himself for now. And it wasn't as if she was pouring out her heart to him either. He knew she liked him, hell, she *had* to like him—at least a little, especially after the weekend they'd just spent together. But she sometimes still acted like a skittish colt, backing away every time he got too close. So, he just needed to keep things light and remain a safe distance away—don't let himself get too close— for both their sakes.

"Mornin', cupcake," he drawled.

She let out a tiny shriek as she jumped and dropped the colored pencil. It rolled across the table as she pressed her hand to her chest. "Holy crickets. I didn't see you there. You scared the fork out of me."

He chuckled and sauntered in to peer over her shoulder. "Whatcha working on?"

"Just a few things for practice tonight. Some drills and a few skate sequences. I've been researching techniques and secrets to teach kids how to improve their hockey skills and have some great ideas for setting up some passing- and shooting-skills practices."

"Wow. These are great ideas. You don't even need me." He pulled one of the pages toward him to study a detailed puck protection drill. "But you do realize these kids are eight, right?"

She snapped the paper back and straightened it in one of the piles. "You do realize I like to be organized, right?" She pushed back her chair, and he stepped away to avoid getting plowed into. "I made coffee. You want a cup?"

"Yeah, thanks. That would be great."

He crossed the kitchen to stand behind her as she pulled a cup from the cabinet and reached for the coffeepot. Brushing the hair from her neck, he leaned down and pressed a tender kiss to her neck. "You smell nice."

Her hands shook, and a bit of coffee splashed over the edge as she tried to pour it into the cup. He reached around her, lifting the cup from her hands and taking a sip. "Mmm. It's good," he said, wrapping his arm around her stomach and pulling her back against his chest.

He expected her to melt into him, or maybe turn around and kiss him good morning. He was standing there in his underwear, and it was pretty clear some parts of him were unmistakably ready to wish her a good day, but she didn't turn around or do any kind of melting. Instead, her shoulders tensed against his back, and she reached for the washcloth folded neatly across the middle of the sink and used it to clean up the spilled coffee. Okay. Not the reaction he was hoping for, but even in the short time he'd known her, it didn't surprise him that she wouldn't be able to leave the mess on the counter.

He took another sip of coffee and tried again. Lowering his voice, he playfully whispered against her ear. "I was going to hop in the shower. You want to join me? I could wash your back. Or your front. Or anything else you think might be dirty."

"Oh, um, no thanks. I already took a shower."

He hadn't actually been interested in getting clean.

She fumbled the spoon she'd been trying to put in the sink, and it clattered against the stainless-steel side. "I mean, of course, I know that's not what you meant. I just have a meeting at school this morning, and I've been focusing on the stuff for practice tonight. I committed to the kids to be their coach, and I don't want to let them down."

She was acting squirrelly again. And he could feel her pulling away, just the slightest bit, but it was there—in the tightness of her shoulders, the firm set of her lips. He couldn't quite figure her out. One minute she was calm and joking around with him, and the next she was as nervous as a long-tailed cat in a room full of rocking chairs.

"Sure, of course. I don't want you to be late to your meeting on my account. Give me ten minutes, and I'll be showered and ready to go."

"You don't have to rush that fast. We don't have to leave for twenty." She'd turned away, and her attention was focused on collecting the pages of notes she'd been making.

He touched her arm. "You're going to do great tonight. I know the kids, and Logan and I, all appreciate the effort you're putting in for the team."

Her shoulders relaxed, dropping just the slightest. "Thank you. I appreciate that. And I'll feed Watson while you shower. There are clean towels under the sink."

The dog had been waiting patiently by the back door, and Colt let him out. He'd thrown a few things in a duffel bag before he'd left the cabin—his razor, a clean shirt, a stick of deodorant, and some dog food. He'd brought the bag in the night before, after Chloe had fallen asleep and he'd gone out to do a walk around her property and check on his truck. He'd dropped the bag by the door, his mind preoccupied with getting back to the warm woman he'd left in bed. "I can feed him if you wouldn't mind giving him some water. I think he's been drinking out of the cat's bowl," he said, unzipping the duffel and pouring some dry dog chow into a traveling dog dish.

Watson could hear the sound of food hitting a dish from a mile away and was wiggling and whining outside the back door to be let back in. Colt opened the door and smiled as the dog went right for his food. "I'll clean up the yard when I get back."

"Get back? What do you mean?"

"I was planning to come back and fix your front door after I dropped you off at school and hit the hardware store."

"But you don't have to…"

He cut her off with a kiss. "I want to," he said against her mouth, then left her in the kitchen as he headed for the shower.

Twenty minutes later, he dropped her off in front the

school. They'd seen Tina through the window next door, and she'd waved them off, mouthing that she'd take the kids to school that morning.

Chloe passed him a single gold key on a ring. "This is my spare house key. It fits the front and the back doors. And I'll pay you back for the door and any other supplies you have to buy."

"Don't worry about that now. We'll figure it out later. I'll pick you up at four."

<hr />

He didn't pick her up at four as he'd planned. In fact, nothing had gone as he'd planned that day. He'd stopped by the hardware store, and they didn't have the right size door and couldn't get it in until tomorrow. The dog must have gotten into the cat's food too because he'd hurled all over the bed of Colt's pickup when he'd stopped for gas, and Mason had called and said he needed his help on the ranch that afternoon.

He'd texted Chloe to fill her in about the door and tell her he was stuck at the ranch. He'd said his mom was coming to town to pick up Max and would be happy to drop her at her house, but she'd replied with a perfectly polite response that it was no problem and she'd find a ride with another teacher.

Vivi had told him she'd tried to find Chloe after school, but she hadn't been in her room. He had no idea if she was upset with him, or simply fine with grabbing another ride home. Sometimes he felt like he could tell exactly what she was thinking, and other times he didn't have a clue. Although it didn't take a genius to figure out she didn't like to be a burden or a bother to anyone, and she'd flat-out said he didn't have to pick her up every day.

But he liked picking her up, liked seeing her and getting a chance to hear about her day. He'd figured they could catch up on the way to practice until she'd texted him to say she'd grab a ride to the ice arena with Tina and Maddie. He couldn't win for losing today.

At least I'll see her here, he thought later that night as he sat on the bleachers at the ice arena and finished lacing up his skates. He yanked the laces so tight, he stripped the cap off the end of one and it cracked off in his hand. *Great*.

There was no reason for him to be so jumpy about seeing her. He'd just been with her that very morning, for cripes' sake. But something about her behavior that morning, the meticulously organized charts and the barest tightening of her shoulders as he'd leaned in to kiss her, had his nerves on edge, and he'd been fidgety and uneasy for the better part of the day.

He figured it probably had something to do with the day before. He knew it was too soon to thrust her into the folds of his family. They were a lot to handle, and they'd been in rare form the day before. He'd watched Chloe shrink into herself as the noise level in the room rose. He'd tried to assure her with light touches, but it took some restraint. He'd wanted to wrap his arm around her, hold her up for display, shout out to his whole family that he really liked this girl, that she was something special. But he'd figured she had enough being thrown at her, so he didn't want to come on too strong. And holding her up like a prize calf was definitely coming on too strong.

He was sure the time spent with his nutty family was why she'd wanted to come home the night before. The craziness must have got to her. Hell, it got to him sometimes too. No wonder she had a headache. And he'd tried to give her space, to leave her alone and sleep in the truck. But dammit, when she'd crawled into the cab wearing only a jersey with his name on it and a tiny pair of panties, he couldn't help himself. He had to have her.

That must be what was going on. Why she was retreating into her charts and organized schedules. He and his family must be too much for her. He should back off. Give her some room to breathe.

"Hiya, Coach," Maddie called, racing toward him. Tina sauntered along behind her, and he craned his neck around her shoulder to try to catch sight of Chloe. But she wasn't with them.

"Don't worry. She's here," Tina said, giving him a knowing smile. "She just stopped to talk to one of the parents."

He shrugged. "I wasn't worried." But he knew he wasn't fooling her. She'd known him the better part of his life, and he hadn't fooled her when he was nine and tried to sneak a snake into his room, so he was sure he wasn't getting anything past his former babysitter.

"I'm sure you weren't," Tina answered with a smirk. "Just like I'm sure she didn't blush and try to hold back a smile every time your name came up in the car on the way over here." She nudged him on the shoulder, then her face turned serious. "Chloe is a great person. She's really helped me out the past few years. She deserves a good guy."

His shoulders slumped. Chloe did deserve a good guy. He only wished he considered himself one.

"Let's get your skates on," he told Maddie as she climbed onto the bleachers next to him. She was already decked out in her pads and a faded red practice jersey that looked two sizes too big but was probably the only one available at the local thrift store. He knew her brothers hadn't played, so that was his best guess as to where the jersey came from. He'd have to see if he could find her an extra one.

She didn't seem to mind as she kicked off her shoes and pulled on her new skates. He had to admire her enthusiasm. He'd brought an extra lace puller to give to Tina and showed her how to hook the metal tool in the laces and use it to pull them as tight as possible.

When he'd finished, he stood and nonchalantly peered over the heads of a group of parents, looking for a certain petite woman. He finally spotted her. She was standing by the door talking to the goalie's parents. Her body was relaxed, her face open and pleasant as she listened intently to whatever Gordy's mom was telling her. She lifted her hand and tucked a strand of hair behind her ear.

Then she turned her head, almost as if she felt his gaze—like an invisible thread ran between them—and drew her chin toward him until she met his eyes, and her face lit with a smile. A smile just for him. And it felt like the force of a flying hockey puck hit him squarely in the chest.

It was just a smile, for frick's sake. But it lit something in his gut and squeezed at his heart the same as the vise grip he'd used to mend a gate that afternoon. This woman was tearing him up inside, and all she'd done was grin. But that one simple grin made his entire night.

Damn. He had it bad. And he hadn't realized just how anxious he'd been about seeing her tonight until that very moment—the moment she'd smiled and he'd felt like a half-ton weight had been lifted from his shoulders. He hadn't known what to expect. She'd seemed so standoffish earlier in the day. But that grin told him all he needed to know.

He stood where he was, not sure if he should go to her or let her finish her conversation. Stuffing his hands in his front pockets, he waited, trying to keep the dopey grin he felt from taking over his face.

She finally excused herself from Gordy's folks and walked toward him, the grin turning bashful as she drew closer. "Hi," she said when she got close enough.

"Hey, cupcake." He leaned down and lowered his voice so only she could hear.

Her lips curved higher, and she stood a little taller, her shoulders drawing back just the barest degree. "That's Coach Cupcake to you."

He chuckled, his hands itching to touch her, to stroke his palm down her back or tangle his fingers in her hair. Heck, he wanted to do more than stroke her back. He wanted to kiss her, good and thoroughly, until neither of them could catch their breath and they forgot where they were. But he didn't.

There were too many people around, and Creedence was too small a town for that kind of public display of affection. The last thing he wanted was for people to make assumptions about them or to start the rumor mill circulating about her. She didn't deserve that, and he didn't imagine she would appreciate it either. His truck had already been parked in front of her house all night, and he planned to park it there again tonight. He was sure that little kernel of information had spread through the gossip wire before he'd even finished his first cup of coffee that morning.

He'd been dying to see her, couldn't wait for her to come over to him, and now he couldn't thing of a dang thing to say. The woman seriously messed with his brain. "Sorry about not getting your door fixed today."

"It's fine, really. I appreciate the time you took to go down and get a new one ordered."

"It was nothing. I was happy to do it." Her smile set off something in his chest, and all he wanted to do was keep it there. And know he was the one responsible for putting it there in the first place. He gestured toward the bleachers where he'd left his things. "I've got something for you."

Her eyes widened. "For me?"

"Yeah, come on." He reached for her hand but touched her arm instead. She followed him to the bleachers where he presented her with a square box with the Bauer logo printed on the side. "I thought the assistant coach deserved a pair of her own skates." He'd known her size from the rental skates she'd been wearing.

She lifted the lid and peered in at the new white-and-black ice skates. "Gosh, they're gorgeous," she gushed. Her brow furrowed, and she tilted her head at him. "Are these from Rock? Like as part of the team budget?"

He'd let his brother have all the credit for outfitting the team, but he wasn't letting Rock get the credit for these. "Nope. These babies are just from me. And don't worry, I did my research, and these are good, solid skates. They should be comfortable and still provide great support for your ankles. And I already got them sharpened, so you'll be good to go as soon as you lace them up."

She closed the lid and pushed the box back toward him. "They're beautiful. And a really thoughtful gift. But I can't accept them. They're too much."

He held up his hands, refusing to take the box back. "Chloe, come on now. I know we haven't had the most conventional start to our relationship, but if it hadn't been for a homicidal maniac threatening you, I would have already bought you flowers and taken you out for a nice dinner and a movie, which probably would've run me about the same cost as the skates. So how about you consider taking them in lieu of our first date. They can be your first-date skates." He'd been so intent on convincing her that he hadn't realized he'd used the words "our relationship" until it was too late. But he couldn't take them back now. And he wasn't sure he wanted to.

He put his hand on the box next to hers and let his fingers graze the side of her wrist. "And if you haven't figured it out yet—I like you. And I'd like to do something nice for you. Please let me. Just accept the skates."

She peered into the box again, chewing on her bottom lip as she appeared to mull it over. Finally, she raised her eyes to meet his. "In lieu of our first date, huh? Okay, I'll accept them." An impish grin tugged at the corner of her lips, and she pulled back her shoulders and raised her chin. "But only on the condition that you'll let me treat for our second date."

He grinned, not just for the fact she was accepting the skates and her easy condition, but at the idea that she'd just suggested going out on a date with him at all. *Another* date. It seemed like a promising turn. "It's a deal."

"Good. Now go round up our team while I get these on, and let's get practice started. I've got a schedule to keep."

"Yes, ma'am."

Fifteen minutes later, they had the kids assembled and out on the ice. Logan had something else going on and couldn't make practice, but he'd promised to make it to the game on Wednesday. So for tonight, it was just Colt and Chloe. And she'd worked so hard on the schedule and drills for that night's practice, he let her take the lead.

She might not know a lot about hockey, but she knew a lot about kids. She was amazing with them, getting them set up in lines and running drills like she'd been doing it for years. Her skating was improving too. Having a good pair of skates instead of the stock rental pair had to help.

For the second part of the practice, they split the kids up. Chloe worked with the offensive lines, running them through passing and shooting drills, while Colt took the defense. Some of the kids had some obvious skills, while a few were still learning the basics. He put the red-haired twins, a.k.a. Fred and George, in charge of the drill while he took the three least experienced kids and spent some extra time working with them on their skating and building their confidence with stickhandling.

"Skate side to side," he told them, leading them around the ice. "Shift your weight, feel the edges of your skates on the ice." He tossed down pucks and had them pass to each other. "Cradle the puck. Don't send it—sail it." He nudged one of the smaller kids on the shoulder after he'd sent a beautiful pass. "That's it. Great job. You're totally getting the hang of this."

The kids finished their drill, and Colt lined them up and showed them how to shoot one-timers toward the net. He skated up to the puck and fired it toward the goal. The puck went wide and pinged off the side of the post.

Gordy ducked and turned an angry scowl to Colt. "Hey! You almost hit me with that."

Colt chuckled. "It's supposed to hit you. You're the goalie."

"I don't know if I want to be the goalie if everyone's gonna be trying to hit me all the time."

"Too late. We already bought the pads to fit you." He wasn't letting the kid get out of his responsibility that easily. He waved over all the kids and tapped a spot on the ice about fifteen feet in front of where Gordy stood in front of the net. "Hey, come over here, everybody."

He had the kids line up in a long row, all facing the goalie. Then he grabbed a bag of pucks and dumped a couple on the ice in front of each kid. "I want everybody to fire a shot at Gordy as hard as you can," he told them.

"Wait, what?" Gordy said, crouching back into the net.

"Go," he called, and the whole row of kids started whacking pucks toward the goal.

"Ah," Gordy yelled, blocking the pucks with his arm. "Cut it out." But his yelps turned to laughter as he realized the thick pads deflected the impact of the pucks. "Hey, that doesn't even hurt."

"I told you," Colt said, rounding up the pucks and sending them back to the kids. "Fire them again."

Now that Gordy's fear was gone, he twisted and turned, deflecting pucks and blocking shots as they flew toward him. Colt tapped him on the top of the helmet with his glove. "You're doing a great job, Gordy. You're gonna be an awesome goalie."

The boy's shoulders pushed back, and he stood taller in the goal. Colt looked up and caught Chloe smiling at him, and he felt like he'd already led them to their first championship game.

"Can I give you a ride home?" he asked her after practice as they were taking off their skates.

"Sure," she answered and looked like she might be going to say something else, but instead glanced up as Rock and a guy wearing jeans and a burgundy Colorado Summit jacket approached. "Hi, Rock. Max did a great job out there tonight."

"So did the two of you. You guys are quite the coaching pair. It's almost like you're made for each other," Rock said, giving his little brother a sly grin.

Nice, Bro. Real subtle.

Rock turned to the man next to him. "This is Joe Forsberg, he's the head defensive coach for the Summit. We had some business to discuss, so we met for dinner, then I dragged him to my kid's practice."

"Nice to meet you," Colt said, shaking the coach's hand, but thinking about how cool it was that his brother was adopting Max and already considered him his kid.

"Good to meet you too. I was watching you with the kids out there. You were doing a great job with them."

"Thanks. I consider that high praise coming from a coach of your status. And I didn't do much. Sometimes a kid just needs some extra attention and a little confidence-building to reassure them they play an important role on the team."

"I couldn't agree more."

They spent the next ten minutes making small talk while Rock helped Max take his skates off and get ready to go. It was cool talking to one of the coaches from his brother's NHL team, but Colt's mind kept wandering to the woman standing next to him and thinking about how soon they could get out of there and he could get her naked and into his arms.

So much for backing off.

The next afternoon, Chloe blew out a breath as she dropped her pen for the third time that day. The kids had gone home, thankfully, and she was finishing up a few things before Colt picked her up.

She'd been frazzled and out of sorts and hadn't quite been able to get it together all day. Every time she thought about Colt standing in her kitchen in his underwear, or wearing only a towel in her bathroom as he shaved, or lying naked in her bed, her brain turned to mush.

That morning, she'd come out of her bedroom to find him in the kitchen drinking coffee wearing only briefs and his cowboy boots. Her mouth went dry thinking of his muscled chest and the way he'd scooped her up and set her on the kitchen counter to kiss her good morning. A kiss that turned into him tugging off her panties and having his way with her on the counter as she wrapped her legs around his waist.

She was going to have to bleach that countertop. And come to think of it, she never did get a chance to ask him why he had on his boots.

Chloe wasn't sure why she was so unnerved today,

but little things with the kids and with her work space had unsettled her. It should have been an easy enough deduction—she'd had a hunky guy sleep over two nights in a row now, and it was disrupting her precise grip on her tidily controlled world. Which seemed ridiculous. Who in their right mind would choose tidily controlled over steaming-hot fantasy-level sex with a ridiculously handsome cowboy?

She should be over the moon with delirious happiness. And some moments she was. She'd caught herself smiling several times that day and was even humming while she graded papers over her lunch break. At times, her heart felt as light as gauze, then other times felt twisted and confused. It didn't make sense to her why a guy like him would be interested in someone like her, and her mind tried to discern reasons and put them into some kind of logic.

She was a nice person, yes. Put that in the plus column. She was thoughtful and kind and good with animals and kids. But did that make her attractive? How could being sweet to puppies and grade-schoolers make her seem alluring? Those were great qualities in a pet-sitter or a childcare worker, but did they count in the relationship department?

So, her personality counted for her, but her body fell hard into the negative column. Sure, she'd lost weight and she was more comfortable with herself— but only when she was wearing clothes. Naked and on the countertop in the kitchen was a whole other story. Every part of Colt was hard and toned, and he had muscles on top of his muscles. Her workout routine consisted of chasing after kids on the playground and running to the ladies room on her two-minute breaks during the day.

Colt was outgoing and funny and so easy to be around. Everyone liked him. He had tons of friends. She was shy and introverted and had to have everything in her life just so, or it would make her twitchy. And her best friend was a cat. And that was touch and go, depending on Agatha's mood and if Chloe had just opened a can of food. How could she and Colt be any kind of a match?

And what could Colt possibly see in her? His and Logan's comments about Colt saving her snuck back into her thoughts. Did he still see her as a wounded sparrow? As someone to save?

He was staying over every night, and he made it seem like it was to protect her from Rank, but it had to be more. Their relationship and their comfort level with each other had grown. She'd grown. With each day spent with him, she'd stepped further and further out of her comfy organized box.

And over the last several days, she had discovered a new facet to her personality and found she could be quite the wanton lust-bunny in the bedroom. Maybe it was because in her heart, she knew this was all temporary—that a guy like Colt would never stick around so she was going for broke and having wild and reckless sex while she had the chance.

A grin stole across her face. The idea that she would ever use the words *wild and reckless* to describe anything in her life seemed outlandish and bizarre, which was probably the exact kind of business that was throwing her body and mind into turmoil.

Focus. Take a breath. Take care of one task at a time. Breathe.

She continued her litany of self-talk as she collected the pages she needed to copy for tomorrow's lessons and headed for the teachers' lounge. She could do this. She was the master of keeping her life under strict control.

Except where did a six-foot-four half-naked cowboy drinking coffee in my kitchen fall under anything resembling control? Distracted again, she felt the file folder slip from her hands, and the papers scattered across the floor. She bent to retrieve the papers, and her hand froze on one of the pages as she heard laughter and her name spoken in a derisive tone by another teacher in the lounge.

Chapter 19

CHLOE RECOGNIZED THE NASALLY VOICE OF JOYCE Ledbetter, David's fourth-grade teacher—the one who had assigned him a book report without making sure he had access to a book. She'd been wanting to tell Joyce what she thought of that stupid idea, but hadn't seen the other teacher. Maybe now was her chance. And maybe she could draw on her newfound bravery. Except boldness in the bedroom didn't exactly equate to courage in confrontations.

Still. She could do this. For David. And for herself.

She drew in a breath, then let it out in a rush when she heard Joyce mention Colt's name.

"I'm telling you," Joyce was saying. "I saw Chloe get out of his truck."

"Are you sure it was Colt James?" The other voice scoffed. It belonged to Jane Hoffman, the music teacher. Jane was still in her first year of teaching and had always been kind to Chloe. Until now, apparently.

"As sure as I'm standing here. And it isn't the first time I've seen him drop her off."

"Maybe he was just giving her a ride. They could be friends, you know."

Joyce gave a haughty snort. "Yeah right. As far as I've seen, Miss Perfect doesn't have any of those." She lowered her voice, and Chloe leaned toward the door, tears pricking the backs of her eyes, her courage seeping out of her like air from an old balloon. She should leave, back away, stop listening, but she couldn't.

"They didn't look like *just friends* to me," Joyce continued. "Not the way he had his arm around her shoulder as he tried to kiss her."

"Wait. You saw him kiss her?"

"I saw him *try* to kiss her. But she turned away."

"What? No way. Now I know you've got your story wrong. Why would anyone turn away from a kiss from Colt James? That guy is seriously hot."

"Precisely my point."

"There must be something more going on."

"Oh, I'm sure of it. Although I can't figure out what. And I've been racking my brain trying to figure out what he could see in her."

"Oh, come on. Chloe is nice."

"You say nice, I say boring. That woman is total dullsville. And besides, *nice* doesn't get guys like Colt James."

Chloe let out a shuddering breath. She had to get out of there. Sure, Joyce was being a total witch, but her words carried a ring of truth to them. All the wicked things she'd said were confirming Chloe's own thoughts about herself. She *was* boring and dull, and there was no reason for Colt to be interested in her. Everything Joyce had said was true. And even though Chloe had just been cataloging her faults to herself, hearing them from someone else—a colleague, no less—had every word stinging like tiny sharp daggers to her heart.

She sank against the wall, the papers no longer a concern as she wrapped her arms around her stomach in an effort to hold herself together, afraid if she didn't, her body would fall apart, and her broken heart would leak onto the stained linoleum floor.

Chloe pressed her hand to her chest, willing her rapidly beating heart to slow down. What if she had a heart attack? Right here—on the floor outside the teachers' lounge? It would serve those nasty gossips right.

As appealing as a revenge heart attack sounded, Chloe would prefer to simply melt into the floor and disappear. Dipping her chin to her chest, she buried her face in her hands.

"Chloe? You all right, darlin'?" a deep voice asked.

She shook her head. *Seriously?* Could Colt have picked a worse moment to come around the hallway corner—just in time to see her huddled on the floor, burning with shame? She squeezed her eyes shut, attempting to gain her composure and trying to ignore the sudden hush in the teachers' lounge followed by an embarrassed giggle.

Gathering the fallen papers, she pasted on a smile and gave an Oscar-worthy show of pretending everything was okay. "Of course, I'm fine. I just dropped my papers."

"Let me help you," he said, reaching down to capture a loose page and hand it to her.

"I've got it," she answered, brusquer than she'd meant to sound. "I just needed to make some copies before I finish up for the day."

"Sure, no problem. Although I am anxious to get you home. I've got a big surprise for you."

A short burst of laughter came from the lounge followed by a shushing sound, and heat flamed Chloe's cheeks as Colt walked into the lounge before she could stop him. Tempted to turn tail and run, she instead let out a sigh, then held her chin up and followed him in. Her coworkers might have guessed she'd heard them, but no way would she let on that their words bothered her.

"Ladies," Colt said, tipping his cowboy hat as he crossed to the copy machine.

"Hi, Colt," Joyce replied, casually leaning her hip against the side of a chair. "What's new?"

"Not much. You?"

Chloe pushed her stack of papers into the tray on the copier and hastily punched the buttons to make thirty copies.

"Nothin' new or exciting with me. But did I just hear you say you had a big surprise for our friend, Miss Bishop, here? Do tell."

Our friend? A minute ago, she'd said she didn't think Chloe had any friends. Now suddenly, she was claiming to be one. The nerve of this woman.

"Did I say that?" He was teasing her, and she was eating it up.

Gag. Chloe grabbed the warm finished copies from the machine. "All done. Let's go."

"You don't need to rush out on our account," Joyce said, her voice saccharine sweet. "We want to hear all about this surprise." She raised her hand and pointed back and forth between them. "I hadn't realized you two knew each other."

A secret part of Chloe—the small part that was occasionally brave and snarky and confident—wanted to slide her arm around Colt's waist and flippantly state she and Colt had been shagging their brains out for days now. But of course, she didn't. Because the realistic part of her—the sane, responsible part—knew that was a bad idea and would only come back to bite her in her smart-alecky behind. So instead, she kept her lips pressed together and tried to smile as she let Colt field the question.

"Oh yeah, we've been friends for a while now," he said. "And Chloe...er...Miss Bishop is helping me coach the eight-and-unders hockey team."

"Oh, we thought we saw you drop her off at school a couple of times," Jane interjected.

So much for her being the sweet one. She was just as nosy as Joyce. Not quite as obnoxious about it, but still just as nosy.

"Yeah, her car's been in the shop so I've been giving her a ride."

Joyce narrowed her eyes at Chloe. "A hockey coach, huh? I didn't realize you knew so much about hockey."

Chloe pushed back her shoulders—she did have a little pride left, dang it. "There are quite a lot of things you don't know about me, Joyce." She turned to Colt, flashing him what she hoped was her most dazzling smile. "Shall we go? I can't wait to see this surprise you have for me."

"Yep." He tilted his hat once more, then followed her out.

They didn't say anything else as they walked back to her room, collected her things, and headed for his truck.

"You want to tell me what that was all about?" he finally said when they'd buckled in and headed toward her house.

"What do you mean?" she asked, trying to keep up the feigned innocence act.

"I mean that little scene in the teachers' lounge."

She let out a heavy sigh. "Oh, you mean the one where I walked up and overheard Jane, the music teacher who I had thought was my friend, and Miss Nosy-Nellie Joyce, who is apparently a mean-spirited witch, gossiping about me and a certain cowboy who has been dropping me off at school and contemplating how such an amazingly hot guy could have any interest in someone as dull and boring as me?"

"Ouch. That sounds terrible. But on the positive side, did they really say I was amazingly hot?" He gave her a teasing grin.

She answered with a hard glare.

"Too soon?" He chuckled as he turned the corner.

She held her glare.

"You know I'm just teasing you. And that had to be rough. But seriously, who cares what they think?"

"I care. I have to work with them every day."

"So what? They were obviously just being petty and jealous. You want me to go back and set them straight? Tell them how it really is?"

"You already did that. You very cleared explained that we were just friends, and you were only dropping me off at school because my car broke down." She tried to keep the anger out of her voice but failed. Miserably.

He drew his head back, and his brow furrowed in confusion. "I thought I was helping. I was trying to protect your reputation."

"My reputation?" She shook her head, trying to understand what he meant. "As what? A dull spinster who couldn't possibly get a man, and especially not one of your caliber? Well, you did a great job there. Now they know for sure that's true."

He pulled up in front of her house, cut the engine, and turned to look at her. His teasing tone softened. "Hey, come on now, are you really upset about this thing?"

She crossed her arms over her chest. "Of course I'm upset. I overhear two gossips talking about how I couldn't possibly have someone as good-looking as you interested in someone as dull and boring as me. Then you confirm their suspicions by telling them you're only hanging out with me because we coach a hockey team together and you're doing me a favor because I don't have a car."

"Chloe, I'm sorry. I wasn't trying to upset you. I really was trying to protect you. This town is full of gossips and folks who don't have anything better to do than talk about other people, and I was trying to keep you from becoming the center of one of those rumors. I'm not ashamed of you or us, but I do feel like what's happening with us is still pretty new. I thought it was better to keep it just between us until we figured out what we wanted it to be first."

What he was saying made sense, and she wanted to believe him. But there was still a part of her that had to wonder if that was all an excuse, a well-spoken justification for not telling anyone they were involved. She stared into her lap and used the edge of her fingernail to scrape at a spot of dried glue on her thigh. It somehow seemed significant that a cute guy was rationalizing his reasons for not telling other people he was involved with her while she was trying to scratch a chunk of craft glue and some glitter off her jeans.

He reached over and touched her chin, turning her head to face him. "Chloe, don't let those women get to you. They don't even matter. You are beautiful—inside *and* out. And anyone who sees us together knows the truth—that you're the pretty one who is way too good for a chump like me."

Tears burned her eyes, but she blinked them back. Was he serious? His words were sweet but totally untrue. She didn't know how to respond, how to argue without it turning into a contest of who could flatter the other one more. And she didn't want to go there because she knew she'd eventually lose. "You're not a chump" was all she could manage to say.

He grinned. "There are a whole passel of people who would line up to disagree with you. And my brothers would probably be the ones forming the line."

She studied his face. He was grinning like he was teasing, but there was true pain hidden in his eyes. How did they even get to this place in their conversation? And how could she get them out of it? Her head was pounding from the whole crazy afternoon, and she just wanted to go into her tidy little home and have a hot cup of tea and quit talking about who was the better catch.

"Did you say something about having a surprise for me?" She couldn't imagine what it could be. Well, she *could* imagine. She could imagine a lot of things and could probably be persuaded to forgo a cup of tea in favor of a cup of cowboy, but he didn't act like that's what the surprise had to do with.

As he jumped out of the truck and came around to get her door, the smile on his face was more like an excited kid who couldn't wait for someone to open his hand-made Christmas gift. "I thought of it while I was fixing your door and spent the better part of the day trying to get it ready for you."

He led her up the path, and she gasped as she caught sight of her new front door. Her last door had been scarred and battered and made from pressed wood. This door was gorgeous and changed the whole look of the front of her house. "It's beautiful."

He unlocked the shiny new brass doorknob, then passed her the key. "I installed the door and put in new locks and a dead bolt."

She ran her hand over the beautiful oak and marveled at the intricately designed stained-glass window in the center. It was lovely, and most certainly out of her price range for home repairs. "This is so wonderful, but it's too much. I can't afford this."

"Sure you can. I got a great deal on it."

"I can't imagine any kind of deal that would put this kind of door into my budget."

"Really, Gus barely charged me anything," Colt insisted, referring to the owner of the hardware store. "He got it for a song, then gave it to me at cost."

She arched her eyebrow. "Let me guess—he owed you a favor?"

Colt shrugged. "Something like that."

Somehow, she knew arguing with him would get her nowhere, and he seemed so excited about the new door that she didn't want to ruin it by arguing over the price. "Well, this really is a great surprise. I love it."

His face broke into an even more excited grin. "Oh, this isn't even the surprise." He took her purse and tote bag from her and set them on the bench inside the door, then closed it behind her. "Follow me." He led her through the living room and into the kitchen.

Everything looked the same as she'd left it that

morning, perfectly neat and all her things in their place. He opened the door to the garage and flipped the light switch. A proud smile beamed from his face as he waved his hand toward the center of the room. "Ta-da!"

The garage was her weakness—the one messy out-of-control spot in her house, a good tip-off that whatever he had to show her wasn't in the sexy category. Not unless he was going to strip down to just a tool belt.

A spark of heat coursed down her back at the mental image. But the spark fizzled and died as she stepped through the door and into the sparkling-clean garage.

The dusty recliner and the heaps of boxes filled with the remnants of her father's life were gone, and the remaining cartons were stacked neatly against the side wall. The floor had been swept clean, and her car sat in the center of the room, the crumpled door repaired, the new paint job gleaming in the overhead light.

She pressed her hand to her stomach and gasped again. But this time is wasn't from delight. Not even close. "What have you done?" she cried.

His excited expression crumpled. "What do you mean?"

"I mean, what have you done? What happened to my dad's stuff?"

"I took it to the thrift store."

"You did what?"

"Don't worry, I only took the boxes that were clearly marked to be donated. Then I stacked and organized the others against the wall so you'd have room to park in here."

"Who said you could do that?"

He rubbed his hand across the back of his neck. "I guess I thought you did. You told me more than once that you wanted to get rid of all those boxes in the garage, but you just haven't had the time or the means to do it."

"So, you thought you'd do it for me?" Chloe could hear her voice rising to a near-shrieking volume.

"Yeah, I was trying to help. Justin called to tell me your car was finished, so I picked it up this afternoon and figured I'd clean out the garage to give you a safe and dry place to park it. I wanted to surprise you." Colt glanced around the room as if looking for answers. "I don't get it. I thought you'd be happy."

"Well, that's what you get for thinking," she snapped.

His head jerked back like she'd physically slapped him.

She didn't care. This, combined with the events of the last week, swirled around her, twisting and roiling in her gut. Nausea churned inside her, and she swallowed at the bile burning the back of her throat. Who did he think he was, touching her things, organizing her space, throwing away her belongings?

Those things were her barometer, the catalyst that would finally let her prove to herself that her father no longer controlled her. She knew that when she finally let go of his things, she would let go of him and the hold he had over her. That she would be free.

Getting rid of the stuff was her final hurdle to proving she was courageous enough to live her own life. And now Colt, another man, had taken that away from her.

So many things had changed in her life this last week. Her whole reality felt altered and distorted. She craved control, routine. Her life was a set of carefully managed schedules. And this man had come crashing in and changed everything. She was going to bed at erratic times, eating differently, changing her shower routine to accommodate another person in the bathroom. Being with him was changing everything—from sharing her bed with someone else to her coworkers laughing at her and mocking her behind her back.

This was all too much, and she couldn't take it. "You had no right to come in and take my things. I barely know you. Do you think just because we're sleeping together you have the right to do whatever you want?"

He shook his head. "No, of course not. I was trying to help, to do something nice for you."

"Something nice would be picking up a pizza. This is too much. This is crossing a line. Before I met you, I had a perfectly controlled life. I knew what to expect and how my day, my week, would go, and now you're here and everything is changing. I'm changing. My routines are changing. You're messing everything up, and I can't handle it." All the anger and frustration and feelings of inadequacy of the past week whirled together as if in an emotional spin cycle. Her voice was shaking, and she clasped her hands together to keep them from trembling.

He flinched, then gave a slow, disbelieving head-shake. "Well, gosh, I'm sorry, Chloe. I sure as hell didn't mean to mess your entire life up. Here I thought I was doing you a favor."

"Like you do for everyone else?" His sarcasm wasn't lost on her, but she was mired too far into her own self-righteousness to back down now. "Is that how you see me? As one of your charity cases? Poor little Chloe, a wounded sparrow, how sad she doesn't have anyone in her life. Maybe I'll throw her a bone, pay a little attention to her, try to save her from her pathetic life."

He took a step back. "What the hell are you talkin' about? How could I possibly see you as a charity case? You honestly think I've been with you the past week because I feel *sorry* for you?"

She crossed her arms, her indignation like a ball of fire burning and raging in her chest. "I honestly have no idea why you've been with me."

The hurt expression on his face changed to one of frustration mixed with anger. "I guess that makes two of us." He shook his head as he strode out of the garage.

Chloe held herself tighter, pressing her lips together as she listened to his bootheels stomp across her kitchen floor. She waited until the front door slammed before she let the sob escape her as she crumpled to the neatly swept floor of the garage.

Chloe turned off the water and reached for a towel. She'd spent the last several hours power-cleaning her house, and her back and knees ached from the effort. The hot shower had felt good on her muscles, but had done nothing to soothe the ache in her heart.

She finished drying off, then dropped the damp towel and pulled on her robe. The warm steam had filled the room, and she was glad the condensation covered the mirror so she didn't have to face herself. Leaving her hair on top of her head in a messy bun, she washed her face and brushed her teeth. It wasn't quite six o'clock, but she considered crawling into bed anyway and trying to sleep off this awful day.

What a horrible person she'd been to Colt. She couldn't believe the things she'd said. He didn't deserve that. He'd only been trying to help. And she *had* told him she wanted to take those boxes to Goodwill—had very emphatically explained there was nothing in them she wanted, and they were only taking up space in an otherwise functional space.

She hadn't told him the stuff was important. In fact, she'd made a point of acting like it wasn't. So why wouldn't he think he was helping by getting rid of it?

Now he probably thought she was crazy. She'd acted completely out of character. She should have just taken a deep breath and explained why she was so upset.

Why did she freak out on the one man she'd been dreaming about for months and had finally been given a chance to be with?

Because she knew it wouldn't last, knew there was no possible way it could be real? Because some desperate part of her figured if she pushed him away first, it would be easier than having him leave her later?

I'm such a fool.

He hadn't pushed her away. He'd done something nice. And she'd wrecked it—wrecked everything.

The doorbell rang, and her heart lifted in hopes it was him. She raced down the hallway, the words of her apology and explanation already on her tongue.

She didn't even think as she grabbed the doorknob and yanked the door open.

But it wasn't Colt standing on her doorstep.

Chapter 20

"WHAT ARE YOU DOING HERE?" CHLOE'S BROW FURROWED as she stared at the two women standing on her doorstep.

Quinn raised an eyebrow. "We're here to pick you up for our girls' night out. I know we're a little early, but geez, quit looking at us like we've got religious pamphlets in our hands and we're here to save you."

"We *are* here to save her," Tess piped in, then winked at Chloe. "Save you from that hideous bathrobe and a boring night spent at home."

"True," Quinn agreed. "And you look like you could use a little saving. Why the long face?" She and Tess walked across the fresh vacuum tracks and plopped themselves onto the sofa.

Chloe cinched the belt of her apparently hideous bathrobe and followed them in. She'd totally forgotten about girls' night out. How was she going to get out of this? And dang it, why did everyone think she needed saving? "I don't know if I feel up for going out tonight. I've had a pretty rough day."

Agatha wandered by the sofa, and Tess pulled her into her lap and stroked her back. "Margs and girl time is the perfect antidote to fix up a rough day."

Somehow, Chloe didn't think a margarita would be the best remedy for what ailed her.

Quinn patted the seat next to her. "What's up,

buttercup? Come over here, and tell us all about it. You look like you lost your best friend today."

She might as well have. Emotions swelled in her throat, and she bit down on her lip to keep from crying.

"Uh-oh." Quinn's teasing grin turned to dismay. "You really did have a bad day. What happened? Do you want to talk about it?"

Chloe shook her head. "Not really." What she really wanted was to crawl under the covers and pretend this day hadn't happened.

Quinn pushed up from the sofa. "Okay, we don't have to talk about it, but we *are* going to feed you and make you laugh."

Chloe looked down at herself. "I just got out of the shower, and I'm a mess. Really, you all should just go on without me."

"Ha," Tess blurted. "Have you met Quinn James? She takes her girls' night out seriously, and she doesn't take no for an answer."

"That's right," Quinn said. "And your hair looks amazing—like you styled it that way on purpose." She pointed to her watch. "Happy hour ends in one hour, so you have fifteen minutes to put on some clothes and a swipe of mascara. We'd offer to clean up or wash the dishes for you or something, but obviously you're a stress cleaner, because I don't see a speck of dirt in your whole house. Lord almighty, girl, dust bunnies must be terrified to show up around here."

Chloe twisted the belt of her robe in her hands. "I don't know…"

Quinn tapped her watch again. "Clock's ticking. Better hurry up. If you take too long, Tess and I are going to start messing up the place. Surely we can find some dirt to track in here, or we might even mix up your spice cabinet. I haven't seen it, but I'm sure it's alphabetized. If you're not out here ready to go in fifteen, your cumin is getting switched with your oregano, and all hell is going to break loose."

A grin tugged at the corners of Chloe's mouth. Maybe a night out with friends would help. If nothing other than to prove she did have friends. And to save her spice cabinet. She shivered at the thought of Quinn moving her cumin. "Fine. I'll get dressed. Keep your hands off my oregano."

"Fourteen minutes now. Chop. Chop."

She heard them laugh as she raced down the hallway to get dressed.

―――――

Thirty minutes and two swipes of mascara later, the waitress set frosty salt-rimmed glasses down in front of the three women.

Something about being with these women, feeling accepted for just being herself, gave Chloe a much-needed boost of assurance, and she hadn't even balked when Tess ordered a round of margaritas for the table.

Quinn raised her glass. "A toast. To friends and sharing good days and laughing off the bad ones."

"Cheers." Chloe clinked her glass against Tess and Quinn's. "And to keeping my spice rack intact."

They laughed and ordered tacos and munched on salty tortilla chips. Rock had offered to drive them all home later so they didn't have to worry about how many drinks they had, and by the second round, Chloe was laughing and for a few minutes had almost forgotten what a horrible person she'd been to Colt earlier.

The other women were funny and sweet and liberally shared their problems and offered each other advice and commiseration. Tess had just told them about an annoying and condescending coworker, and Quinn had offered to send Rock down to punch him in the throat.

"Thanks for the offer, but since I *am* a writer, I'd rather slay him with my sharp wit and cunning wordplay."

Quinn tapped the side of her head. "Smart." She tipped her glass toward Chloe. "All right, it's your turn. You've had food and almost two drinks. It's time to tell us what's eating you. I have a feeling it has something to do with my handsome brother-in-law." She turned to Tess. "Well, *one* of my handsome brothers-in-law."

Tess nodded. "After last Sunday at Vivi's, it's obvious the two of you spent some *quality time* together. Did you all have an argument or something?"

"More than an argument. I chased him away, and I'm sure he's gone for good." Chloe let out a sigh. Maybe it would help to talk about it. She'd never really had girlfriends before, yet she felt she could trust these women. Like they really cared about her.

Interesting how I can accept they like me but have such a hard time understanding that Colt does.

The thought of Colt had her throat burning again, and she knocked back the rest of her drink, then told them about her flustercluck of a day. She told them about her coworkers making fun of her and about her insecurities with Colt and how she couldn't comprehend what he saw in her. They listened and commiserated and made her laugh but never judged her or made her feel less about herself.

She shared a little about growing up chubby and her struggles with control and her routines. And she told them how her need for routine and organization had got the best of her and how she'd lost her skittles with Colt earlier that day and how he'd walked out. She didn't go into details about the symbolism of her father's things. She liked these women and wasn't ready for them to think she was a total looney ball.

"I've seen the way Colt looks at you *and* heard how he talks about you. Like 'constantly' doesn't begin to describe it," Quinn told her. "And he has for months. I know the guy really likes you. Just because you got in a fight doesn't mean he's gone for good."

"I agree. On all accounts. We've all seen how smitten he is with you. And I don't think the James men give up on something they want that easily." Tess set her hand on Chloe's. "Honey, you're not giving yourself enough credit. And you're holding on to way too many old issues. You don't have to be that insecure little girl anymore. You are a beautiful woman who went to college, who earned a degree, who has a successful career and takes care of and educates this town's children."

Chloe shook her head. "I'm not insecure about my value as a teacher. I know I'm good with kids. I'm also a darn good knitter and can bake an excellent quiche. But none of those things make me good girlfriend material. They just make me a proficient spinster."

"Stop it. You've got to quit putting yourself down. Tess is right. You're gorgeous, and everyone who meets you loves you. And so what if you're a little curvy? Men love curves. You need to own them. You've got a great hourglass figure."

"Yeah, except I've got a little too much sand." She laughed. These women were good for her soul. She was feeling a little better and wasn't sure if it was the camaraderie or the buzz from that second margarita.

"Seriously, Chloe. You need to believe that you're worthy of catching a guy like Colt. Heck, any guy for that matter." Quinn gazed around the bar. "I think we should do a poll of all the men in here, just to prove you are every bit as gorgeous as we say you are."

"Don't you dare," she ordered.

"Oh, I do dare." Quinn stood up on her chair and lifted her fingers to her mouth to let out a whistle. Apparently the margaritas were making her fairly feisty as well.

Chloe grabbed her arm and pulled her back into her chair.

Quinn plopped down in her seat but narrowed her eyes at Chloe. "This is for your own good. I want you to believe in yourself. But, I will let go of the bar poll idea on one condition. You have to pick one person in this bar and ask them to dance."

"Okay." She turned to Tess and smiled. "Tess, will you dance with me?"

Quinn waved her hands like a referee calling "no goal." "No way. It has to be a man. You have to pick someone in this bar, *and* he has to be under sixty years old. No fair asking old Doc Saunders to dance." She nodded toward the eightysomething-year-old man sitting at the end of the bar enjoying his weekly Taco Tuesday night out with his bride of sixty years.

Rats. He was going to be her next idea. Chloe scanned

the rest of the people in the bar, hoping for another out that would still satisfy Quinn's conditions. An evil grin pulled at her lips as she spied a familiar muscled physique playing darts.

"Fine. If I can get one man in this bar to agree to dance with me, then you'll leave me alone?"

Quinn nodded. "But he has to be under eighty, remember? And older than eighteen," she tossed in, although there weren't any kids in the place at the moment. "And you have to stay out there for the whole song."

"No way. You said one condition. All I have to do is get him to agree and to go out on the dance floor. You didn't say how long we had to stay."

"She has a point," Tess agreed, then pulled a ten-dollar bill from her pocket and plunked it on the table. "Go for it, Chloe. My money's on you."

She waved the money away. She wasn't about to take it, not with knowing she had an unfair advantage and was already planning to sneak one by Quinn. Crossing the bar, she approached the man playing darts. "Hey, Huge." *Oh crud*. She cough-laughed into her hand, trying to act like she had something stuck in her throat.

The gym teacher didn't seem to notice as his eyes lit with recognition. "Hi there, Chloe. I don't usually see you out on Taco Tuesday."

"It's my first time. But the tacos were great." She glanced back to where Quinn and Tessa were watching her from the bar.

"Do it," Quinn mouthed.

"Hey, listen," she said, turning back to Hugh. "I know it's kind of silly, but my friends dared me to ask you to dance. Would you be a pal and indulge me? Just for like half a song?"

His lips curved into a wolfish grin. "Your friends dared you, huh?"

Uh-oh. Maybe this wasn't such a great idea. "No, really. This is just to prove a point."

"Yeah, sure, whatever you say, Chloe. I'll bite." He waggled his eyebrows.

Ugh. It wasn't too late to back out. Although what could Quinn do? She wouldn't really ask every man in the whole restaurant if he thought she was pretty or not. She glanced back at Quinn. Shiznuggets. Yeah, she would. She wouldn't put anything past that woman.

Hugh grabbed Chloe's hand and pulled her toward the dance floor, spinning her into his arms just as a fast country song came on the jukebox.

Thank goodness for small favors. Not that she was any good at dancing to any kind of music, but at least she didn't have to endure an entire slow song of being trapped in Hugh's embrace. That would have been about three and half minutes longer than she could handle.

She figured she could put up with this for about sixty seconds as Hugh spun her under his arm and wheeled her around the dance floor. He was actually a pretty good dancer. Come to think of it, she remembered now that he had spent a week or two last spring teaching the fifth graders some basic dancing skills during their gym class.

His hand rested on her hip and guided her movements using slight pressure to lead her left or right. She let out a laugh as he spun her again and landed her in the cradle of his right arm. The song was ending, and he gave her a last spin that finished in a dip.

He followed her down with his head, and she tensed as she feared he was going to try to kiss her, but instead he leaned close to her ear and whispered, "Tell your friends thanks for the dance."

He kept his arm around her as he pulled her back up and brought her face-to-face with Colt.

She shrugged out of Hugh's arm. "Colt, hi. I didn't know you'd be here."

He leveled a cool stare at her, his lips drawn tightly together. "Obviously," he said through gritted teeth, then turned his back and strode toward the door.

"Wait, Colt." She ran after him and caught him just as he started to open the door. "I'm glad you're here."

He jerked back and hit her with another steely glare. "Why are you glad? Were you hoping I'd catch you dancing with Huge? What is this, just another calculated move in whatever game you're playing?"

His words hit her like a slap to the face. "Game? I'm not playing any game. And I was only dancing with Hugh because Quinn dared me to."

"Sure. That sounds like a reasonable excuse."

"It's not an excuse. I wasn't even planning to come out tonight. I only did because Quinn and Tess made me."

"Gosh, it sounds like you aren't able to stand up to anyone tonight. Although you were doing a pretty great job earlier this afternoon with me."

"That's what I'm trying to talk to you about. I wanted to apologize. I was completely out of line. And I'm sorry."

He stared at her a moment longer, then let out his breath and relaxed the tension in his shoulders. "I'm sorry too. I never would have done that if I'd thought it would make you upset. I swear I was only trying to help."

"I know you were. I just had a really bad day, and I was taking it out on you."

"I'm well aware of that fact. But why didn't you call me or send me a text if you wanted to talk?" Apparently, he wasn't totally ready to let it go. "And why would Quinn dare you to dance with someone? She knows how I feel about you."

Chloe swallowed. He was being honest, or had at least just declared that he had feelings for her. Maybe she should be honest with him. "She was trying to prove a point to me."

He narrowed his eyes. "What kind of point?"

She stared at the floor, unable to meet his eyes. "A stupid one. I told her how my coworkers were laughing at me today, and she was trying to convince me it didn't matter, I guess."

"This again?" He huffed. "I told you those women don't matter."

Before she had a chance to reply, the door of the restaurant opened, and two women walked in, one a gorgeous blond whose face lit up when she saw Colt.

"Colton James," she cried before launching herself into his arms. "I didn't know you'd be here tonight."

"Hey, Ash. I didn't know I would be either, but Dale had his regular guy call in sick and needed someone to cover the bar for the next few hours." He gave her a quick hug then tried to peel himself away, but she was clinging to him like a spider monkey.

She gave Chloe a contemptuous glance. "Sorry. Are we blocking your way? We're old friends and haven't seen each other in a long time."

That's awesome. Any self-confidence she might have

gained from talking to Quinn and Tess flowed out of Chloe like water flushed down a toilet. This beautiful woman assumed she was trying to leave the restaurant instead of even considering she was standing there having a conversation with Colt.

"I was actually talking to Colt," she said, trying to sound bold, but coming off flat.

The other woman brought her hand to her mouth in a coy gesture. "Oops. My bad."

"Chloe, this is Ashley. She's an old friend."

Ashley playfully slugged him in the gut, still not letting him go, her arm tucked possessively around his waist. "Old friend? Seriously? I'm his old *girlfriend*. And you know they say you never get over your first love."

"You sure did," he muttered, not quite under his breath.

Ashley laughed a little too loudly. "Oh, Colt, still hilarious."

"What are you doing in town?"

"I'm back for good this time. Mom needs me to help run the shop, and I'm tired of the scene in LA, so I agreed to come home." She looked up at him and tenderly touched the side of his cheek. "It's really so great to see you. I should get over to my table, but I'll come keep you company at the bar in a bit. We can catch up."

His expression softened just a little as he gazed down at her. "Sure. I'll see you later."

She gave him one last squeeze, and Chloe's heart twisted as she realized how well the two of them fit together. They had a shared history that would always belong to them. Colt had told her about Ashley, how serious they'd been and how he'd pushed her away after the accident. *And* how she'd broken his heart when she'd left him.

But now she was back. For good, she'd said. And obviously still interested in Colt.

And from the affectionate look he'd just given her, it didn't appear he was completely over her either.

Who was she kidding? This whole idea that she could have a future with Colt James was an exercise in futility. Seeing him standing there with Ashley brought it home to her in stark, clear color that he was completely out of her league, and he deserved someone as beautiful as he was. Someone like Ashley, not like her.

The door swung open again, and Rock stepped into the restaurant, accompanied by a burst of cold wind as icy as the feeling in Chloe's heart.

"Hey, guys," he said, seemingly oblivious to the tension between them. "I'm here to provide taxi service to the party girls."

Quinn and Tess, who had been casually waiting at the table to give her and Colt space to talk, came walking up. Quinn leaned in and snuggled against Rock's side. "Thanks for picking us up, babe."

"Of course. I've been considering a job as an Uber driver when I retire from hockey, and this gives me some good practice."

"Sure you have."

"Hey, I just got married, and having a family costs a lot of money. Especially my new wife. She's always racking up charges on my account like Taco Tuesday night with the girls."

"Another crack like that, and I'll be racking up more than your charges," Quinn teased.

He grinned down at her, obviously enjoying her sassy talk. "I'm just kidding. Put your meals and drinks for the night on my tab."

"Oh, I already did."

He chuckled. "Nice. Are you all ready to go? Rock's Uber Service is leaving the station. But just so you know, I'm charging you all extra if anyone barfs in my car."

"We've each had two drinks. I don't think you have to worry," Tess told him. She handed Chloe her purse and lowered her voice. "Are you ready to go, or do you want us to wait a little bit so you all can finish your conversation?"

Chloe shook her head. "No, I'm ready to go. I don't think there is anything left to say." She turned to the door, avoiding Colt's eye, knowing if she looked at him, her steely resolve would melt faster than a Popsicle in the hot sun.

Thirty minutes later, Chloe had changed into her pajamas and performed her nightly rituals with a vengeance. Her cheeks stung from scrubbing them so hard.

She wandered through the house, checking the locks and peering through the front windows, both hoping and dreading she would see Colt's pickup parked on the street. But so far, the street was empty. She'd turned away and taken two steps down the hall when she heard the familiar rumble of a truck engine. Her heart leapt to her throat as she hurried back to the window and peered through the curtain.

But it wasn't Colt's truck at the curb. And it wasn't his tall, lean body walking toward her door.

Chapter 21

CHLOE HURRIED TO THE FRONT DOOR AND FLUNG IT OPEN. This felt like déjà vu of a few hours earlier. "What are you doing here?"

"I'm asking myself the same question," Logan said, suppressing a yawn behind his hand. "I was already tucked in bed when I got a call from Colt telling me I needed to grab my toothbrush and spend the night on your sofa."

"What? Why?" She was horrified Colt had gotten Logan out of bed and sent him into town for her.

Logan walked past her and dropped a small duffel bag onto the bench inside the door. He sank down next to it and pulled off his boots. "Because Rank Johnson is still on the loose. And Colt can't make it himself, so he sent me in his place."

"Oh Mylanta. You didn't have to come all the way over here. I can take care of myself." Once again, Colt had stepped over the line and crossed into her perfectly balanced territory in order to do something nice for her. "This is humiliating."

Logan shrugged out of his coat and pulled her into a hug. "Hey, I'm just joking around. I was glad to come. Colt's my best friend, and I would do anything for the guy. And he'd do the same for me. And you're my friend too. So don't worry about it. This isn't a big deal." He pulled back and peered down at her. "Neither of us are going to let anything happen to you."

How could she argue with that? And it didn't matter if she did have an argument. He'd never let her win.

"You don't have to sleep on the sofa. I have a guest room with an actual bed. Agatha usually sleeps in there, but she'll share."

Logan cocked an eyebrow. "Who is this Agatha creature, and is she single? Or more importantly, does she hog the bed or steal the covers?"

"Yes, she does hog the bed. And she *is* an actual creature. Agatha is my cat. And I was just teasing. I can keep her in my room."

He shrugged. "It's okay. I don't mind a little feline company." He offered her a grin, and she couldn't tell if he meant the line to be dirty or if her mind was just in the too-much-sex-on-the-brain-lately gutter.

But after two margaritas and the emotional night she'd had, she couldn't find it in her to care. "Come on. I'll show you to your room." She led him down the hall and pointed to the guest room. "Sheets are clean. Bathroom's across the way. My room's at the end of the hall. I'll scream if I need you."

"You're funny."

"I'm not sure I was trying to be. I *will* scream if I need you."

"Okay. I'll probably get up a couple of times in the night, just to check things out. I'll try not to wake you."

At this point, she wasn't sure a freight train barreling through her bedroom could wake her. She put a hand on his arm. "Thank you, Logan. I appreciate you being here." Her heart ached at the thought of Colt not being here, and she could only let herself think that it was because he was either too mad or had to work late at The Creed. The alternative—that he'd gone home with Ashley—was too terrible and heart-wrenching to imagine.

"No problem. Good night, Chloe."

"Good night."

—∾∾—

It was after one when Colt finally got the bar cleaned up and closed down for the night. He'd had a feeling it was going to be a late night, which was why he'd sent Logan over to keep an eye on Chloe. It was killing him not to be there himself, but he knew if he couldn't be there, he could trust Logan to watch over his girl.

Except she wasn't *his* girl. Or maybe she was. Or maybe she could be. Hell, he didn't know anymore. The way she'd been so pissed earlier that day, then hightailed it out of there that night like a raccoon with its tail on fire, gave the distinct impression she didn't really want anything more to do with him. But then why had she said she was looking for him? And why had she apologized?

Because she's a nice person, you dope.

That was probably it. He was sure it had nothing to do with him and more to do with the fact that she was just a kind person in general. He should have known this would happen, should have been more prepared for the curse to kick in.

But he'd forgotten. For just a fraction of a second, he'd forgotten about the curse and had let himself believe he and Chloe could have a future, could be happy together. What an idiot he was.

But maybe he was dodging a bullet. If she was going to get that worked up every time he tried to help her, maybe he was better off without her. The pain in his chest told him he didn't think so, but his head was trying to get him to see reason. She'd walked out, so now was the time to cut her loose, get on with his life, forget about Chloe and this crazy idea that he could get a chance at sharing a real life with someone.

Colt scowled as he trudged across the parking lot, distracted by his anger and frustration, and didn't notice the figure huddled inside the cab of his truck until he'd almost reached the pickup.

"What the hell are you doing in my truck?" he asked as he yanked open the door.

A pair of miserably sad eyes peered up at him from under the hood of a jacket that wasn't near warm enough for this cold a night. Nobody left their cars locked in small towns. But usually the worst you expected to find was a bag of extra zucchinis or tomatoes from someone's garden, not a disheartened teenager who appeared to be carrying the weight of the world on his shoulders.

"Jesse?" Colt climbed into the truck and started the heater. "Sorry I yelled at you, kid. You scared the tar out of me. What are you doing in here? Are you all right?"

The teenager shrugged. "No. Yes. I don't know. I don't even know what I'm doing here, man. I've been out looking for my dad, and it was too damn cold to walk home. I saw you inside and figured I'd wait in your truck and see if I could bum a ride home with you."

He'd seen Jesse inside the restaurant earlier, but hadn't had time to talk to the kid. "Sure, of course. I'm glad to drop you on my way out to the ranch." He put the truck in gear and pulled out of the parking lot.

"Oh. I don't want to cause you any trouble. I just seen your truck parked at Miss Bishop's the last few nights and figured you'd be heading that way anyway."

Kid was too smart for his own good. "My truck will not be parked there tonight, but I *was* planning to drive by to check on her anyway, so it's cool to drop you off. And the only reason I've been staying there is to make sure she's not alone, in case, you know, your dad comes back for her."

"Whatever." Jesse shrugged his thin shoulders and stared out the window. "I don't think you have to worry though. It doesn't matter what he said; he's not very good on his follow-through. And he never comes back. Even if he promises he will."

Poor kid—he wasn't talking about the threat to Chloe anymore.

"That's a tough thing you got going on with your pop, Jesse. I'm sorry."

The teen shrugged again.

"Why were you looking for him? It seems to me you'd do good to stay out of his way."

"I know. But I need to talk to him. I need to tell him something."

"Are you sure it can't wait until he's had a chance to cool off?"

"I'm sure. And he doesn't ever really cool off, so that doesn't matter. But I need to talk to him anyway. He thinks I'm the one who ratted him out and got him sent up."

"But you didn't."

Jesse jerked his head back and narrowed his eyes. "How do you know?"

"I volunteer with the sheriff's department. I can't say,

but I do *know* who snitched on your dad. And I know it wasn't you."

The boy's shoulders caved even further into his chest. "It might as well have been."

"What does that mean?"

"It means I may not have been the actual one who snitched, but I wanted to. I tried. I placed anonymous calls to the police station. I even rode my bike down there a couple of times after he tore into my mom. I *wanted* to turn him in and get him sent to jail, so it may as well have been me, because I wanted him gone. I just didn't have the guts to turn him in myself." He swiped the back of his sleeve across his nose. From the tremble in Jesse's voice, Colt figured he was crying but didn't want to draw attention to it. There was nothing wrong with a guy needing to get out a good cry once in a while—especially a conflicted teenager who had an abusive father who he obviously both loved and hated.

"Jesse, you gotta quit being so tough on yourself. None of what happened was your fault, or your siblings' fault, or your mom's fault. The blame for your dad getting sent to jail falls solely on *his* shoulders. He did the crime, so he's doing the time. And he hurt people, hurt you and your mom. It's totally understandable you'd want to tell someone and get your family some help. That doesn't make you a snitch. It makes you brave."

Jesse shook his head. "I don't feel brave. I've never felt brave a day in my life. All I feel is scared. All the time. I'm scared he'll come back. And I'm scared he won't. I'm scared of him coming home, and I'm scared he'll never come home again. I'm scared he'll find me and beat the shit out of me, and I'm scared he won't find me because he doesn't care enough about me to look."

"That's rough. But everything you're saying still makes sense. It's hard when you have a father like Rank. It's hard to love a man like that."

"I didn't say I love him. How could I love a guy who nearly killed my mom? He knocks my head against a wall as easy as he passes the salt. He's punched me more times than he's hugged me. What kind of stupid asshole would that make me if I still loved a guy like that?"

"It wouldn't make you a stupid asshole. It would make you a son. A son who keeps giving his dad a chance. That right there is what being brave is all about."

The boy shook his head and picked at a seam on his jeans. His head was bent so low, his chin practically touched his chest.

"I mean it, kid. I think you have more courage than you realize. And it takes courage to love someone. You gotta be strong to put yourself out there. Especially when you know there is a good chance they might not love you back."

"Love is stupid. I don't get why everyone is always getting so worked up over this love deal. If you ask me, love sucks. It doesn't make you feel good. It only makes you feel like shit. Like someone reached inside your chest and ripped your dang heart right out. Why would anyone wish for that?"

"Because it's not always like that. Sometimes it's pretty great."

"I wouldn't know about that."

"Sure you would. I've seen your family and the way

you kids take care of each other and your mom. And I've seen the way your mom is with you kids. It's obvious you love each other, and she loves you. It's a tough deal she's got—hard to be both parents—but I know she's doing the best she can."

Jesse shrugged again. If shrugging were an Olympic sport, this kid would take home the gold. "Whatever."

"Well, I can tell you being lonely and cutting yourself off from everyone is a lot more painful than taking a chance and letting yourself love someone."

And letting someone love you.

Another shrug.

"Nothing good ever comes easy, kid. Just like in hockey, you can't win games if you don't train and play hard and give it all you got. And sometimes it feels like you're stuck in the penalty box or you're afraid or you never even get a chance to get off the bench. But I can tell you—you're never going to win if you don't get out on the ice and actually play the game."

"What if I don't care about the game? If I never sign up for hockey at all, I'll never lose a game."

"If you never sign up, you'll for sure never get a chance to experience what it feels like to play."

"This is all stupid. Life isn't some dumb hockey game. And from what I've seen, sometimes it's easier to bail first than be the one who always gets left behind."

Colt pulled up in front of the Johnson's house.

"Thanks, man. I appreciate the ride," Jesse said, opening the passenger door before the truck had even come to a full stop. He'd apparently had enough of this mushy heart-to-heart talk.

"See ya, kid. And you want my advice, stay away from Rank. It won't matter what you tell him. He's not the kind of guy who listens to anyone else anyway."

Jesse gave him one last shrug, then slammed the truck door and trudged up to his house.

Colt watched him go in and shut the door, then his eyes cut to Chloe's yard. Nothing seemed amiss, and except for the front porch light and a small glow of the aqua nightlight he knew she kept on in the kitchen, the house looked dark and buttoned down.

His chest ached as he wished he could walk across the yard and through the new front door he'd just installed. He also wished he could drop his clothes and climb naked into bed with her and curl her body against his. But he couldn't. And he didn't know if he ever would again.

Was this morose, shrugging teenager right? Was it better to leave before he got left? And had he already been doing that? Already been pushing her away?

Chloe came from the same kind of home life Jesse did. So, had she been doing that to him? Was that what this afternoon had really been about—Chloe pushing him away? Had the combination of her coworkers mocking her and him tossing her dad's things sent her over the edge? Was she using the garage and her insecurity issues as an excuse to leave him before she got hurt?

All this conjecture and speculation hurt his head. Jesse was right about one thing though. Love could suck. Colt felt like he'd gone two rounds with a bull and come out on the losing side. His heart hurt, his body ached. He just needed to go to bed and think about this in the morning. Somehow things always seemed better when you examined them in the light of day.

He gave Chloe's house a last once-over, then put the truck in gear and headed for the ranch.

———ᴍ———

The next morning started cloudy and gray and accurately reflected how Colt felt as he set about to do his morning chores. He'd been neglecting a few things at the ranch in order to help Chloe and had more than enough to keep him busy. It was good to use his muscles, to haul bales and swing a hammer to repair a wall in the barn, to sweat out some of his frustration and aggravation. But the work only required his brawn and left his brain unattended to think and stew and fester over what he was going to do about Chloe.

As if it were a dried scab, he spent the morning picking and scratching at it, until he felt like the whole thing with her had turned into an open bloody wound. And that was not the way he figured a good relationship should be described.

But the more he festered, the more heated he got until he was slamming things around and ready to throw in the whole towel. He didn't need this kind of grief. He had shit to do, a ranch to help run. All this thing with Chloe was doing was messing with his head and keeping him from getting his work done.

She had her car fixed now so he didn't need to be running into town to ferry her around, which worked in his favor. The more he could stay away from her right now, the better. Breaking this thing off, if there was even anything left to break, was going to be tough enough. He knew it had to be done, that he had to get out before he got in any deeper and really got stuck. Just like driving his pickup through the mud, the faster he went, the less likely he was to get mired down in it.

He'd made the decision to call it quits, and now he needed to stick with it. The real tough part was going to be getting through the next several weeks of hockey practice. But he'd make sure Logan came with him and could partner the two of them up to work with the kids and keep him and Chloe focused on different lines and out of each other's way. Yeah, this would work out fine.

Sure, keep telling yourself that, buddy.

He needed to take a break for lunch and from all this thinking. It made his head hurt. He whistled for the dog and made his way back to the cabin. They were predicting snow, and a few light flurries spun in the air. Colt rubbed a hand over his chilled neck and realized Chloe still had his good blue scarf. That would be awkward trying to get that back. Oh well, she could keep it. It looked better on her anyway.

Watson ran into the cabin ahead of him, and Colt pushed the door shut with his foot as he shrugged out of his coat and hung it on an empty peg. His cell phone buzzed in his pocket, and for the briefest of seconds, his hopes lifted that it was her. *Shit.* He needed to get over that business right now.

He pulled his phone free and frowned at the screen. Denver area code, but he didn't recognize the number.

"Hello. This is Colt."

"Hey, Colt. This is Joe Forsberg. I'm the head defensive coach with the Colorado Summit. We met the other night when I was at the game with your brother and his boy."

"Oh sure. I remember. But if you're looking for

Rock, I'm pretty sure he's down in Denver today. Did you try his cell phone?"

"No. I'm not looking for Rock. I'm actually hoping to talk to you."

"To me? Why's that?"

"I was thinking about what you said the other night at practice. Remember when you were talking about how you were spending a little extra time with a few of the kids, building up their confidence, making them feel more like part of the team, that sort of thing?"

"Yeah?"

"Well, I got to thinking about that, and we got a couple of rookies in the draft this year who I think have some really great potential, and I think they could benefit from a little of that specialized attention. And I was thinking you might be the guy to help with that."

"Me? I'm not sure why you would want me, but I guess I could help. I'm a big fan of the team and usually have a little wager on the Summit making a run for the Cup. And I already do a lot of volunteer stuff. I could probably give them some time, if you think I could help."

Joe chuckled. "Well, I appreciate your offer to volunteer your time, but I was thinking more along the lines of a paid position. We'd like to schedule an interview and have you meet the team, of course. But we're looking to add you to the coaching staff, if everything works out and that's something you think you might be interested in."

Colt opened his mouth, then closed it again. He didn't know what to say. His knees threatened to give way, and he sank onto the edge of the couch. After his accident, he'd thought his career in hockey was over. He'd never dreamed he'd have a chance to be a part of the sport again in a coaching capacity.

"Hello? You still there?"

"Uh, yeah. Yeah, I'm still here. And I think that sounds great. I'd love to meet with you and the guys. Rock talks a lot about the team, and he says they're a great bunch of people to work with."

"Good. That's real good. Listen, I know it's short notice, but we're having a special practice tonight followed by a team dinner. A couple of the head honchos will be there, and I think it will be a great opportunity for you to get to meet everyone and spend some time with them both on and off the ice. What do you think?"

"I think that sounds great."

"About six o'clock then? At the stadium. I can text you the address. Do you need directions?"

"No, sir. I've been there with Rock. I know where it is."

"Great. We'll see you tonight then. And we're excited about making you part of the team."

"Yes, sir. Thank you, sir." Colt disconnected the call and sank back against the cushions. *Part of the team. Part of the motherfreakin' Colorado Summit team.* The NHL. This was it. The big time. What he'd always dreamed of. Maybe not the *way* he'd dreamed it, but after all he'd been through, this was the best chance he had to still be a part of the team.

A smile cracked across his face, and he let out a whoop. Watson barked, getting in on the excitement as he ran over to grab a tennis ball from his box of toys.

Colt's smile fell as he realized he'd said yes without hesitation and without even considering if he had other plans for the night. And he *did* have other plans. He had plans with his real team, the one he'd committed to first. The eight-and-unders had their first game tonight.

But this was his chance. He had to take it. And the kids still had Logan and Chloe. He wasn't leaving them all alone.

This morning he'd thought the curse was in full swing, that losing Chloe was what he was due and that his chance at happiness was once again slipping through his fingers. But maybe the curse was coming to an end. Maybe there was no stupid curse. Or maybe the curse only applied to his love life.

Because he'd just been offered a coaching position with the NHL.

The decision to go to the interview would change everything. He'd spent the morning making the call to break things off with Chloe, but taking this job, deserting the team for their very first game, leaving her to clean up the aftermath of his decision, that all would clinch the deal. There was no turning back from that.

He would gain the job, gain his dream to work in the NHL, but he would lose the girl, lose any chance he had at building a future with her.

He'd never really had a chance with her anyway, he tried to convince himself.

So that was a risk he'd have to take.

Chapter 22

CHLOE PACED THE LENGTH OF THE BLEACHERS AND BACK. She checked her watch. Again. Where the h-e-double-hockey-sticks was Colt?

He should have been here by now, should have been here thirty minutes ago. She'd called his phone three times and left him two messages. Surely he wouldn't desert her, or the kids, for their first game—which could only mean that something had happened to him, and he was lying in a ditch somewhere bleeding out. Which was better than imagining he was lying in a bed somewhere curled up naked with Ashley.

Stop it. He wouldn't do that.

Well, who the heck really knew? She hadn't known him all that long. Maybe that *is* something he'd do. But she didn't think so. He might let *her* down, but there was no way he'd let these kids down. Which sent her back into a tailspin of imagining him still in the ditch, bleeding and hurt.

Logan came out of the locker room, a grim expression on his face. He took her elbow and pulled her to the side.

Oh no. Here it came—the bad news. She steeled herself to hear what hospital Colt was being sent to.

"He's not coming," Logan said.

"Why? What happened? Where is he?"

"He's on his way to Denver. He's got an appointment."

"An *appointment*? What the fork are you talking about? What kind of appointment is more important than this game with these kids?"

Logan shrugged. "You'll have to ask him. But don't worry. We've got this."

That wasn't the point. The point was Colt should be here.

The kids filed out of the locker room and onto the ice to warm up. They had ten minutes before the game started. Chloe looked around, her stomach sinking like she'd swallowed a rock.

Maddie wasn't here either. And she hadn't seen her all afternoon. Tina's car hadn't been in the driveway when she'd pulled out of her shiny clean garage.

Now that it was done and she'd parked her car in there, the new organized garage was pretty amazing. She'd hoped to tell Colt again tonight how sorry she was and how much she truly appreciated being able to park in the garage, especially with the snow, which had been falling all afternoon. Plus, her engine was running better than ever. She had a feeling Justin had worked on more than just the door. She'd called him earlier to thank him for doing such a great job on her car and invited him to bring Spencer and Milo to tonight's game. She'd have to find him later and thank him again. The conversation with the mechanic would be much easier than the one with Colt.

Especially since Colt wasn't here. And neither was Maddie. What was going on?

Her anxiety was shooting through the roof, but it wasn't just worry anymore. Now she was getting good and mad. She stepped behind the bleachers and tried Colt's phone one more time.

"Hello?"

Finally. Relief tinged with irritation swirled in her chest, and she tried not to grit her teeth as she spoke his name. "Colt? Where are you? The game is starting in five minutes."

"Didn't Logan tell you? I'm not coming to the game."

Her fingers cramped as she clutched the phone tightly to her ear. "What could you possibly be doing that is more important than this game?"

"I'm going to a job interview. In Denver."

She sucked in her breath, and the side of her face went tingly. "A job interview? What kind of job?"

"It's a coaching position. With the Colorado Summit."

"A coaching position?"

"Yeah, with the NHL. It's a once-in-a-lifetime offer. I had to try for it."

"And leave everything else behind?"

"What everything else? I'm missing one game, and you and Logan can easily field it without me."

She swallowed. He sounded different—his voice more callous, and he hadn't mentioned her or anything about them. Maybe that was because he hadn't given any thought to them. Or maybe there wasn't a "them" to even think about it. This didn't really seem the time to be hashing out their relationship, not with the game starting and her working up a good steam of mad. But she had to know—had been dying to know. Had been waiting all day for the game to get a clue to where they stood. And now the only way she would know was to ask. "What about us?"

"What 'us'? You made it pretty clear yesterday in the garage and again when you left the restaurant last night that you didn't want anything to do with me, so I'm respecting your wishes and giving you what you wanted."

What *she* wanted? Or what *he* wanted? "But…"

But what? What could she say? She wasn't convinced there was an "us" either. Or if she even wanted there to be. Her heart ached, but what else was there to say? He obviously wasn't interested in fighting for them, and she'd already decided she didn't need the distraction and agitation of the chaos he brought to her life. But if this is what she'd wanted, why did her chest feel like a hole had just been ripped from it? Like a spiked hand has just reached in and torn out her heart, tearing her skin and muscles and leaving a gaping, bloody hole, the edges raw and burning.

She swallowed, trying to make her voice sound somewhere in the range of normal. "Well, good luck on your interview then."

"Thanks." Did she detect even the slightest hint of remorse in his voice?

"Bye, Colt."

"Bye, Chloe."

She disconnected the call and pressed the phone into her pocket. Well, that was that. Easy come, easy go. She'd had a life before Colt James; she'd have one after. Not that the life she had was anything to write home about, but it was a life, nonetheless. And despite the gaping hole in her chest—wounds healed—she was fine getting back to it. No more recently shaved whiskers trailing across her bathroom counter, no more pools of sudsy soap dripping down the side of the shower, no more boot tracks on her kitchen floor.

That all sounded perfect. It sounded wonderful, in fact.

No more warm, hard body curled around me when I sleep. No more stolen kisses and passionate encounters on the kitchen counter or in the shower or in front of the fire in his cabin. No more laughter or companionship or playful affection. No more Colt.

But by golly, her forking house would be clean, and her spice rack would stay organized. She blinked back the tears burning her eyes and pulled the clipboard from her tote bag as she walked out from behind the bleachers. She straightened the edges, lining them up perfectly with the corners of the board, trying to get a semblance of order back into her world.

"Chloe!"

She turned as someone yelled her name. Maddie and Tina rushed up to her, the girl's skates swinging perilously over Tina's arm. Maddie threw herself against Chloe's legs and wrapped her arms around her waist. Her cheeks were stained with smudged tear tracks.

"Chloe," Tina said again, the word coming out in a rush of breath. "Have you seen Jesse?"

"Jesse? No. Why? What's wrong?"

"What's going on?" Logan asked, as he and Quinn came up behind her.

"It's Jesse," Tina said. "He's missing. Rank called while I was at work and left this terrible message on our home answering machine about how he was going to track down Jesse and have a 'man-to-man talk' with him. Which in Rank-speak means he's going to beat him within an inch of his life. Jesse had brought the other kids home, but he left after hearing the message. I haven't been able to find him all night. I've been calling his cell phone, but he won't answer. And it's really starting to snow. He could be out there, cold and alone. He could be hurt." A single tear escaped the corner of her eye, but she rubbed it away with the back of her hand. "I don't know what to do."

Logan stepped around Chloe and pulled Tina against him. "Don't worry. We'll find him. I'll help you look."

Panic tore through Chloe's chest. She knew Logan leaving was the right thing to do, but that meant she was left to handle the whole team and their first home game by herself.

Logan reached out a hand and gripped her shoulder. He narrowed his eyes as he stared into hers. "Chloe, you got this. It's three twelve-minute periods. We've already created the lines, and you know how to rotate them in and out." He glanced up at his sister. "Quinn can help. She can find a parent to man the penalty box, and she can assist with the defensive lines. Right, Sis?"

"Sure. Whatever I can do to help," Quinn said. "Just find Jesse."

They all knew how dangerous Rank was, and it went without saying that they needed to find the boy before he did.

"Quinn can get Maddie's skates on," Logan continued. He fixed Chloe with a hard stare. "You go get the team ready. You can do this."

She nodded and gave Tina's arm a squeeze. "Don't worry. You'll find him. And we'll help look after the game is over."

"Thank you. I already called Mike—you know the policeman who took your statement—and he's got the police looking too. But there are only a couple guys on duty tonight."

"It's going to be okay."

Tina leaned down and squeezed Maddie's small shoulders. "I'm sorry I'm missing your first game, baby."

"It's okay, Momma. Just find Jesse before Daddy does."

Her mother nodded, then rushed out of the ice arena, Logan on her heels.

"I'll get Maddie ready," Quinn said. "You go take care of the team."

Chloe nodded and hurried toward the box where the boys were already getting rowdy and playing keep away with a water bottle. Taking a deep breath, she reached for the door to the box. She could do this. She dealt with rowdy kids every day. But her classroom was organized and tidy and didn't smell anything like these kids and their sweaty pads. She had her third-graders trained and held a modicum of control in her classroom—it was her domain.

This was nothing like her domain. This domain was loud, and smelly, and chaotic. It was more like a wild jungle. And Tarzan was nowhere to be found.

Stop. I can do this. It's not even a whole hour. She wasn't helpless, wasn't a victim, not anymore. She'd done things this week that before she'd only dreamed of. She could do this too.

I am large and in charge, she told herself, using the quote she often gave her students to build their confidence. In this case, she *was* in charge. She was their coach. And she'd just been promoted to head coach. These parents and this community had entrusted her with their kids, and unlike a certain cowboy she knew, she wasn't going to let them down.

She pushed back her shoulders and channeled her inner Jane of the Jungle, then opened the door of the box.

Colt squinted into the thick flurries of snow spinning through the air. Several inches covered the road, and the storm was getting worse the further he drove down the pass. His chest felt tight, and a sick churning rumbled in his gut.

The snow wasn't what was bothering him. He'd driven in storms before. And he was heading toward the opportunity of a lifetime.

No, the roiling in his belly wasn't from what he was heading toward. It was from what he was leaving behind.

He felt like a total shit. It was bad enough he'd ditched the kids for their first game, but the real issue that had his chest hurting was the way he'd acted with Chloe. He'd been a real douche, and that wasn't like him. He usually tried to be a nice guy, so why had he been such a jerk to the person he was starting to really care about?

Starting to care about? That's an understatement. He knew it. He knew he was way beyond just *starting* to care. He'd started to care the first time he'd met her, back during the summer when he'd been at the drive-in with his family, and they'd met while she'd been generously taking her four neighbor kids to the movies. But spending time with her the last week, talking to her, laughing with her, touching her, he'd moved beyond caring and was falling head over bootheels in love with her.

He'd seen her endure crisis and catastrophe, and he'd seen her giggling and teasing him as she'd lobbed snowballs at his butt. He'd seen the serious side of her, the messy side, which was actually the super-neat and sometimes too-organized side, but he'd also seen the tender side, the sweet side, the caring side. And he'd seen the sexy-as-sin side, and he somehow knew that wasn't a side she'd shared with many other people.

So if he'd seen all these sides to her and still wanted her, what was the problem? What was holding him back from grabbing her and not letting her go? Hell, he'd already let her go. With that stupid comment about there not being an "us." What had he been thinking?

He hadn't. He hadn't been thinking. He'd been knee-jerk reacting and assuming if he started to get too happy, the curse would knock him back on his ass. But the curse hadn't done anything. Maybe it had *never* done anything. Maybe everything that had gone wrong for him had been his own doing. The car accident that destroyed his hockey career had been his fault for driving too fast. Losing the girl he loved had been his fault too for acting like such an asshole and pushing her away, and the list went on and on.

His conversation with Jesse played through his mind as he looked back on all the times he'd blamed the curse for what had gone wrong in his life, and he wondered if he hadn't been doing the same thing as the teenager. Had he bailed before the good things in his life had a chance to bail on him? Had he pushed Ashley away all those years ago because he assumed she was going to leave anyway?

Was that what he was doing with Chloe? Was he pushing her away, not because he was afraid she'd stay, but because he was afraid she'd leave? Not because he didn't like her or hope for a chance at a future with her, but because he was afraid she would figure out what an idiot he was and leave him?

He'd told Jesse it takes courage to love someone—
that a person had to be strong to put themselves out
there. He'd given him the whole "love is like the game
of hockey" analogy. It had all sounded great at the time,
but Colt suddenly realized he wasn't following any of
his own advice.

He was sitting on the bench, missing the game,
because he was afraid to get out on the ice. He'd learned
the sport, but he wasn't giving it his all or working hard
at trying to win. In fact, he wasn't trying at all.

He couldn't win if he didn't play. That's what he'd
told Jesse and what he needed to tell himself.

He wouldn't know if he and Chloe had a chance—a
chance at something real—unless he tightened his skates
and got his ass out onto the ice. Unless he got in the
game and played to win. And Chloe was a prize worth
playing for.

His phone was in the mount on the dash, and he tapped
the screen to call Joe. The coach didn't answer, but Colt
left him a message explaining that he wouldn't be able
to make the special practice tonight after all because his
team had a game and they needed him. He said he hoped
Joe would understand, and that he truly appreciated the
offer and wished he could take him up on it, but he needed
to put *his* team, his ragtag band of eight-and-unders, first.

As Colt tapped off the phone, a smile tugged at the
corners of his lips. As much as he wanted that job, he
wanted Chloe more. And he sought to be the kind of
man she would want and one she would be proud of. He
felt good, and if he could find a place to turn around, he
had a fair chance of making it back in time for the last
half of the game.

He spotted a turnoff and slowed to take it, but the brakes didn't respond. The tires hit a sheet of black ice, buried beneath the layers of snow, and slid across the blacktop.

Losing traction, Colt spun the wheel, trying—and failing—to turn into the spin as he skidded off the road.

The screech of metal as the truck hit the guardrail had his mind and body flashing back to the accident he'd had in high school, and on reflex, he raised his hands as the vehicle plunged down the embankment and crashed through the trees.

His head slammed into the steering wheel as the hood of the truck smashed into a huge pine tree.

The curse is real were Colt's last thoughts before he slumped against the wheel and everything went black.

Disorganized was a generous word for the first two periods, but by the time they'd made it halfway through the third, the game had dissolved into utter chaos. Chloe had accidentally sent the defensive line in to cover for the offense, they'd gotten a penalty for too many men (or kids, in this instance) on the ice, and the other team had scored four goals on them. And to add insult to injury, one of the goals had accidentally been kicked in by their own player. They'd had a couple of chances but hadn't scored, and the game was thankfully dwindling down to the last few minutes.

As the game progressed, Chloe noticed that one of the bigger kids on the other team had been knocking into Max way more times than necessary, trying to trip him and using other bullying tactics. She'd seen it so many times, a big kid automatically targeting a smaller one they assumed was weak. But Max wasn't weak. He wasn't strong, but he *was* smart. And focused entirely on the game.

So he was either oblivious to the other kid's actions or was just really good at ignoring him, because Max didn't seem to be bothered and wasn't letting it affect his focus. Until the other kid pushed him into the boards and grabbed him in a choke hold.

"Hey! Come on, ref!" Chloe yelled as Quinn tried to climb over the boards. She opened the door onto the ice and took a few precarious steps.

The other boy had his arm wrapped around Max's neck, but to her surprise, Max bent his knees, dropping his weight and dug his chin into the other guy's arm. The combination of his deadweight and the dig of his chin must have put enough pressure on the other kid's arm that he let him go, and Max skated deftly away.

Huh. Colt's trick worked. It really worked. That kid was twice Max's size and a foot taller, yet the combination of the moves had been enough to get him to release the smaller boy.

Quinn thankfully held her tongue as the ref ushered the bully into the penalty box. All they needed was to have Chloe's only helper get tossed from the game for laying into one of the opposing team's players. Not that he didn't deserve it—stupid bully.

Chloe held the door and waited for Max to skate back to the bench. "Good job, buddy. Way to outsmart him." She wanted to hug him and tell him how amazingly brave he'd been, but instead she gave him an encouraging nod and patted his shoulder pad in a more coach-like move.

A grin the size of Montana covered Max's face as he smiled up at her before being engulfed by the rest of the team as they cheered and high-fived him as he stepped into the box.

She let them have their moment, then waved them closer and huddled the team together. "Okay, guys, this is our chance. They've got a penalty so they're down one man on the ice, and we've got a full minute and a half to try to score." She held up her clipboard and outlined a play they'd worked on in practice a few nights before.

The kids were all over it, and she sent the yellow line out to execute the play. Colt had tried to set the lines as one, two, and three, but she'd talked him into using colors instead so none of the kids felt like their line was better or worse. He'd gone for the idea and acted like it was a good one, and she'd really felt like part of the coaching team.

"You can do this," she yelled and beat the palm of her hand against the boards like she'd seen Colt do.

The ref whistled and dropped the puck, and her team's forward sent it sailing down the ice. Max had insisted he was ready to play again, so he was back on the ice and caught the puck, cradling it in his stick as he pushed it down the ice. The other team's two defensemen doubled up and barreled down on him, leaving Maddie wide open at the net.

As the two opposing players focused on Max, he looked up, caught sight of Maddie, and passed the puck straight toward her. She bent forward, her lips pressed together around her mouth guard, and gripped her stick with the concentration of an Olympic medalist.

The puck hit her stick with a crack, and she shot it toward the net.

The goalie deflected the puck, but instead of trapping it in his glove, he sent it back toward her. She caught the rebound and changed her angle, then hit it right back. This time, it sailed past his skate and landed neatly in the corner of the net just as the buzzer sounded, ending the game.

The team broke into a cheer and scrambled out onto the ice to scream and hug Maddie and Max. They tossed their helmets and clapped each other on the back, every face lit with happiness.

Chloe looked at Quinn. "I don't get it. This whole game was a crazy mess of chaos, and we lost miserably. I thought I'd have to pick these kids up off the floor, they'd be so bummed, but look at them—they're cheering and laughing like we just won the Stanford Cup."

Quinn chuckled. "It's actually called the Stanley Cup, but you get points for the effort." She wrapped an arm around Chloe's shoulder. "I think you're missing the big picture. These kids are brand-new to the game. They know they're not going to always win, and there will be teams better than they are, but they're so excited just to be part of the game. They don't care if it's messy or chaotic. They're just excited to play."

Her friend's words stuck with her as Chloe herded the team into the locker room and talked to parents as they helped their kids change. She gave the kids instructions for the next week's practice and reminded Gordy's mom she was on snack duty for the next game. They still hadn't heard from Tina, and Quinn offered to take Max and Maddie out for celebratory ice cream so Chloe could go home and check her neighbor's house to see if she'd returned.

Chloe was feeling pretty proud of herself and the way she'd handled the game and the team as she drove home. But the things that were giving her the most pause were the insights Quinn had given her about the kids and their attitude toward the game.

She'd spent so much of her life trying to make sure things went an exact certain way, to keep everyone around her on an even keel, to try to manage everything—from her surroundings to how many scoops of food her cat ate. She somehow had it in her mind that control equaled happiness, but the kids had shown her tonight that even through crazy chaos, they could still have fun.

This last week had been totally chaotic. So many things had been out of her control. Some, like Rank's attack, were things she couldn't control if she tried, and others—like the way she'd let her hair down a little and been willing to act wanton with Colt—were in her control, but she let loose of the reins and simply allowed things to happen. And some of those moments were the best of the week.

She was running from a relationship with a man she really liked because she was afraid it was too messy and because she couldn't dictate the outcomes, but she was missing the point. Love *was* messy. It was chaotic and emotional and could put her heart through the wringer with a thousand different feelings and sensations. But the thing she wasn't getting, the big-picture piece she'd been missing, was that chaos and messy were apparently okay.

Just because something was muddled or disorganized didn't mean it couldn't still be wonderful and amazing. Just because falling in love was illogical and irrational, that didn't make it bad. Sometimes doing things that were a little wild and reckless—like dropping her towel and seducing a cute cowboy—could end up having the best results.

She just had to weigh the decision of whether she could handle the chaos or not—if letting herself fall in love with Colt was worth the risk of letting go of the command she had on her life. It didn't seem that hard to decide when the alternative was not having Colt in her life at all. She could kid herself about them staying friends, but there was no way she could handle being around him now, knowing she'd blown her chance to be with him in a way that was beyond friendship.

She'd convinced herself tonight to take control, to not be the victim, and to step into the game as the coach and the one in charge. That's how she needed to treat this relationship. Or what she hoped would be a relationship. She wasn't a victim, so why was she letting everything happen *to* her? Forget the stupid crap of her dad's that had been taking up space in her garage. This was the real thing she needed to fight for. So why was she still standing in the box, afraid to even get into the game?

Tightening the strap on her imaginary helmet, she stepped out of the box and whacked her stick on the ice, calling for the puck, ready not just to play, but to score the winning goal. The only way to win was to get in there and play, to fight for what she wanted. *Fight for love.* It sounded corny, but it was the truth. She'd fallen in love with Colt, and she was ready to drop the gloves and fight for a future with him.

A plan formed in her mind. She'd wanted to be daring and courageous, to act fearlessly. Well, this was her chance. And she was going to take it. She'd feed the cat and change her clothes, then drive out to the ranch and wait for him to come home. She'd sit in front of his cabin all night if she had to.

Distracted by thoughts of his reaction upon coming home and finding her there, she pulled into the garage, cut the engine, and pushed the button on her visor to shut the garage door.

As she opened her door and stepped one foot out, she caught a flash of color in the side mirror and turned in time to see Rank Johnson slip under the closing door and walk menacingly toward her.

Chapter 23

CHLOE SCREAMED AND TRIED TO PULL HER CAR DOOR SHUT, but Rank was too fast. He had the element of surprise on his side, and he kicked his foot out, sending the door slamming back open. He reached into the car, grabbed a handful of her hair, and tried to drag her from the seat.

When he'd stepped under the garage door, his body must have caused the sensor to trip because the door was going back up, and a cold gust of snow blew in through the wide-open space. Sharp pain made Chloe's eyes water, but she held on to the steering wheel, trying to get her keys out of the ignition. The sparkly can of pepper spray Sassy had given her was hanging from her key ring, and if she could get hold of it and give Rank even one squirt, it might be enough to give her a chance to get away.

He gave another yank, and Chloe's head snapped to the side, but she'd gotten a finger through the ring, and it came out of the ignition. She let loose another scream, this one a mix of pain and frustration, as the keys and the small canister slipped from her finger and dropped to the floor of the car.

It was hard to think with the searing pain in her head, but Colt had told her to use whatever she could as a weapon—her hands, her feet, her fingernails and teeth. And she was prepared to bite and kick and scratch Rank's eyes out if she had to.

She'd worn a pair of heavy, thick-soled boots to the game tonight, thinking they'd keep her feet warm, but they also gave her extra weight as she kicked her foot toward Rank's legs. Her foot connected with his knee-cap, and he let out a howl of pain and released his grip on her hair.

She scrambled forward, sweeping her hand across the floorboard in an effort to locate the key ring.

Got it. She closed her fingers around the canister, trying to twist the lid to the side to release the safety.

Rank grabbed her legs and hauled her out of the car. Chloe fell, going down hard and smacking her tailbone against the cement floor of the garage. Fighting the pain, she held the canister up, pointing it toward his face.

His fist shot out, but she pressed the button an instant before his hand connected with hers.

A stream of spray fired out, barely missing his eyes but still hitting him in the cheek as the canister went flying from her hand and rolled under the car. The air instantly filled with the chemical, and Chloe choked, her throat and nose stinging and her eyes tearing up. It didn't seem to matter if she breathed it in or out; it stole her breath either way.

Rank howled in rage, swiping the back of his arm across his face. "You bitch! You're gonna pay for that!" His eyes were red and squinted, but the pepper spray didn't seem to have deterred him. It only fueled his fury.

Chloe scrambled backward, blinking away the tears, her tailbone stinging, the freezing cement cold against her hands as she tried to gain purchase. Her gaze whipped around the garage, looking for a weapon or a way out. The garage door stood wide open, but a very pissed-off

Rank remained between her and that escape. The pepper spray was under the car, but it hadn't seemed to stop him anyway. She needed a weapon, something to disable him just long enough to give her a chance to escape.

Her dad's tools were in the drawers on the back wall next to the workbench, if she could just get there.

The drawers! She'd forgotten that's where she'd stashed Colt's gun. He'd said it wasn't loaded, but Rank didn't know that, and so far the man was strong but hadn't proven himself to be very formidable in the brains department. Chloe rolled over, trying to crawl away and get her legs under her at the same time. If she could just get to the drawers, just get to the gun…

A meaty hand landed on her calf and yanked her backward. Terror ripped through her chest. She couldn't let him get her. Letting out another scream, she kicked her legs, hearing a grunt from Rank as her foot connected with his chest.

But she was no match for his anger and rage, and he hauled her up and jerked her against him. She could smell the sweat and body odor on his clothes, and the sound of her racing heartbeat thrashed in her ears.

His arm cut across her chest, and she tried to fight, to kick and punch, but her hits were ineffectual against the hard mass of angry man. His breath smelled like sour booze and tooth decay as he scratched his rough-whiskered cheek along hers. "You stuck your snooty nose in where it didn't belong, and now you're gonna pay."

Black spots danced in front of her eyes as his forearm pressed into her windpipe. She clawed at his skin, digging her nails into his flesh, but nothing she did had any effect.

"You are nothing. A nobody. Just a stupid school-teacher that no one will even miss." His cigarette-scarred voice rasped menacingly against her ear, and shivers of terror surged through her blood as sweat formed on her back and her bladder threatened to let loose.

She'd been fighting so hard, but his words burrowed into her brain and threatened to immobilize her. The intimidating words and threatening tone he used mingled with the memory of her dad's voice, and she blinked, tears from the spray and the pain coursing down her cheeks as she tried to discern this man from the abusive one who'd raised her. She sagged against him, her chest throbbing as she tried to breathe, unable to find the strength to keep fighting.

As she sagged back, she remembered Colt's instructions about using her body weight. But Rank was so strong. He could toss her across the room with one hard throw. How could she do anything to match his strength?

The image of Max at the game tonight came rushing back to her. He'd escaped a bully so much bigger than him, and he hadn't used his brawn. He'd used his brain and simple physics. Courage welled in her. If an eight-year-old could find the strength to do this, so could she.

She wasn't the scared little girl she'd been in the past. She wasn't even the timid schoolteacher she'd been last week. She'd changed so much, done so much more than she'd imagined she was capable of.

She'd just made the decision to fight for Colt. Now she needed to fight for herself—to defeat the memories, to face the demons of her past, of her father. She couldn't fight this by controlling the situation. The only way she could win was to let go, to give in to the fight.

She bent her knees, letting the full weight of her body pull her down. At the same time, she dug her chin into Rank's arm and twisted her body toward him.

Gagging on the scent of him, she kept twisting, knowing she had to stare him in the eyes, to defeat him by actually facing him. All her fears, her insecurities, her past abuse had culminated in the worn and leathered face of Rank Johnson. If she could face him, stare him in the eye, and fight, she could face anything. If she could find the strength to fight this solid mass of a true monster, then she could surely defeat the fictional creatures that fought to gain purchase in her mind.

Rotating her head another inch, she met his eye, his pupils huge and his cheeks swollen and red from the pepper spray. He stared at her with all the fury and rage of a mythical beast, but she didn't back down, didn't wither and wilt or curl into a ball. She pulled on her armor and drew her sword and, with a primal scream, drove into battle as she sank her teeth into the skin of his arm and bit down as hard as she could.

The coppery taste of blood struck her tongue, and she wanted to gag. But she didn't. Instead she tensed, ready to escape. The muscles in his arm loosened, and she wiggled from his grasp and ran toward the drawer where she'd hidden the gun.

He screamed and lunged for her, but she eluded his grasp, feeling the tug of his fingers as they slid off the back of her coat.

Reaching the drawer, she yanked it open and fumbled for the gun. The freezing metal stung her already cold fingers, but she grasped it tightly and turned to face him, holding the revolver out in front of her.

Rank froze and held his arms out to the side. He might be stupid, but he knew the impact of a firearm, and he took a small step back. Tears still leaked from his eyes, and his lips drew out in a pressed line. "Put the gun down, teacher. We both know you don't want to shoot me."

She clasped the gun with both hands, extending her arms as she pointed it straight at his chest. Her hands shook, but she kept them trained on him. "I may not want to, but I will. As God is my witness, if you take one step closer, I will shoot a hole right in your chest."

He narrowed his enflamed eyes and studied her, as if trying to decide if she really would do it.

She held her ground, never more serious about anything in her life. She only had Colt's word for it that the gun wasn't loaded. It *could* actually have a bullet in the chamber for all she knew. She'd never fired a gun, but she'd seen a lot of television and got the general idea of pointing the thing and pulling the trigger. Not knowing if the gun would go off, her biggest weapon right now was making Rank believe it would. And convincing him she'd be willing to shoot him.

She planted her feet, drawing on every ounce of courage she could muster. "I want you to leave. To leave me and Tina and the kids alone. Get out and never come back, or I will shoot you. If not this time, then the next."

Daggers of rage shot from his eyes, but he didn't move. "You can't threaten me. You think you scare me?"

"I think you *should* be scared because I've never wanted anything more than to put a bullet in your chest—to shoot you right here and right now. And remember I'm a teacher, and I teach science and chemistry, so I know how to dissolve your body in acid so there won't be a single trace of you left." She really had no idea how to dissolve anything in acid or what kind of acid would even do that. The last science curriculum she'd taught had been about space and the solar system and learning the names of the planets, but she'd read about the acid thing in a book, and it sounded plausible and scary as heck to her. And she didn't need to be able to do it, she reminded herself. She just had to *convince him* she'd be able to.

She raised the gun and took the slightest step forward. "Now. Get. The. Fuck. Out. Of. My. Garage."

He must have detected the change in her because he backed away, slowly stepping toward the open garage door. "I'll leave," he sneered. "But I'll be back."

"Good," she said, making her voice as hard and steely as she could. "I'll be waiting."

He turned and started to run just as Jesse's battered Toyota pulled into the driveway.

The door opened, and Jesse stepped out. Rank sprinted toward him, grabbing the door and shoving the teenager back inside. He pushed Jesse over as he slid into the driver's seat, then threw the car into reverse, spinning out of the driveway and almost sliding into a huge Dodge pickup with a snowplow implement on the front.

The pickup screeched to a halt, the passenger door opening before the truck had even fully stopped. Colt jumped out and ran toward her.

What was he doing here? Chloe couldn't comprehend the sight of him as he ran across the snow, but she didn't have time to think it through.

"He's got Jesse," she cried, falling to her knees and sweeping her arms under the car, desperately searching for the keys. Her fingers touched the key ring, and she pulled it out and slid into the car, tucking the revolver in between the seat and the console next to her.

"I saw," Colt said, jumping into the passenger side and slamming the door. "Go!"

Chloe backed out of the driveway and tore after Jesse's car, her car's back end fishtailing over the slick black ice. The taillights of the Toyota were up ahead, and she stepped on the gas, trying to catch them.

Colt had his phone out and pressed to his ear. He must have called 911, because he was relaying the situation into the phone and telling them the streets they were driving down.

They came out the back side of her neighborhood, and the Toyota sped toward the edge of town. Lights flashed in Chloe's rearview mirror, and she realized the truck with the snowplow was also in pursuit behind her.

Rank turned onto a dirt road leading up into the mountains, but the back end of the Toyota slid out. The car spun in a complete three-sixty before sliding off the road and rolled half a turn before landing on its roof.

"Jesse," Chloe screamed, braking to a stop and flinging open the door. She grabbed the revolver, then jumped out of her car and ran toward the Toyota upside down in the ditch.

The driver's side window was shattered, and Rank was crawling out the open space.

Chloe planted her feet and held the gun out. "Stop! Don't move!"

But Colt sprinted past her and grabbed Rank by the shoulders, heaving him out of the car and landing a punch directly in his face. Rank's nose shattered, and blood splattered across the front of his jacket and ran down his face as Colt punched him again.

Flashing red and blue lights shot through the night sky as a police car pulled up and two cops jumped out and ran toward Rank. Mike, the cop Tina had called, grabbed Colt and dragged him away as the other officer snapped a set of handcuffs on Rank's wrists. He hauled Rank up and dragged him toward the car as Colt wrenched himself away from Mike.

The other man, the one driving the truck with the snowplow, had run after Colt and flattened himself on the ground to reach into the car to pull Jesse out.

A sob escaped Chloe's lips, and she ran toward the car as the teenager half crawled and was half pulled from the vehicle, then stood up next to it. "Jesse, are you okay?" She threw the revolver to the ground and wrapped the boy in her arms.

"I'm okay. My dad was driving crazy, so I put my seat belt on."

Thank goodness. Chloe pulled him tightly to her. "You clever boy. That was so smart."

Another truck pulled up, a silver one Chloe recognized as Logan's, and Tina came flying from it, her expression a mix of terror and relief. "Jesse!"

"Mom!" The boy let Chloe go, and tears pricked her eyes as Tina reached her son and clasped him to her. The boy was taller than her, yet she held on to him as if he were still a little boy.

Colt reached for Chloe and pulled her to him, burying his face in her hair. "Are you okay?"

She nodded against his chest, unable to speak as emotion clogged her throat.

"What the hell happened?"

She pulled back and took a shuddering breath as she pushed her bangs from her forehead. "Rank was waiting for me when I got home. He slipped under my garage door as it was closing."

Colt's eyes hardened, and he searched her face. "Did he hurt you? I'll kill him myself if he hurt you."

She shook her head. "He did, but I'm okay. I stood up to him, Colt. I fought, and I got away. I used the stuff you taught me, then I used your gun to get him to leave."

"My *gun*? What gun?" His face paled as he looked to the ground where she was pointing. "Geezus, Chloe. That's not a gun."

"What?"

He picked it up, pointed it toward the trees, and pulled the trigger. She braced herself for the sound of a shot, but instead a flare of flame popped out of the hammer. "It *used* to be a gun, but now it's a lighter. That's why we were all laughing about it the other day. I thought you knew."

Her knees went weak, and she sagged against him. *Holy fork.* She'd just fought off Rank Johnson using a few self-defense techniques, her own bravery, and a cigarette lighter.

An ambulance pulled up, and two EMTs set to work checking out her and Jesse. They had an assortment of bumps, bruises, and scrapes, but were both in surprisingly good shape considering the trauma they'd gone through. The EMTs didn't think either of them had concussions, and there was no reason to suspect anything was broken. They were both released with the promise they would go to the doctor the next day for a more formal checkup.

Colt stayed by Chloe's side, touching some part of her body the whole time the EMT was with her. Tina and Mike stayed by Jesse's side, and Chloe couldn't help but notice the tender and protective way Mike stood with Tina, either holding her arm or resting his hand on her back or shoulder.

He seemed like a good man, and the idea that Tina and the kids would have the cop as their friend, or maybe more, filled Chloe's heart with joy and put her mind at ease. He could do a lot more to protect them than their neighbor who had just used a lighter to fight off a maniac.

She shook her head, still astonished at that fact. And a little embarrassed as she relayed what had happened to Mike when she gave her statement.

Colt put his arm around her shoulders. "I think she's had enough," he told the officer. "I'm taking her home. If you need something more, she can come down to the station tomorrow."

He led her to the car, easing her into the passenger seat, then driving them back to her house. They didn't talk on the short drive, but she noticed his hands weren't quite steady as he held the steering wheel.

They pulled into the garage, and this time the door shut behind them without incident. Exhaustion overtook her as the shock and adrenaline started to wear off. Her eyes and skin still burned from the pepper spray, but it seemed to have dissipated from the air.

As they walked through the garage and into the kitchen, Chloe tried to figure out what she was going to say, rehearsing different scripts in her head. She wanted to fight for him, to tell him how she felt, but now that he was here, all six-foot massive something of him, her words seemed to have escaped her.

Just say how I feel. Be honest. Start with that.

He hit the switch to turn on the kitchen light, and she turned to face him, ready to tell him how much she cared about him. But words failed her as she took in the smeared blood surrounding a cut above his eyebrow and the purple bruise around his eye.

"Oh my gosh, you're bleeding. What happened? Did Rank hit you?" She thought back to him pulling the other man from the car but couldn't remember Rank getting off a single hit aimed at Colt.

He raised his hand and gently touched his cheek. "Nah. I think I hit my head on the steering wheel."

"On the steering wheel?" She'd already moved to the sink and was wetting a clean blue washcloth with warm water. "What happened?" She pulled out a kitchen chair and pushed him into it, then raised the cloth to his face.

He pulled his head back. "It's nothing. A little cut and a minor goose egg. I had the EMT give it a quick look when you were talking to Mike, and I'm fine. It's no big deal, and I don't want you to get blood on your nice washcloth."

"I don't care about the washcloth." And she surprisingly didn't. *I care about you*, she thought as she dabbed at the blood on his forehead and tried to clean the wound.

He winced, but didn't draw his head away this time. "I put my truck in a ditch and must have hit my head when I slammed into a couple of trees."

"You were in an accident?"

"Not much of one. I was trying to turn around and hit a patch of black ice and slid off the road. Thank God the truck didn't roll. But I might have passed out when I whacked my head. I remember coming to, then climbing up the embankment, and I just started walking until I hailed down a passing truck. It was a stroke of luck that it was Guy, a buddy of mine, who happened to be plowing that particular stretch of road. He gave me a ride back to town."

Chloe's hand stilled in the middle of his story. Her mouth had gone dry, but she was afraid to hope for his answer. "Why were you turning around?"

He lifted his hand and set it on top of hers. "To come back to you."

She caught her breath as he wrapped an arm around her waist and pulled her onto his lap. "Me? Or the team?"

"Both. I was trying to get back for the game, but my main focus was getting back to you. I had some stuff to tell you, and when I realized I'd missed the game, I had Guy bring me here."

"What kind of stuff?" she whispered.

"Stuff like I'm an idiot and a fool. I'm sorry for what I said and how I treated you." He reached up and tenderly touched her face. "I really care about you but was afraid to tell you because I thought I would scare you off."

"I *was* scared." She set the washcloth on the kitchen table, then turned to look into his eyes. She swallowed. "I was terrified. Not from imagining you cared about me, but from knowing with all certainty that you couldn't possibly like someone like me."

"Someone like you?" His brow furrowed. "You mean someone smart and beautiful, and one of the kindest, most thoughtful people of anyone I know. Someone who is funny and sweet and sexy as hell?"

She shook her head. "No, someone like me who is a shy introvert and a control freak who alphabetizes her spice rack. Someone who had mousy-brown hair and leads a dull and uninteresting life. I'm an ordinary schoolteacher who spends her spare time reading, watching British dramas on PBS, and knitting. How could that possibly interest someone like you, a man who is handsome and charming and has muscles where I didn't even know muscles existed?"

He chuckled and shook his head. But before he could respond, she touched her finger to his lips. "I was raised to believe I was nothing, an insignificant speck who wasn't even wanted by her own mother. I had this small existence that included my students and fixing up my little house and buying matching blue accessories for my kitchen."

"Aqua," he said against her finger.

A small smile tugged at her mouth, but tears of shame burned her eyes. "Yes, aqua. I had convinced myself I was happy—that aqua measuring spoons and perfectly knitted rows of yarn could equal a contented life. But then you came along, and you smiled and touched my hand and made me cupcakes. You laughed with me and seemed to like my cat."

"I do like your cat."

"I know. But it was more than that. So much more. You kissed me and said such sweet words, and you opened my eyes to what happiness could be. When we were together, I felt like a different woman. Then you would drop me off for work or go home to the ranch, and I would lapse back into my insecurities. My emotions were all over the place, and I was terrified of all these big feelings I had for you. They took over my every waking thought, and I was feeling smothered by my doubts and fears and by the sheer enormity of how much I was feeling and how utterly petrified I was that you weren't feeling the same way."

"But I was feeling the same way. How could you not tell? I came over every day. I asked you to coach the team with me. I fixed your door. I brought you to Sunday dinner at my mom's house."

"I thought you were just being nice. I thought you just wanted to be friends."

His eyes widened. "At what point could you possibly think that? Did you think I just wanted to be friends when I carried you naked into my bed? Or how about when I stripped off your clothes and soaped you up in the shower? Or maybe when I did that thing to you in front of the fireplace? Or was it when I wanted you so badly that I tore off your panties and took you on the counter of your aqua kitchen?"

Heat warmed her cheeks—from both embarrassment and the sudden heat that coiled between her legs as he talked about wanting her and stripping off her clothes. "That was all great—amazing. All that was mind-blowingly incredible. For me. But I didn't know what it meant for you. I don't have a lot of experience with that stuff. I didn't know if that was just sex or if that's how you were with everyone." She lowered her eyes, unable to face him. "I thought maybe you were just being nice to me—you know, doing me a favor, like you do for everyone else—because you felt sorry for me."

"Doing you a favor? Are you kidding me? A favor is shoveling the snow from your walk or passing you the salt. It's not spending hours in bed with you, exploring your body and looking for ways to get you to make that sexy sighing sound you do when I touch you just right."

She ducked her head, feeling the heat in her cheeks but also secretly pleased at his words.

"Where did you even get these ideas?" he asked, shaking his head.

"From you. And Logan. That day at your mom's house. When he was teasing you about Tina. He said you were into saving wounded women, and you said you didn't need another person to save. Like I was already enough."

He scrubbed a hand across his face and let out a sigh. "I wasn't talking about *you*. I was talking about how much work it was taking to try to save *myself*. And I have never seen you as a wounded sparrow, so it never crossed my mind to try to save you. When all that stuff happened with Rank, I wanted to *protect* you, but that's not the same as *saving* you—not the way you're saying it. I never believed you weren't strong enough or capable enough to take care of yourself."

He lifted her chin until he could see her eyes. "I felt bad for what happened to you and angry at your father for the way he treated you, but I have never once felt sorry for you or pitied you or thought I was saving you. And I sure as hell didn't kiss you, or do any of the other things I did to you, out of pity or as some sort of charity. I did them because I liked you, and I wanted you so bad I couldn't take another minute of not being able to get my hands on you."

His bold statements were like balm to her wounded soul. And she wanted to believe him—wanted to trust everything he said. "Why didn't you tell me?"

"Because I was an idiot, and I was afraid. And I wasn't sure how you felt about me. Especially after I saw you dancing with Huge at The Creed. You looked like you were having so much fun. And I was so jealous, I wanted to punch the guy in the throat."

"I wasn't having fun. I was just trying to prove something to Quinn and Tess. And I tried to apologize for that—tried to talk to you that night, but I couldn't."

"Obviously not. You didn't seem like you wanted to talk."

"I did."

"Then why did you leave?"

"Because your ex-girlfriend, Ashley, showed up, and all I could think about was how she was your first love and how you'd told me you screwed up when you lost her. And now she was going to be back in town, and I figured you'd want a second chance with her. She seems like such a perfect fit for you—she's pretty and so much better suited for you than me."

He shook his head. "What in the Sam Hill are you talking about? Why would I ever want Ashley back? She left me the summer we graduated—ran off with a carny who'd been in town for two weeks working the carnival at the county fair. She took off with him, and I didn't see or hear from her for years. We only just started speaking again a few years ago. Why the hell would that make her a good fit for me?"

Chloe winced. "Why are you getting angry at me?"

He sighed. "I'm not angry at you. It just pisses me

off to think about that time and reminds me what a tool I had to have been to make a carny seem like a better choice than me."

"Well, I don't even like carnivals. I detest cotton candy, wouldn't eat a corn dog on a bet, and just the thought of the Tilt-A-Whirl makes me want to barf."

He chuckled. "Good. That somehow does make me feel better. But I still can't imagine how you could possibly think I would want Ashley over you."

"She seemed perfect for you."

He brushed her bangs from her forehead, and the light touch of his fingers sent a dart of heat down her spine. "*You're* perfect for me. You're kind and thoughtful, and you make me want to be a better man. I've been falling for you since the first time I met you. But I couldn't tell you, because I was afraid if I said it out loud, the curse would kick in, and I would lose you. So, I tried to show you how much I cared about you. I tried to show you every time I kissed you, every time I touched you. I tried to show you by doing things for you, but I kept getting them wrong, like when you were upset the other day when I picked you up from school and then you got so angry about the garage."

"I'm sorry about the garage. I was upset about what I'd overheard the other teachers saying about me, and I overreacted. That was more about my issues and things that happened with my dad, and me using the act of getting rid of those boxes as a way to break free from the control he still had over me. But I know now that getting rid of all that stupid stuff wasn't the key to my freedom. It was all the risks I was taking with you, all the times that I took a bold step out of my box, that I tried something new, challenged myself to try something different, *be* someone different—those things were what truly set me free.

"And I really do love what you did in the garage. It was thoughtful, and I know it must have been a lot of work. I do appreciate it, and I was going to apologize and tell you that when I saw you at the game tonight." A sudden thought struck her. "You said you turned around on the road, so what happened to the interview?"

He shrugged. "I don't know. I didn't go. I called the coach and told him I couldn't bail on my team."

"But, that job sounded like a dream—like you would finally get your chance to be with the NHL. I know you dreamed of being a player, but this would still let you be part of the game."

He rubbed a hand up her back. "Funny you should say that. I was talking to Jesse last night. I gave him a ride home, and we were talking about life and relationships and getting in the game. That's what made me turn around tonight. I realized I'd been sitting on the sidelines, so sure I was going to lose, that I was afraid to even get in the game. But that's not what I want.

"I'm tired of being afraid—tired of letting this fictional curse rule my life. So much of what's happened to me has been my own fault, like I'm my own worst enemy. But I don't want to live like that anymore. I don't want to get in the way of my own chance at having something real."

She nodded. "I get it. I feel the same way. I think I was pushing you away before you had a chance to hurt me."

He lifted his hands to her cheeks, holding them on either side of her face. "How about we stop pushing each other away? Can we do that?"

"Yes," she whispered. Her heart pounded in her chest, and she couldn't tear her eyes from his.

Still holding her face, he dropped his gaze to her mouth and grazed her bottom lip with his thumb. He took a deep shuddering breath. "So here goes. I'm stepping into the game, darlin', and telling you flat-out I'm in love with you. I love your smile and the way you hug my dog. I love the way you treat people and the way you take care of everyone else's kids. I love the way you touch the side of my hand with your pinkie, and I love the way you gnaw your bottom lip when you're thinking really hard. I don't care that you have to alphabetize your books or color-code your kitchen. I don't care that you have to check the locks three times every night, or that you can't swear to save your life. I want to protect you, to keep you safe, to ease your mind, and to make you laugh. I want to kiss you and touch you and hold you when you're scared. I know I keep talking, but I really just want to say one thing. I love you, Chloe. That's all."

"That's enough." Tears welled in her eyes. He'd taken the first step, skated into the rink, and passed her the puck. Now it was her turn, and she was taking a shot at the goal. "I love you too."

His lips curved into a grin, and he leaned forward and kissed her. Tenderly at first, but then he deepened the kiss as he picked her up and carried her to her room.

Score.

Chapter 24

CHLOE STAGGERED INTO THE KITCHEN THE NEXT MORNING, drawn by the scent of bacon and in dire need of coffee. What she found gave her more energy than any shot of caffeine. A hot cowboy was standing at the stove dishing her up a plate of scrambled eggs.

"Good morning, beautiful," Colt said, leaning down to give her a kiss before handing her the plate.

She grinned. "Yes, it is. Especially since the district gave us a rare snow day. So, it's a good morning *and* was an excellent night." She scooped a bite into her mouth and groaned at the delicious flavor of eggs, bacon, and cheese.

He passed her a cup of coffee. "Just the way you like it, two exact teaspoons of sugar and a full tablespoon of cream."

She put her plate on the table and took a sip. "Perfect. Just like you." Setting the cup on the kitchen counter, she reached up and pulled his face down to press a kiss to his lips.

As he deepened the kiss, he bent his knees and slid his arms down her back, over the rounded curve of her rear, then lifted her up and set her on the counter next to her cup. Heat bloomed along her spine as she wrapped her legs around his waist, pulling him to her as she ran her fingers through his thick hair.

A low growl sounded in the back of his throat as

he slid his hand under the hem of her jersey and up her thigh.

Oh boy. This was shaping up to be a *really* good morning. She arched into him, anticipating his touch, but was interrupted as his phone buzzed on the counter. She swallowed, her mouth dry as he pulled his hand free of her jersey and reached for the phone.

He peered at the screen, and narrowed his eyes as he held it up for her to see. The display read "Joe Forsberg." He answered and put the phone to his ear. "Hello, this is Colt."

Her head was still so close to his, she could hear the booming voice of the coach.

"Hey, Colt, this is Coach Forsberg. Sorry to call so early, but I wanted to talk to you about last night."

"Yes, sir. I'm sure you do. I'd like to apologize again for not showing up. I really appreciated the offer, but I couldn't let my team down."

"That's what I'm calling about. It takes a lot of guts to turn down an opportunity like this one for a bunch of kids."

"Beggin' your pardon, sir, but they're not just a bunch of kids to me. They're my team."

"I understand. And that's why I wanted to call you. To tell you the job is yours, if you still want it."

"But, I don't understand. I bailed on the interview."

"That's right. And you bailing on the interview to take care of your team tells me you're just the kind of man we need for this job. I'm looking for someone who will make a difference, who cares enough about the team to inspire that kind of loyalty and dedication. I'd still like you to come down and meet the team, and we'll need to talk about salary and benefits, but the job is yours if you want it."

Colt looked up at her, a question in his eyes, and if she'd had any doubt about his feelings, that slight hesitation, that moment where she knew he was putting her above everything else, even his dream job, told her everything she could ever wish to know.

"Say yes," she mouthed, nodding to the phone. "Take the job."

A grin spread across his face. "Thank you, sir. I'd like that."

"Great. Why don't you check your schedule, and I'll call you later to set up some times to come down to Denver."

"Yes, sounds good. I'll do that, and I look forward to hearing from you." He hung up the phone, and his face lit with happiness. "I guess I got the job anyway."

"Yes! Congratulations." Chloe threw her arms around his neck and pressed a kiss to his mouth. "Screw the forking curse. That thing is dead and gone."

He laughed, a low rumble she felt against her chest. "You know, I think you're right. Screw the forking curse." He chuckled again and leaned in to pull her to him, but her hip hit the handle of her cup and coffee swirled over the sides and splattered around the counter.

"Shit, sorry," he said, pulling back to grab a towel.

She grabbed the towel from his hand and tossed it back toward the sink. "Leave it. It's just a little mess." Picking up his hand, she put it back on her waist. "We've got more important things to worry about than spilled coffee. We've got celebrating to do."

He raised an eyebrow. "Why, Miss Bishop, I do believe you're flirting with me."

She batted her eyes and let out a tinkling laugh. "I do believe I am."

His eyes darkened with a hunger she recognized, and her breasts tightened in anticipation. He dropped his voice to a low, slow drawl. "Suddenly, I'm getting real hungry for dessert."

"Dessert? We haven't even finished breakfast."

"I don't care about breakfast." He winked, and a devilish grin curved his lips. "I'm craving a cupcake."

She grinned, looking at her future standing in front of her. A future that was messy and unpredictable—that she couldn't control, that would hold chaos and disarray, but would also be filled with laughter, and delirious joy, and love. And suddenly, the messiness didn't matter. In fact, she couldn't wait to get messy, as long as it was in the arms of this man.

She leaned close to his ear, a laugh on her lips and her heart full to bursting as she whispered, "I'll get the frosting."

*Keep reading for an excerpt of the first book in
Jennie Marts's Cowboys of Creedence series*

CAUGHT UP
in a
COWBOY

Chapter 1

BITS OF GRAVEL FLEW BEHIND THE TIRES OF THE CONVERTIBLE, and Rockford James swore as he turned onto the dirt road leading to the Triple J Ranch. Normally, he enjoyed coming home for a visit, especially in the late spring when everything was turning green and the wildflowers were in bloom, but not this spring—not when he was coming home with both his pride and his body badly injured.

His spirits lifted and the corners of his mouth tugged up in a grin as he drew even with what appeared to be a pirate riding a child's bicycle along the shoulder of the road. A gorgeous female pirate—one with long blond hair and great legs.

Legs he recognized.

Legs that belonged to the only woman who had ever stolen his heart.

Nine years ago, Quinn Rivers had given him her heart as well. Too bad he'd broken it. Not exactly broken— more like smashed, crushed, and shattered it into a million tiny pieces. According to her anyway.

He slowed the car, calling out as he drew alongside her. Her outfit consisted of a flimsy little top that bared her shoulders under a snug corset vest and a short, frilly striped skirt. She wore some kind of sheer white knee socks, and one of them had fallen and pooled loosely around her ankle. "Ahoy there, matey. You lose your ship?"

Keeping her eyes focused on the road, she stuck out

her hand and offered him a gesture unbecoming of a lady—pirate or otherwise. Then her feet stilled on the pedals as she must have registered his voice. "Ho-ly crap. You have got to be freaking kidding me."

Bracing her feet on the ground, she turned her head, brown eyes flashing with anger. "And here I thought my day couldn't get any worse. What the hell are you doing here, Rock?"

He stopped the car next to her, then draped his arm over the steering wheel, trying to appear cool. Even though his heart pounded against his chest from the fact that he was seeing her again. She had this way of getting under his skin; she was just so damn beautiful. Even wearing a pirate outfit. "Hey, now. Is that any way to speak to an old friend?"

"I don't know. I'll let you know when I run into one."

Ouch. He'd hoped she wasn't still that bitter about their breakup. They'd been kids, barely out of high school. But they'd been together since they were fourteen, his conscience reminded him, and they'd made plans to spend their future together.

But that was before he got the full-ride scholarship and the NHL started scouting him.

And he had tried.

Yeah, keep telling yourself that, buddy.

Okay, he probably hadn't tried hard enough. But he'd been young and dumb and swept up in the fever and glory of finally having his dreams of pursuing a professional hockey career coming true.

With that glory came attention and fame and lots of travel with the team where cute puck bunnies were ready and willing to show their favorite players a good time.

He hadn't cheated on Quinn, but he came home less often and didn't make the time for texts and calls. He'd gone to college first while she finished her senior year, and by the time he did come home the next summer, he'd felt like he'd outgrown their relationship, and her, and had suggested they take a mini break.

Which turned into an *actual* break, of both their relationship and Quinn's heart.

But it had been almost nine years since he'd left; they'd been kids, and that kind of stuff happened all the time. Since then, he hadn't made it home a lot and had run into her only a handful of times. In fact, he probably hadn't seen her in over a year.

But he'd thought of her. Often. And repeatedly wondered if he'd made the right choice by picking the fame and celebrity of his career and letting go of her.

Sometimes, those summer days spent with Quinn seemed like yesterday, but really, so much had happened—in both of their lives—that it felt like a lifetime ago.

Surely she'd softened a little toward him in all that time. "Let me offer you a lift." The dirt road they were on led to both of their families' neighboring ranches.

"No thanks. I'd rather pedal this bike until the moon comes up than take a ride from you."

Yep. Still mad, all right.

Nothing he could do if she wanted to keep the grudge fest going. Except he was tired of the grudge. Tired of them being enemies. She'd been the best friend he'd ever had. And right now, he felt like he could use a friend.

His pride had already been wounded; what was one more hit? At least he could say he tried.

Although he didn't want it to seem like he was trying too hard. He did still have a *little* pride left, damn it.

"Okay. Suit yourself. It's not *that* hot out here." He squinted up at the bright Colorado sun, then eased off the brake, letting the car coast forward.

"Wait." She shifted from one booted foot to the other, the plastic pirate sword bouncing against her curvy hip. "Fine. I'll take a ride. But only because I'm desperate."

"You? Desperate? I doubt it," he said with a chuckle. Putting the car in Park, he left the engine running and made his way around the back of the car. He reached for the bike, but she was already fitting it into the back seat of the convertible.

"I've got it." Her gaze traveled along the length of his body, coming to rest on his face, and her expression softened for the first time. "I heard about the fight and your injury."

He froze, heat rushing to his cheeks and anger building in his gut. Of course she'd heard about the fight. It had made the nightly news, for Pete's sake. He was sure the whole town of Creedence had heard about it.

Nothing flowed faster than a good piece of gossip in a small town. Especially when it's bad news—or news about the fall of the hometown hero. Or the guy who thought he was better than everyone else and bigger than his small-town roots, depending on who you talked to and which camp they fell into. Or what day of the week it was.

You could always count on a small town to be loyal.

Until you let them down.

"I'm fine," he said, probably a little too sternly, as he opened the car door, giving her room to pass him and slide into the passenger seat. He sucked in a breath as the scent of her perfume swept over him.

She smelled the same—a mix of vanilla, honeysuckle, and home.

He didn't let himself wonder if she felt the same. No, he'd blown his chances of that ever happening again a long time ago. Still, he couldn't help but drop his gaze to her long, tanned legs or notice the way her breasts spilled over the snug, corseted vest of the pirate costume.

"So, what's with the outfit?" he asked as he slid into the driver's seat and put the car in gear.

She blew out her breath in an exaggerated sigh. A loose tendril of hair clung to her damp forehead, and he was tempted to reach across the seat to brush it back.

"It's Max's birthday today," she said, as if that explained everything.

He didn't say anything—didn't know what to say.

The subject of Max always was a bit of an awkward one between them. After he'd left, he'd heard the rumors of how Quinn had hooked up with a hick loser named Monty Hill who'd lived one town over. She'd met him at a party and it had been a rebound one-night stand, designed to make him pay for breaking things off with her, if the gossip was true.

But she'd been the one to pay. Her impulse retaliation had ended in an unplanned pregnancy with another jerk who couldn't be counted on to stick around for her. Hill had taken off, and Quinn had ended up staying at her family's ranch.

"He's eight now." Her voice held the steely tone of anger, but he heard the hint of pride that also crept in.

"I know," he mumbled, more to himself than to her. "So, you decided to dress up like a pirate for his birthday?"

She snorted. "No. Of course not. One of Max's favorite books is *Treasure Island*, and he wanted a pirate-themed party, so I *hired* a party company to send out a couple of actors to dress up like pirates. The outfits showed up this morning, but the actors didn't. Evidently, there was a mix-up in the office, and the couple had been double-booked and were already en route to Denver when I called."

"So you decided to fill in." He tried to hold back his grin.

She shrugged. "What else was I going to do?"

"That doesn't explain the bike."

"The bike is his main gift. I ordered it from the hardware store in town, but it was late and we weren't expecting it to come in today. They called about an hour ago and said it had shown up, but they didn't have anyone to deliver it. I was already in the pirate getup, so I ran into town to get it."

"And decided to ride it home?"

"Yes, smart-ass. I thought it would be fun to squeeze onto a tiny bike dressed in a cheap Halloween costume and enjoy the bright, sunny day by riding home." She blew out another exasperated breath. "My stupid car broke down on the main road."

"Why didn't you call Ham or Logan to come pick you up?" he asked, referring to her dad and her older brother.

"Because in my flustered state of panic about having to fill in as the pirate princess and the fear that the party would be ruined, I left my phone on the dresser when I ran out of the house. I was carrying the dang bike, but it got so heavy, then I tried pushing it, and that was killing my back, so I thought it would be easier and faster if I just tried to ride it the last mile back to the ranch."

"Makes sense to me." He slowed the car, turning into the long driveway of Rivers Gulch. White fences lined the drive, and several head of cattle grazed on the fresh green grass of the pastures along either side of the road.

The scent of recently mown hay skimmed the air, mixed with the familiar smells of plowed earth and cattle.

Seeing the sprawling ranch house and the long, white barn settled something inside of him, and he let out a slow breath, helping to ease the tension in his neck. He'd practically grown up here, running around this place with Quinn and her brother, Logan.

Their families' ranches were within spitting distance of each other; in fact, he could see the farmhouse of the Triple J across the pasture to his left. They were separated only by prime grazing land and the pond that he'd learned to swim in during the summer and skate on in the winter.

The two families had an ongoing feud—although he wasn't sure any of them really knew what they were fighting about anymore, and the kids had never cared much about it anyway.

The adults liked to bring it up, but they were the only kids around for miles, and they'd become fast friends—he and his brothers sneaking over to Rivers Gulch as often as they could.

This place felt just as much like home as his own did.

He'd missed it. In the years since he'd left, he'd been back only a handful of times.

His life had become so busy, his hockey career taking up most of his time. And after what happened with Quinn, neither Ham nor Logan was ever too excited to see him. Her mom had died when she was in grade school, and both men had always been overprotective of her.

He snuck a glance at her as he drove past the barn. Her wavy hair was pulled back in a ponytail, but wisps of it had come loose and fell across her neck in little curls. She looked good—really good. A thick chunk of regret settled in his gut, and he knew letting her go had been the biggest mistake of his life.

It wasn't the first time he'd thought it. Images of Quinn haunted his dreams, and he often wondered what it would be like now if only he'd brought her with him instead of leaving her behind. If he had her to wave to in the stands at his games or to come home to at night instead of an empty house. But he'd screwed that up, and he felt the remorse every time he returned to Rivers Gulch.

He'd been young and arrogant—thought he had the world by the tail. Scouts had come sniffing around when he was in high school, inflating his head and his own self-importance. And once he started playing in the big leagues, everything about this small town—including Quinn—had just seemed…well…small. Too small for a big shot like him.

He was just a kid—and an idiot. But by the time he'd realized his mistake and come back for her, it was too late.

Hindsight was a mother.

And so was Quinn.

Easing the car in front of the house, he took in the festive balloons and streamers tied to the railings along the porch. So much of the house looked the same—the long porch that ran the length of the house, the wooden rocking chairs, and the swing hanging from the end.

They'd spent a lot of time on that swing, talking and laughing, his arm around her as his foot slowly pushed them back and forth.

She opened the car door, but he put a hand on her arm and offered her one of his most charming smiles. "It's good to see you, Quinn. You look great. Even in a pirate outfit."

Her eyes widened, and she blinked at him, for once not having a sarcastic reply. He watched her throat shift as she swallowed, and he yearned to reach out to run his fingers along her slender neck.

"Well, thanks for the lift." She turned away and stepped out of the car.

Pushing open his door, he got out and reached for the bicycle, lifting it out of the back seat before she had a chance. He carried it around and set it on the ground in front of her. "I'd like to meet him. You know, Max. If that's okay."

"You would?" Her voice was soft, almost hopeful, but still held a note of suspicion. "Why?"

He ran a hand through his hair and let out a sigh. He'd been rehearsing what he was going to say as they drove up to the ranch, but now his mouth had gone dry. The collar of his cotton T-shirt clung to his neck, and he didn't know what to do with his hands.

Dang. He hadn't had sweaty palms since he was in

high school. He wiped them on his jeans. He was known for his charm and usually had a way with women, but not this woman. This one had him tongue-tied and nervous as a teenager.

He shoved his hands in his pockets. "Listen, Quinn. I know I screwed up. I was young and stupid and a damn fool. And I'm sorrier than I could ever say. But I can't go back and fix it. All I can do is move forward. I miss this place. I miss having you in my life. I'd like to at least be your friend."

She opened her mouth, and he steeled himself for her to tell him to go jump in the lake. Or worse. But she didn't. She looked up at him, her eyes searching his face, as if trying to decide if he was serious. "Why now? After all these years?"

He shrugged, his gaze drifting as he stared off at the distant green pastures. He'd let this go on too long, let the hurt fester. It was time to make amends—to at least try. He looked back at her, trying to express his sincerity. "Why not? Isn't it about time?"

She swallowed again and gave a small nod of her head.

A tiny flicker of hope lit in his gut as he waited for her response. He could practically *see* her thinking—watch the emotions cross her face in the furrow of her brow and the way she chewed on her bottom lip. Oh man, he loved it when she did that; the way she sucked her bottom lip under her front teeth always did crazy things to his insides.

"Okay. We can *try* being friends." She gave him a sidelong glance, the hint of a smile tugging at the corner of her mouth. "On one condition."

Uh-oh. Conditions are never good. Although he would do just about anything to prove to her that he was serious about being in her life again.

"What's that?"

"I need someone to be the other pirate for the party. I already asked Logan if he would wear the other costume, and he refused. I was planning to ask Dad, but I have a feeling I'll get the same response."

He tried to imagine Hamilton Rivers in a pirate outfit and couldn't. Ham was old-school cowboy, tough as nails and loyal to the land. He wore his boots from sunup to sundown and had more grit than a sheet of sandpaper. The only soft spot he had was for his daughter. And Rock had broken her heart.

If there hadn't been enough animosity between the two families over their land before, Rock had sealed the feud by walking away from Quinn.

And now he had a chance to try to make it up to her. And to keep an eight-year-old kid from being disappointed. Even if it meant making a fool of himself.

He squinted one eye closed and tilted his head. If he was going to do it, might as well do it right.

Go big or go home.

"Aye, lass," he said in his best gruff pirate impression. "I'll be a pirate for ye, but don't cross me, or I'll make ye walk the plank."

Her eyes widened, and she laughed before she could stop herself. An actual laugh. Well, more like a small chuckle, but it was worth it. He'd talk in a pirate accent all afternoon if it meant he could hear her laugh again.

She took a step forward, reached out her hand as if to touch his arm, then let it drop to her side. "All right,

Captain Jack, you don't have to go that far." She might not have touched him, but she offered him a grin—a true grin.

Yeah, he could be a pirate. He could be whatever she needed. Or he could dang well try.

The front door slammed open with a bang, and Quinn jumped. As if on cue, her brother stepped out on the front porch.

Anger sparked in Logan's eyes as he glared at Rock. "What the hell are you doing here?"

Acknowledgments

As always, my love and thanks goes out to my family! Todd, thanks for always believing in me and for being the real life role model of a romantic hero. You cherish me and make me laugh every day and the words it would take to truly thank you would fill a book on their own. I love you. Always.

Thank you to my sons, Tyler and Nick, for always supporting me and listening to a zillion plotting ideas. And for all of your technical help when I call you with crazy oddball questions. I love you both with more than my heart could ever imagine.

I can't thank my editor, Deb Werksman, enough for believing in me and this book, for your amazing editing talents, and for always making me feel like a rock star. Thanks to Dawn Adams for this incredible cover that perfectly captures the awesomeness of Colt James. I love being part of the Sourcebooks Sisterhood, and I offer buckets of thanks to the whole Sourcebooks Casablanca team for all of your efforts and hard work in making this book happen.

Huge shout out thanks to my agent, Nicole Resciniti at The Seymour Agency, for your advice and your guidance. You are the best, and I'm so thankful you are part of my tribe.

A big thank you to my parents—all of them. I appreciate everything you do and am so thankful for your support of this crazy writing career. Thanks to my mom, Lee Cumba, for so many lunches where we talk writing and plots. And thanks to my dad, Bill Bryant, for spending hours giving me ranching and farming advice and plot ideas.

Special thanks goes out to Jonathan Maberry for indulging me at the very end of the Pikes Peak Writers Conference and offering me technical advice and your ideas for my heroine's self-defense moves.

Special acknowledgement goes out to the women who walk this writing journey with me every single day. The ones who make me laugh, who encourage and support, who offer great advice and sometimes just listen. Thank you Michelle Major, Lana Williams, Anne Eliot, Kristin Miller, Ginger Scott, Selena Laurence, Cindy Skaggs, and Beth Rhodes. XO

Big thanks goes out to my street team, Jennie's Page Turners, and for all of my readers: the people who have been with me from the start, my loyal readers, my dedicated fans, the ones who have read my stories, who have laughed and cried with me, who have fallen in love with my heroes and have clamored for more! Whether you have been with me since the first book or just discovered me with this book, know that I write these stories for you, and I can't thank you enough for reading them. Sending love, laughter, and big Colorado hugs to you all!

About the Author

Jennie Marts is the *USA Today* bestselling author of award-winning books filled with love, laughter, and always a happily-ever-after. Readers call her books "laugh out loud" funny and the "perfect mix of romance, humor, and steam." Fic Central claimed one of her books was "the most fun I've had reading in years."

She is living her own happily-ever-after in the mountains of Colorado with her husband, two dogs, and a parakeet that loves to tweet to the oldies. She's addicted to Diet Coke, adores Cheetos, and believes you can't have too many books, shoes, or friends.

Her books include the contemporary western romances of the Cowboys of Creedence and the Hearts of Montana series, the cozy mysteries of The Page Turners series, the hunky hockey-playing men in the Bannister Brothers Books, and the small-town romantic comedies in the Cotton Creek Romance series.

Jennie loves to hear from readers. Follow her on Facebook at Jennie Marts Books, or Twitter at @JennieMarts. Visit her at jenniemarts.com and sign up for her newsletter to keep up with the latest news and releases.

CAUGHT UP IN A COWBOY

USA Today bestselling author Jennie Marts welcomes you to Creedence, Colorado, where the cowboys are hot on the ice

After an injury, NHL star Rockford James returns to his hometown ranch to find that a lot has changed. The one thing that hasn't? His feelings for Quinn Rivers, his high school sweetheart and girl next door.

Quinn had no choice but to get over Rock after he left. Teenaged and heartbroken, she had a rebound one-night stand that ended in single motherhood. Now that Rock's back—and clamoring for a second chance—Quinn will do anything to avoid getting caught up in this oh-so-tempting cowboy…

"Funny, complicated, and irresistible."

—Jodi Thomas, *New York Times* bestselling author

For more Jennie Marts, visit:
sourcebooks.com

YOU HAD ME
AT COWBOY

These hockey-playing cowboys will melt your heart,
from USA Today bestselling author Jennie Marts

Mason James is the responsible one who stayed behind
to run the ranch when his brother Rock took off to play
hockey for the NHL. Women have used Mason to get to
his famous brother before, but he never expects to fall—
and fall hard—for one of them…

Tessa Kane is about to lose a job she desperately needs—
unless she's clever enough to snag a story on star player
Rockford James. But when her subject's brother starts to
win her heart, it's only a matter of time before he finds out
who she really is… Can the two take a chance on their love
story after all?

For more info about Sourcebooks's books and
authors, visit:

sourcebooks.com

RECKLESS IN TEXAS

He's a hotshot in the ring...but
love is a whole new rodeo.

Violet Jacobs is fearless. At least, that's what the cowboys
she snatches from under the hooves of bucking horses
think. Outside the ring, she's got plenty of worries rattling
her bones, including her family's struggling rodeo. When
she takes business into her own hands and hires a hotshot
bullfighter, she expects to start a ruckus. She never expects
her heart to be on the line.

Joe Cassidy didn't plan on staying in Texas, but Violet is
everything he never knew he was missing. And the deeper
he's pulled into her beautiful mess of a family, the more he
realizes this fierce rodeo girl may be offering him the one
thing he never could find on his own.

"Look out, world! There's a new cowboy in town."

**—Carolyn Brown, *New York Times* Bestselling
Author, for *Tangled in Texas***

For more Kari Lynn Dell, visit:
sourcebooks.com

COWBOY SUMMER

Fall in love with Joanne Kennedy's sweet and sexy cowboys in a brand-new series!

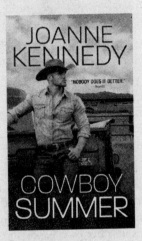

Jess Bailey left Cade Walker years ago, trading small-town simplicity for city sophistication—but she's still a cowgirl at heart. She heads home when her dad announces he's selling the ranch, and comes face to face with all she left behind. As for Cade, he's ready to win back the woman he still loves—but can she really abandon the career she worked so hard to build?

"Get set for the ride of your life."

—Fresh Fiction for How to Wrangle a Cowboy

For more info about Sourcebooks's books and authors, visit:

sourcebooks.com